the long shot

ISBN-10: 1090787294
ISBN-13: 978-1090787293

Library of Congress Control Number: 2019903333

Cover design: akira007 at fiverr.com
Printed in the U.S.A.

the long shot

Joyce Derenas (signature)

joyce derenas

11/2/19 Rutland, MA

a french canadian
saga— book 1

DEDICATION

To Gloria Hamilton and Norman Poulin, my double

second cousins and

my connection to Nazaire Poulin.

IN MEMORIAM

To Norma Poulin-Riddall, I know you would have

liked more fish.

They're coming in Book 2.

Contents

THE STING OF

GOD'S LOVE

Louis   Nazaire Poulin   Joe

CHASING PROSPERITY

Big Mountain Row

Saint Joseph of Beauce, Quebec ❧ January 6, 1907

N azaire searched the sky and saw colors, glowing reds and greens. He yelled at the kitchen window. "Come, Victoria, come outside and see this."

Wrapped in a wool shawl, Nazaire's petite spouse joined him outside in the farmyard. "What is it?"

He stretched as he pointed to the twilight sky behind her, and asked, "Do you remember our wedding night and the sky like this?"

Together they raised their heads. God had dimmed the stars with a canvas of blues and reds that shot down, then zigzagged up like a splatter of paints thrown against the horizon. Everyone knew it was good luck seeing the northern lights. Nazaire stood behind his spouse. He cupped open palms on each

1

side of her belly, and held them there until he felt a little push.

"The first time we saw the lights, I knew we would be right together." Nazaire laughed when Victoria oohed and aahed, exhilarated to witness the spectacle above. They had been married seven years and this next child would be their fifth. It seemed ready to break free from her body with little punches that reshaped her stomach against Nazaire's hands. Their breaths rose in the air like pale exhalations of a brighter tomorrow.

"Are they all asleep?" Nazaire asked.

"All but this one."

They stood and watched the show of lights. Each arc, ribbon and spiral dazzled them. No two auroras were alike. Nazaire rubbed Victoria's shoulders, so proud of her, the ideal spouse. With Christmas gone and the Epiphany behind them, Victoria could rest before this baby came.

"It's too cold for you, go in. I'll tend the animals."

"Don't waste your time singing to those horses." Victoria said as she turned to leave.

Nazaire shrugged his shoulders as he lightly tapped her on the behind, "I don't sing to my horses."

"Oh, fresh," she giggled.

At thirty-three years, Nazaire was long in the bone with a thin face and quiet eyes. His worn cap and torn mackinaw, a short wool coat of plaid, spoke of a modesty steeped in near poverty. His farm sat in the middle of Big Mountain Row on a raised ridge that enjoyed the protection of high ground, three miles north of the village gates. Nazaire's eyes were bright and alert, aware of his surroundings. His receded hairline created a center triangle of fine fuzz and he sported a full mustache that ended in thin points on each side of his cheeks. He walked to the barn and opened the doors, hanging the kerosene lantern on a nail.

"I might be able to barter my largest sow for some seed. That gives me all spring and summer to fatten the smaller sows on house scraps and the last of the crab apples," he said to his team of horses.

But what would he gain if next year's harvest prices were no higher? He felt a stabbing in his stomach. He wasn't sentimental, rather he had a practical, no-nonsense way about him. But when it came to his work horses, Louis and Joe, he found comfort in their daily companionship. The three of them were a team. With the air clean and icy, a calm descended like a wool blanket that covered his world.

With spotless black-velvet coats, the geldings stomped their feet, content in their wide stall. Behind them, his spouse's mare nickered in her own stall. He emptied the feed bags and stored the leftover grain back in the wooden bin, then upended a pail and sat. He chuckled and plunged both thin hands into his coat pockets.

"Did you see the lights in the sky? It's good luck."

The horses turned their long necks to watch Nazaire as he hummed to them in a low voice. With great flourish, he removed a paper bag from his pocket. Nazaire fought to empty the bag as the horses shuffled, heads tossed back and nickered with delight.

Once the horses' nostrils caught the smell of juicy, tart cranberries and leftover raisins that filled his palm, he separated an equal number into three piles while their muzzles pivoted in the air.

He presented crab apples smelling of cinnamon and too ripe for the vinegar jar, while the horses pushed the farmer's shoulders aside to get at them.

"Come Joe, you get just as many as Louis, so don't be selfish," he said as he fed his spouse's mare first.

Farming was a struggle, but at that exact moment, Nazaire was content. What more would a man want or need?

The Annual Reckoning

Village Center ❧ January 8, 1907

Nazaire Poulin gave an impatient huff as he squeezed into the crowded storefront of the tobacco shop among a group of neighbors, and hoped that the government would raise prices for grains this year. The ranchers, growers and farmers of the village had all come to hear the Registrar of Agriculture deliver the annual reckoning of last year's harvests.

Would the government finally loosen its restraints on prices? Every sheep rancher, dairy farmer and grower hoped so. The men greeted each other with forced smiles. The storefront entrance opened wide and the Registrar entered with a greeting.

"Everyone hello. Let's begin."

He bent toward the oil lamp and squinted as he called out the first name in his ledger. The man followed the Registrar into a small back room. Hopelessness curled the shoulders of the men waiting their turn.

After an hour, the Registrar barked, "Poulin, Nazaire."

Nazaire entered the back room while others continued their hard wait. Even the stove complained with a constant tick as it glowed cherry. He closed the door and stood in silence; his thin frame stiff while his head slumped to miss the low ceiling. The lingering aroma of balsam curled in the air.

"You have thirty acres of prime grain, but the final count fights against you," the Registrar said.

He puffed on a pipe. His eyes didn't leave the sprawl of papers on the desk. "Grain prices have dropped. This is out of our control."

Nazaire swayed and strangled his dirty wool cap like he was wringing the neck of a turkey.

"The government sets the prices. For you, it might be better to leave the fields and go chop wood in Michigan or Wisconsin for a few years. Give the prices time to rise again. You're in the same bed with everyone else."

Nazaire gritted his teeth. "My tally?"

"Not good. Nine dollars and fifty cents. Cash now or let it ride until spring?"

Nazaire hesitated and looked at his feet.

"Cash," he said and stretched a swaying hand to receive the money.

Nazaire left the back room straight out the tobacco shop with a finger of steam escaping close behind. He walked to the village livery where his spouse's mare was tied deep in the back of the barn. He wiped the horse's eyes with a rag, held the reins and led her out to the main road while a hard knot pinched his stomach.

Any passersby would think Nazaire calm and serene. In truth, a storm festered within him. He was caught, trapped in his thoughts while rage burned his insides. He had hoped for fifteen dollars, eighteen maybe, but nine dollars and fifty cents? Not enough to buy seed for spring planting.

He was in trouble and had no idea how to deal with it. Outside the livery, a broadside advertised gold in the far north. The Yukon they called it, with a drawing of three men and pick axes. The drawing looked almost comical compared to the harshness of life in Quebec. The Yukon was a dream and Nazaire had no time for foolishness.

Nazaire sat ramrod straight as the horse settled into a gentle gait up the steep hill and through the village gates toward home. Once the Registrar moved on, the whole village would buzz with the hard news. Sheep farmers, dairy farmers and grain growers would all crowd into saloons and smoke shops to discuss how to outlast the remaining winter, going into a harder-looking summer.

In the past, spring floods of the Chaudière River had drowned people and destroyed homes, yet the river did more than take, it also gave. In the Beauce Valley, no barley, nor alfalfa was as hardy as grain from the village of Saint Joseph of Beauce, fifty miles

south of Quebec City. Chaudière topsoil was known
as the richest in the region.

But the Beaucerons had struggled in past decades
to survive wet springs that yielded nothing but rot,
while scorching summers grew new shoots stunted
and brittle. If summers were ideal, a cold autumn
might come down fast, or rains scatter the grain.
Images flashed in Nazaire's mind. He envied the
dozens of men from the village who had left for the
quarries of Maine and the lumber camps of
Wisconsin, but it was too late now for him to leave.
Snow and mud roads could get him stranded
anywhere. He was numb. What could he do with a
meager nine dollars and fifty cents?

Maybe the recruiters from the states were right,
these men who came and spoke to people after mass
about ready jobs in the mill towns of New England.

"Come, we have higher paying jobs," they
promised.

Nazaire wasn't one to ask for help but the fixed
prices set by the government left a taste of deceit and

betrayal in his mouth. There was no one to ask for help. While the government laced their pockets, praying to a God that was deaf and dumb was a waste of his time. No matter how hard he worked, his head was never above water. He touched his mouth with a finger and tasted blood, his lip bitten in anger.

Call the Doctor — Call the Priest

Nazaire's Farmhouse ❧ January 15, 1907

Sweat dotted the doctor's forehead as he braced his knees, his hands bloodied to his wrists.

"I can't save them both," he said.

The priest rushed the attending women out of the small bedroom, closing the door in their faces. He snarled as his top lip curled. "You listen to me. This village has widows to spare. You save that baby. God wills it."

The doctor's eyebrows raised.

"I leave the warmth of my presbytery fireplace and miss my afternoon brandy and hearty meal for this?" The priest pointed to the woman in bed.

"Who do these farmers think they are? I'm missing the best part of my week for a peasant who won't drop her brat. My uncle, the Archbishop of Quebec will hear of this bruise on my time," the priest huffed. He stormed from the bedroom across the crowded kitchen and right out the farmhouse door.

The attending women scowled as they walked back into the bedroom. They heard the crack of the whip on the dun and the warning bells of the priest's surrey dissolve in the air outside.

In the bedroom, the doctor considered the sweat-covered face of Victoria Poulin. He knew her well and had warned that she was too torn inside to bear another child. Exhaustion had overtaken the woman. What would Nazaire do with a newborn infant but no spouse to manage his household? Victoria would grieve the loss of a child, but she would recover. After all, she had four others.

"Damn!" The doctor breathed deep and encouraged the farmer's spouse to expel the baby.

With renewed effort and a long push, a limp boy, blue and lifeless, gushed from Victoria's body. The attending women held clutched hands to their chests. Neither the suck of breath nor a cry cut the air from the newborn, whose pallor was blue-black when the doctor held him upside down, slapping his bottom. The doctor raised an index finger to his lips, then grabbed a small vial of sacred water in one hand and cradled the baby with his free arm. His neutral face swore the attending women to secrecy.

"I baptize this boy in the name of the Father and Son and Holy Ghost," the doctor said as he spilled a few drops of water over the child's head.

Men of the cloth resented emergency baptisms by outsiders. They wanted their nickel no matter what. The priest had been called to give Victoria Last Rites, but since he dared to leave early, Nazaire and Victoria would find comfort in the physician's attention to their son's soul.

Victoria closed her eyes and groaned as sleep overtook her. Everyone in the farmhouse held their breath as they waited for sounds of life. In a bit, a faint cry broke the quiet of the afternoon. It sounded like a kitten, fragile and weak. The latch on the bedroom door rose as Nazaire entered the bedroom.

"You wait," one of the attending women said, and exiled Nazaire to the kitchen. All he could do was wring one long hand in the other.

Victoria's Fight

January 25, 1907

Nazaire's frame filled the bedroom doorway. He stared at Victoria, who lay motionless in their bed. The wet nurse comforted their infant son in the kitchen. The ten-day-old boy had struggled for many days and nights before his strength turned a corner. Today he was pink-faced and more active.

Beside Victoria, the doctor's remedy of milk laced with strychnine remained untouched on a small table in the bedroom. A clean strip of cloth looped around her head, securing the jaw. Two cabbage leaves still covered her breasts, the country remedy for drying up mother's milk. Victoria's ivory skin was dull and waxen. The doctor looked sheepish as he placed a firm grip on Nazaire's shoulder.

"I'm so sorry, I did everything I could."

The same priest stood beside the bed. He turned toward Nazaire, and raised a hand while tracing the sign of the cross in midair. Nazaire's chest tightened. He flung the priest's hand to the side and slammed it against the wall.

"Get out, GET OUT," he yelled.

Both doctor and priest ran from the room.

"NO. NO!" Nazaire clutched fingers into tight fists while he stumbled out of the bedroom and sucked gulps of air.

He tore across the farmyard to the barn and collapsed on his knees. Why couldn't he breathe? His chest was so tight. Pain shot toward one shoulder. He bent over, gasping for air. He closed his eyes and held a firm hand to his heart.

"How can this be? Victoria gone? NO, NO. It can't be."

Home Viewing

January 26, 1907

"She stays here," Nazaire yelled as white knuckles squeezed one edge of the coffin. Spit flung from his mouth as he rocked on his heels. They want. They want. What about him? What about what he wanted?

Victoria's family wanted the home viewing of her body at their parents' house. They got their way in most matters when pressed, but wouldn't it be a kindness to let everything be? Nazaire would make the decisions. Wasn't it his spouse who had died!

The farmhouse jumped with activity as family members and neighbors unpacked a wagon filled with borrowed chairs. One of Victoria's sisters rummaged in the children's bedroom for clothes, packed a small bundle under her coat and left, taking the children, all of them. She didn't even ask. The blood in Nazaire's chest pumped double-time when it dawned on him. What would he do without his children? His world was falling apart.

Varis, Nazaire's father, had worked on the rough-cut coffin in his drafty barn all night, smoothing the edges as best he could with numb fingers. Victoria's brothers arrived and immediately helped to milk the cows, water and feed all the animals. They talked of decisions to be made but Nazaire wasn't ready. He sat apart, too stunned to talk, as preparations were made.

Victoria's family spoke little as they prepared the kitchen to receive dozens of relatives. The farmhouse had no sitting room and no salon; therefore, the coffin remained on the old kitchen table. The room held scant space to walk around. The wives of Nazaire's brothers made the funeral cake of honey and flour.

Victoria's sisters fixed her hair in a loose bun behind her head, the way she liked it, with her delicate swan barrette. The house had no silver, only four cups in the cupboard. The wicks of lanterns were nothing but stubs. Bright, new lanterns with fat wicks bathed the room in soft shadows while two full candles burned in ornate silver candlesticks, one on each side of the cross. Someone had placed a beautiful silver crucifix near the head of the coffin. Victoria's face, light and creamy, held a waxen cast.

Once an hour, the family knelt to recite the rosary. Nazaire picked up a vague pealing as a distant sound moved in the wind. Then a distinct second stroke of the bell. Two strokes for a woman. The bells rang in the village church for his Victoria, their sounds bouncing off the surface of the frozen Chaudière River and then climbing to the high ridge.

A white sheet covered the wobbly kitchen table, another inside the coffin. Upon the sheet, Victoria lay on a hidden bed of cedar chips. A soft white cloth draped over her lower body and legs while the coffin lid stood sentry outside the back door. More family poured into the kitchen, lowered their heads and shook Nazaire's hand. Victoria's sisters kept vigil over the body while the eldest brother greeted people who had traveled far. By the head of the coffin, another of her brothers stood ready to add strong spirits to the men's coffee cups. Nazaire half-listened to the voices around him.

"Did you hear? Over eleven dead in the last two days, and that's just in Saint Joseph of Beauce," someone said in the kitchen.

"Influenza," a cousin commented.

Other relatives spoke in hushed whispers of 'the grippe.' Quarantine, a very new practice, was becoming popular, but not among the poor, so deaths continued. From Frampton just up the road, more bells rang day and night. One stroke for a child, three for a man. If people were dying all around his farm, were his children safe? Were they warm? Endless questions tormented him.

"Nazaire, have some coffee," someone said.

In his kitchen, Nazaire didn't eat, nor drink. Victoria's brothers wanted to transport her to church, and pay for the funeral. They pressed for control. Couldn't they let him be? Let him bury his spouse the way he wanted? All these suggestions crowded in his head. His father, Varis, and his brothers took turns, one always with Nazaire. They stared at the floor or stood by the kitchen window. Nazaire's eyes became murky, swollen lids with pale slits. Sometimes he barely registered what his eyes gazed upon, but still he sat and stared.

"It isn't funny, the life of the people," a neighbor said.

The day was awkward with as many as six of Victoria's brothers in the kitchen, quietly criticizing the hard life this marriage had imposed upon their delicate sister. Whispers of 'never enough to eat' rose in the room. Nazaire's chest tightened, and his back became rigid with rage; he raised his head and threw his shoulders back in pride. When he struggled to listen further, Varis walked up to the men and looked each one hard in the eyes. The whispers stopped.

For three days and nights, Nazaire sat by the kitchen door, knuckles white, fists clenched, his lips one angry line that wouldn't part to speak a word. Go ahead, kneel again, he thought; see if your prayers bring my Victoria back. Already they had taken his children, carted them off to the Vachon home. All of them gone. He valued the help Victoria's family offered, valued everyone's help, but at the same time he hated them, hated them all.

"The women will take care of the kitchen. Come now. We go to my home and have a drink. You stay with me for a while," Varis said to his grieving son.

His wife gone, his children taken from him, what did he had to live for? At Varis' farmhouse, Nazaire sat with arms by his side. In front of him, a full glass of whiskey remained on the kitchen table. His brain swelled. His skull twitched and his eyes floated in his head, unable to find a horizon.

What does a man do? How does he fight a family entitled by rank and prestige in his own village, by a government that squeezes your profits to nothing, and a God that is deaf and dumb to your pleas of help?

In the middle of the night, Nazaire stood and mumbled "There's nothing for me here. Nothing."

He walked outside with neither hat nor coat in the frigid cold, followed by his brothers, who guided him back inside. His thoughts returned to the reckoning just days ago. What did he have to live for? A few days before, his family's well-being had been sealed by low grain prices. Now his wife was gone and his children were taken from him. He was a man lost.

The Letter

February 8, 1907

In Varis Poulin's farmhouse, a worn letter sat on the kitchen table. The letter, written in his son Gaudias' hand, read:

mai 1900   parents   we arrive dawson 30,000 men
romeo robbed in winnpeg   so we go swif curan then
calgarie   prairies full of wheat   horses + indiens
dam cold   we hear gold in yukon so we walk 3
monthrockys terrible   indiens guide us   we hear many
tongues every day we cut trees + build boats
1st day150 boats sink   19 smash on bolders many die
rapids you no believe the power   rivers mighty fast
dawson steady work $6 day   many go Nom but still
gold herewe suffer for nothing
work for foreman 300 + good to us

we buy no extra   here everything 4 X back home

pricewe stay   make a go   work Hunker creek

8 men in cabincome winter board gran fork

cut trees for firewoods to cold for work in mines

hunt moose or grouses

if things bad at home   tell brothers come

bring mamas green soap   Gaudias

The letter had arrived the year Marchand's pig

burned down the big barn. At sixty-five years and six

feet nine, Varis was still taller than his five sons, most

long in the bone. He had been a dairy farmer all his

life. With hollow eyes and a lean jaw, it was easy to

see Varis' reflection in Nazaire's face.

Varis slipped the yellowed letter into his Bible

where a permanent crease in its spine would cause

the book to fall open. The three-cent stamp still

remained on the envelope. News had spread

throughout the village that now people must pay

three pennies to receive a letter. It had sparked an

outrage that brought the village mailman to his bed for a week.

Two of Varis' sons, Romeo and Gaudias, had been gone several years when the letter appeared. Romeo had been a man of thirteen when the boys left home, Gaudias almost twelve. The letter caused a scare throughout the village. Menfolk figured that one of the boys must be dead, maybe both.

In the spring of 1896, newspapers reported that starving wolves in Wawa were killing people. All these years Varis worried much with visions of his sons being ripped apart, dying alone. Until that letter arrived, his chest had burned like a heated anvil every night.

Varis read the letter again before placing it in his open Bible on the kitchen table. If Nazaire saw the letter, he might believe it was his idea. Maybe he would see the wisdom in this opportunity to turn his life around. Varis hoped that if Nazaire went north to find gold, then he would have a chance to gain back everything.

More than once, Varis had heard wages in Dawson were up to ten dollars a day, an incredible sum compared to the fifty-three cents a day that most men earned in the valley.

The pain of losing Victoria, a lovely daughter-in-law, reminded Varis of his own spouse. Her death had come about the same way. Within weeks of giving birth, she had bled out. The tiny boy she presented didn't see two complete days. Swallowing that grief had kept Varis sane the first year, with eleven children to raise. His oldest daughter had come home to say her worldly goodbyes when his spouse had died. Varis had no choice but to pull her back from that convent in Quebec City. She would take over household duties and raise her siblings. This is what people did. Those were black days that turned into gray years.

Now his eldest son's grief was spreading like poison from a snakebite. Nazaire was not feeding his animals, not even mucking the barns. The cows suffered from heavy bags and too little water. Even with Raoul's help each day, Nazaire's animals were at risk of falling ill.

Raoul was the youngest of Varis' sons and as big as a tree. His thick neck and wide shoulders stood atop a body of Herculean strength but with the gentleness of a lamb. He still worked Varis' farm, living there with his new bride, Lucia and their two tots. Since the death of Nazaire's spouse, Raoul helped his oldest brother with farm chores.

Varis raised his eyebrows and offered another prayer. Wasn't it best to push Nazaire into the most promising possibility? With hard work, he could rise out of the grief that had gripped his heart. If his son could save the farm and the land, then he surely could reunite his family.

SET TO RIGHTS

Talk in the Barn

February 12, 1907

N azaire sat in his barn, mind and body numb against pressures that cut into his shoulders like steel suspenders. No amount of work pulled him from his murky sorrow. For two weeks now, Victoria lay dead. A chill crept up his legs and onto his thighs as he imagined his delicate spouse in the biting cold.

Raoul arrived to give Nazaire a hand with chores. At twenty-two, Raoul was ruddy-cheeked with brown eyes, a barrel chest and bear-sized hands. Like most of his brothers, he had the strong chin and straight nose that marked him as Abenaki. His naked face revealed a light fluff where other men sported a beard, maybe coarse whiskers.

They shoveled the winter coop and laid out fresh bedding. Every day Raoul helped, and every day Nazaire dragged his feet. Cows needed milking, horses fed, barns and stable shoveled, more wood cut for the stove. Nazaire sat, his mind and body paralyzed.

"You need to work. The animals, they don't feed themselves," Raoul complained.

"You're right. I need to work, but not here. I have no taste for it. I can't do it, I can't be here," Nazaire said as he put down feed for the chickens.

"It'll pass, it takes time."

"No, it won't."

Nazaire's thin fingers reached for the letter and pressed it into his brother's hand. Raoul read it, then handed it back.

"You want to leave home and everyone you know? Your children?"

"No. But none of this is of my making. I'm out of choices, and out of time."

They mucked the back stalls and put down straw. They fed the small animals, and filled feed carts for the horses and cows.

Raoul stared at his brother with an open mouth. "Think on this thing. This is a big thing."

"I can't buy seed for the spring. I'll lose it all."

They threw down fresh hay from the loft into the stables, broke ice cover in the troughs and water buckets so the animals could drink.

"Victoria is everywhere I look. There's nothing for me here. I'll go find Romeo and Gaudias — find our brothers and gold. Come with me. What you say we go?"

"You think I want to leave my woman? My little ones?" Raoul asked.

Nazaire sat down on a bale of hay, and sighed. "What do I have without my children? If I go, I have a fighting chance."

"You think hard on this. This is a big thing."

"It's a long shot, I know, but I take the long shot."

Raoul stood, looking at his feet. The brothers walked back to their father's farmhouse.

"It's a big decision for the both of us. Want to end up like me? One day your spouse is gone, your children ripped from your home, torn from your heart? What you've worked for, come to nothing?"

A tight knot clenched inside his stomach.

"What will Lucia think? What about father?"

Nazaire licked his lips. "Lucia is your spouse, not your courage. Father will think we're carving out our future."

"You need more than gold, Nazaire. You need a mother for your children."

The men walked back to Varis' farm. Lucia would accept any decision Raoul made; this was what women did. But what would his father say about this?

For Nazaire, no decision could be harder to make. Every good thing that had happened to him came after he had met Victoria. It wasn't that she was good luck, or that she was good for him, it's that all the goodness in the world came to him through her: his

children, his farm, his land, his entire life — and now
it was gone.

All gone.

Hard Planning

February 15, 1907

Nazaire pulled the letter from his pocket and set it on the kitchen table while Varis sat and rubbed his head with both hands.

"I can understand you going, Nazaire," Varis said, then turned toward his youngest son. "But why you, Raoul?"

"Together, we protect each other," Raoul said.

He leaned back against the water pump at the sink and stretched his arms like spreading wings, closed them, then stretched them out again.

"How can I run my farm without you here? No, you can't go, too!" Varis raised his hands in the air and shook his head back and forth. "No, better you go alone Nazaire, and Raoul stays," Varis continued.

Nazaire shuffled from one foot to the other.

"No, Raoul needs to stay," Varis said, spit spewing from his mouth.

Varis appraised his eldest son, Nazaire, the dependable one, steady and true. He released a long breath and raised his eyes to the ceiling.

Nazaire counted the fingers of one hand while he worked it out. "We'll have three years to find gold," he said.

"Yes and no," Varis explained. "It's not how many years your fields will be fallow that matter. You've declared yourself a farmer and a yield is what your fields must bring. What needs concern you is when your land will be abandoned by law, taken by the government, and that's in the spring of the fourth year. Brings you to maybe May tenth of the fourth year," Varis said. "Miss it and you'll lose your land."

Nazaire stood and turned from his father's view, a blush of red rising up his neck and face. With a nod of his head, Varis consented. They agreed to hire on a neighbor's two sons, steady men and hungry for work. The neighbor's sons agreed.

"Father, make sure the farmhands stable my team together so as not to upset them, and feed my taller gelding first or he'll bite," Nazaire instructed.

Raoul stifled a laugh while Varis paced in the large kitchen, his eyes shifting from the table to the farmhouse door.

Varis continued, "OK Nazaire, you'll need to take into account snow and ice; they'll slow you down. Be back May the fifth, not one day later. Talk to Connolly; you need advice about the journey."

With a final nod, Varis gave his blessing to both of them. Raoul would go as well.

Nazaire smiled as his shoulders lowered. He took in a deep breath and felt the smallest quiver. Maybe tomorrow could be better.

Seeking Advice

February 17, 1907

Nazaire struck Michael Connolly's front door with a loud rap. An old man known for his blended gin and far travels, Connolly lived in Frampton, in a one-room cabin that leaned heavy on the front side and pushed against anyone who found themselves at his door. Solid green at one time, the clapboards smelled of rot where the paint stopped and moisture crept. Wooden steps wobbled, shifting under the weight of the men as they stood outside. Nazaire heard feet shuffling near the door.

"Who is it?" Connolly yelled.

"Nazaire Poulin from Saint Joseph of Beauce."

Heavy wheezing followed a sudden pop of the iron latch. The door pulled back, and Connolly stood with his mouth ajar at the extended arm before him, which held out a block of aged cheese.

"My father, Varis Poulin sends us. I'm Nazaire. This is Raoul, my brother. Can we talk?"

Frampton, a pioneering village of Irish Catholics surrounded by the French, was known for its gin. Unlike bathtub gin or that Saint Lawrence seaweed gin, Frampton raised gin to an elixir of the Gods, a miracle for the lips. Men could knock on any door, day or night, for a dime bottle.

A man of eighty, Connolly had a bent back with a thick head of iron-gray hair, and a greasy beard he wore like a bib on his chest. To the back, a sheet hung from the ceiling, separating the kitchen from his one-legged pallet, while a small fire glowed in an old wood-burning stove. The smell of skunk oil seeped from a lantern with a broken globe on a slanted cupboard.

Nazaire placed the cheese in front of Connolly as the old man caught his breath and settled himself at the table. He pointed to chairs with a shaking hand.

"Know your father, worked with him one winter. We lost eleven houses in 1900. They floated down the

Chaudière, one with five men still on the roof."
Connolly eyed the brothers, sized them up while he
stroked his beard.

"The men who lived by the river, they'd move a
house off its foundation in three minutes flat, haul it
up to higher ground," Connolly said.

Could this man be trusted? Nazaire wasn't sure.
He rubbed his hands and asked, "We want to go to
the gold fields of the Klondike," Nazaire said.

"Men have come for advice about the Yukon, and
many never came back. You be going into the deep
cold there."

Connolly stretched as if rowing a boat, winced
and rubbed an elbow. "In my green years, I traveled
throughout Ontario and Quebec as a yeoman, worked
on Lake Nipigon three years, hauling cargo for the fur
trade."

Connolly paused, turned his bottom lip into a
pout, his jaw working and took a pull from his
Imperial tin. Nazaire and Raoul leaned in, hands and

forearms on the table. Connolly squinted while he worked his mouth, caught saliva for the lecture.

"First, bring oils and spirits to break the frost in your rifles. Second, use castor oil for mosquitoes, rub it on your face, neck, ears, wherever skin shows."

He pointed to Raoul, "You have the look of your mother." He turned to Nazaire, "And you, your father."

Nazaire wondered if the old man was clear-minded.

"Third, there's goin' to be wind like God is walkin' the earth. Bring a good scarf for your face. After the Prairies, expect rock and snow, more cold than you've ever known."

Nazaire and Raoul leaned harder on the table, felt the top give a little, straightened their backs and pushed away.

"Fourth, at the first sign of snow, make snowshoes, watch the Indians and do what they do," Connolly advised.

Did the old man know what he was talking about? Nazaire wasn't sure. Maybe he was crazy with memories too long passed.

Connolly turned in his chair, gasped hard and gathered his thoughts. "Fifth, there's empty work camps all over. When you must rest, take a day or two, build a rhythm to refresh yourselves."

Raoul's chair squeaked against the warped floor as he repositioned his legs.

"Where do we cross the Rockies?" Nazaire asked.

"The Rockies? How you travel will tell you where you cross. The rivers are faster than land. You'll cover in one day on water what it'll take you ten or more on ground. Less animals to hunt you or steal your sleep with worry."

"How do we not get lost?" Raoul asked. A red flash spread up his neck.

"Nobody crosses the Rockies without a guide. Many have died, found frozen or never found. There's plenty o' guides in Edmonton."

joyce derenas

Nazaire lowered his head and looked up at
Raoul. They both remained silent while Connolly
continued, relishing the conversation.

"Beyond Edmonton, always walk with a long
rope around your waist. If'n one of you falls into a
hole, throw the rope and th'other can pull you out."

The old man rose and shoved the sheet aside.
Nazaire watched as he walked to his pallet. Next to it,
a small table held a pipe in a swan dish, its double
wings and graceful neck painted gold. It mimicked
the same colors as Victoria's barrette, a wedding gift
Nazaire had surprised her with, the hairpiece delicate
and petite like his new bride. It was then Nazaire
knew in his bones that Victoria would approve, and
Connolly's advice was solid and true. This journey
was the only solution to Nazaire's miseries.

The old man returned with a black book, opened
it and thumbed some pages before beginning again.

"Get to Ottawa before April the one, look up a
man name of Sherman. He'll take you through the

Prairies, guarantee you food and water, no trouble from Indians. Find him in Carlington."

"Don't believe we can afford the luxury," Nazaire said.

Connolly became sterner as he explained, "Listen boys, Sherman parleys with prairie Indians; he'll get you through and cut out the rigmarole. Don't think you can put out snares anywhere you want, do you? Take moose or elk? Take water from any stream? Not in Indian territory. Maybe twenty years ago, but not today. The more north you go, the more Indians there are, not like hunting on someone's land around here."

Raoul sat like a frightened turtle, his head tucked into broad shoulders, two useless flippers clenched on his lap.

"The most important thing to remember is — everything about that country wants to kill you."

Raoul and Nazaire gave thanks with ready smiles and handshakes. The lecture complete, Connolly pulled out a bottle of his proper Irish gin and got three greasy glasses from the cupboard. They shared a toast for good luck, then the brothers left.

Outside, Nazaire heard Connolly through the cabin door. "Wonder if today be the last time I see these men?"

Goodbyes

February 20, 1907

Nazaire had said his goodbyes the evening before, during a large meal of meat pies, cheese quiches and blood sausage at his in-law's house. The aroma of roasted duck had hovered over the dining room like ambrosia.

The evening was both glorious and bittersweet, like a cruel gift Nazaire was grateful for, yet dreaded to accept. Thomas, his oldest son, remained silent beside his father the entire time, his bottom lip pushed out. He was tall for his eight years, with narrow shoulders and sandy hair. The men had asked one question after another of Nazaire, avoiding the issue of returning back home, so talk of this stayed outside.

During the meal, Nazaire insisted his oldest move in with the boy's Uncle Arthur, in the center of the village. He would help out in the convenience store.

He was too old for school now and must learn the ways of the world and what it was to be a man.

After the meal, Victoria's parents had assembled the children for a last hug and kiss from their father. How Nazaire cherished the smell of his newborn's head, all talc and rosewater.

"Uncle Raoul and me, we're going away for a bit. When we get back, you'll all come home," Nazaire told his children.

Some of Victoria's family, the Vachons, rolled their eyes at the promise, igniting a fire in Nazaire's stomach while the weight of the night lay heavy on his heart. He loved Victoria's family but hated them at the same time. Should he go? They had all but pushed him into this dangerous journey when they took his children. Were they right?

———

The next morning, Nazaire gathered everything they would carry, spread out on Varis' kitchen table. Nazaire's resolve strengthened. He would show them, show all the Vachons. He would go, and with hard work and determination, he'd be back, the better for the leaving. In an upstairs bedroom Raoul and Lucia were saying their goodbyes with the rhythmic squeak of their old bed. Thomas helped as his father barked instructions. It was time for a last check.

"Are you ready? Let me look," Varis asked.

Nazaire took two rucksacks and filled them with a small pot and utensils, then foodstuffs. A line of small bottles sat on the table, each labeled castor, spirit, turpentine. Thomas touched Nazaire's forearm and handed him the hunting knives.

"Grab my water canteen and fill it. Do the same for Raoul's, boy," Nazaire said.

Thomas filled each canteen from the water pump. Raoul joined them in the kitchen as they rolled their rifle packs with care, folded wool balbriggans, added pistol and shot, then secured the bundles with cat gut. Nazaire's pack held his .50 Winchester while Raoul grabbed his .351 Remington.

Each man covered their rifle pack with waterproof canvas and extended the butt end of their firearms in the air for quick grabbing. Nazaire rubbed his hands together while everyone else held their breath, the air thin in the large kitchen. Restless arms and bodies bumped into each other.

"Thomas, get Grandpa's whiskey under the sink, and four glasses," Nazaire said.

The men stopped to watch the boy.

"Come father, Raoul, let's sit and have a shot together. You too, Thomas — just a little taste," Nazaire said.

Varis poured out the strong whiskey. The four of them had never sat like this before, but here they were, raised glasses in the air.

Nazaire nudged his son's shoulder. "Sip it slow, boy."

A huge smile replaced the thin line that was Thomas' lips while the men watched him struggle to sip the strong home-brew. Thomas shook his head and wet his lips with his tongue, closed one eye as he drank. Raoul let out a chuckle followed by a guffaw, and that got everyone started. The kitchen exploded with raised shoulders and bellowing laughter. Around the table, the men relaxed as Raoul spoke of old man Connolly and retold some of his fierce cautions.

Varis watched while his sons knelt on the floor and spread out their bedrolls. He threw down hunting knives, cat gut and leather ties. Raoul grabbed small bottles of oils, placing the items into various pockets.

Nazaire shuddered as he grabbed a tin of matches, two candles, a compass, an old map, and green soap similar to their mother's. His head ached from all the quick decisions. He jammed in wire, a flint, boot laces, cheesecloth for purifying water and a small file. Everyone stood and scanned the kitchen for forgotten items.

"Your kit, Papa. Where is your kit?" Thomas asked.

"It's everything we carry with us, Thomas," Nazaire said as he pointed to the packs and rolls on the floor.

Raoul patted his pants' pockets and asked, "Pipe and tobacco?"

These were added to the inside pockets of their wool mackinaws along with ammo. They lifted their kits, spent five minutes to check heft and counterbalance. They would leave in their warmest mackinaws and old gumboots. Lucia entered the kitchen, added new knit tuques and scarves, placed two mason jars of harvest punch made from apple cider vinegar, molasses and ginger on the table.

The air in the kitchen felt odd, as if unknown law of gravity had sucked some element from the room, making it difficult to think. Nazaire's mind slipped sideways as he questioned the logic of staying against the necessity of going. He paced and shook out restless legs that found no destination. No, he had no choice. He must go.

What would become of his children if he didn't return? What if he returned but failed to find gold? Leaving wasn't what Nazaire wanted. He squeezed his eyes tight, then opened them wide. A chill spread down his spine while he poured himself another shot of whiskey.

Varis grabbed Nazaire by the shoulder and said, "You come back now with your brother."

"Promise," Nazaire said.

Then Nazaire turned to Raoul and stated the same demand.

Raoul answered, "Promise."

They would leave in the darkness of the next morning.

Talk with Thomas

February 20, 1907

Nazaire stopped in the doorway of the small bedroom upstairs in Varis' farm. Thomas turned his head and looked up. Red marks circled the boy's eyes.

Nazaire sat on the narrow cot. "You did good today."

Thomas asked, "Why do you have to go, Papa?"

Nazaire shrugged his shoulders.

"To keep you children and the farm, I need to go."

The boy cried and clung to Nazaire's arms while he pulled his son's hands down under the wool blanket.

"You're my big boy, Thomas. I look to you because you're dependable. Mother would be happy with you."

"Papa, where do you go?"

"On promenade, Thomas. You know what that is, eh? It's when men leave home to go find work, go for a long time. When we leave tomorrow, I'm taking you to your Uncle Arthur's. You're too old for school now so you stay with him until I get back. He's a good man and you'll learn many important things."

The boy pulled a rag from under his blankets and wiped his nose.

"But Papa, what if you don't come back?"

"Of course, I'll come back. Uncle Arthur will teach you your numbers. You'll work with money and understand business. These are important things for a young man to learn."

"When do you come back?" Tears ran down Thomas' face, and his lips quivered.

"I make you a promise, Thomas. You count four springs, we come back in the fourth spring. Sleep now."

Nazaire stood up and pulled the covers to the boy's shoulders. He hesitated as he looked down at his son with eyes and a small chin like Victoria's. The boy turned on his side, facing the wall. Nazaire placed a gentle hand on his son's shoulder then squeezed, surprising himself with the gesture. He couldn't help but think of all the changes the boy would go through in the coming years. Nothing could be done about it. As a father, he was doing right by his eldest son. Wasn't it time for Thomas to become a man?

Wayside Cross

February 20, 1907

Rarely did Raoul Poulin pray. A practical man, he found happiness each day while he expected hard work to make good things happen. When it came to God, womenfolk offered intercessions; however, this journey and all the risks that it entailed demanded the added pull of prayer.

He walked to the bend in Big Mountain Row and turned the corner, his target an old wooden wayside cross with clover endpoints. He bent a knee on the weathered frame that doubled as a kneeler. This was Raoul's favorite. Wayside crosses were everywhere in Quebec, offering rest and comfort for the road-weary. Each was unique, some made of wood, even discarded farm equipment, whatever could be hammered or welded into shape.

Raoul didn't want an audience, his being here a private matter, a moment all his own. The sound of hoofbeats gained his attention, faint at first, then louder until the whoosh of front skis on the road slapped in his face. He stood and turned from the spray of slush and took a knee. He bit his lip and started.

"God, you know me and my heart, help us to be safe and find gold when we get to the Klondike. Don't let any bears or Indians get us, you know how I feel about Indians."

He shivered with cold as visions of the settlers who died by the hands of fifteen hundred Mohawks in the Lachine Massacre turned in his mind. That the massacre had happened at least two hundred years earlier made no difference to him.

"Make sure we find our way."

Deep in his chest, he felt the same twinge of sorrow that had marked his mother's last days. The lamented sobs came through the bedroom walls as his mother cried, calling for Romeo and Gaudias, his brothers, far from home and surely lost. Even the one letter received years later offered no proof that they remained alive. Raoul breathed in, took his time to get all the words right, proving how much he was in earnest.

"Help my Lucia and the farmhands, protect my two little ones and watch my father." His words dissolved in the crisp air as dusk signaled vespers from the peel of bells at the small, nearby chapel.

"You know how many lives depend on us, Lucia and my children, Nazaire and his. We'll give it all we've got in the mines, but I hold you to your part."

———

Raoul walked home, a little spring in his step as he considered the issue closed. The day had exhausted everyone, and with time running short, Raoul and his spouse, Lucia had much to settle before they slept.

He had grown to depend on Lucia. She was thin but solidly built, and smart. Her skin glowed with a milky complexion. In Varis' farmhouse, Raoul and Lucia shared an upstairs bedroom while their two toddlers slept in an alcove at the bottom of the stairwell.

In their bedroom that night, Raoul began, "It'll be difficult, but the farmhands will do the bulk of the work. I'll make maybe ten or twelve dollars a day compared to fifty-three cents I would make here. It's a chance for us to get ahead, maybe get our own farm."

"You're right, the time for sacrifice is now when the children are little. Are you sure you'll find gold?" Lucia asked, clutching her fingers under the covers.

"Newspapers have said that there's plenty still there. Yes, I believe it."

Raoul's mind raced with excitement. In bed, he wrapped his arms around Lucia, took in the softness of her hair, the curve of her chin, how her eyes sparkled. How would he manage without her?

For two years, Lucia had filled most of Raoul's nights and days, and he needed her as much as loved her. She was steadfast and constant — what a farmer needed in a spouse. In the morning, he would leave and might never return. His eyes hurt from all the thoughts that roiled in his head, but he'd think about that after he was on the road. Now he wanted to concern himself with nothing but her white shoulders and those delicate pink pearls rigid against his chest.

"Woman," he whispered as he pulled her atop him, felt the lightness of her body, the shimmer of her breasts.

Lucia tucked a hand under his chin while the light scent of vanilla rose from the back of her ears, a farmer wife's perfume. His passions flared with the creak of the bed springs, encouraged by her sweet laugh. How can I leave this woman? He cursed the sacrifice this journey would demand of him.

Again, he moaned, "Woman."

NORTHBOUND

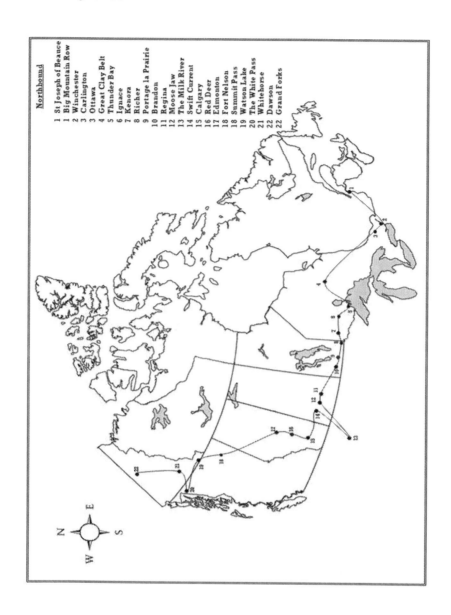

Northbound

1 St Joseph of Beauce
1 Big Mountain Row
2 Winchester
3 Carlington
3 Ottawa
4 Great Clay Belt
5 Thunder Bay
6 Ignace
7 Kenora
8 Richer
9 Portage la Prairie
10 Brandon
11 Regina
12 Moose Jaw
13 The Milk River
14 Swift Current
15 Calgary
16 Red Deer
17 Edmonton
18 Fort Nelson
18 Summit Pass
19 Watson Lake
20 The White Pass
21 Whitehorse
22 Dawson
22 Grand Forks

TRAVELING MEN

Winchester

Ontario ✎ March 6, 1907

Men walked in loose groups on country roads that led up from the northern shore of Lake Superior and beyond. Many traveled to reach bunkhouses where they hoped jobs awaited. Men would spend all their monies to reach a job hundreds of miles away just to be pushed aside or told no, not for another twelve weeks. Most camps paid a dollar and a half a day for a six-day week with a ten- to twelve-hour workday. A week's board was four dollars and a half.

Every village and town revealed tent cities. As many as a dozen men filled a tent, most speaking the same tongue, congregating to survive until a hint of the next job might take them more miles with neither food nor transport provided. The open road could be a dangerous place. You could meet wolfers or roustabouts, ready to offer you tea one minute, and steal your kit the next.

Nazaire spotted an Indian one night, an Ojibway by the look of the bead work on his mocks. He wore hide leggings with a breechcloth and a collarless, home spun shirt. A curled blue sash collected long black hair across his forehead and hung down his back like two bright snakes. The Indian stayed to the rear of the group, keeping company with two youths in similar dress. The next morning, the youths had left and the Indian trailed behind all day, walking easy with a striking mare, a leopard appaloosa with rich brown spots like new leather.

Beyond the village of Winchester, where the roads played out, groups of people walked together, strangers all. The rowdier men merged into one noisy crowd leading the pack. The temperatures had been unbearable across the last seven days, dipping to 3°F. March finally brought days above freezing and nights more tolerable for camping outdoors.

In some places, the wagon trail slumped into ground water with slush ice and frozen leaves, making walking treacherous. Where rot was thick in the air, people fanned right or left, seeking rail ties or tracks that followed higher ground with dry, surer purchase for each step. They camped the same way they walked — at separate campfires with the feistiest up front, the meek in the rear. Few people shared fire, not wanting to be shamed into offering food. The trail was hard, and no place for generosity.

Nazaire motioned that the Ojibway join his small fire. The Ojibway's long hair held small braids and at the front of his forehead, two long feathers were bound by gut. Rings of beads fell from his neck. He had a strong chin and deep-seated eyes. Rawhide tassels adorned his shoulders and cuffs. Most prominent was the copper medallion marking him as a Midi, a medicine man.

"I'm Peter Coppaway. I come from Curve Lake in Peterborough," he said.

An aura of calmness lit Coppaway's face. His eyes were gentle, and he looked not at Nazaire but somehow into him. At once, Nazaire felt that this was a man he could trust, and on whom he could depend. These were valuable traits on the trail. If Coppaway was a Midi, a member of the Grand Medicine Society, then it was wise on the road to have someone who knew natural medicines.

One night, Raoul was awakened from a deep sleep by a hand that brushed against his mouth. "What?" Raoul pushed a shoulder deeper into his bedroll.

Nazaire flicked his brother's earlobe. Raoul gasped in surprise as he opened his eyes to see Nazaire peering down at him. Nazaire raised a chin toward the sounds of many men fighting. Shouts heaved through the branches, with squeals of blasphemy and rowdiness.

"Come now," Nazaire whispered.

In the inky darkness, five shots rang out, their echoes stretched in the air like greasy smoke. Nazaire

and Raoul gathered their bedrolls and kits as
Coppaway motioned them back toward the empty
trail. Whatever the cause of the fight, Nazaire wanted
nothing to do with the mischief. The three men
walked off the trail and settled back down to sleep.
Sounds of men walking among brush continued
during the night.

In the early morning, Coppaway left his horse
and the sleeping brothers as he circled to the front of
the ruckus. He walked on fallen leaves, squatted to
listen while whispers sometimes rose with the dawn.
He soon discovered the cause of the commotion.

"I hit something, I know it," once voice said.

"He ran over there," a second voice insisted.

Coppaway heard three hunters move off to the
east. They were wrong. They had wounded an elk,
and she lay on the ground, shivering with pain.
Coppaway slit her throat, giving silent thanks for a
life that would feed many. Her milk glands were
swollen. She had a calf nearby; Coppaway was sure of
it.

He gutted the cow and carried her to the road, walking toward the rear campfires where travelers were more civil. Coppaway cut away chunks of meat and left them on the ground or next to cooking pots at a number of small fires. He remembered seeing women who stood by their cooking pots, anxious to get a small slab of steak or anything for their hungry children. When he had the neck and head left, he dropped those at the fire tended by men dressed in large fur hats and woven vests. They would make good brain stew.

Coppaway rejoined the two brothers from Quebec. Raoul was awake and had built a small fire. Tired from their broken sleep, they coffeed up and planned what they ought to do next. Coppaway pulled out a large chunk of rump from a bloody pouch. It would sustain them for a few days.

Coppaway said, "I know what the commotion was last night. Those drunks shot an elk, but lost it in the dark. I helped her out of this world and then gave some of the meat to the women who tend the small fires."

Nazaire and Raoul both smiled at the size of the rump. They rummaged in their kit to find a pot and salt.

"A young one remains, left to starve. We could find it, it won't be far," Coppaway said.

As the dawn broke into a honeyed sky, Nazaire grabbed ammo and a good boning knife.

"Raoul, stay and tend the fire."

Coppaway disappeared into the woods followed by Nazaire carrying his rifle and a small rucksack. When they returned, Coppaway laid a young gutted elk down near the campfire.

Raoul smiled. He had cut the meat into chunks, and added them to the pot with the last of the vegetables, a ripe squash. He topped the pot off with wild onions that he had pounded into a mush.

"Where're you headed?" Nazaire asked.

"Near Ottawa to meet a friend," Coppaway said.

"We're going to meet a wilderness guide named Sherman at a town called Carlington," Nazaire said.

Coppaway turned his head in surprise. "Sherman? Carlington? Sherman and my father are good friends for many years. He is like an uncle to me. I go with him to Edmonton."

By the warmth of the fire, the men ate and laughed at their coincidence. Coppaway spoke of his father, the Ojibway Chief of the Curve Lake band who had accompanied Sherman into Indian territory and introduced the wilderness guide to many chiefs throughout the west. Coppaway explained how his father helped establish Sherman as a man to be trusted, his word as good as that of any chief.

Perhaps others on the same road were headed to find Sherman and gold. Each night while settling down, Nazaire and Raoul spoke of the Yukon and gold. They had read a newspaper article that reported the gold in tons taken from the Dawson area.

Raoul asked Nazaire with excitement, "Sure sounds like there's more than enough for you and me.

If they report gold by the ton, don't you think it'll be easy for us to get a small shovelful each week?"

"Listen, they ain't just giving it away. You gotta get it out of the ground first," Nazaire said. "Never sell the skin before you kill the bear."

No one followed drunks that fired their arms in the night-it was dangerous business. The three men gladly lagged behind to stay safe from the mischief makers ahead of them. They would find the edge of Carlington and camp in the forest nearby, awaiting the start of April.

Carlington

April 1, 1907

Nazaire, Raoul, and Coppaway were the first to walk into the small tavern in Carlington. They found a long bench at the side and sat, dropping their kits by their feet. Nazaire held his breath, squirming on the rough wood. Two pioneer men dressed in rawhide pants entered next, their faces ruddy. The two groups looked each other over. Coppaway stood and grabbed a man by the shoulders.

"Uncle," Coppaway said as they embraced.

"Boy, you've grown into a man. I got your father's message. How is it that you're going all the way up to Edmonton?" Sherman asked.

"My father marries me off to a woman there. I'll join her band if her father has me," Coppaway said as the two men laughed. They embraced and spoke for a few minutes, then Coppaway introduced Nazaire and

Raoul, who shook hands with Sherman and his guide,
Lennox.

Nazaire looked Sherman over, remembering
Coppaway's words about the wilderness guide who
had walked with his father and followed old Indian
trails. They had struck negotiations with bands
throughout the Northwest Territories, through the
Prairies and south in Ontario.

Sherman introduced himself and Lennox to
Nazaire and Raoul. Sherman and Lennox looked like
rugged frontiersmen, calm and clear-eyed. Sherman's
ink black hair and long nose suggested a mixed
background while Lennox' gray eyes proved him to
be a true Scot.

Coppaway had spoken of Lennox, the Scot who
trapped and hunted for Sherman's chuck wagon.
Lennox checked water crossings for safety, and over
the years, met with agency Indians or the Royal
North-West Mounted Police to parley when entering
conflicted territory where fighting was often over
water rights.

Nazaire and Raoul paid Sherman. A stone fireplace burned with many pops at the back of the tavern. In the corner, two navvy men played a game of cards on a wooden barrel. Nazaire found comfort in Coppaway's presence. The shaman was calm, which was more than Nazaire could say of himself. Inside, his stomach lurched with knots that jumped at every sound. His eyes took in the sweep of the dark tavern while loud customers clinked glasses.

Nazaire knew in his heart that he could back out right now, turn around and ask Raoul to follow, that they would be going home. Raoul would do it; he would follow Nazaire wherever he went.

"Am I crazy? Should we even be here?" Nazaire asked Raoul.

"What," Raoul said.

Nazaire lowered his head. How could he consider such a foolish notion? How would he earn enough to feed his children if he returned home? How could he plant a crop or hope to turn his sweat into cash come autumn? No, he had to continue north. He was here, outside Ottawa. Nazaire remembered old man Connolly's words-"You are quarter way there by Ottawa. Winnipeg is halfway, and Edmonton starts the last quarter." Nazaire shook his head.

"What," Raoul asked again.

"I don't repeat the mass for the deaf," Nazaire whispered in a harsh voice, gritting his teeth.

He fidgeted as more men walked through the tavern door. Sherman greeted each one, his rawhide jacket fringed with tasseled chest pockets and forearms signaling him as head of the party. One man entered the tavern, gray-haired and round in the stomach. He pulled up a chair near Nazaire and spoke of often traveling with Sherman's outfit and knew the crew to be reliable, the conversation putting Nazaire's mind to ease.

The next man came in with a young boy. Both wore long, black coats sweeping the floor. The man's words cut the air like guttural swords. Sherman said they were Hutterites from Bavaria. He paid up and sat on a long bench, his shy son clinging to his arm, not daring to look around.

Nazaire glanced at the boy as thoughts of his sons flooded his mind. No, Nazaire would avoid the boy. The pain of homesickness was too raw for him to bear. Two men arrived next, Americans who were loud and ill clad with felt bowlers, those stiff felt hats that would do nothing to warm their heads.

"We need passage to the Klondike," said one.

Sherman looked the pair over, and replied, "I can get you as far as Edmonton."

They paid up and sat at one side of the tavern where they called for ales. Nickleson, the younger of the two, flopped an exquisite, custom-tooled leather satchel on the table. In the center of the flap was a silver compass secured by silver snaps. Nickleson turned the bag around, revealing a sketch of an automobile and 'Nickleson Electric Car Company' worked in a handsome cherry stain. The grooves and curves of the tooling were magnificent and together with decorative silver on the flaps, straps, and compass all gleamed.

Nazaire wondered why a traveling man would advertise a bejesus bag where he kept his cash. This was a man who had little experience with the world. The older American, Cochran, scanned the room. With subtle smirks, he influenced Nickleson's brash behavior. It was clear who was the hen and who was the cock.

Three more men entered, looking for Sherman. They were dressed like merchants, with wool vests and new mackinaws. They were strangers to each other, and all had business in Edmonton.

Nazaire felt Raoul grab his arm as three Indians, Gros Ventre, arrived and parleyed with Sherman in their Sioux dialect. Nazaire learned that two were helping the youngest, Longfox, a thirteen-year-old who was stranded and needed to return to his reservation in Montana. Longfox wore a breechcloth and leggings with a dirty, old blanket for a coat. The shy Longfox stood with downcast eyes while he scanned everyone in the tavern.

Sherman explained, "I can take him as far as Moose Jaw or Swift Current, but then he'll have to make his way south to Fort Belknap on his own."

The two Gros Ventre paid and left. Longfox made his way to the bench against the wall and nudged Raoul to squeeze aside of Coppaway, seeking his own kind. Raoul's eyes widened as he stiffened on the bench, unsure what to do. He was shoulder to shoulder with a wild Indian.

Nazaire whispered to Raoul, "You're OK."

More men entered and shook Sherman's hand before seating themselves.

Sherman checked his pocket watch, stood and spoke.

"I'm Sherman, the expedition leader. This is my forward guide, Lennox."

At the mention of his name, Lennox gave a small nod. Lennox had soft gray eyes and was all business and rugged as a tree.

"Both of us are experienced trappers, and we're here to protect you. Whenever one of us needs a helping hand, I expect that you'll oblige," Sherman said.

Nazaire caught Nickleson and Cochran as they threw out their lips, a slight sneer on their faces. Lennox walked by the side tables and stopped in front of Nickleson, waiting for him to lower a bent leg so he could pass unimpeded. Lennox gazed down at Nickleson and smiled, continued to smile as he waited. Nickleson read the intention and delayed longer than necessary to pull back the extended leg. Meanwhile, Cochran looked up, two black eyes riveted on Lennox. Cochran placed a light hand on Nickleson's forearm and squeezed.

Nazaire's eyes met Coppaway's. Both men caught Nickleson's hesitancy. From the looks of it, the older Cochran rode a steady hand on Nickleson's emotions. Lennox passed by and left the tavern through the back door, then re-entered a minute later.

Sherman raised his rifle in the air, a Ross Mark II, a handsome five bolt, pull action weapon. He looked around the room and asked, "OK men, who's loaded?"

Nazaire, Raoul and the Hutterite raised their hands.

"Let's unload right now. What you've paid for is protection, clean water and grub. Between me, Lennox and the chuck wagon cook, we'll take care of you."

As the three men pulled shot from their rifles, Sherman continued.

"Each man is to help with general duties every day."

Nazaire and Raoul nodded in agreement.

"They're gonna be trouble," Nazaire whispered to Raoul with a nudge toward the backside of the room.

"Huh," Raoul said.

Lennox spoke next. "You'll each be assigned a job in the next day or two. Most of you are without a horse, and that's an advantage. Beyond Edmonton, there's neither feed nor hay for horses unless you pay a prime rate."

Sherman took over the lecture. "If you risk anyone's life, or raise hell, we'll leave you to yourself. My word is final with any dispute, understood?"

Sherman's eyes met each man's long enough to gain consent. "OK, let's go."

The men spilled outside where a string of horses stood, saddled and ready to be mounted. The party formed a mixed line of men carrying sacks, poles and carpetbags of every size and description.

Nazaire overheard Sherman whisper to Lennox, "Maybe half of them will make it there and back alive."

"Maybe less," Lennox said.

Each man had their own reason for walking to Edmonton. As cities expanded, so did the need to move livestock or cargo, always cheaper on the trail than using rail. With Sherman at the front and Lennox taking up the rear, they made for a rawboned-looking bunch.

Nazaire swallowed hard. This was it. He was headed to Edmonton and there would be no backing out now. Each mile put distance between where he wanted to be and what he must do for his family, his farm, and his land.

City of Ottawa

April 3, 1907

Nazaire turned when he heard a buckboard approach from behind. The driver slowed his four-horse team as Sherman's party split, hugging the sides of a wet road. In the back, most of the work crew stood, faces and clothes covered in dust. The driver was a muscular man with mahogany skin, ferrying a work crew of ten men who clung to the wooden rail boards of the wagon, all with skin the same rich dark color.

Nazaire asked Sherman, "Who are these men? Where do they come from?"

Sherman explained, "Third-generation Canadians. Descendants of American slaves who ran for their lives toward freedom. There's over thirty thousand of them in Ottawa now."

The party made its way into the city of Ottawa. As the dirt road widened, muddy ruts fell away. The backs of wooden cabins and rows of filthy tents came into view. It was a sorrowful sight of tattered and torn canvas, patched up sheeting, even broken crates used as window frames.

More tent cities fronted the shoreline of the Ottawa River to the Northwest, bleached tents, some painted with the words 'Laundry', two to three acres of them smelling foul with wet ruts along the back rows where men and women alike relieved themselves. Lines of wash hung in disarray as dirty-faced children played in dried gullies. Women pushed creaking wagons whose wheels complained as the women greeted one another, plying their trade. People of all ages and colors moved about, bound to make a penny by mid-morn.

At the train station, men, many of them grandsons of former Georgian slaves, worked as porters and station men. Never had Nazaire seen such lustrous chestnut skin as that of the rail workers. Neither were his ears prepared for the languid drawl of southern dialects. Near the river's edge, men worked in severe cold, some with torn jackets, others missing sleeves. A small crowd poured out of streetcars and trolleys. Most were black.

"Are we still in Canada?" Raoul whispered.

"I don't know," Nazaire said.

Nazaire exchanged grimaces with Raoul, shocked to be outnumbered ten-to-one by dark-skinned people. The group continued through the main streets in silence, eyes wide and mouths open in disbelief. The city stretched out before them, bordered on the east by the winding Ottawa River. Four-story brick buildings lined the main thoroughfares while a group of buildings, all looking to be ornate, stone fortresses rose above all others.

"Parliament," Lennox said.

"Oh, this is where my grain profits go," Nazaire complained.

Small shops and eateries lined the riverside heading up to the city center while every four blocks, bells announced the city rail cars as they stopped at major crossroads, letting people escape like mice, trapping others behind pivoting doors.

People on the streets spoke languages and dialects difficult to understand. Every fourth person, it seemed, had just arrived from England. The city abounded with the soft inflections of the Irish, the slow drawls of the southern freedmen, and the clipped vowels of the Brits. Sherman's party made their way on the broad sidewalks. They carried pans and tin cups that hung from shoe laces slung on their chests, and blanket rolls or rucksacks strapped to their backs.

An impressive brick building, the Eaton Company Limited loomed before the group. Eaton's was an emporium of delights and the largest retail seller first in England, and now Canada. Every village postman had an Eaton catalog that town folks used to order necessaries. The catalog, some two hundred-fifty pages, included hundreds of drawings and ample descriptions with prices. The necessaries pictured were enough to stop a strong man's heart, and loosen a shy wife's tongue.

Sherman called for his party's attention. "If you need mosquito netting, rifle shot, or anything else, get it here. It'll cost more the closer we get to Edmonton. Lay your kits down and Lennox will watch them. We'll wait twenty minutes."

Lennox stood apart from the men, guarding the kits some men had shed on the wooden walkway and said, "If you've got little money, don't go there. It'll taunt your soul to see all those sparkles."

"They sell whiskey?" Nickleson asked.

Lennox hesitated, then pointed to a storefront across the street. "Yonder, lad. Best you change your greenbacks for Canadian dollars first at the bank up a few doors."

Nickleson crossed the busy road, his short wool jacket collecting snow and mud from the horses that trotted by. Cochran ran after him like a nursemaid, brushing slush from the underside of Nickleson's fine leather satchel.

The Hutterite boy pressed his nose to the large department store window, his hands cupped around his eyes as he squinted through the frosty glass. A few minutes later, Longfox and then Coppaway joined him, all three bent over with their backsides sticking out, each awed by the glitter and mystery inside.

Nazaire remembered old man Connolly's caution as he and Raoul entered Eaton's and faced the costumed doorman inside the entrance.

"Mosquito nets?" Nazaire asked.

The doorman pointed. "Down the left staircase, sir, to the right, against the wall."

Nazaire found the netting and paid. Both couldn't help but examine every counter, crate and display on the ground floor before leaving. The group reunited outside.

"There's things in there nobody needs," Raoul said.

"Frenchy, some of us are perhaps more civilized than you," Nickleson snickered.

Raoul glared at the remark with hard eyes, but
Nazaire placed a calming hand on Raoul's shoulder as
he seethed, standing motionless and saying nothing.

———

At nightfall, the group arrived at a livery barn
north of the city. Coppaway rode next to Longfox and
tried to temper the boy some. To that end, Lennox
approached Longfox about his chores during the
journey.

"Feed and water the horses. Give them a
rubdown and take the curry to whichever horse is
terrible dusty. Wipe any that are wet. They sleep
inside tonight; otherwise, build a tether line to hitch
up the animals at night. Picket them. You know what
that means?" Lennox asked.

Longfox nodded.

"Each rider saddles and unsaddles their mount.
The rest will be your job each morning and night."

The youth agreed with a shallow grunt. Sherman
and Lennox rode geldings. Two mares followed, one
designated more a spare in case of injury. The mares

would carry small water barrels when necessary. Coppaway rode a beautiful leopard appaloosa, white dappled with brown spots while one merchant rode a skewbald mare. The chuck wagon would arrive in the morning, pulled by two flea-bitten grays. With Longfox's mustang, the count was nine horses. In snow or rain, Coppaway would give a hand. Sherman didn't like his animals wet. He prided himself on healthy mounts for the two-thousand-mile journey.

Sherman had bartered a good night's rest for his party in an empty barn, waiting on the cook to sort out the chuck wagon. The men would enjoy a hot meal, served in a nearby logger's warehouse, and sleep indoors on clean straw. The meal of beef in thick gravy with potatoes and carrots would be the first and last time that the group would eat so well.

Sherman rousted the men in the morning to the sounds of dragging chains as horse teams entered the livery yard. "Come on boys, pack your kits, then breakfast before we break camp."

Outside, the camp cook drove up to the outside of the barn, his chuck wagon filled with victuals and necessaries. He prepared the first of many breakfasts for the men. The camp cook, fat and near forty, offered a ready smile. Once coffeed up, he stood by the largest fire, leaning over bubbling fry pans and pots.

He started his sermon, "Hey boys, I'm Cookie. You just line up with your plates, and I'll dish the grub to each of ya. Help yourself to coffee in those pots. Hot biscuits are on the grate-two for each man."

The men lined up behind Sherman and Lennox, presenting their tin plates for beans and bacon. As the men finished eating, Cookie removed a pail of hot water from the fire and set it aside with a few rags for each man to clean their cup and plate.

True to his word, Longfox led the horses to the water troughs, then led them to hay. Coppaway helped Longfox with his chores and then and there, a bond began between the two. As Longfox fed and watered the horses, he took a mighty shine to

Coppaway's appaloosa with a beautiful chocolate and ivory coat.

The day before had been long but Nazaire knew that the memory of a cozy barn would fade as sleeping outside would be one of many sacrifices each man would endure.

The Great Clay Belt

T he forests at the edge of the Great Clay Belt were unnaturally spaced, a landscape of dead timbers, mainly black spruce and aspen for hundreds of miles with ground that sunk from poorly drained soils. Great stands of tamarack and stunted black spruce, skeletonized by insect damage and long-past fires, followed Sherman's party for miles. Even the horses found walking difficult as they fought to raise their hooves in the sucking clay soil. Around them, the stench of rotted salt brine lay in a fogged layer, a foot off the bare ground.

Time stretched out like the unending steel rails of a train track as the boredom of walking seeped into the men's bones. Nazaire and Raoul had left Quebec three months earlier, yet already their feet were sore. Each night, both men pulled green soap from their kit, spit a little, and then rubbed the pine-smelling soap against their heels and the sides of their feet. Cracks and sore spots were healed by morning.

The party followed the train tracks, climbing north until the trail reached the sheltered town of Cochrane that grew out of the summer campgrounds of the Wahgoshig, a band of Ojib-Cree Indians. The area was once an active canoe stopover for fur traders and Indians going north.

Over the decades, the town had become a rail transport junction for the Temiskaming and Northern Ontario Railways, as well as the Canadian National. Tents and rough-looking boarding houses sheltered hundreds of railroad workers.

Sherman had traveled through Cochrane every year but had yet to encounter one polar bear, despite many warnings posted to broadsides nailed on the outside of buildings and hanging from tent flaps. Town folks called them white ghosts and would tell how they wandered down from the arctic tidewaters of James Bay some four hundred miles north on the Old Overland Packet Trail in Moosonee. Polar bears could be heard bristling in the pine and spruce bush, throwing deep huffs while scratching out food with their huge paws.

People recognized Sherman and waved hello. In this town, his men hunkered indoors in a comfortable barn loft, free from worry of the wandering white ghosts.

Come nightfall, the men in the loft heard Sherman instruct Cookie.

"Clean up pronto tonight. We don't want no white ghosts coming in. I had Lennox throw Nickleson's and Cochran's kits down on the lower level. When you bed down, lock the door and when they come in from town, make them sleep down with the slush and horse piss. If they object, tell them there's no more room up here. That should teach them."

Above the dank, dirt floor, the men slept in comfort in the second-story loft on soft straw, warmed by the breath of horses below.

———

Town folks heeded the bear warnings this time of
year; Nickleson and Cochran, however, preferred to
roam the small town after dark, looking for cheap
whiskey and fast women. At a noisy tavern,
Nickleson bragged of his fortune, lifting the hidden
flap of his cherry bejesus satchel with ease.

The laggards in the barroom had missed curfew,
but the promise of money held back two barmaids
hopeful for a dollar toss on their hay mattresses in a
worn-out shanty a few streets away. The act, poorly
performed by Nickleson, left both he and Cochran
wandering through town alone, bringing attention to
themselves with rollicking songs, teasing night
monsters out of the dark and remarking on the
northern lights, a site that mesmerized them at that
hour of the night. They heard a rustling and they saw
the thing, huge with an open mouth and teeth that
gnashed.

Nickleson and Cochran ran as they screamed and
pounded on the livery doors but weren't fast enough
to escape the deep roar of a bear. A juvenile of

perhaps six hundred pounds jumped upon them, catching its front paws on Nickleson's bejesus satchel. The bag dragged in the purple-black clay before it tore free with one long scratch. The broken strap lay in the slush like the long jutting tongue of some primordial insect, shiny with the wet. A block away, one sleeve of Cochran's coat lay submerged under the bejesus bag and slush ice; the other was missing.

The roar of the village siren washed the quiet fog with two blasts that struck terror into every sleeping soul. Lanterns lit, and men pointed rifles and shotguns as they ran from open doorways and out of tent flaps, half asleep and angry. White men and Cree alike smirked at the drunks reveling at the northern lights that painted the sky.

––––

Nazaire shuddered in his bedroll. Downstairs, Cochran and Nickleson, both liquored up with their green common sense, had broken curfew. The town's acting constabulary considered the infraction a punishable offense that put people's lives in jeopardy.

The men were examined for injury, then thrown in the town's livery, nothing more than a ramshackle shed, to sleep it off.

The next morning, in the midst of waving arms and dramatic apologies, Nickleson and Cochran explained that after escorting the good-time girls to their pallets, they'd lost their way and soon heard the pitching and gulping of a large creature behind them. From his wet bejesus bag. Nickleson paid five dollars each for both his and Cochran's fine.

Cochran's coat was nowhere to be found. From a dirty box of rotted clothing, he pulled out a coat short at the sleeves and in the length but better than nothing. As they were let out of jail, Nickleson dragged his mud-coated bejesus bag by the broken strap.

A drunk yelled after them, "he just wanted to play with yous, that's all."

Some of the town folks laughed as Cochran and Nickleson chased after the retreating steps of Sherman's party.

CORDUROY ROADS

Thunder Bay

The party entered Thunder Bay welcomed by the stink of rotted fish. By the waterfront piers, broken Quebec carts filled one shallow cove gone still while a blanket of frigid air two feet off the icy ground trapped the stench of scales and fish heads, an assault to the men's noses. Everywhere, nets and ships' cordage hung off barrels.

A shelf of high cliffs rose to the west resembling a reclined man. His feet, torso, shoulders, face, chin and nose were visible from shore. Across the bay, Nazaire pointed to the rock formation once he saw it.

"This your sleeping giant?" Nazaire asked Coppaway.

Coppaway followed Nazaire's pointing finger, stopped and took in the long sweep of the thing, a massive rock formation on the shore of Lake Superior.

"I learned of the sleeping man as a boy. The stories tell about trust and betrayal," Coppaway said as he leaned over his horse and grabbed Nazaire's shoulder, a gesture of thanks.

The party meandered toward the center of town, fighting through the crowded thruways noisy with buckboards and horses. Streets, no more than muddy wagon paths, were lined with clusters of hitching rails. Boardwalks fronted the buildings with every entrance and doorway filled with bits of bark, broken branches and curled wood shavings clinging to the hems of clothing. Fine sawdust hugged everyone's boots while saws growled. Their buzzing teeth rose like cries for mercy falling on deaf ears and Sherman's party felt the annoyance. In Thunder Bay, lumber was King and the town enjoyed its newfound prosperity.

The railroad had built a dedicated north track that sent empty flatbed cars up to Winnipeg. Another dedicated south track brought down open cars of potash or huge trees to slip from Winnipeg into Thunder Bay's switching yards, then be offloaded.

Watching the cars coming and going mesmerized Sherman's men. Few outsiders had seen the sheer efficiency of these two majestic loops of steel, continuous lines of rail cars, each making money for the lumber yards. The buzz saws in Thunder Bay cut the trees to boards day and night, creating a boom industry for the tired fishing city.

Nazaire watched Nickleson break from the group and run into J. Hastings General Mercantile. When he caught up with Sherman's party, he sought out Cochran, hiding the bottle of whiskey.

"They've electrified the damned street. I didn't know there was electro hereabouts," Nickleson said.

"What's electrified?" Lennox asked.

"Street lights all the length of Arthur Street. We've arrived at a piece of civilization here. Even the mercantile has an electrolier on the ceiling. It lit up the entire store like you were standing in the presence of God or something."

On the back end of town, busy rail yards held dozens of flat cars loaded with rough-dressed lumber, their size and colors few of the men had ever seen. One car held a single tree so thick in girth that straps couldn't contain it. Along its length, braided ship cordage hammered flat and covered in tar fought double to secure it. Mixed smells rose from the rail yards, seeping from the cuts of the blade mixed with gentle balsam and pungent spruce.

At the north end of Thunder Bay, the corduroy road lay across the trail toward open forests as the party entered the Canadian Shield. A landscape of coniferous trees changed to hardwood, many strange to the men's eyes. There would be faster walkingwith the log road that continued onto Winnipeg, built using young trees, all tied and bundled, lining across the muddy road like a carpet. For over four hundred miles, men and horses would be free from the muddy ruts that turned horse hooves and sucked men's boots at every footfall. Within the Canadian Shield, the party would have harder sleeping on such thin topsoil atop bedrock.

Beyond the town, the railroad had laid double tracks. One brought down raw timber and potash from Winnipeg and horses from Saskatchewan. The other track offered northbound travel, hauling empty lumber flatcars and passengers. A separate north and south track defied custom but in this town, every activity favored the lumber industry. Sherman caught up with the group riding double with a thin stranger behind, the last member to join the westward party. He was a tall Norwegian engineer accompanied by a large wolfhound.

Sherman called "make camp," near a large rail spur.

———

The open land near the railroad spur was level space, ideal for Cookie to settle his chuck wagon for the night. The men set up tents under small trees and on soft grasses, content to sleep without lumps and away from the screeching saws of Thunder Bay. Near dusk, a train slowed to a stop at the spur. This train was a colonist train waiting to proceed northward to the Prairies. On this train there were no first-class passengers, no cargo, no dining cars with their double smoke stacks.

"What is this?" Nazaire asked.

"Immigrants going to open homesteads in the Prairies. These here are colony cars," Lennox said.

Electric lights illuminated the interiors of every coach, throwing shadows through the trees and setting a scene like the camera tricks of Melies' early movie, *A Trip to the Moon*. Silence fell over the camp as the coaches came to a full stop. Young children in some of the coaches noticed the men outside and waved. They pointed out the windows and jumped in excitement.

The cars looked to be ordinary passenger train coaches, except that every seat folded down into a sleeping pallet or folded back up to a table top for eating meals. At the front of each coach, women cooked on a stove built into one wall while on the opposite wall, a woman drew water from a spigot.

Some of the passengers saw Sherman's group and motioned for the outsiders to approach. From opened windows, smoking stoves in the coaches created a screen of haze with the aroma of grilled sausages wafting out. Sherman's men stood, breathing in the pulsing stench of thick oil from the locomotive wheels blended with the faint whiff of cooking meat. The persistent tick of the train engine echoed through the trees. A few children laughed from high berths that swung above folded tabletops.

The men in camp kept their distance but walked in front of the windows as the train started rolling by, one slow revolution of the wheels at a time. Sherman's men couldn't resist peering inside each colony coach.

Four coaches carried men, young to old. They looked to be a work gang dressed in dirty, worn clothing. In one coach, all the men wore the same color tunic in homespun wool with a bright red sash at the waist. They had black, oily hair that curled at their shoulders.

"Who are these men?" Nazaire asked.

"Looks like Prussians to me," Lennox said.

"Why all men in some coaches?"

"Pickers, seasonal help. They ride cheap, cook their food on the way up or back home. They'll work the sheep or horse ranches, maybe break their backs in greenhouses. Some will get jobs around grain elevators or for the railroad switching yards."

In another coach, a woman washed a young child in front of a window, and looked out with tired eyes. When she noticed Sherman's group, she screamed. Outside, Cochran stood holding his Johnson as he passed water in full view while Nickleson laughed and jumped up and down in giddy excitement.

"Ever seen anything this big?" Cochran yelled with pride.

"Hey, shame on you. Proper men don't act that way," Nazaire shouted.

Nickleson ran up to Nazaire, raised two arms and reached for Nazaire's shoulders. Then he pushed. Down Nazaire went, twisting as he fell. Some of the men who caught Cochran's misdeed shook their heads, whereas Raoul moved at the quick to help his brother off the ground. Nazaire wiped blood from his nose and turned to face Nickleson.

Lennox intervened, blocking another blow intent on finding Nazaire.

"Stop," Lennox said.

Cochran and Nickleson moved about, arms swinging as the two jostled to get closer to Nazaire.

"You're an offense to all good manners. Quit now," Lennox said.

"That damned bastard Canuck don't have nothing to say to me," Nickleson insisted.

Lennox raised a flat palm toward Nickleson, the other to Cochran.

"We're in a country full of Canucks. You two need to make friends wherever you can."

Sherman walked into the skirmish, stopping in front of Nickleson, "Give me the bottle."

Everyone stopped moving and watched as Nickleson hesitated, then walked to his bejesus bag and passed the whiskey into Sherman's outstretched hand. Nazaire wiped more blood from his face.

"I ever see you two do something like that again, I'll knock you dead asleep, you hear me?" Sherman barked as he peered at Nickleson and Cochran.

By chow time the silence had grown to quiet murmurs. During the meal, someone asked the distance to the gold fields of Dawson.

Lennox puzzled it out by stretching his hand open and counted fingers. "Three thousand miles maybe."

Other men shook heads in disbelief.

Later, searching the night sky, Nazaire wondered if those gold fields might be further than the entire north of Canada, maybe at the top of the world? He was still unsure of himself. Was this the point of no return? What did it matter; he could never go back. What would he say to the in-laws or his children? He knew of one man, a blacksmith from Cacouna who had lost his woman and never got his children back. Could the same catastrophe happen to him? The longer he stayed away, the further Nazaire was separated from his children.

Nazaire thought of home — some twelve hundred miles behind him. How he longed to be with Victoria, on his own piece of land. He remembered walking to the edge of his fields before the sun cut into the sky. He missed the first birds of the day squabbling by his back pasture. He needed to open the barn doors in the morning to milk his cows and rub the mare. He itched to look Louis and Joe in the eye and talk about his plans for the day.

No. Best he continue.

With every fiber in his core, he didn't want to, but sometimes a man does what is best, not what he wants.

Ignace

Nazaire felt a growing unease and could not place the source. Thoughts of stinging words from his brothers-in-law collided in his mind.One ghost town after anotherdisplayed a lack of civilization for hundreds of miles.How had all these villages come to nothing? The isolation became too much for his unsettled mind.It seemed the world had come to an end.

The only signs of life bore pictographs of braves in canoes on cave walls, and once, painted red on a rock, an impressive Thunderbird above a herd of bison. Nazaire pointed out each discovery to Raoul. To be so cut off from civilized society was unnatural, but in another manner, exciting. One morning, Ignace appeared on the shores of Agimak Lake, another nothing village surrounded by nothing for hundreds of miles in every direction, and home to less than thirty souls.

Everywhere, the ghost town held remnants of bygone gold mines and quarries. Abandoned bits of scaffolding sat half-built, resembling bones of a skinned whale. A silent roadhouse made up the entire affair. Would Dawson look like this when he got there? Two years after the Klondike Gold Rush, over forty thousand men left for the beaches of Nome, Alaska. Might all of the Yukon be a ghost town?

"What's this?" Nazaire asked.

The town's main feature seemed to be an old steam warping tugboat used in the lumber boom years that all the men were looking at with severe interest.

"Alligator, they called it, on accounta it moved in water, then crawled up on land," an old villager said.

He pointed to the rusted cable lying idle on shore. "The steel cables or 'warping rope' wound onto a winch drum thirty inches wide, the first amphibious craft of its kind. The winch would drive onto the main line shaft from its steam engine, a West and Peachy engine, it was."

Sherman's men examined the rusty body with high interest and circled it for a better look-see.

The old villager pointed to an edge of black near the ground and said, "They're good 'n' rotted out now, but down here, the black was once white oak runners on the flat bottom there."

"I'll be damned. How big was she?" Nazaire asked.

The old villager scratched a chin and gave it a think. "The hull stretched thirty-two feet long and four feet deep with a beam of ten foot."

"How'd it work?" the Hutterite asked.

"The alligator would tie up to a log boom on the river there and hold back hundreds of logs. The head logger moved the boom with a cable, one-mile long it was, tied to some tree on the other side."

The men found a welcome distraction in inspecting the odd, flat bottom tug and enjoyed hearing the old villager speak of bygone years.

———

Sherman's party advanced a few miles beyond
the village with the banks of Agimak Lake still
visible. A sudden whack struck the dank air. Some of
the men crouched down, surprised and unmoving.

Nazaire pointed as he whispered to Raoul, "Look,
so many runs and tracks on shore."

Sherman signaled to stop by raising his right arm.
Nazaire saw otter and beaver signs everywhere near
the tree line, smeared and uneven. The rodents had
run to their dens in fear.

Nazaire caught Cookie's quick movement as he
raised a chin to Sherman. He recognized the silent
signal. Cookie wanted whatever the lake would yield
in his cook pot. With jerky now overripe and sharp to
the tongue, any chance to lay a few snares might perk
the men up with fresh game. The whack of a beaver
tail excited Cookie what with supplies in the chuck
wagon getting low. Sherman turned on his horse and
without a word, set a task for Coppaway, Nazaire,
and Raoul with three quick pushes of his finger in the
air.

The shoreline brought predators day and night, no different than ringing a dinner bell. The three men lowered their packs, pulled out knives and snares. Coppaway grabbed his rifle and checked for shot. Behind Sherman, Nickleson started to unwrap the Hutterites' rifle sitting in the back of the chuck wagon, but Sherman stopped him with a firm hand on his shoulder.

The hunters disappeared into the tree line. It would be easy-hunting with the wind behind them. They might even snag a badger. Meanwhile, the rest of Sherman's party moved a mile further down the road and made camp in an open clearing. They set up tents and started the evening fires.

An hour later, Coppaway, Nazaire, and Raoul walked into camp with two beavers, gutted and ready for the fire. The large one was over forty pounds and a tad longer than three feet. The small one not much less in weight.

Sherman announced, "We'll stay for two nights," as Lennox returned with good news of dry land ahead.

The three hunters got busy. Nazaire grabbed an ax to cut the tails off for Cookie to deal with later, then found a level clearing. First Nazaire soaked the skins in water, then mixed alum and coarse salt for the skins to sit in a busted barrel with a rock keeping them submerged. Tomorrow, he and Coppaway would ring the skins out and rub the stretched underbellies against small trees to break flesh and cord attachments from the leather. Nazaire helped Coppaway cut willows to make frames on which the skins would stretch and dry.

Meanwhile, the chuck wagon sprung to life as Cookie let out a whoop, as if a firecracker had alighted under him. Nazaire had never seen Cookie move so fast. He laid out a clean piece of tarp and cut up those beavers into thick steaks. This action alone got everyone's attention as the camp became mesmerized, beaver not being common on their home fires.

"Get some potatoes a boilin' right quick," Cookie ordered.

Raoul obliged. He unhitched the tail bone on the chuck wagon and dug into Cookie's wooden boxes for a pot.

"Get me the cast iron pan with little legs and some string," Cookie said.

Raoul came back with waxed cooking string in one hand, the cover of a Dutch oven in the other. On a flat rock whose surface Cookie swept clean with the back of his hand, he scored and chopped the flat tails as best he could with an ax, then hung them with string from tree branches to drip throughout the night into a deep cauldron. He laid out frying pans on the fires and dotted each one with a careful dripping of the rich oil oozing from the cut tails.

"Raoul," Cookie barked, "come over here and learn. Get me blackstrap and vinegar."

Raoul pushed crates and bottles aside in the chuck wagon. Cookie pulled out three racks and set them above each fire, checked the potatoes, then set cut steaks to sizzling on the grill. The entire camp watched in rapture.

"Come see how I pour the blackstrap and vinegar, Raoul. I mix it up fine and it'll thin out a bit on its own. Then I'll coat each steak with the mixture."

The magic of Cookie's actions dazzled everyone with the rich aroma of seared steaks lingering low to the ground. Some men squatted near the fires just to suck in the smell before Cookie called chow.

Cookie went loco with the pouring and slathering, licking a finger now and then to test the mixture. The camp watched transfixed as Cookie led Raoul to the cauldron with the hanging castor tails dripping from their strings.

Cookie turned to the men and said: "Let me splain it to ya. By tomorra, the pot'll overflow with the beav oil. I'll pound the tails some, then clean the oil through fine burlap. We could have two quarts maybe."

Everyone raised a cheer to Cookie as he passed out the delicious meal. After supper, Coppaway and Nazaire walked to the clearing to check their pelts. Nickleson cut in front of Nazaire, his arm swinging as it caught Nazaire's shoulder in a deliberate swipe that twisted Nazaire clear around.

"Why do you always get to hunt?" Nickleson spit.

He seemed itchy for a fight. Nazaire stopped and faced Nickleson, took a step back and considered the question.

"Do I?"

The two men were a few feet apart. Nickleson seethed with anger, his teeth clenched in a tight jaw. Sherman walked over and stood between them.

"Nickleson, he didn't snare the beavers alone. You had your chance early on to show me your skills. Once you spoiled that wolverine pelt with more shot than necessary, and ruined the fur's value, you proved yourself a hot head."

"That's not fair," Nickleson yelled. His face turned red as he held a glare.

"Fair's got nothing to do with it. You let every damned wolf and bear know our whereabouts for nothing. You don't have a good eye or ear for hunting and no good sense for shooting."

"I got a right."

"You got nothing of the sort. No one's going off shooting game that needs snaring or trapping instead. This is hard country boy, and you don't decide what you'll shoot because you feel like it."

Outside their tent flaps, the men spoke in low murmurs and watched as Sherman stood dead still, staring Nickleson down.

"Why does he always get to hunt?" Nickleson persisted.

Sherman stepped right up to Nickleson's face. "Look, this morning, the chuck wagon needed fresh meat and we got it. Ain't nothing for you to complain about."

"But ..."

"But nothing. You got a nice piece of steak tonight, right? You don't have any damned cause to fret. End this now."

Nazaire said nothing but watched, tense and hesitant. After long moments, Nickleson turned toward his tent, his bottom lip thrust out about as far as next week.

"Let's get some sleep boys," Sherman said as the night thickened. "Cookie's going to be after us to pound those beaver tails of his tomorrow."

Nazaire and Coppaway checked the beaver skins. They broke branches and gave the mixture a hard stir. Nazaire walked back to his tent and sat uneasy on the ground, stiff-backed.

What was it that got Nickleson riled up so? Nazaire couldn't figure it out. Had he bruised Nickleson or Cochran in some way, made them feel betrayed by him? Those boys had no cause. They didn't know what betrayal was.

When Nazaire lit his pipe, the old thought came again — Victoria on the kitchen table and all the sorry words that filled the air about her life and what their union had wrought. He felt the searing burn of betrayal from his in-laws as if it were last evening — men he sometimes worked with. How could Victoria's brothers dare insult his home, put out the thought that his spouse starved in his house, that Victoria was less than happy or pleased with their marriage. Was this what her people thought? What everyone thought?

He wasn't sure how things got turned around so bad with whispers he heard during her home viewing. They said the house never had enough food. Victoria had plenty to eat, didn't she? Didn't she take what she wanted from the table? How was he to know now? He would go crazy with doubts that buzzed in his head like pestered bees.

Nazaire remembered their insults, the petty resentments that stung. Were her brothers on the attack because she died? Would they be happier if the coffin were his? It was such a scornful thing, betrayal.

Nazaire rose to enter his tent. He spotted a rusty plate on the ground and kicked it with a hard whack.

Victoria was gone. He had given her the best life he could. Grant you, he was plain and so was his house. Even his table was plain, but Victoria had kept it that way, hadn't she? No, she found happiness in each day, Nazaire knew it. He knew it at his core. She was faithful and loyal, more tender than anyone he had ever known. There was not one falsehood about her.

Kenora

Gone were the red and white pines of the Saint Lawrence corridor, replaced by rocks with thin layers of topsoil, remnants of the ancient lava flows that made up the Canadian Shield. The party crossed into Kenora, a small city of five thousand where Mennonites shared power with the Turtle band of woodland Ojibways.

The Mennonite farmers and ranchers wore black wool clothing with stiff black hats as they drove their teams from one farm to another. The women and children also dressed in black. They painted a somber picture of drabness that didn't match their wide smiles and wholesome cheeks.

The Mennonites lived on large adjoining homesteads with neat, clean farms and ranches. They raised pigs and goats, goslings and chicks to sell. They grew almost all their food and built churches where they kept to their own in homespun black clothing.

On one end of town, the Ojibways numbered sixty-one and most suffered terrible from the dog bark, a few from the prairie itch. The terrible whooping cough would not allow for sleep and some Ojibways died from suffocation, their ribs bruised coughing day and night. Just as terrible, prairie itch caused endless scratching from mites.

Over forty of their band had died; the most recent loss was their chief. Leadership now rested on the shoulders of their shaman, also ill with the dog bark. As Sherman's party crossed in front of their teepees, the Turtle band noticed Coppaway and his shaman medallion and immediately sought him out for a pow-wow.

"Come, speak with our shaman," an Ojibway youth begged.

Coppaway agreed and followed the youth into a domed-shaped birch bark hut. Inside, the shaman rested on a pallet, too sick to stand. Nearby, two corpses reeked of decay, coiled in rigidity.

"Help us," the shaman whispered. "Here, take these. I fear we'll all be dead soon."

Coppaway could not believe what was happening. The shaman reached a hand into a wicker basket filled with sacred migis shells. The shells were powerful symbols of spirits. Smooth and shiny, the egg-shaped shells had a porcelain finish, often in colorful patterns while their flat undersides included a slit opening that resembled an eye with fluted eyelids.

The youth explained. "People of the Turtle band ask that Thunderbird guides our chief, dead five days now. Many have the dog bark or prairie itch. No white man's medicine helps. All around, bands are dying. Soon there will be no one to walk the straight path of a good Ojibway."

Their shaman spoke, "Accept these migis shells from the last of the Turtle band."

This desperate plea cut into Coppaway's heart. With the few Ojibway that remained, the whooping cough would continue to spread. The band would never survive. He knew it, and they knew it. Coppaway might have stayed with them but for his father's promise that he go to Edmonton and there marry a young woman from a sister band. By accepting the shells, a bond now existed between the two holy men, the spirits of their moieties connecting them. The helplessness of the meeting brought both shamans to tears.

———

For weeks, Coppaway sat apart by a small fire every evening and smudged himself with sacred sage. He lamented in whispered wails that frightened many in Sherman's party. All kept their distance while Sherman and his crew knew better than to ask questions.

When he reached Edmonton, Coppaway would marry as planned. He would give some migis shells to his new bride's father, the others he would keep until opportunity might show itself. He swore to someday hand the largest to his first-born son. He vowed to protect the sacred shells and the spirits held within them.

A SEA OF WHEAT

Richer

Manitoba ❧ April 30, 1907

Coppaway stopped at the edge of the roadhouse, the lone going concern in the small village of Richer, home to twenty members of the Roseau River Ojibways, a number of Métis and a few Chinese families. A crooked sign read "Start of the Dawson Trail."

An old Ojibway sat on the ground, back bent and squinting into a comfortable April sun. A dirty blanket covered the old man and a yellowed drum rested on his lap.

"Are you well, Father," Coppaway asked.

As Sherman's party crossed the village, Cochran reached down and slapped the old Indian's drum. Nickleson chuckled and pretended to do the same, swatting the air instead. The old Indian straightened and spit at Cochran in disgust. Coppaway remained calm but inside, he felt the bruise of injury atop insult.

Coppaway remained on the edge of town, determined to stop misbehavior from Nickleson or Cochran. They often lagged behind to search out whiskey and good-time women. When they did saunter into camp, all the work setting up camp had been done. They would curse as they stumbled while they put their tent up in the dark. But Richer was another no-account ghost town that lacked both liquor and women. Coppaway hid behind some trees and waited for the pair to pass.

To the side of the road stood an inuksuk, a small stone structure built to resemble a man. Inuksuit could be found everywhere in the Prairies, warning of a fork ahead, or with instructions to veer left or right for safety.

In front of a small stone figure, Nickleson swiped his foot wide, aimed for the inuksuk and missed. With his head pushed up from the momentum, he stopped, stepped back and again swiped at the inuksuk. This time the figure flew apart, with stones scattered in all directions. He and Cochran laughed as they continued down the road.

Coppaway pulled his lips into his mouth and wondered how many times these men had repeated this disrespectful act. He waited for them to be out of sight, then approached the spot, bent on one knee and tried to rebuild the toppled figure. From behind, Coppaway felt a rush of air as a young Roseau River Ojibway emerged in the road behind him. It reminded Coppaway of his tenth summer when his father and Sherman had first met.

At the Curve Lake Reserve, Coppaway's band had opened their summer camp for gatherings. Two Cree from James Bay had arrived with this man, Sherman, seeking a route for white travelers. They wanted clean water, safe shelter and the privilege to hunt when their food stores were low. For these things, Sherman offered sugar, salt, and skunk oil. The Curve Lake Chief judged Sherman to be a man on the right path, responsible and fair.

The Roseaumeant Coppaway no harm but he had seen Nickleson and Cochran from under cover, and this fact changed everything. There would be a reckoning now. Coppaway took a deep breath then spoke in his Ojibway dialect.

"I travel with these white men that broke the inuksuk. The leader, Sherman, is trusted by many bands and would never allow this. Let me handle this matter, and I'll make the white men stop," he said.

The Roseauheld the insult between clenched teeth and stayed silent. Coppaway remained on one knee and continued to gather pieces of the sculpture. Within minutes, the inuksuk was restored.

The Roseaustood aside of Coppaway, chanting powerful words to restore the spirit of the inuksuk. Coppaway rose, showing respect to the injured spirit with outstretched hands and open palms, whispering sacred words.

"How can you make these white men stop?" The Roseau asked.

"I'll guard every inuksuk I see while they pass."

"No. It's three times these men have kicked our sacred stones. My elders ask for blood."

Coppaway inhaled as his chest filled with dread. He fought to give a neutral face and reached for his copper medallion, the symbol of his shaman status. The medallion, however, might be of no influence in this situation.

"Tell your elders I return here tonight with these white men. We will talk."

———

Coppaway and Sherman arrived on mounts at dusk to the exact spot. Their horses nudged Nickleson and Cochran ahead, on foot. Sherman made sure that Nickleson brought along his bejesus bag. Ten agitated Roseauformed a wide circle, all anxious to receive justice.

Grievances mounted against the reckless pair, whose ways were reported some twenty miles east of Richer as word that Nickleson and Cochran's disrespectful acts reached other towns. To the west, knowledge of their actions spread by moccasin news.

Already Indians yet to meet Sherman's party promised to kill the pair if they were seen misbehaving. Cochran and Nickleson had caused destruction along with taunting injury and loathsome insult.

Coppaway translated the Roseau words as the pair stood with bowed heads, acting the penitents. Shrieks of terror rose from Nickleson and Cochran at hearing that their lives hung in purgatory. Some of the Roseauhowled and yipped behind them. They tightened a circle around them, jabbing rifles into their backs.

"I can't stop them. If they want you boys dead, you're dead," Sherman said. "They want blood."

"You couldn't. You wouldn't allow it," Cochran insisted. A red flush crawled up his face as he smacked dry lips.

"There's no 'allow' in this. You two have dared to insult their ways. You beat another man's drum and damaged their sacred stones. No amount of talk is going to change their mind," Coppaway said.

133

Nickleson's face drained white. "But we're sorry. We won't do it again."

The offending pair looked from Sherman to the surrounding Indians with shifting eyes.

"That's the point they're taking, that they'll see you never do it again," Sherman said.

Nickleson yelled, "Damn, are you just going to stand there and let them at us?"

"What would you have me do? You two break the rules and act like you're on your Sunday best."

The Roseau elders turned their backs on the white men. Tensions ratcheted up among the younger members of the band.

"We can pay, can't we, Nick? We can pay money for any damage. They'll take money, won't they?" Cochran insisted.

Sherman explained, "I'm thinking money isn't what they're wanting. By kicking the inuksuk, you could have put someone's life in danger. Maybe more than one someone. How do you pay for that? See, you boys just don't get it. If they want blood, I can't stop them."

The remaining Roseaucrowded nearer Nickleson and Cochran. Sherman and Coppaway backed off.

Nickleson gasped. "We won't be breaking any more rules, I promise!"

"What the hell good is *your* word?" Sherman asked.

Another Roseaupushed Nickleson, flinging him to the ground.

"I'll back my word with money. Will five dollars do?" Nickleson asked, staying on the ground.

"What is that? Three days' wages? I don't think so."

"Ask them. Ask if five dollars will do? Five from each of us? Ten each?"

Nickleson rose and turned around. Cochran turned as well, and searched who might inflict the next blow.

Two Roseau elders spoke with much head turning, and flared nostrils. The Roseaustomped their feet and shook arms in the air. Another Roseau elder motioned at both penitents and the inuksuk. They growled with agitated faces.

Coppaway blocked Nickleson and Cochran's bodies with crossed arms, then turned and moved aside to give clear view to the troublemakers less they think they were being defended.

After an hour of rattled talk, Sherman stood, mounted his horse and spoke to the miscreants. "You give ten dollars apiece to Coppaway, and he'll pass it to the Roseau elders with high apologies. Then you sonofabitches return to camp without a sound. I don't want any bullshit from either of you."

Sherman whipped his horse around without delay and left while Coppaway took over the negotiations. Again, he fought to keep a neutral face in front of the men. After ten more minutes of angry words from the Roseau, Coppaway left, his horse rudely uncoupling Nickleson to one side of the road, and Cochran to the other. They walked back to camp in the dark.

The next morning, both men received chuck duty for a week under threat of being left behind. Once camp broke, all eyes stayed on Nickleson and Cochran who were ordered to walk close behind Sherman for the balance of the journey.

Coppaway wasn't convinced that the pair had learned a lesson. He knew stupid was just plain stupid. Although he added nothing to the camp gossip, Coppaway would now watch Nickleson and Cochran from a distance at the rear of the party.

Portage la Prairie

The party had crossed rich grasslands flat with wheat and sugar beets for weeks. The number of horses, Indians and immigrants surprised Nazaire beyond imagining. Gone was the corduroy road, replaced by soft-packed dirt. Some sections were no wider than a cart trail, others wide enough for one of those new-fangled electric cars.

Portage la Prairie fell away as the landscape turned into quilted farms of cabbages and beans. Acres of new-sprouted plants jutted from the ground in parallel rows. Nazaire looked upon fields that took on every shade of growth possible from celery white to dark purple, to black shadowed in green.

As far as the eyes allowed, homesteads flourished with the earthy smell of black, new-turned soils. Breezes swept over shallow valleys. Some sunsets reflected blocks of blinding white wheat, while others shone bronze with goldenrod or pale blue from tiny prairie crocus.

The walking was easy on the wide stagecoach roads, where Indians wore bib overalls with store-bought collarless or calico shirts. Farmers and ranchers alike spoke languages both exotic and strange, from guttural German to Portuguese that flowed like the feel of a woman's tongue or the grunts of the stern Mennonites.

Sleep evaded Nazaire for two days and nights as he fought a raging toothache. The chill of the morning air crept into the root of his tooth as he rode on the tail bone of Cookie's chuck wagon, favoring his jaw and unable to focus his feet for sure purchase. He stretched his mouth with ever-larger clumps of balled up burdock leaves, packing the angry boil until his lips began to crack.

The party passed a hops farm worked by a large family of Métis, descendants of pioneer Scots and local Indians. Tall stakes, thirty feet high lined the rows from which mature vines would cling. Right now, hop heads were just lifting off the ground, their vines spreading in every direction like tentacles.

Coppaway noticed the large farm and let out a whoop, catching Sherman's eye as he signaled his intentions. He handed the leather lead of his appaloosa to Longfox, and from the chuck wagon, he pulled Nazaire by the shoulder and led him to the open farmyard. Members of the party turned to see where the pair had gone. Coppaway approached an elder Métis and in Ojib-Métis parlance, asked for help with Nazaire's toothache.

The heady aroma of hops burst from the ground as the three men walked up the rows of crowning heads, releasing their bitter citrus aroma. They made for an open barn by the back of the main house. Wooden crates lined a wall, and the Métis searched inside them. He pulled a box of last season's withered garlic bulbs from a crate.

He handed one full bulb to Nazaire and instructed, "Chew a button a day, add water to spit if need be. Sleep with it in your mouth. Come morning spit out then start with another. Do until they're all gone."

Coppaway looked around the barn at piles of netting that sat in large wagons.

"What you do with these?" he asked.

"We pound poles in the ground in long rows, then string up nets so the hops will climb. They get the sun right good. It saves the lower heads from rain rot," the Métis said.

Nazaire pointed to the workers in the field and commented, "You have good strong men here."

"My sons. They help at planting time. Two raise hops like me. One keeps bees. Right now, we add the nets to trellis the hops."

The Métis found a small glass jar of honey by the barn door. He handed it to Coppaway as they spoke with their strange-sounding words.

Nazaire fished in his rucksack to present a half-empty bag of cut tobacco, payment for the garlic. The Métis farmer laughed.

"No need. We smoke our hops instead of bacco."

Nazaire, all red-necked, took back his dwindling supply. The Métis yelled to a worker who ran in the barn and returned with two burlap sacks of dried cut hops.

"You try. Half cherry bacco, half hops. You'll like. This kind mild, less bitter. Soon, you can smoke with no bacco."

The pair said thanks and resumed their walk on the road. They passed long fields of noisy workers, all Métis. The men dug fresh holes to set up more poles as womenfolk climbed ladders, stretching nets like unwinding sheets of lace.

Nazaire chewed on a garlic button while Coppaway picked trailside sarsaparilla leaves and adding them to his spirit pouch. Coppaway kept the honey and handed the bacco bag to Nazaire.

"I no smoke," he said.

The sun warmed the men as they walked on the road and came to a small stream. They both knelt and cupped water in their hands, sat a while and rested. Then Coppaway surprised Nazaire.

"You are long missing your woman, but you do her no honor."

"What?" Nazaire said.

"Naz, I had beautiful squaw and young daughter, two summers. Lost them to the fluenze."

"I didn't know that. I'm sorry."

"Many know pain of loss, but you wear your hurt like a black hand over your face, blocking the good that waits to come to you."

"What?"

"You think your sadness shows esteem to your woman, but no."

"Why talk to me this way?" Nazaire snapped. A collar of heat encircled his neck and climbed up his face.

Coppaway explained, "What do white men say? You languish for her, but you do not honor her, nor do you honor yourself."

"What would you know about my spouse?" Nazaire barked.

"Your sadness brings nothing to your gone-woman, and no prepare you for your ahead-woman."

143

Coppaway looked long and hard at Nazaire, then placed a hand on his shoulder. "Look at you, always angry or sad. You only see the thing that has already happened. You do not walk in balance with the new sun."

Nazaire dropped his eyes and shrugged his shoulders.

"I count you friend, Naz. We are same, me and you. When you are best today, then you honor yourself today. Do each day, and whatever comes that you no see, yoube ready."

"How do you know this?"

"I, like you, after my squaw and little girl dead, sad and much angry. It does loved ones no honor to live like this."

"You see this in me, in my face Coppaway? Every day?"

"Yes, Naz, and I hope better for you, my friend."

Coppaway grinned as he touched the little jar of honey inside his possibilities bag, a nice present for his bride whom he hoped would be as sweet.

Nazaire thought about his friend's advice and to his surprise, he agreed. He smiled and laughed at the two nice bags of half-hops and half-tobacco that were now his. Yes, maybe it was time to see tomorrow and let yesterday go.

Brandon

For miles, Sherman's party watched as wild horses galloped through coulees and over scrappy plateaus from a south ridge. Nazaire pointed at the wild horses as they broke into open fields of rich pastureland bordered by fields of wheat grasses, golden against vermilion canyons in the distance.

Everywhere wheat was waist high; red wheat and white barleys; golden wheat and hardy blues; rose-colored durum and pale-yellow spring wheat.

When the party reached Brandon, they found a pioneer town settled by agency Indians and immigrants who had become farmers and ranchers. Newcomers seeking homesteads added to the chaos along with Brandon's ten thousand citizens. Everyone, it seemed, wore calico shirts. Dirty canvas tents outnumbered the poorer cabins littered with accumulated trash and horse dung everywhere.

Commerce and industry boomed from the downtown brick buildings and an inner-city rail system for its people. The streets were lined with red river carts thanks to the huge Doukhobor settlement that numbered more than fifteen hundred, established northeast of town. The Doukhobors were a Russian sect of religious people who believed in an inner voice that rejected taxes, military drafts and organized religion.

The flurry of business buzzed with life while the railroad added wealth to the town as it carried goods southeast to Minnesota and southwest into Calgary.

Nazaire saw grain elevators at each end of town that gave evidence of a rising middle class, enjoying their first taste of prosperity. In the outskirts, farmers grew as many as sixty different legumes and raised livestock. For Sherman's party walking through, the longer the men stayed, the more reasons beckoned their purses open.

Chinamen filled one end of Brandon's tent city, doing an outstanding laundry business while next door, Sherman's party discovered more Chinamen running a public bath inside a large tent. Nickleson and Cochran walked into the tent in their all-together, happy to part with a quarter for a hot soak while their clothes were being washed in an adjoining tent. A few men cared not to acquaint themselves with soap.

Nazaire and Raoul were itchy from dust, but gladly parted with a shinplaster, a twenty-five cent note that bought them both a barrel of hot water with their trail clothes on to save a few pennies. Once refreshed, the party pushed through the pioneer town with the men's clean, wet clothes rolled-to be laid out on dry bushes during the coming night.

Townsfolk who recognized Sherman yelled warnings about the dangers that the wild horses wrought. They stampeded onto ranches, farm fields and camps while their sheer numbers destroyed everything underfoot.

The whole of Brandon Township included almost thirty thousand horses. They came in every possible size and color: flea-bitten grays, liver chestnuts, rich

buckskin browns, skewbalds and velvety blue roans.
Every kind of sock a horse could wear appeared on
mismatched legs. Stars and blazes emerged like
smudged paint that glowed on their muzzles as they
galloped by in sheer abandon.

The horses would bolt at the least flash of
heatstroke lightning and run themselves slavered,
with mouths foaming white or crusted yellow. No
trough of clear water, nor open stream was safe from
the nuisance of their thieving ways. To lasso one was
a sure way to get bitten. Angry clouds of trampled
wheat followed them everywhere. To dare take up
their rear threatened temporary blindness from a
whirl of speckled prairie grasses that rose above the
ground in a violent dance.

Summer rains brought blow flies and tiny, biting
no see ums, mites that plagued the animals. They bled
the muzzles of wild horses into an angry maroon as
the animals struggled to shake the wretched pests
from swollen eyes. No flicking of lips, nor flapping of

their muzzles would bring the horses comfort from the biting midges.

———

Beyond Brandon, Sherman called 'make camp' and instructed tents and bedrolls be placed in a safeguarded pattern with more campfires to protect his party from the dangers of the stampeding beasts. Nazaire helped drag some of the tents into a square arrangement with fires on the outer perimeter and Cookie's three cooking fires around a protective curl of fallen trees. Most of the camp was relaxed from their soothing baths.

Longfox arranged a lead line between trees for the horses, and then fed and watered them. The young Longfox thought back to how it came to be that he was with Sherman's party, isolated and in strange company. He had left his reservation, Fort Belknap, Montana, in the summer of 1906 alongside his aging uncle who was desperate to visit an ailing sister.

They had followed old Indian trails until they reached Ottawa with its forty thousand, third-generation freedmen. Neither Gros Ventre had seen a 'midnight' man or woman before and the site of so many African-Americans frightened them both. The uncle became sluggish and died right after entering the city. Longfox feared that authorities might find him guilty of murder. He wrapped his uncle's body in a stolen blanket and left the corpse at the back of a church. After three days of wandering with no feed for the two horses, nor food for himself, Longfox entered a Chippewa reserve near Grand Traverse Bay, hungry and exhausted. Chippewa women fed him while band elders discussed the youth's challenges in unknown territory.

The Chief asked Longfox to relinquish the better of his two horses in exchange for food and proper clothing until the spring when they would seek Sherman, a wilderness guide who could get him closer to his reserve in Montana. Longfox agreed. With the uncle's old nag, broken tail and all, Longfox

would join Sherman's party in the spring. As for the
dead uncle, the Chippewa elders claimed the body
and buried it among their own dead.

Coppaway had often stood up for the youth, but
after months of travel, Longfox grew to hate everyone
he traveled with. He had never consented to tolerate
coarse jabberings from Nickleson and Cochran. As
tents went up for the night, the pair approached
Longfox. The youth wore a rawhide vest and dirty
leggings with a rawhide string circled his gray neck
with blue beads strung between small white ones. His
one blanket served as both bedroll and coat.

"This a good horse?" Nickleson asked Longfox.

Longfox ignored him.

"What ya call your horse?" Nickleson asked, his
voice jeering.

"Horse."

"No, what ya call him so he'll come?" Cochran
asked.

Around camp, Nazaire and others stopped settling in to watch what Nickleson and Cochran would do next.

"Come horse."

The pair laughed at Longfox, whose face colored red.

Nazaire walked over to Longfox' side. "Why don't you let the kid alone?"

"Ya," Some of the other men chimed in.

"Mind your God damn business," Nickleson said.

Nickleson sneered at the intrusion while he complained under his breath, "Damn Canuck, good for nothing but messing up the work floor in my father's automobile factory."

He stared at Longfox for a full minute, both hands clenched by his sides. The men in camp continued to watch, some shaking their heads in disgust. Every other day, it seemed, someone caught Nickleson and Cochran up to some mischief. Cochran grabbed Nickleson's shoulder, and edged him toward their tent at the opposite side of camp.

Longfox pulled a long face as his shoulders and arms went stiff. In foul weather, he tented with Coppaway, but tonight Longfox wouldn't dare leave his horse's side. He placed his mustang flush against a tree and tied a rain-slick, no more than a greasy piece of deerhide, from the tree to its flank. The mustang looked sad with a full head dirty white and the rest all ash gray. His tail hung limp, broken. Coronas decorated all four feet in the same dirty white.

"Rain coming tonight?" Nazaire asked.

The shy Longfox lowered his head. "No rain," he whispered, "But wonder what hurt these white men might bring my horse."

Regina

Saskatchewan ❧ May 19, 1907

Nazaire tossed throughout the night. Sleep came in short bouts of hovering dreams and restless moments. Awareness plunged deep as if e were in a gorge, then surged upward as Nazaire reached wakefulness in a jittery rest that left stiff joints aching the length of his body.

Rustling branches threw him into sudden consciousness with a panicked start. The wind blew all night without cease, which added to his agitation. Nazaire opened the tent flap, and a wall of fog pressed against the camp as high as the surrounding trees. The air was thick with the decayed smell of broken bark peeled from damaged trunks. No other tents were visible in the gray, dim light. He couldn't make out the horses hobbled nearby.

She appeared to his right, beyond the smoke pit. He knew it was her, come to fill his empty heart until it would burst from being so many months without her.

"Victoria," he said.

She returned the coffee pot to the grate and straightened her upper body. Then she turned to face him.

Nazaire's arms swung above his chest at the shock of seeing her. His eyes took in the full measure of her small frame. His chest burst with a flicker of desperate hope.

"I know you aren't real," he said. "Never you mind. I'm happy just to see you, to be with you."

Her lips parted in that subtle grin he recognized. Those sweet, curved lips that would open slow, then turn into a beaming smile. How this drove him to distraction. It would drive a man mad to look at her — the delicate waist, her ivory skin.

"Take coffee, husband?" Victoria asked.

He approached the smoke pit and found a suitable rock to sit on while Victoria poured out a cup.

"I'm so tired, Victoria, tired of living so many days and nights without you."

Nazaire coffeed up and turned to face her.

"We've four, maybe five more months to walk. Will you be there when I arrive?"

"I'm here now, aren't I, Nazaire? I'm always near when you need me."

His thoughts struggled to form words. "I can't do more."

"Yes, you can. You need to do all that is necessary for the children, for the farm."

Nazaire lowered his head in shame. Doesn't she know how hard he'd worked all this time? How often he thought he might turn back? Maybe not make it to Dawson?

His shoulders rose and lowered as he fought tears. He lifted his eyes, and she was gone. In his core he knew that she was right, that he must fortify himself, resolve to fight any challenge that stood in the way of his success. Was he going mad?

A light flicker of air pushed behind him.

"Coffee still hot?" Sherman asked.

———

As the party walked that day, they came to a network of grain elevators and water towers aside a railroad spur. Dozens of storage bins stood, ready to be packed with produce into rail cars. Beyond the cluster of cars, set off to the side, young children poured into four rail cars used for prairie schools. Their cheerful laughter brought a smile to Nazaire's face.

Nazaire and Raoul often discussed Dawson but preferred to keep their business between themselves. This evening they sat with Sherman and Nazaire put his saved-up questions to him.

"Do you bring many with you that go to the gold fields of the Klondike?" Nazaire asked in a low voice.

"Not as many as before. When news of the rush spread, Lennox and I, we had maybe thirty to forty men that journeyed north each spring. Nowadays, most take the train but still, there are some who just can't afford it."

"Will there be men returning with you from Edmonton, men who were in Dawson?" whispered Nazaire.

"Maybe. I never know until I get there."

Nazaire and Raoul left for their tent. Nazaire was at peace with Sherman's answers but with a fire building in him, a fire that glittered like gold.

Moose Jaw

Right out of his tent, Nazaire's foot slipped at his first step. Down he went with a thud. "Sonofabitch," he yelled. Nazaire sat on the ground and pulled off one boot. He howled in disgust. Heads turned as eyes looked to see the commotion.

Sherman walked over. "Who did this?"

He turned to see which men were already dressed and out of their tents.

"I don't know," Nazaire said.

No one answered. Sherman grabbed the boot from Nazaire's hands and found the wolfhound outside the Norwegian's tent. He held the boot under the dog's nose. "Find."

The wolfhound sniffed the insulting odor, meandered among the men and eventually sat down with both paws outstretched in front of Cochran. Sherman strode over with the offending boot in hand.

Cochran crouched with round shoulders; the word guilty all but painted on his blood-red face. Nazaire watched from his tent flap and held his anger in check.

"Are you so stupid you don't know where to crap?" Sherman barked.

Sherman threw Nazaire's boot at CochranSherman hissed. "Don't dare risk the safety of somebody's easy walking for your goddamn amusement, you understand me?"

Cochran turned his face away and struggled to swallow a laugh.

Next to him, Nickleson gushed pink with delight.

"You clean the bottom of this without one speck of your shit left on it, and then you return it to its owner."

Nazaire removed his remaining boot and packed it in his kit. The ground was refreshing against the bottom of his feet and before he knew it, Raoul had joined him, both men bootless and saving their leather.

———

Lennox and Coppaway met Sherman on the
narrow road by noon. The party had not gained half a
day's walk. Out front, Lennox swung wide for
support as he fought bushes. He pushed thorns away
from his horse's flank with a pole and widened the
space to clear the travois. Lennox' jacket shone deep
cherry with blood and a few hanging thorns.
Coppaway took up the rear as the pair returned from
their reconnoiter — a successful look-see. Was it a
bull moose or a bear? Everyone in camp was
jumpified with excitement over the height of the tarp.
Sherman ordered 'make camp for two days' and led
the party onto a level clearing.

Coppaway's horse dragged the travois heavy
with the high-mounded tarp. Nazaire and Raoul
rushed to the sides of the travois and beat down tall
willows. They cut stalks heavy with devil's club, those
tight stemmed thorns, from the small entrance to the
clearing. The travois needed to be freed. In the cold
air, hoarfrost shown from the horses' muzzles.

From Lennox' side hung a beautiful cinnamon skin, rolled and hooked to the saddle pommel. With one hand, Coppaway removed the bearskin, slapping Lennox on the back with whoops and heehaws. Cookie would need to smoke all the meat. The men would eat well for several days.

Raoul helped Cookie set up the portable abattoir. On the trail, all you needed were a couple of mature trees with thick branches, a pulley, some ropes and at least one long spreader bar, either steel or hardwood to open the pelvis.

The two men pulled out long poles from the chuck wagon and tied the pulleys that would suspend the meat. To quick-cool the carcass, they needed to break the chest and hind quarters and slit the game open to the air. This needed to be done immediately or the flesh wouldn't cure.

Nazaire gathered broken branches and set to lighting three large fires. He pulled out the larger pots and filled them with water from the side barrel roped to the chuck wagon. The wolfhound jumped to the edge of the abattoir, vying for position to catch any scraps. He sniffed with curiosity.

Raoul unfurled the largest tarp on the ground. Cookie laid out the heavy legs, thick hunks of shoulder and rump, readying them for cutting. He tossed smaller chunks of flesh in a frying pan, out of the wolfhound's reach. He removed large rolls of fat from the travois and threw them in a cauldron for rendering later on. Cookie handed Raoul one of his prized, long knives as the cutting began on the ground.

"This kill will set the chuck wagon to rights for a few days, boys," Cookie said while he beamed with delight.

Lennox attached rawhide to the tops of the main long poles that would serve as the outer skin for the smoker. The heaviest hunks of glistening flesh dripped blood from the pulley that now hung from a large tree branch. Cookie threw salt against these.

Raoul grabbed a canvas bag and turned it inside out. It held the huge heart, thick and difficult to cut.

He plunged the bag into a wooden bucket with water and vinegar to clean it out. Most everyone in camp helped. The Hutterite raised his son atop the chuck wagon seat with the wolfhound following, the two out of the way. The Hutterite built up the fires while Nazaire and Coppaway filled more cauldrons with water.

Coppaway wrapped heavy rawhide around the poles and closed it up, closeting the larger pieces of meat. He left an opening at ground level to add the smoke — a magical mixture of herbs that would transform the greasy meat into ambrosia. Meanwhile Cookie opened his tinder bag and pulled out bits of cedar and crushed bulrush heads to start the smoke. Coppaway gathered twigs and ghost beard, a fine moss, shaping the tinder bed into a rough circle in his palms. He laid out Cookie's tinder on top of the tinder bed, adding alder chips to give the meat a fragrant flavor.

Building up the tinder bed took patience and skill, which Cookie demonstrated as he searched for a handful of bird feathers to add to the small branches that would sit beneath the tinder bed. The smoker would burn throughout the night and most of the next day, seasoning the meat with mellow flavors.

Custom held that the person who made the kill would get the roasted heart. The shooter could also choose front or back paws or both. Coppaway claimed the skin and front paws, giving Cookie the back paws which he could trade at the next town. Coppaway and Lennox would both split the heart seeing as how they worked hard field-gutting the beast. Lennox and Coppaway sat by Sherman, catching their breath.

"The bear was due west about twelve miles," Lennox said to Sherman.

Coppaway added, "A few wolves were about, but they left us alone. More interested in what we left in the bush."

"I'll search for water," said Lennox. "We're almost into the Badlands — nothing but stone there. There'll be no water once we leave ground."

Longfox busied himself, wiping down the appaloosa and Lennox' mount. He gave them water and checked their legs and flanks for thorns.

Nickleson made his way to the chuck wagon and in all the chaos, grabbed an empty burlap bag. Near the edge of the abattoir, he snatched the front paws from the tarp on the ground. He pivoted his body as he wrapped the front paws in a bag, sliding the bag inside his coat and walked away. Men who worked at the abattoir said nothing, but all eyes widened. Lips scowled in disgust.

Sherman led the Scot into his tent, where maps lay open on top of the canvas flooring. The two knelt while carving out the next leg of the trail. The irritating issue of Nickleson floated in the background like some annoying scratch that Sherman couldn't satisfy. By the grates, Coppaway reached into his sling bag and presented Cookie with two tins of juicy, ripe Saskatoon-berries.

"For you. Good berries. Make nice gravy," Coppaway said.

167

"Hot damn, where did you get these, Coppaway? They'll be in tonight's gravy alright," Cookie smiled wider than his face, parting his thick beard in two.

Following Cookie's instructions, Raoul started to make bear butter from a large tub of rendered fat. He cut a chunk of meat into small pieces, threw in a handful of salt and added water to cover. The tub would sit all night atop a low fire and by morning the mixture, a coagulated mess of chocolate-colored liquid, would be strained and seasoned before being poured into clean galvanized quart cans.

Coppaway and Nazaire moved away from the activity, finding a level spot to clean and scrape the bear skin. The skin and bear paws would be welcomed gifts to his new bride.

They spread the skin out flat and built a rigid frame around the outer edge of the pelt. With stiffened deer gut, they threaded the outer skin to the frame and hung it by two ropes to nearby trees. It swayed in the air, dripping blood and congealed fat. They scraped the wet side with the edge of long knives, forcing tissue to roll into spirals that gleamed in the hot sun. When Nazaire tired, Coppaway spelled him. After a few hours the skin shone clear, and it was time to wash off remaining bits of fat and grit with hot water.

Cookie ladled one small wooden barrel filled with strips of cut up meat with a brine of molasses, Saskatoon-berries, and vinegar.

"Best jerky recipe I got," Cookie boasted.

The Hutterite helped hang the jerky strips to dry overnight in the smoker while Sherman instructed Longfox to hobble the horses. Lennox would keep watch during the night for animals coming into camp, following the smells of the smoker.

Nickleson sauntered over to Cochran and bent down. He packed something in his leather satchel, piling his bedroll on top. His bejesus bag would stink, attracting ground varmints, a fact perhaps lost on both Americans.

Cookie separated out chunks of meat to be smoked into roasts. These he wrapped tight against surplus air and packed in his cleanest, waterproofed bags.

As for the evening meal, Cookie served thick steaks, blood-soaked and seasoned with saltpeter. The wolfhound gloried with a propeller tail that knocked the Hutterite boy down twice. The wolfhound gobbled up chunks of oily, gristle meat that many of the men threw at him.

"How big was this bear?" The Hutterite asked.

"I'd say 'bout fourteen hundred pounds," Lennox said.

"Who gets the heart?" Cochran asked.

"Lennox and Coppaway. They worked hard to field-gut the bear," Sherman said.

"Who gets the liver?" Nickleson asked.

"Liver? Left to the wolves. You can't eat bear liver. It'll kill ya. You slickers don't know nothin," Cookie said.

———

As the night darkened, Sherman's eye caught Coppaway moving fast behind the camp toward

Cochran. What was Cochran doing there? Hiding? Cochran had walked into the tree line. He raised a rifle and took aim toward the chuck wagon at Nazaire. A whisper of air crossed Cochran's cheek.

"You fire, you die," Coppaway whispered as he held his blade against Cochran's windpipe.

Cochran stiffened. He had picked up Lennox' Ross Mark II rifle and had loaded the firearm with a .303 shot. He never heard a sound as he stood by the tree and took aim. Coppaway yanked the rifle from the American's hands. With a light touch, his knife brushed against Cochran's throat, leaving a bloom of red. Cochran rushed back to his tent, shaking and holding his hands to his throat.

With the rifle in hand, Coppaway approached Sherman's tent. Sherman had seen the entire event unfold in stretched seconds. He called Lennox to his tent, holding the flap open for Coppaway to also enter. The flap closed while the three men parleyed inside.

Something would have to be done now.

Cookie's Concoction

At mid-morning, Sherman called Cookie into his tent.

"I want you to listen to me, and listen good. Make up some of that special concoction of yours, plenty of it."

"Sure thing."

"Enough to knock out Nickleson and Cochran, so they'll sleep through the noise of camp breaking tomorrow. I don't want them waking up while we're just out of earshot."

Cookie knitted his eyebrows in thought. "Theys always dipping their store-bought whiskey into their coffee before they turns in. I'll take care of it," he said.

The day filled with activities surrounding yesterday's influx of fresh meat. Lennox and Coppaway left with the chuck wagon to refill the water barrels. Longfox went along, leading all the mounts in tow. That night, Cookie served stew laced with gravy and a heavy dose of fresh biscuits. As usual, Cookie passed a coffee pot around after the meal.

When he got to Nickleson and Cochran, Cookie claimed, "This one's out. I got another."

Cookie grabbed the second pot and filled Nickleson and Cochran's tin cups. After the meal, men crouched on the ground in loose circles by the fires. They tamped their pipes or rolled their cigarettes for an evening smoke before bedding down. Some pulled out picture cards and amused themselves until dark overtook the sky.

Longfox walked in front of Sherman's tent, raised his arms and began to speak in his broken English, wavering into his native Gros Ventre or an Arapaho dialect here and there. In a halting voice, he palavered on the hardships of his people, carving out an existence with little else but wild yucca to eat. He spoke of the many box canyons that trapped and drowned valuable colts his people hoped to trade. He sauntered back and forth like a caged animal.

In the waning moonlight, his face looked old and his hair greasy, with breechcloth and leggings soiled beyond washing. All this day, his last before leaving, Longfox feared that the Americans might follow him and bring some disaster into his life.

Longfox praised the Blackfoot bands who led great herds of buffalo to their death at Head-Smashed-In ridge, where the beats stampeded into a death plunge before starvation cut down the number of his people. He praised the many bands that crossed the Medicine Line, stealing mustangs and trading them as far south as Billings or Hole in the Wall.

He remembered the stories of the great Sioux leader, Sitting Bull, and those who rode with him at Little Big Horn thirty years past. Longfox scorned the states for forcing his band to share their reservation with the likes of the Assiniboine outside Fort Belknap, Montana.

Sherman and Lennox nodded now and again, but Longfox continued his rant. He regarded well the power of the Writing-on-Stone caves; a sacred place guarded by the mystical hoodoos of the Milk River. All these thoughts he shared with maladroit jeers and a warrior's pride while the men sat with silent tongues and uneasy movements.

Longfox held a poppy seed rattle and told of its mystical powers, released when heated on a dying fire. He feigned prowess about his long journey home. Resentment rose in his cracked voice and pursed lips. With hesitant bravado, he lowered his arms to his sides and stopped.

The men took it as a sign to break from squatting and head to their bedrolls in double time. Lennox entered Sherman's tent for a parley, this time about Longfox's uneasy lecture.

The agitated Longfox crossed the camp and stood, motionless, as he watched the men disperse. With piercing eyes, he held Coppaway's gaze a flickering second, then walked to his blanket.

When Sherman raised his tent flap to enter, he seized upon Coppaway's eyes. Sherman lowered his hand to his gun belt, fingering the six-shooter. Coppaway caught his meaning with full intent.

Inside, Sherman looked at Lennox and whispered, "What the hell was that all about?"

"Makes no sense, this one," Lennox said.

"That young pup ain't said more than ten words since we picked him up, and now he gives us the Easter sermon? Do you think he wants to kill us all before he leaves?"

"Wouldn't disregard that notion. No one's going to sleep good tonight."

Settling down in his tent, Sherman could think no more but that Longfox felt hurt — a hurt that comes from betrayal when people you love have suffered, and you can do nothing about it. He knew about that kind of pain; his Sioux mother had died from flea-infested blankets while his father was out trapping, the family near starving back home in their small Scottish community.

Run to the Milk

Old Fort Assiniboine Trail   ✤   May 29, 1907

Before first light, Coppaway listened as Longfox moved to Nickleson's tent, then doubled back. Longfox untied his mustang and led it out of camp. Twenty feet away, Lennox also lay awake, listening and waiting for Longfox to leave. Had Longfox taken something from Nickleson's tent? Neither Coppaway nor Lennox were surprised at what they heard.

Although it was still dark, Longfox' mustang pushed himself away from brambles and rode in open clearings with his sixth sense. Coppaway heard Longfox ride south, where an old Indian trail led to the Milk River. Beyond the Milk, Fort Belknap beckoned the youthful Longfox home.

The rising hills of the Badlands were an hour away, and Longfox's gelding needed to be cautious with his footing, or both rider and horse could come to grave danger. With so many coulees and canyons with eroding sides, a horse's feet would never stop once in a severe skid with the soft-packed ground.

Coppaway and Lennox left their tents a few minutes later with Lennox snapping a finger against Sherman's tent, a signal that the two would follow Longfox if any mischief were at hand.

———

Coppaway unhitched their mounts. Lennox knew some of the old Indian trails, so with quick riding, they circled around and in front of Longfox, waiting at a switch-back some thirteen miles south on a long, broad curve of crumbled rock.

Coppaway stilled his appaloosa when the milky white muzzle of Longfox's horse cut through the morning mist. The pale animal looked like a ghost with its head bobbing atop Longfox's dirty buckskins, the rest of the ash mount near invisible.

Longfox had grabbed Nickleson's leather satchel by its broken strap and dragged it almost to the ground for miles. Its front face and one edge, scuffed and torn against the canyon walls, resembled talon marks of some wild raptor.

Coppaway caught sight of the damaged bag. The silver snaps that held the silver compass were no more. Gone also was the handsome, solid silver compass. On the front flap, the fancy leather craft had been all but scraped off. Blood had dripped from the bear paws and saturated the entire bottom of the bag. The secret flap that hid money inside would no longer stay flat and closed.

At the bottom, fine scissors and a bar of Mitchelsen's shaving soap united in a thick gob of congealed burgundy. Under the toiletries, a wad of hundred-dollar bills wrapped in a thin paper bag festered in cerise clumps of fur, melded together in a solid unit.

Letters of introduction stuck to one inside wall, indecipherable. Scattered at the bottom was an opened metal tin of tablets used to curb inflammation of Gonococci, Nickleson's curse for his whoring ways. The expensive tablets imported from England looked like small cranberries. Some of Nickleson's fifty-dollar bills lay fanned out against the opposite inner wall, soaked. Other bills swam, submerged in half-dried, maroon globs, stuck as one unidentifiable stew. Who knew how many dollars were scattered along the Old Fort Assiniboine trail?

Longfox pulled on his horse's reins when he saw the two men appear at the switchback. He raised his head in pride and looked from one to the other, a full sneer covering his face. The youth was in no mood to fight them off and so, with insult smack dab atop injury, Longfox dropped the bejesus bag to the ground, and turned toward Montana as mosquitoes buzzed near their delightful morning treat.

Coppaway grabbed Longfox's reins and held fast. "Brother, be careful of prairie rattlers. The voodoos be full of them," Coppaway warned.

The sides of the Old Fort Assiniboine trail were lined prairie scrub but beyond, maybe ten miles or so, buttes rose in the sky, carved by the wind into cliffs eroded into sandstone ravines, marking it a place of both mystery and stark beauty. The surrounding hills were cone-shaped with corrupt formations, mimicking tree trunks of petrified sandstone with gnarled fingers looked like twisted, dying men.

The low hum of constant wind hovered in the men's ears as they returned the way they had come. At Maple Creek, Coppaway used a pocket knife to cut away putrid flesh and fur as he separated claws from foot pads as best he could. Running creek water hurried the job. At least the claws were tolerable for travel.

Coppaway understood what had motivated Longfox's actions and could even sympathize with him. At least now the youth wouldn't have to tolerate two white men who poked fun at him at every turn. Tonight, Coppaway would begin working the bear claws into a neck piece for his future bride's father. He hoped that Longfox would make it back to his reserve.

———

Coppaway and Lennox caught up to Sherman, and gave a report.

"Threw the satchel into Nickleson's tent. They were still asleep," Lennox said.

As Sherman's party moved west toward Swift Current, they glimpsed the first edge of the Great Sand Hills to the north. The hills were scrub turned into a series of rolling hills, golden but treacherous to enter. Each footfall in the fine sand could drag man or horse deep into the dunes. To get caught there meant death from exposure while giant kangaroo rats applied aggravation upon unlucky trespassers.

Swift Current

Saskatchewan / Alberta Border

Sherman considered it strange to pass this stretch of trail surrounded by majestic mountains rising gracefully from flat, treeless plateaus and shallow valleys, with not a dip or buffalo wallow where wolf or coyote could hide. Imagine God had taken a nice stretch of open flat country and crushed it together in a fit of anger, creating a godforsaken set of crowded hills and valleys. That was Cypress Hills.

The summer was at its peak, with prairie grasses lush and tall, their crowns yellow and tan in the brown soil. Sherman's party had left Swift Current behind when Sherman felt a great movement. It swelled from the ground and traveled up his body. His horse's ears pulled back. Could it be a few deer running out of Cypress Hills? The vibrations deepened. Couldn't be buffalo, they were all but gone.

From the bushes a wrangler, tall and wiry, skinny as a starving calf, rode out of a gulch to the right of the road. His horse jumped the gully with five more wranglers riding hard behind him. They near bolted into Sherman with no time for 'xcuse me's, the wild crew rode hard across the road, oblivious to the long line of men and horses they had forced to a rude halt. The stink of whiskey followed them into the dusk.

Sherman reined in his horse, and yelled at the wranglers' backs.

"What the hell you think you're doing?"

An old buckboard trailed last, piled high with pelts, bundled tight and smelling of rot and the stink of old blood. Despite the agitated thrust of the wheels, large black flies held fast while they gorged on the edges of the bundles, sucking out the last of the crimson nourishment from the skins. Steel traps and pole springs jangled from the rear of the buckboard. Both sounds and smells agitated Sherman's horses and put his entire party at great unease.

"If'n you's stands back a mite, we'll be outta your way sharpish," a crusty old codger said.

The wagon bounced hard, the axle stiff against each rut. The old man continued on his way with not a hint of hesitation and ignored the dangers of cutting into a road as he brought needless risk to himself and his horses. In the wake of the wagon, the metallic stench of blood rushed up the noses of all Shermans's party, stinging each man's nostrils.

Lennox rode to the front, ready to offer aid.

"No, let them be," Sherman said. "We want them miles from us."

After Sherman called 'make camp,' and the tents unfurled, four Blackfoot rode into camp, accompanied by a mountie and a U.S. marshal. All activities stopped as men circled to get a proper listen. Sherman greeted the group, chin up in surprise and hands on both hips.

"You seen any wolfers hereabouts?" the mountie asked.

"Not twenty minutes ago, headed south to the Medicine Line," Sherman said.

"That's got to be Skerrit," the marshal said.

He explained that Skerrit and his crew had come up from Montana through Billings and into the Badlands of Alberta, where the likes of the Sundance Kid and Butch Cassidy had hidden in miles of caves years earlier. Skerrit and his crew had made their way into Cypress Hills and caused aggravation. Most of Sherman's men squatted, listening to the talk.

The marshal continued. "Montana allows five dollars' bounty for adult or pup. With Skerrit's crew almost sitting on the border, they can go out on an idle morning and come back with as many as ten pelts per man to present for bounty. Now that wolves are scarce in the states, sonofabitches like Skerrit come into Canada to trap."

"They never stay long enough to clean up their treachery", the mountie explained.

He shook his head and continued, "They bring trouble wherever they go. They use strychnine to salt rough-gutted elk and come back later to gather up the dead adults and pups. They clean out dens like nothing. Birds and other small game feed on the carcasses and spread the poison to waterways, across ranches and homesteads, leaving a chain of dead game."

The marshal added, "Birds and insects spread the poison. It's the homesteaders, the hard-working settlers who pay a dear price for their quick-kill methods."

"Best make many fires so Skerrit sees your camp," the Blackfoot leader suggested.

"We will," Sherman said. "Thanks for the warning."

"He's got a point, them rowdies could be atop you before you know it," the marshal said. "What'd he look like?"

"Skinny and half starved. He stopped in front of me for a second — his eyes flickering like the strokes of a Morse code machine at the Telegraph office. Not the first time he crosses my path," Sherman said.

Lennox walked over and stood next to Sherman. Wherever they camped, the stink of their withering trophies brought predators and raptors alike.

"I heard tell he laid still like a newborn deer for near two days and nights," the mountie said, "ferreted out a den of twelve pups at thirty dollars a skin. That was back in '05. They drank to their hearts' content coming back over the Medicine Line that time."

"He's a general nuisance then?" Sherman asked.

"Damn yes," snapped the marshal. "The cattle ranchers who suffer serious losses each year argue that wolfers are a necessary atrocity, but theirs is a strange dance. Cattle farmers hate them, yet revere them. Paying a bounty for skins cost little when the wolfers protect ranchers' prized bulls, some worth thirty, sometimes forty thousand dollars. Some ranchers have three or four of those damned high-priced bulls."

"Imagine they're on their way back with so many pelts on their buckboard. Those pelts couldn't be piled much higher," Sherman said.

Sherman invited the group to a meal, but they declined and watered their horses before leaving.

That night Sherman thought of his father, a proud Scot who knew the land where he trapped with his Sioux wife. He had taught Sherman respect for the animals that nourished them and for the land that grew their food.

Sherman hated the wolfers and their atrocious ways. What a damned rough way to make a living. No Indian would trouble himself for the bother. For them, there was happier work breaking horses for prosperous settlers or competing for jobs at grain elevators or railroad stops. No Indians wanted to live this way, abusing the harmony of wolf spirits. There was no honor in it.

Calgary

Alberta ❧ June 6, 1907

Nazaire had marveled at the town folks in Lethbridge who worked clay in brick kilns that fired day and night, some as high as two stories, curing clay pots and ceramics taken by rail to market.

The area had once teamed with fast rivers and fish, but a new dam stopped spawning migrations and left no fish in many of the rivers, and now most waterways had lost their currents. Sherman's party had arrived at the foothills of the Rockies, north of Calgary.

———

Nazaire found the coach road to be indistinguishable from the hard rock plateaus of the Badlands, but the terrain changed to a brutal wind-whipped forest of felled trees with broken limbs, a violent sea of scattered bark and rot. Then it changed again.

"This is a goddamn strange place," Nazaire said.

Other men agreed, and many looked to Sherman for an explanation. A few men coughed. Soon Nazaire and other men plied kerchiefs to their mouths and tried not to breathe. The road turned from hard-packed, with spots of softer dirt that oozed a congealed grease, like oil on butcher paper.

Everywhere on the road was odd ground, with air that smelled syrupy and burnt, almost ominous. Had God forgotten this place and allowed demons to take over? Branches on trees hung heavy as if they lacked the strength to reach the sun. The horses snorted in protest, sensing something rotten. Pools of oil, hard-bottomed and shallow, spotted the road. Other, much deeper spots could ensnare men, as they would sink right quick to a foot deep.

"This air is unnatural thick," Nazaire complained.

Raoul agreed, "Even the horses are skittish."

The men came to a dead stop in the middle of the road.

"Be glad we're not in the tar pits near Fort
McMurray," Sherman said. "You could lose a horse
and rider in those tar pits."

"What's a tar pit?" Nazaire asked.

Sherman explained, "It's oil trapped in heavy
sand. Trapped for maybe hundreds of years. These
pockets of oil find one another and form a huge pool
of tar, sticky and foul."

A few of the men knelt with raised brows and
touched the top of one pool, smelled and examined
the grittiness of the congealed syrup.

"Where does it come from?" Coppaway asked.

"Deep underground," Sherman said. "Pools of it
squeeze up to the surface and lay flat, it's so thick."

The men learned to recognize and avoid them at
all costs, in particular, the men with mounts. They
needed to protect their horse's hooves. Sherman's
party walked a good twenty miles with their heads
down, scanning each footfall. Before long, the back of
their necks ached from the effort.

Lennox cautioned the men, "This is rough country. Look where you walk, and you'll be fine. These pools show up all around here until about Edmonton."

Chinook winds raged all day and night, coming down east of the Rockies, dry and warm. The men wrapped their heads as best they could against ear and throat ailments, winding cloths and whatnots to cover all but their eyes. The winds grew stronger, agitating the horses, who snorted in protest with tails clamped down between their hind ends. Then the winds grew merciless. Never had Nazaire felt winds this fierce. Might they all be blown up into the sky? The whole affair painted a sorry looking lot as they trudged down the road and sought shelter.

———

In a clearing, Nazaire helped build a lean-to out of tarps, using the side of the chuck wagon to keep victuals from blowing away. Cookie struggled to make a supper that wasn't half dirt and grit. Temperatures plunged to -10°F within a few hours as the men struggled to stay warm in their tents, hunched over and praying that the wrath of God wasn't upon them.

The winds howled like wolves all night but the party woke to calm and silence the next morning. A heavy sense of dread lifted with the fog and the sun gave off a golden warmth that curled around every man. Nazaire was excited to be heading true north as Sherman took to the road posthaste toward Calgary, Red Deer, and beyond, Edmonton.

Nearby, the wolfhound loped in the soft sand, growling and snarling, his head twisting from side to side at a feverish pace.

"Hundenkommer her," the Norwegian called.

"He's got somethin', see how he's all jumpified?" Cookie said.

The wolfhound returned with something in his mouth, alive but injured.

"What's this? Some kind of squirrel?" Nazaire asked.

Sherman laughed, "No, not with those big jumpy feet. That's a kangaroo rat. They live in the sands."

In the distance, two mule deer bent to nibble on scrub brush off the high dunes as the men continued to walk the difficult road. The sands kept them company for over eighty miles. Nazaire heard the Hutterite boy snivel. He was road-weary and frustrated from the long night's ordeal. All day, the boy stayed close to the wolfhound, both curled in a tight circle in the back of the buckboard.

The Hutterites would be leaving in the morning. After months of avoiding the boy, Nazaire could now look at him and not feel pain from longing after his own sons.

Raoul had been whittling two wooden horses and two riders for the boy. He had stayed up late the entire week. Now Raoul cut the legs of the riders wide so they would each sit a horse well. One rider had long legs, the other shorter, and Raoul needed a third hand to finish the job. Nazaire lay on his bedroll next to Raoul, eyes diverted from his whittling brother.

Raoul had already braided string to make the reins and tacked the tails on the horses and the dog.

"Hold this horse?" Raoul asked in a low voice.

"I'm tired, leave me alone," Nazaire said.

"But I need three hands."

"Get Coppaway."

Raoul leaned over as close as he dared to Coppaway. "He's with sleep," Raoul whispered.

Nazaire gave in and stretched as he rolled over.

"What you want?"

Raoul handed over the wooden horses, then the riders.

"Hold one horse by underneath. I need to tie the bridle on."

He looped the small braided strings under the horses' necks, crossed them behind the ears and back down under the neck, drawing each long end together. He knotted the ends and inserted them into the little notch at each rider's hands, securing each rider to its animal. He did the same for the other horse and rider.

"OK, I'm done," Raoul said.

The carved dog took on the color of the real wolfhound from a mixture of mud and ash. Nazaire lay stiff with eyes that watered as he pushed his body into the side of the tent. He thought of his sons back home. Who would be making a toy for them? No one.

Nazaire stifled his tears. How could he hold those wooden toys and not feel a twinge of sadness? He relaxed and decided that he would hand the boy one of the toys when the Hutterites left tomorrow.

In a few days, the party would travel through Red Deer. Nazaire and Raoul had a choice to make. They could continue to Edmonton a hundred miles farther north and face the Rockies or break the monotony of their journey and rest for a few days at their cousin's home.

Red Deer

June 10, 1907

Nazaire and Raoul asked directions, then arrived at the home of Cameron Fraser, a horse rancher who had married their cousin, Julia, ten years before when the couple had left Beauce Junction to build a life on the empty plains of Alberta. The brothers could count on back-home hospitality from Julia for a few days and were eager at the prospect of a warm, soft bed and a level table for meals.

The two-story ranch house was a long, sprawling affair. The front porch stretched ten columns across with screened in sections ready to stop annoying midges. A short fence stood out front. Beyond that, the brothers could see horse stables, a hay barn, smithy shop and other outbuildings nestled among corrals and open pastureland. Rich black soil gleamed in the sun beyond the outbuildings. It could not be more magnificent.

Julia received her cousins with kisses and hugs,
then asked endless questions about family back in the
Beauce; but the men, dirty and road-weary, asked to
nap. Hours later, they awakened to fresh towels and
hot bath water that Julia had at the ready. That
evening, they opened all the large, screened windows
in the parlor while laughter graced the serene quiet of
the property.

The next day, Raoul passed the morning with feet
soaked in oil and crushed peppermint on the front
porch while he collected his thoughts. In the
afternoon, he joined Julia in the kitchen with the
children, reminiscing about their childhood.

Cameron and Nazaire toured the barns and side
stables, looked over the prized studs. Nazaire
couldn't help but stroke the jowls of each horse,
fighting tears. He ached for his hard-working team.
He took the halter of one curious blue roan, cupped
his hands and blew his breath into the animal's
nostrils, the proper way to introduce yourself to a
horse. The fresh smell of new-mown hay hung in the

air. Galvanized water troughs bordered surrounding barns and stables. Water pails hung from outside faucets.

"My father started this ranch and passed it to me when he was struck with yellow fever. I built up the stock and improved on the land. It's a good life," Cameron said.

Both men leaned against a fence post.

"Me, I got a small farm, growing grain with my team of geldings, Louis and Joe. They're black, so black you can see the smallest bits of dirt on them," Nazaire said.

He stood silent a few moments then shrugged his shoulders as both men walked up to the largest corral.

"Joe, he has white socks in the back and is the funny one, always defies me before the work's finished. Louis is taller and serious. He never relaxes, him."

Nazaire pulled out a tin of Stag fine cut, packed his pipe, then fired up.

He explained, "Sometimes I sit and sing to them when we come in at night. Louis's always in a hurry to get back to the barn. Not Joe — he would take the long way home if he could. But Louis, he's the boss, and poor Joe can't even nibble a little extra clover. Louis even bosses me around."

"How many hands?" asked Cameron.

"They're small, compared to your animals. Canadiens, a short breed, fourteen hands the both, with long necks and full chests, good for pulling, you know."

"Most of my stock are difficult eaters. You want the best for them but they can be stubborn."

Nazaire continued, "Sometimes I put something good in my pockets, they know it before I even see them. Sometimes I put dried berries in their feed. They like that."

"No mares then?"

"The mare, that's my woman's. I use her for town." Nazaire lowered his head and grew quiet.

The following day, Cameron seated the brothers in his small study and discussed the perils they would face. "People say every wild animal you meet wants to kill you, so better be alert and sure-footed. Rivers are fast, and with the melting snow and rotting ice, their edges are hard to see. Carry one or two strong walking poles and feel the ground under the snow or ice before stepping on it. The water'll kill you within five seconds if you go under."

Cameron opened a desk drawer, pulled out a Cannon Ball tin, and took a plug of spit tobacco into his mouth. He offered it to the brothers. Both declined, but pulled out their pipes instead, and tamped a good pinch into their bowls, then fired up.

"In Edmonton the stores will try 'n' sell you everything. If your rifles are good, fine; just make sure you have shot for them, powerful enough to stop a brown bear."

Both brothers shuffled their feet under their chairs as they listened.

"Never sleep near the opening of your tent. You don't want a grizzly pulling you out by your feet. You'll come across wolves, big ones, and lots of rough Indians, hostiles, not mild-speaking ones like we got in town."

"How do we keep ourselves safe?" Raoul asked.

"If I were you, I'd sign on with an outfit."

Raoul coughed while he stared at Nazaire.

"If you come to water and hear a buzzing, it's a pool of mosquitoes. Don't doubt it for a second. Get the hell out of there and cover your face and hands with strong, fine netting. You must have netting," Cameron emphasized.

"How about crossing the Rockies?" Nazaire asked.

"The Rockies are treacherous. Men say that this time of year you can't see rocks in the bottom valleys and canyons because of leftover ice. Most rock faces are loose, you could break a leg going up or down. I'd take whatever rivers you can. It's faster travel with much less risk."

"And work? Is there work?" Raoul asked.

203

"I hear tell there's work everywhere. The general mercantile in town claims that if you work for someone rich, you get seventeen, maybe eighteen dollars a day plus you use their tools. No one around here gets that kind of money."

———

The brothers rode out with Cameron to meet the sergeant at the Royal North-West Mounted Police station housed in a crude log cabin in town. A pot belly stove stood at one end of the small structure. The cabin was done up neat with a wooden floor and one window of waxed parchment. Broadsides filled a back wall and advertised homesteads in the Prairies. The sergeant was a husky youth in his late twenties, efficient in the way the British are. The sergeant cut a fine line in his clean, red uniform.

He opened a gazetteer to maps of the Rockies. "The days will get longer as you get closer to the arctic. Expect a damn short summer and a hell of a long winter. The winters are dark, and maybe hard to take but you'll get used to it."

Nazaire asked about a guide.

"Join Nelson Peck's crew. He's the most reliable outfitter in Edmonton. He values common sense, and his people will get you across the Rockies as far as Whitehorse," the sergeant said.

A large broadside hung behind the sergeant's small desk. It depicted a pasture with two grazing cows and the words, 'Own your own farm in Canada and apply for a ready-made farm to the nearest Canadian Pacific agent.'

Nazaire stared at the poster as he thought of his own land — all the wet springs that rotted his sprouted grain, and the hot, dry summers that burned his crops before they gained height. These were the losses he and Victoria had struggled through in the last six years, and for what? Here is this rich soil and the government was giving away homesteads!

"Know what gold miners get for pay?" Raoul asked.

"Last I heard, twenty dollars a day."

"Holy Jesus," Raoul said. He slapped a hand on the sergeant's desk and laughed.

"Some jobs can kill you so you might want to ask around before taking on new work. Ask the old-timers, they'll set you to rights," the sergeant said.

Nazaire was flush pink in the face, happy at the thought of Raoul earning as much as twenty dollars a day. He had been right to encourage Raoul to come. After the men had left the mounties' station, Cameron led them around the small town of Red Deer on his well-behaved mares.

The railroad station, cargo warehouses, and large grain elevators brought pride to the area. The town featured a two-story hospital and a new bridge for crossing the dangerous Red Deer River. Stone and brick commercial buildings lined the two main roads. Red Deer even had a denim overall factory.

"Everything looks good now, but fifteen years ago there was no one here but a few Métis, maybe some Cree and hundreds of Blackfoot. Julia and I, we were smart to come when we did," Cameron said.

The three men turned back toward Cameron's ranch as he continued, "The Prairies are settled and producing a solid economy, but we saw over two million immigrants struggle to get a homestead going.

Nazaire's eyes widened.

"Some families, the women and children lived off soup and bread for maybe three years before their men had raised a rough cabin. Women and children crowded in immigrant warehouses filled with lice and weevils, no way to wash. Many drowned in the Red Deer River trying to wash or get across. Today, few farms are smaller than a hundred sixty acres and the government buys as much sugar beets, cabbages, potatoes, vegetables, wheat and other grains the framers grow."

Nazaire held back from sharing the bitter depression that had gripped the entire Quebec Provence. Just under one million Quebecers had abandoned the country for better wages in the New England states. Businesses were boarded up overnight and farms of all sizes lay vacant, including his own. People couldn't even give away their stock. No one had enough feed to take over the care of an extra animal. Banks large and small had left people penniless overnight, wiping out years of lifesavings.

He couldn't get the image of that poster out of his mind. If he were alone and without Raoul, Nazaire might have slapped down coin for a homestead there and then, but what of his farm back in the Beauce? He thought of his children parceled out to relatives like orphans. His brothers and sisters and aging father. His team, Louis and Joe. His untilled fields and good crabapple trees, his grove of maples that each year gave more syrup.

No, he needed to focus on the job in front of him. Get to the gold fields and dig. Dig to save his children, his farm, his land. Dig to make a future. Nazaire was happy for Cameron and Julia, but it was a shock to see all this growth, compared to conditions back home. Could his family ever believe the miles of good land and rich soils he had passed through these last months? The strain he and his family had endured were a nightmare he could not shake, like a grinding fist tearing away at his heart.

Everyone back home was helpless to do anything about this. It was like walking in wet clothes, bogged down in layer after layer, almost drowning from the weight. Instead, he stayed quiet and motioned Raoul to ask his questions.

They rode back to Cameron's ranch through fragrant groves of spruce and aspen. Above them, flocks of jabbering swans and their cygnets flew south to their summer nesting grounds in the Platte River basin of Nebraska. The brothers rode on either side of Fraser, lost in their thoughts before preparing to enter a land known both for its magnificent beauty and its vicious cruelty.

Nazaire felt alive, a whole man again — certain he was looking at the dream he wanted for himself, and all that was standing in the way was fifteen hundred miles of the roughest terrain on earth and a whole lot of digging.

THE WILDERNESS

Edmonton

Alberta ❧ June 17, 1907

Nazaire wandered the main street of Edmonton while Raoul sought pipe tobacco at the general mercantile. They had arrived that morning on the new gravel road, the first of its kind anywhere in the Prairies. Their feet much approved.

Nazaire sought someplace quiet to think as he stood at the entrance of an odd church with a splayed roof and onion dome. Ukrainian, someone said. Whatever God he found inside didn't matter.

He closed his eyes when he heard the bells and remembered being six years old in the forest with his mother, carrying firewood that his father had just cut. They had held the cut wood in their arms. The hollow sound of an ax against a tree had echoed in the woods, and the scent of pines hung in the air, clean and bright. The village monseigneur had ridden by in his carriage with its warning bell breaking the morning calm. Nazaire's mother had knelt in the muddy slush with bowed head until the monseigneur had passed. Nazaire had not.

The top chunk of wood had slid in his grasp and fallen. He looked up to see the holy man's scowling face. The monseigneur's clenched fists painted his palms white. For years, Nazaire had held the guilt of that dropped firewood. He never wanted to feel that helpless again. Tears spilled down his face, and the knot in his belly loosened. He crossed the street, wiping his eyes before searching out Raoul.

Edmonton was a scruffy town filled with people speaking more languages than Nazaire and Raoul had heard in Ottawa. Horses overran the pioneer town. Behind a few cabins, shipwrights were rough-carving small boats with chisels and scrapers. Branches and bark littered the streets, wood curls dragging on the men's long coats. The new wooden steps outside Queen Avenue School and the new gravel road were Edmonton's first symbols of modern living. Telephone poles lined the main thoroughfare, as yet unwired while coal power plants threw black smoke into the air, following the current of the North Saskatchewan River.

Off a main road, five shorter alleys bustled with activity. Rope corrals held horses, saddles, and tack. With wood a premium, few trees remained at the north end of town. Most had been chopped years earlier for boats. Wooden crates of foodstuffs and coiled ropes fronted each alley alongside canvas tents. These were the domain of Edmonton's five wilderness outfitters. An endless procession of men meandered in and out like a carnival.

"Peck. Where can we find Peck?" Nazaire asked a man in a moosehide coat.

"Two alleys down," the man pointed.

Nazaire and Raoul made their way through the crush and found the back of Peck's tent with a crowd of prospectors all at attention. Peck wore a long wool coat that added to his height. A dirty, blue cravat at his neck swallowed his curly hair. Peck had started his lecture, so Nazaire and Raoul stood silent and listened while men shuffled their feet as they took in his words.

"Things are going to be different. You'll need to friend every man here. You never know who might save your life, eh? You got this new way of living right now and here 'tis. Wake at four, take coffee and bannock, piss and then run."

Peck continued, "You run Indian file 'til noon, when you take a ten-minute rest. Start walking slow, then fast, then run again 'til dusk."

"Indian file. What's that?" A cowboy asked.

"Walk in the footsteps of the man in front of you. Indian file, you know. Tarry, and you'll be left behind, do you hear? If you don't make the next camp before dark, no one'll be lookin' for you. Dark comes smartly, and when it does, you can't see your hands afore your face."

The audience numbered forty men, all with their kits by their feet. Some looked disheveled and worried by the words just spoken. Aside of Peck, a grizzled man dressed in rawhide twitched and spoke up.

"There's wolves out there, some large cats, and fierce Indians that don't take to white men. We got mosquitoes, black flies and all kinds of prickles. There's dead falls, mud holes that'll near sink a man complete, and muskegs that masquerade as solid ground. The Rockies got every kindof quicksand known to man."

After a moment, Peck took over the lecture. "Never go anyplace alone, always in twos. In camp, you get coffee and supper, then rest for the next morn. The guides change every day, but pay that no never mind. Do as your camp boss says, and you'll be fine."

Prospectors lined up in front of a broken, lopsided table to sign up and pay. Word in the saloons was no one dared cross the Rockies without a guide. Most Indians knew the way, but only through their particular territory. Nazaire and Raoul lingered, picking up all manner of conversation. Each trail boss left with twenty-five men, Nazaire learned, the most each camp could sleep and feed at a time. Some camps handled men moving east through Montana or west into Vancouver, while a few ran north to Whitehorse.

They were nearly there. Months ago, old man Connolly had said that the Rockies were the last quarter of the trip. There would be no turning back now. He had seen his dream when he and Raoul had visited with Cameron and how he would get it. What he had wanted all along. He was ready to work, sweat and dig for gold. He would dig for his children and for his future.

Nazaire and Raoul approached the lopsided table and paid their fee. A cowboy stood behind them, his red scarf tied around his neck. Men nearby were dressed in every sort of work clothes: woolen coats, tipped caps, Russian fur hats with full ear flaps, long otter coats that dragged on the ground. One prospector had shiny, new Wellington boots, rugged but with a height that would cut into the back of his knees with steep climbing.

"You two together? Two days' wait. Be here 4 a.m. on Thursday," the money collector said behind the table. He wrote down their names and took their money.

He looked at Nazaire's kit. "You got more than sixty pounds there?"

"No, less. How far to Dawson?" Nazaire asked.

"Little over fifteen hundred miles," the man said.

Nazaire and Raoul looked at each other, then walked off. They hoped to see a familiar face from their old party. He and Raoul both held out a ready hand when they caught Sherman's husky voice outside a saloon.

"Could we sleep in your camp for two nights?" Nazaire asked.

"Sure, but best get your meals in town," Sherman said, "Cookie's not provisioned up yet."

"Have you seen Coppaway?"

Sherman hesitated before answering. "You haven't heard? Shot dead yesterday, not an hour after his wedding."

"But how? Why?" Nazaire asked.

Nazaire and Raoul gasped while Sherman's eyes went idle. The three men stood stiff without saying another word. Nazaire and Raoul offered their sympathies to Sherman, who had known Coppaway since he was a child.

"An Indian stole a blacksmith's tool bag. Some say the blacksmith mistook Coppaway for the thief. Who knows? This frontier town is about as wild as it gets." Sherman paused, turned quiet and surly-mouthed, then disappeared into a crowded street.

Nazaire mourned Coppaway's death. His mind flooded with cherished memories as he recalled Coppaway's words to "honor what you have today." He thought of the bear skin and claw necklace that Coppaway had worked on.

"Make clothes for new squaw. Show I can provide," Coppaway had said.

Nazaire remembered the small jar of honey that Coppaway saved for her. When he got those migis shells from the dying shaman at Kenora, Coppaway had separated out one particular one that he planned to give to his firstborn son. All Coppaway's dreams, gone.

Nazaire grieved for this man — an improbable friend who had become more father than brother by the time they parted at Red Deer. Not often were men were thrown in together but since the drunken men's fight in the road, Nazaire had grown to like the Ojibway a lot. Over supper at a quiet eatery, Nazaire talked out the differences this new outfitter would present.

"It won't be like with Sherman," Nazaire said.

"No?" Raoul asked.

"With Sherman, we brought food and water with us the whole way. We set up tents each night and broke them down each morning. With these outfitters, the camps are setup permanent. We're in a new camp every night and food's already there. Our guides will change with the territory."

"I see."

"No horses travel with us, so you can bet the forest is damn thick. They said the guides bring water to us when we rest at midday. It's a different kind of traveling."

"Who said that?"

"Peck. So are you pleased now that we didn't stop earlier and take some job at a dollar a day?"

Raoul nodded yes.

––––––

For two days, Nazaire and Raoul listened to the hawkers of Edmonton push their ceaseless bushwhacking wares. The vendors sold gold pans, nails, firearms and ammo while they insisted everyone needed their warm clothes and gold-digger outfits. Nazaire and Raoul each bought a pair of leather gloves and fresh pipe tobacco. They followed Cookie's suggestion and ate as many Cheechako potatoes that they could find — no powdered stuff.

Each meal was a large glass of milk, Cheechako potatoes, and eggs with sausages laced with saltpeter, the tang sharp on their tongues.

With the extra time in Edmonton, Nazaire and Raoul searched out the route across the Rockies at the Royal North-West Mounted Police office, where people were welcome to look over their maps. There was no one way to get to Dawson, but several depending on the season, with forest fires in summer, or rivers whose banks overflowed in the spring. They might head to Fort Nelson, go up the Liard River and onto Watson Lake or not. Who was to say?

Blind Swale

The Rockies ❧ June 20, 1907

After weeks of walking through fields of tree stumps, the true forest of the Rockies surrounded Raoul. The camp bosses warned everyone to cut sturdy walking poles that would steady a man when climbing or jumping down from felled trees. The prospectors admired the cowboy's pole whittled with a wide forked notch on the top that caught branches from snapping into his face.

Each night a new camp and each day new guides, one at the front and one at the rear. A quick start was automatic with everyone sleeping in their clothes, but Raoul cradled his boots in his arms during the night. Broken trunks, tipped branches, old growth, first-generation trees whose cores were split by lightning or some god-awful happenstance faced Raoul every day.

Sphagnum moss covered everything, concealing holes and pits in the ground, giving off the stink of old mold, thick and earthy. Some trees too large to climb over lay on their sides, so Raoul followed the reclined giants until he reached the root ball, a black wall of snarled prickles and rocks imprisoning the roots. No one dared walk too close for fear of having their dungarees caught.

In the tangle of dark growth, a prospector at the front turned and raised a finger to his lips. Muffled sounds of heavy snorting carried in the air. The prospectors stopped to listen.

"Old moose. No good eat," a Kaska Dena Indian said as a weak grin appeared on his hard face.

The prospectors continued their march in Indian file. By mid-morning, the trees had thinned out, and the forest floor grew wet between tussocks, those clustered areas of tangled grasses. The earth became miry and soft, yielding under each footfall. The area surrounding the tussocks shook, frightening prospectors as they sank into sphagnum bogs concealed by decayed vegetation.

Raoul found it difficult to maneuver out of clumps of devil's club with his feet finding no purchase on firm soil. Before he realized it, he and one other man trailed behind.

Raoul glanced ahead when the last Kaska Dena had passed, keeping him in sight. A dreaded noise sounded behind him and broke his focus. Raoul stood abandoned with no idea which way to advance. He dared not look behind, but ran forward, questioning what malevolence might manifest itself. He stopped, steeled himself and then turned around to see the man behind him gone. No trace of him remained. What sort of menace was responsible? He shivered in place, listening for any sign.

"Hey, you OK?" Raoul called to the empty space. Silence.

He listened for a solid minute. Not a sound registered where moments before, the suck of dozens of boots filled the swales with echoes, those decaying ridges marshy and unstable underfoot. At his back, soft footfalls grew until a Kaska Dena and the cowboy were at his side.

"Run. Why you no run?" The Kaska Dena asked looking up at Raoul.

"A man was behind, somewhere," Raoul said as he pointed.

"Show."

"I don't know," Raoul said with eyes widening in disbelief.

"One? More?"

"No, only one."

"You come, follow," the Kaska Dena said as he pulled Raoul's pole from his hands and retraced his steps, examining trampled vegetation. The Kaska Dena prodded with the pole at different spots until a splash of water broke the silence. Bushes rattled as if being swept from side to side.

"Come, come help," the Kaska Dena yelled to Raoul and the cowboy.

They ran toward the noise and discovered the
Kaska Dena on his hands and knees, his pole pushing
a limp body to one edge of a muskeg. Raoul offered a
huge hand as the Kaska Dena squat and leaned one
foot at the edge of the swamp, reaching for the man's
shoulder.

The cowboy pried his notched pole, trying to
hook the body's suspenders. The Kaska Dena
managed to turn the man's head above water. Mud
coated the man's hair, and his eyes were idle. Raoul
and the cowboy struggled to wrestle the Kaska Dena
free of the suck, while the man lay limp in his arms.

Once out of the muck, the Kaska Dena turned the
body on its side and bent the man's knees while he
slapped his back. Over and over he slapped. The
cowboy pulled out his water canteen and cleared the
man's mouth. Back slapping turned to forceful
pounding as the Kaska Dena fought to bring the man
to life.

But it was too late.

Raoul and the cowboy dragged the body to the edge of the new camp. The crowd of prospectors circled the pair when they entered the campgrounds, throwing questions at them. The camp boss ushered both of them into his large tent. Nazaire followed with a blanket, ready to cover his brother. The camp boss poured four shots of whiskey and passed them out. He looked from Raoul to the cowboy.

He looked back at Raoul. "Is he dead? It's a terrible thing, this land. You always gotta be looking out for each other."

He swallowed his whiskey in one quick stroke, and then continued, "Relax now, boys. You all stay in here and eat your meal away from prying eyes and gossipy questions."

"We tried to get him out, but we was too late," the cowboy said. His shirt and neck scarf were covered in brown sludge.

The camp boss wrung his hands, and then looked at Nazaire. "You stay and eat with these men. The woman will get your plates. Pour them another shot and one for yourself. I gotta go talk to those Indians."

Nazaire pulled the blanket over Raoul's shoulders while the cowboy sat on a wooden crate and drank his shot of whiskey.

"It could have been me," Raoul said.

His shoulders trembled, and he stared at the ground. Outside, the prospectors raised a nervous cheer when the cook called dinner. Nazaire grabbed the whiskey bottle and poured each of them another round. Raoul remained silent and stared at his big shaking hands. He opened his rucksack and pulled out a long rope, tying it around his waist. Next, he packed away his easy smile, remembering old man Connolly's lecture.

In the Bush

British Columbia ❧ August 1, 1907

Nazaire and Raoul entered the new camp. They had taken to the new routine quick enough with most camps laid out the same. Large canvas tents fronted three main fires, with the largest in the center of a crown of rocks. One large grate held coffee pots and bannock, grilling over the open fire. The two end campfires spat and splattered with boiling kettles of stew, a welcome break from beans.

The prospectors dropped their gear in the damp canvas tents where oilcloths lined most of the floors, and set their kits and gear against the inside walls to keep out the cold. A few point blankets leftover from Hudson Bay days were scattered around, their red, green and yellow stripes faded with dirt and grime.

The camp boss appeared and said, "Anyone so sore they needs to stay more than a night, it's a quarter extra each day, and another quarter for those needing liniments."

Dusk gave way to inky nothingness. The end campfires dimmed as the camp boss tossed more logs on the central campfire. A carpet of mist settled around the outskirts of the rough camp as the black night thickened into a solid wall. The cold settled in. A Cree serving woman emerged from the chuck tent with a tray of hard grain bannocks ready for the grill. The woman threaded her way to the center campfire through a tangle of prospectors' feet. Nazaire and Raoul stood off to one edge of camp and waited for someone to call dinner.

A push of air brushed against Nazaire's cheek as a sharp smell pierced his nostrils. The stench was like a bramble in his throat. A tall intruder ran with such speed that not one man in camp reacted as a blur of putrid furs advanced toward the woman and pushed against her shoulder. She pivoted, her eyes flaring as the grizzled beast hoisted her up onto broad shoulders and bolted from the front of camp right through the back.

And then they were gone.

No camp dogs barked. They stood stiff with their tails between their legs and their ears back. The few horses in camp curled their upper lips and stood with ears flicking back and forth as they snorted gusts of frost into the air. The prospectors were frozen in place, open-mouthed. As the intruder passed a large tree, the serving woman let out a scream when her head grazed the trunk with a hollow thud.

Her screaming stopped.

A few prospectors grappled for their rifles and handguns, but no one rose to follow. Heads turned left to right, some seeking understanding, but not one man stood. Murmurs of disbelief grew into coarse statements around the campfires. The prospectors spoke in whispers. Some joined the line for coffee and others picked up pieces of the raw, broken bread off the ground. Raoul remained in line, stiff and confused as he searched into the black peripheries that surrounded camp.

"Gorille," Raoul whispered to Nazaire.

"Maybe not," Nazaire said.

"What else can it be?"

"Don't know. Smelled more animal than man."

The prospectors ate quick with most settled in their tents early. Everyone spoke about tying their tent flaps from the inside for safety. The camp boss grabbed his rifle, pointed it up, and fired into the air. A few prospectors ducked their heads, some staring in the direction of the shot.

"I posted four guards tonight with loaded rifles, so don't be fearful. The wild man ain't coming back," he said.

The Cut Line

Nazaire watched a Cree come into camp and speak with the camp boss. Wisps of vaporous breath punctuated each word the Cree spoke. As Nazaire bent to tighten his bootlaces, he hoped to catch some of their talk. The camp boss asked how the men would go forward with a large pack of wolves nearby in Doig River Indian territory.

"Doig know where wolf is and where he attack," the Cree said.

"How?" The camp boss asked.

"It game wolf play. Wolf want man fall. If'n one fall, more fall. I send word. Cree push them up. Doig make cut line. Men be good if'n they run," the Cree said as he pointed an index finger in the air and made little stabbing motions downward. "Must run Indian way."

Nazaire and Raoul overheard the talk and looked at each other with raised eyebrows. Prospectors tightened a circle around the camp boss and the Cree, all interested. Nazaire listened harder, trying to capture the sense of it.

The camp boss turned to the prospectors. "There's wolves about. We're sending you out with more protection today."

"What's the fellow saying about some man falling?" A prospector asked.

"You need your best runner out front. Look, you'll be just fine."

"What's a cut line?" Raoul whispered to Nazaire.

"Don't know," Nazaire said, "Something about a wolf."

Nazaire stood next to the camp boss and asked in a whisper, "How cold is it?"

The camp boss lowered his head and hesitated. "Minus eight. It'll get colder for the next hundred miles."

The prospectors mumbled and stood uneasy, pushing their weight from foot to foot.

The camp boss stretched his arms wide and explained, "Today you'll see Doig River Indians, them with red sashes on their heads. Don't stop running and don't pay you no heed. Stay in Indian file. They're experts at protecting you."

Nazaire saw weary looks cloud the prospectors' faces as they started off. Each man searched throughout the day, but no Indians appeared. As the afternoon lengthened, the land narrowed on either side and funneled the men into a tapered path with a rock wall at their right. The thick forest was near impassible.

A distant growl pierced the afternoon air as the Cree guide at the front turned and yelled, "Stay Indian file."

Nazaire's heels almost hit the arm swing of the man behind. He saw a large gray wolf running parallel to his right on the other side of a stone wall. Farther right, a second wolf appeared at a slow run. It snarled. Two more wolves showed themselves behind trees. Each neared the wall as the rock face rose in height, revealing a high ledge cut along the top. The wolves edged closer, their angry-looking muzzles shooting up from the snow. Each wolf jumped in one graceful motion onto the rock ledge that climbed higher above the ground. It was a rout of wolves, a pack lining up above the prospectors like corporals looking down on their subordinates.

One Doig appeared behind a tree to the left, and then a second. Four more Doig walked out from trees far ahead. They each moved in one swift motion with long rifle barrels trained on the wolves. Nazaire looked ahead and watched the Doig line up their shots. Like a circus pinwheel game, the Doig poised their firearms against tree trunks and calculated the space between the prospectors, firing. The skills of the Doig, aim and precision, found their mark. The prospectors panicked. One ran abreast of another, blocking any chance the Doig could take a shot.

"No stop. Keep run Indian file," the Cree yelled.

The rifles fired. Crack, crack. On the upper ledge, one wolf fell and tumbled down onto a prospector.

Explosions ricocheted along the rock face while their echoes sounded off the top ridge after every bang. A spot of crimson bloomed on one wolf's neck. The Doig fired in a shattered assault of smoke and noise. The group was too far from the last camp, and they couldn't go back.

A few animals jumped and backed away from the fight with blood trails following them. Some returned for another try, their loyalty to the pack fierce. The leaves and branches shone white in the afternoon hoarfrost amid the strange contrast of deep red stains splattered on the rock face. Howls and yips mixed with the metallic, bitter smell of blood.

The prospectors were cold to the bone, but didn't dare slow down. If they did, they would be lost in a turmoil of teeth and blood. Nazaire felt the grunts of the wolves vibrate into his shoulders. He was afraid, more afraid than he'd ever been. Did bullets outnumber the wolves? Where was Raoul? He wasn't right behind him. Why not?

Nazaire took in a long breath and felt the first singe of freezer burn on his nostrils and lips. His eyes watered while he tried to brush the ice crystals from his eyelashes and under his nose. He began to panic and struggled to understand what was happening. He remembered one stampeder with a story of men freezing to death and how once it's cold enough, the eyes water, then eyelashes build up ice. When the eye surface crystallizes, the man cannot see because the eyelids freeze together.

"He's a dead soul walkin' but don't know it yet," the stampeder had said.

The temperature must have dropped five degrees. How could the Doig survive in this cold? Nazaire's mind raced, and then he realized: yes, if one man fell, then others would fall. He turned to see the prospectors behind him run with their chests curled in. Where was Raoul?

Terror embraced Nazaire from the deep-throated snarls of the wolves. Teeth gnashed, and muzzles threw spittle from the ledge while the prospectors gasped below. Horror at the speed and power of the brutes overwhelmed them.

Farther left behind the trees, more Doig moved in closer as they fired. Nazaire couldn't believe his eyes. Next to one tree, a Doig stood with feet apart. By his ankles, a young boy no older than ten lay on the ground, his rifle aimed at the line of men. Nazaire looked up at the Doig father, saw his lips moving as he spoke to his son. Below him, the boy changed the angle of his rifle and fired.

Smoke and loud reports broke Nazaire's focus. He watched the grays follow the ledge as its slow descent brought the wolves nearer level ground where they would join with their prey. The wall disappeared and with it, the distance between wolf and man. A bullet whizzed in front of a man's chest and another missed a second man's leg. Reports fired all around the prospectors while the Doig whooped and yipped.

Ahead, large fires marked the entrance of the next camp with two Doig pointing firearms dead into the line of incoming prospectors. One Doig caught a wolf in mid-jump with a shot so precise that the brute tumbled up and over in the air, an extended paw capturing one man's tuque. In camp, the prospectors stopped and caught their breath while they searched out familiar faces. When Nazaire found Raoul, they embraced. The camp boss gave them some minutes to recover, then bellowed his lecture.

"Welcome to Fort St. Nelson territory, boys. I hear the guides did a tip-top job. Not a one of you scratched or lost."

The prospectors cheered. Nazaire heard that all but four wolves had been cut down, making good the promise of their safety. Fourteen Doig came into camp that night, eager for their thank-you meal. Grateful smiles and continuous back slaps greeted them. They were handsome men with red calico bandannas around thick, black hair. They were tall, and wore hide leggings with coats of goat wool that lacked a proper washing.

Nazaire told a camp cook, "It looked like the circus shoot-em-up game where the ducks, they waddle across a board, and the people, they aim and fire."

Nazaire thought of the empty space each bullet had to travel to hit its target, a gap so precise it expanded in his mind and resolved itself in a spell of gratitude and excitement. His blood was on fire from the ordeal. He couldn't remember the last time he'd felt so alive. He and Raoul grabbed each other's shoulders again.

"Damn you, you stay behind me from now on. I don't ever want to lose you like that again," Nazaire said and laughed.

"I tried to stay on your heels but got pushed out of the way," Raoul said.

The camp boss pulled out a bottle of whiskey and passed it around. Some prospectors danced around the fire pits and sang into the black night while guffaws washed over the camp.

———

Doig and Cree squatted by the fires with tin plates in their hands.

"Wolf already given. Good cut," one Doig said to another.

Nazaire turned to one of the Doig and asked, "How many skins did you get?"

"Doig take nine. We give Cree four."

Nazaire watched another prospector raise his eyebrows and ask the Doig, "Nine?"

"Cree slap bushes. Doig use bullets," the Doig said while he shook his rifle in the air.

"Why did the wolves attack?" Nazaire asked a Doig.

"Wolf hungry. Deer sick two years now. Many die," the Doig said.

While everyone ate together, Nazaire searched out the father of the young boy. He wandered through camp among the back slaps and handshakes. At last, he found the man.

"How old is your son?" Nazaire asked.

The Doig turned in surprise and couldn't stifle a proud grin.

"Nine years. You see him?"

"How could anyone miss him between your legs? Nazaire said. "Brave boy and good aim. I been scared before but not like this."

The Doig squatted broomstick-straight and smiled with pride.

"Tell him he did good, excellent good," Nazaire's said.

The Doig raised his chin in agreement.

"It game to wolf. We play too, good practice."

That night, laments of grief kept the men awake. It broke Nazaire's heart to hear the wolves' howls of love and sadness. He thought of the young Doig boy while tears came to his eyes.

Fort Nelson

September 2, 1907

Nazaire watched two Métis enter camp some forty miles south of Fort Nelson. They greeted the camp boss in low voices. The Métis wore deerskin clothes, braided hair, and medicine bags hanging from their waists. The older had bright, gray eyes that betrayed his Scottish heritage. How did they live with one foot in the Indian world and the other in the white man's? Both Métis looked to be father and son by the cut of their chins, but the younger had dark, round eyes, similar to other Métis hereabouts.

"Which way did you come?" the camp boss asked.

"Northeast, four days out," the older Métis said.

"What news?"

"The woman, the one with the tray of bannocks?"

"What about her?"

"The Buick Cree found her five days out, east of Prespatou."

"Where?"

"In a big hole in the ground," the younger Métis answered.

Listening, Nazaire and Raoul bristled at the recollection of the incident. Other prospectors heard the words, and a few fidgeted from foot to foot while they stood.

The prospectors gathered around the fires, rubbing their cold hands and legs while they waited for someone to call the evening meal. Those who sweated while running now found their clothes wet and needed to change before sleep or they would take sick. The line of hungry prospectors elbowed Nazaire and Raoul nearer the camp boss's tent.

Raoul nudged Nazaire, "You hear that?"

"What did you expect? She'd be coming back?" Nazaire said. "She cracked her head but good on that tree."

"You said it smelled like an animal."

"It did, and it didn't. Don't mean that it was. Maybe a holy man. Hermit or something. Some called it a wechuge," Nazaire said.

Raoul's eyes flashed side to side. "Are we safe?"

"Calm yourself."

The two Métis greeted others in camp, then got plates of food and squatted to eat. They leaned over the fire and pushed smoke up to their faces with open palms.

Nazaire watched them, and then asked a camp worker, "What are they doing with the smoke?"

"It stops the No See Ums," he said.

The camp boss stood by the largest fire and spoke.

"Boys, you need to keep your voices down. We're in a tough spot here between the Doig River and Blueberry River territories. The Blueberrys been in a bad way and don't want white men on their land."

"Why not?" one prospector asked in a quiet tone.

"There's not enough game in these parts to feed themselves, let alone outsiders."

"But we'll be OK, right?" Nazaire asked.

"Sure. You boys just be real quiet and tomorrow if you see any Indians, you be real polite."

Nazaire rolled that thought around in his head the rest of the evening. He worried about Raoul, a giant of a man who had an unnatural fear of all Indians. Nazaire scratched his head and joined the others sitting by the fire when the talk turned to gold. One miner held the attention of a small group.

"Where'd you mine?" A prospector asked.

"Worked on the Peace River, then at the Kennecott Mines in Alaska for Guggenheim. Copper mining. I suppose I'm the official Sourdough here," the miner said in a low voice.

"Sourdough? What's that?" The cowboy asked, pulling his red scarf from his neck. He wiped his face and listened.

"That's me — somebody who's been in the Yukon a full year. Before that, you're a Cheechako, a greenhorn."

"Are there different kinds of gold?" The youngest prospector asked.

The sourdough seemed to relish the attention as he explained.

"Starting from the largest, ya got you nuggets. Thems can be small as your thumb nail or a five-pound boulder if you be so lucky. Then you got stone gold, them be pebbles like. You find 'em in the tailings when cleaning the dredges."

"What's dredges?" A prospector with broken suspenders asked.

"And what's tailings?" The youngest prospector asked.

"You got you big dredges that runs on belts, real wide belts, one on each side; its thems what moves the dredge forward and back. A long pole stretches out in front of the dredge and at the bottom is another belt, but this one has attached to it many tubs, like bathing tubs thems be. So this pole has 'bout twenty or so tubs that go round, pulling paydirt outta the ground."

"What's paydirt?" The cowboy asked.

"Paydirt's what you're looking for, cowboy. Dirt that's still got gold in it. The tubs pulls the paydirt into the air til the tubs disappear in the soul of the dredge where it gets cleaned by spraying it with water. Lots of water. The riffles, thems are slanted pieces of metal, captures the gold on accounta gold's heavier than dirt. The dirt that comes out of the dredge, thems the tailings."

The cowboy continued with his questions. "So what's tailings for?"

"Tailings got no purpose," laughed the Sourdough. "It's the leftover mud comes outta the dredge. Nuggets and stones drop outside the tubs as they climb in the air, and it's where yous can pick up some nice nuggets. The problem is, it's dangerous work, cleaning the belts. Chances of getting sucked down are real good. It takes a fast, strong man to do the job. It pays a lot, but it kills lots of men, too."

Nazaire and Raoul took in every word as the Sourdough continued.

"When the belts get filled with rocks 'n such, mens go down and cleans them, but it's all sucking mud, and many a man's been crushed 'cause he couldn't get out an' away fast enough. In all that muck, many nuggets gets tossed to one side by larger rocks, and never goes through the hoppers. What gold you find around the edge of thems dredges is yours. Theys large nuggets, maybe worth two hundred dollars."

More men joined the circle to listen.

The Sourdough continued, "Not all dredges are sitting in water, though. It's after working a spot for a year or more that theys sitting in a pond. Before that, theys standing in sucking mud so thick, it'll take your boots and socks, even your underwears and belt. When a dredge starts to work a claim, it's all dry ground, and gets wetter and wetter over the months."

Some prospectors lit pipes while others rolled cigarettes. The Sourdough threw his cold coffee on the ground when the cook offered a fresh cup. He looked at all the faces staring at him, then raised his cup to signal the next question.

"How many kinds of gold is there?" The prospector with the high Wellingtons asked.

"Ya got you dirty gold, that's half black and yellow and needs a washing with quicksilver to burn off the paydirt."

"Will we need quicksilver?" The prospector with broken suspenders asked.

"No. There'll be one or two guys in Dawson, smelters theys called. They takes your dirty gold and smelts it down in a forge into those shiny bars."

"So there's dirty gold and what else?" The cowboy asked.

"Dirty gold ain't no kind of gold, it's the condition of gold. The kinds of gold that's got value would be dust, flicks, then flakes, then sparkles, thems the most common kind. Lace gold, that's rare. Theys mostly oil trapped in the gold so's theys always moving around. No lace gold around here, it's all up near Fort McMurray."

"Do they still use dust and scales in Dawson?" The prospector with broken suspenders asked.

The Sourdough's voice had gotten quieter as he continued explaining.

"Not for buying booze. No self-respecting miner would walk into a saloon with anything larger than dust, but that was back before nineteen and 05. The scales is all gone, not a one left except in the assayer's offices at the banks or with the few smelters around Dawson, thems still cleans gold. The smelters work for big outfits now, thems got twenty to fifty men working for em."

"What's the hardest thing about working the gold fields?" The cowboy asked.

The Sourdough sat silent for a bit while the closest prospectors crowded in to hear his reply, "I suppose chopping wood and potatoes."

"You chop potatoes?" The cowboy asked.

"No. After the stampeders left Dawson for Nome, all the cabins they built stood idle. If'n a cabin's empty, it's yours, but you gotta chop wood for heat.

Enough for eight months. You got to be chopping wood every day. And then there's potatoes. There's a powerful lack o' potatoes in the north, and you need ems for fighting off scurvy."

The Sourdough chuckled as he looked over the faces hanging on every word.

"You's don't even need an outfit. There's plenty around that men left behind, the ones that packed it in and went back home. Big outfits provide you what you need."

"But the hawkers in Edmonton said we needed a full miner's kit. They advised it," one young miner said.

"Ya needs warm clothing, but the rest is 'xaggerated lies, all bloated trumpery to suck out every last nickel from a man's calloused hands."

Nazaire found the Sourdoughs' words a lot to think on as he and Raoul drifted to their tent while some men stayed at the fire, tamping a pipe or cutting a plug of tobacco and too excited for sleep.

Summit Pass

September 23, 1907

Yesterday had put Nazaire on edge as the prospectors, now a hundred miles west of Fort Nelson, faced the Summit Pass on Mount Saint Paul. It loomed before him, four thousand feet high, the northern gateway to Watson Lake.

"Anyone see cougar or bear droppings, go tell the guide quick," the camp boss said as the prospectors left.

The guide was a short man, a Kaska Dena Indian about forty years old, ruddy-faced with not a whisker on his cheeks. He wore a calico shirt and heavy dungarees under a greasy piece of rawhide. A red kerchief kept his thick hair clinging to his head. With a long knife hanging from his waist and a rifle slung on his shoulder, Nazaire judged him to be serious and dependable. The guide's sled dog carried a haversack with pouches of food and firewood necessary. The

Kaska Dena led the prospectors to the trailhead, scolding his bitch as she growled at the wolfhound.

"You last, so dogs no fight," he said to the Norwegian.

As the party moved through groves of lodgepole pines, Nazaire picked up pine cones that would add pops and a clean fragrance to the night campfire. Indian Paintbrush blanketed the area with pockets of bright red blooms. The air turned thin by midday when the party reached a shallow field with a clear spring. Despite dancing butterflies, not one mosquito buzzed.

The Kaska Dena filled water bags and handed them to the men. "Drink now," he said. "Up there, night no drink, only morning, no more."

All afternoon, a pair of kingfishers squabbled at the intrusion of humans on their territory. The first night, the Kaska Dena offered a cold mash for supper and the soft ground as bed.

By morning the weather had changed, and an easy wind blew most of the day. With each step,

Nazaire's feet fell on more rock and less soil, and the air became colder above the tree line. Easy walking was no more. Ahead of Nazaire, a shower of rubble covered most of the trail.

The scree spread before the prospectors like a bad-luck omen and nearby, the sound of rocks hitting the ground caused everyone to look to the sky. Loose stones filled the slope so Nazaire tapped Raoul on the shoulder and both moved to the outer limit of the scattering. Like a mudslide, the swathe left no easy path except to step on the sharp, angular stones as prospectors slipped and fell on the rocks. Even those with a walking stick could not step out of the scree without falling down.

Nazaire gazed at the coarse and gray slopes where toward the top, herds of dahl and stone sheep created a small shower of rubble. By dusk, the party neared the top third of the pass where out of the clouds, a small cabin emerged filled with cooking pots and canvas tents. The prospectors' legs ached but before they sat and rested, tents needed to be put up where any soft ground could be found.

Two large fire pits sat in a depression, nestled against a flat slab where the sled dog gave up his pack. In the chilled air, the Kaska Dena started roaring fires that warmed the men, and roasted steaks with fresh greens he had picked along the way. Nazaire threw the pine cones into the largest fire, hoping their pops would unsettle a roaming cat.

The prospectors sat and ate in silence. Some rubbed their calves and thighs, easing charley horses while others needed help removing swollen feet from their boots. The Kaska Dena walked among the men. He pointed to the cowboy's boots.

"My feet are just fine," the cowboy said with a pained look on his face.

With no hesitation, the Kaska Dena grabbed a leg and pulled one boot off. Out came bloody toes and skin bloodied at the heel. Nazaire turned his head, unable to look at the cowboy's feet burning in full swell. The Kaska Dena boiled water into a thick tea with greens and a few sticks from his dog's haversack. He painted the cowboy's bare soles with the stinking sludge.

"Be good tomorrow," he said.

The temperature dropped to below freezing as the party of men clustered closer to each other with hoarfrost coating the edge of boulders.

"Come Raoul," Nazaire said as he inched closer to his brother, "we sleep like spoons tonight to stay warm."

———

The next morning brought another hard start with no hot coffee, rather a tin of water and cold mash for each man. The tents were put back in the small cabin and each man could see that they were out of the scree with solid rock under their feet. Climbing would be easier, Nazaire thought, as they approached the summit.

At mid-morning, the Kaska Dena stopped. "We rest little."

The group was very near the top. Pieces of basalt and granite, not the split-edged kind, dotted the area. Nazaire examined a fossilized chunk of dolomite whose underside held dozens of solidified skeletons, a graveyard of oceanic remains.

"Seabed," the Kaska Dena said.

"Seabed? The bed of a sea up here?" Nazaire asked.

The Kaska Dena explained, "Over mile up. Thunderbird create earth, give rivers water and much fish. Some rivers him push up to sky. Now mountains."

A vista most extraordinary took Nazaire's breath away as he counted twenty-two mountain peaks due north. Never had he witnessed so majestic a site and it filled him with a joy and sense of weightlessness as if his body could rise up into the cloud cover. The prospectors clustered around the Kaska Dena, many pointing as they tried to get their bearings. Which way was north? Where was east?

He raised an arm and pointed to the north mountain chain, "You no cross there," he said. He turned and continued, "You go northwest to Watson Lake. Now, this one corner of Cassiars."

Nazaire turned to Raoul, "How can so much beauty be where no man walks? It's a waste."

The Kaska Dena smiled. "No waste. You see."

After they rested, the Kaska Dena stood and demanded, "No boots. All take off."

Nazaire tied his gumboots together, happy to let his toes grab purchase where they could.

The Kaska Dena pointed to the Norwegian, "You with dog, make eat," and held out a pinch of meat, then fed another pinch to his bitch.

The trail cut against the slope of the mountain, funneling the line of prospectors into a wall, narrow and blind. Before them, a hundred feet of ledge offered little room for misstep. A thick-braided rappelling rope hung, tied around huge boulders at the edge of the overhang. Was this the only protection?

The Kaska Dena stood by the rope and again spoke to the Norwegian, "You tie dog on neck. I go, then you."

He turned to the crowd in front of him, "I come back. You watch good."

The guide put a leather lead around his dog's neck, picked her up and nestled her on his shoulders where she remained, asleep.

He tied the back legs to a cord at his waist. Everyone watched as the Norwegian did the same to his wolfhound. They each squat to climb in front of the rappelling rope and grasped the wall before them. They moved with slow steps along the ledge until they disappeared as the rock edge cut back toward the mountainside. A few minutes later, the Kaska Dena returned. Now Nazaire understood — safety demanded bare feet. The men formed a line and adjusted their kits as each positioned the rappelling rope behind their backs and watched the feet of the man ahead. With a raised hand, the Kaska Dena paused the men when too many were on the ledge at once.

As the men jostled into position, the cowboy slid behind Raoul and in front of Nazaire. With feet rosy-colored with puff, the cowboy stepped on the ledge as it narrowed to near nothing. Each man searched the rock face for any surface that fingers and toes could grab. Below, nothing but treachery and rocks awaited.

"Agh," the cowboy howled. His foot slipped and without thought, he reached out and grabbed at Raoul's sleeve. Try as he might, the cowboy couldn't get one foot on the uneven shelf. Raoul grabbed for an outcropping of willow scrub above his head.

Time stalled as Nazaire witnessed the cowboy's slip, his leg dangling over the ledge, a hand snatching Raoul's shoulder and with it, a cry from both men as they each fought toward anything they could grasp. By instinct, Nazaire reached out, and held tight to the cowboy's long coat.

Seconds of panic stretched out as the three men struggled to grab any lip on the cliff face. From below,

a wave of icy air chilled their bare feet. A screech
pierced the air. The cowboy slipped from his coat,
leaving the vacant garment between the two men. The
dull thump of his body echoed up from below.

Once Raoul and Nazaire moved around the
curved corner and out of sight, they were off the
ledge and onto level ground.

Below the ledge, a broad meadow appeared with
not a single piece of scree. The ground turned green
like a lush carpet, and led to a small grove of aspen
and willows protected from the wind. The
prospectors fell to the ground, each relieved to be off
the ledge and on soft soil. Nazaire's blood pumped
with the thought of losing his brother. He looked at
Raoul.

"Damn, old man Connolly was right."

A forest of lodgepole pines spread at an inclined
pitch to the valley floor. Small purple flowers, moss
campion, covered every grassy surface. How could
such fragility remain amid coarse stone? By dusk, the
prospectors were off the pass where the Kaska Dena

claimed the tree line ended in a small river of clear, delicious water. Walking was easy now with soft ground under Nazaire's feet.

Each man turned when they heard the sound of water, but along with it, a faint chirp, and then another. After a few steps, the chirps became more like the sounds of peeping chicks in spring.

On the bank of a pond, frogs leapt, dusky gray with dark blotches. The smell of rotted salt followed the length of the pond where the creatures appeared painted with an ivory streak down the center of their backs-each one identically adorned. They created a moving carpet of green and black bodies, some creatures as long as five inches as they jumped outrageous distances to remove themselves from the prospectors' boots.

One frog leaped up and hit Raoul's wrist. He jumped in surprise and swatted it away.

"No touch. Milk poison," the Kaska Dena warned.

One tall prospector examined a frog at his feet. "I know what these are. They're western toads. Where are they going?"

The guide pointed to the trees. "They go sleep. Warm in forest."

A few brazen toads bled a white substance along their spine, enough of a warning for any living thing.

It took everything out of Nazaire to cross Summit Pass with all its mystery and danger, a memory he wouldn't forget. Snug in his tent at the next camp, Nazaire thought of Raoul as he struggled to hold onto the memory of the cowboy. There one second, gone the next. What would he ever do if something happened to Raoul? He shivered in his bedroll. Damn, that old man Connolly was right.

Watson Lake

The Yukon ❧ September 27, 1907

Nazaire had heard of the 60th parallel when the group got their first taste of elongated day and night cycles stretching in unnatural ways.

Now the men experienced eleven hours of sunlight per day. Next month, that would drop to eight hours of sunlight. The recalibrating of their internal clocks pressed against the prospectors, who struggled in the constant gray. Sleep was near impossible. No calm darkness was to be had. Nazaire pushed thoughts of this severe oddity from his mind, replaced by a headache wanting to bloom.

"You'll get used to it," the new camp boss said.

"Can't we walk away from the sixty line and get back the night time?" One young man asked.

"Not if you want to reach the gold fields."

This morning, the prospectors were led by two Blueberry River Indians. Both were very young, maybe ten or eleven. Wide-eyed and silent, they looked the prospectors over. As Nazaire walked, he gained ground up a small rise, and then everything changed. A fire had come through and revealed the back side of a ridge as the ground gave way to lower valleys. Ash covered the hillside as great trunks curled black with their strangulated roots, akin to maggots writhing in a slight breeze.

"Fire one year old," a Blueberry Indian said.

They were near Watson Lake, home to a small group of Kaska Dena Indians when the camp boss announced that no one need walk Indian file anymore. Relief shown on Nazaire's face for a moment, replaced by tight lips when the camp boss spoke of river crossings ahead with swollen banks, some with sides of clay so treacherous that they could drag a man down to his neck. Nazaire couldn't swim. Neither could Raoul.

Every dawn, great flocks of croaking sandhill cranes headed south to their wintering grounds, often followed by a constant wedge of swans who complained of the coming cold. They brought a smile to Nazaire's face with thoughts of Victoria.

The prospectors walked, slipping over mossy cover. Lazy black slugs thicker than a hog-eye slithered across leaves, dropping sperm in their shadows as clusters of beargrass brightened the slopes with their fuzzy tops. On the underside of a felled tree, Nazaire spotted it, one small stock, gray with new fuzz pushing up toward the cover of sky. Fluffy rivulets were carved into its cap, like worms that struggled to break free. He stopped to pick it up and held it in his hand.

"What ya got there?" One prospector asked.

Nazaire ignored him, walked a few more feet, then gasped. Across an open field he laid eyes on the plumpest mushrooms he'd ever seen. They were everywhere, in different varieties. Some had sturdy stems that carried ginger crowns slanted into a cornucopia on one side like a tipped hat on a grand madame.

"Chanterelle," Nazaire said. "They're delicious and sweet."

He bent to pick a few and threw them in a small bag at his waist. Raoul followed suit.

"The cook will be happy to have these in the stew tonight," Nazaire commented.

He picked delicate sponge morels clustered together in bunches with hollow crevasses and elongated heads. Further on, a prospector brushed against a large red one, and a puff of smoke shot up.

Nazaire ran behind the man and yelled, "It's poison, that mushroom you kicked is poison. Lift your head and raise your arms high."

The man coughed and ran parallel to Nazaire with glazed eyes. When the prospectors stopped for a break, Nazaire splashed water on the man's face and hands. He took him aside and broke a few branches, then brushed off the spores that dotted the man's pants and boots.

"Those mushrooms, bright red on top with white spots, don't touch them. They explode with fine smoke that sticks to your clothes. Clean the spots off. Be careful if your hands touch the poison. When you eat, don't bring poison to your mouth."

"How you know?" A Blueberry Indian asked.

"An old man back home told me. He worked at Lake Nipigon, where they grew. If you walk near them, walk slow and cover your mouth. Once the mushrooms open in the air, don't breathe their smoke."

The lead Blueberry Indian gave a subtle nod of thanks. During the mid-day rest, Nazaire pointed to a notch in a tree. A Blueberry Indian whistled and leaned against the tree as the prospectors watched the other Blueberry Indian jump on his shoulders and raise his arms to groove the tree with a more distinct notch.

When he jumped down, Nazaire asked, "Why make the notch so high?"

"Make mark higher than snow."

After a few miles, the line of men slowed. One Blueberry Indian signaled the men to group together, picked up a broken branch and pointed to some plants.

"Locoweed," he said, "this locoweed, no eat."

The prospectors mulled around, each one trying to see the particular leaf. The guide spotted another plant at ground level and again pointed with his branch, "No touch; you die fast," he said.

"What's that?" The prospector with the high Wellingtons asked.

Someone said, "It's fringed sage. It'll kill a horse right quick if he eats any."

Nazaire sighed as he walked out from the tree line, free from the crowded underbrush that fought each step. The prospectors left the tangle of threaded weeds and thorns that pulled at everyone's clothing and cut the men's ankles. They crossed into sparse meadows filled with rocks, chipped and sliced into layers by wind and ice.

———

In camp, Nazaire repeated the story of old man Connolly's cautions to curious prospectors. That

night, two Doig River Indians entered camp and
asked for the white man who knew about the
erupting mushrooms. Someone led them to Nazaire.

"Tell about red caps," a Doig asked.

Nazaire repeated old man Connolly's words and
his simple remedy. The Doig looked at each other
with neutral faces.

"Red caps never here before. Now many," the
taller Doig said.

"Cut them out in winter when they don't smoke,"
Nazaire cautioned.

They left with grunts of gratitude. Close to Atlin
Lake, Tlingits relieved the Blueberrys as the
prospectors entered into Southern Tutchone territory.
Tomorrow, the group would face rock mountains that
all but kissed the clouds but this night, Nazaire felt
small and insignificant as he watched stars twinkle
and fall in an unending procession in the black sky.

The White Pass

British Columbia ❧ October 6, 1907

Nazaire had not noticed as each day lost four minutes of sunshine to gray twilight. His soul hungered for a warming sun but none would be had. He was in the home of the midnight sun. All the prospectors mumbled among themselves. Some more stubborn than mules.

"It'll take six months to adjust. By then, the winter blackness will eat your soul, and you'll be begging for the sun again but the night won't give you a damn nights' rest," the camp boss said.

"What choice do we have?" The Sourdough asked.

"None. The heavenly bodies will have their own way at the sixtieth parallel," the camp boss tried to explain.

"Right now in October, you still got about ten, eleven hours of sunlight a day — but come November, that'll drop to eight hours a day, so the nights will get longer. Bring in December, and you have maybe five hours of sunlight. January brings you even less, and longer nights still. Look, it's like a yoyo — you get less and less sunshine the closer you are to the winter months."

The prospectors slept in a sluggish fog while their stomachs flipped, and constitutions gained upset. Some men seemed to walk in their sleep. Others complained that their hearts beat faster. Their feet seemed to push forward in a drunken murk. Eating proved difficult in the thin air and each morning, for as much as half an hour, clouds spit icy crystals on everyone's heads. They melted when they reached their hands, the heavens teasing Nazaire with satisfying refreshment.

He stopped counting the valleys that appeared beyond Watson Lake. What looked from afar to be bright green patches of paradise, up close were quagmires of thawed mud and permafrost swelled by the decaying pus of mangled streams. Each quagmire offered a stench so severe, the sole living creatures were biting mosquitoes that wallowed in the festering trenches. Everywhere, the sweet odor of decay hovered above the ground.

Fresh guides appeared to lead the prospectors — this time the Tlingits, who insisted the men tie ropes to each other and walk four men abreast in a front guard, ready to pull out whomever might sink. The Tlingits stopped in one dense forest and bade the prospectors to cut young trees to whittle into staffs.

"Help walk on mountain," a Tlingit explained.

When the trees played out, wind-blown shrubs turned to a hell in damnation, where nothing but rocks and thin, slippery shale plates remained. The group skirted the spines of mountains for weeks, scaling down to seek safe harbor each night.

Over smoking fires, the Tlingits cooked stews from fires of dried moose and sheep pellets. They instructed the men to walk two or three at a time up mountain sides, leaving gaps between the groups as stones tumbled down hundreds of feet. Men and kits slipped until they stopped. Bruised shins and sore ankles were the price of impatience.

On the mountainsides, the camps were no more than open sheds, one roof and two torn canvas sheets giving scant protection from wind-tossed stones.

Nazaire and the others cursed the Edmonton outfitters with their shouts of the "All-Canadian" trail in all the Prairie newspapers, for none existed. Even the Tlingits struggled to travel through the Rockies.

Every night there was angry talk in camp, the fear in men's throats thickening to blasphemy. Because there was no trail at all that the prospectors could see, how could they be guaranteed the Tlingits would lead them to the White Pass on Canadian soil, and not the Chilkoot Trail, where Americans would impose custom fees for everything that the men carried. Peck had guaranteed all the crossings would be on Canadian soil. It was an agitation each man found heavy to bear.

One night, the camp boss addressed the prospectors. "You'll be coming to Dead Horse Trail next," he said, "I knows you're worried 'bout paying money but yous Canadians don't pay no customs, so don't fret."

"How far from Dead Horse Trail to the White Pass?" A prospector asked.

"Theys the same place."

"Why call it Dead Horse Trail?" The sourdough asked.

The camp boss looked the man square in the face, lowered his eyes, then raised them slow. He stretched his lips, then spoke. "On accounta three thousand horses died for nothin'. Beat, bled, abused, and starved, all in the damn name of gold."

Nazaire gasped. Did he hear right? He couldn't believe it. Three thousand? It must be an exaggeration, or a downright lie! He had never heard so horrific a thing. The Tlingits led the group up gentle rises, then at the top of the next gap, a vast plateau appeared.

———

Before his eyes, Nazaire saw it — Dead Horse
Trail. The ground had been beaten up, scavenged by
other travelers, with pieces of broken carts tangled
amid tumbled trees and rotted ropes.

Hovering in a patch of black soil, he questioned
the whiff of burnt molasses in the center of a huge
charred circle. An aged stench lingered, captured in
the shallow plateau. All at once he knew it, and his
blood ran cold. Thee was a syrupy stench of horse
flesh and bones set to fire. The hollow rose on all
sides, creating a six-foot trough in the center — a
crater of charcoal where broken wheel axles and a few
jaw bones remained, black but still recognizable.

Gone was the hard evidence of decaying
carcasses. Wind and rain had washed away flesh and
bone from the rush that fed men's desperation back in
1897. Nazaire's heart broke to think of it. How many
horses, Nazaire wondered, were taken by something
other than men's greed — by wolves or wild cats
maybe? None. He had heard that it was all because of
avarice, the chance to get ahead that drove a man's

desperation beyond his soul, into a place of damnation.

How, when you knew the gentle nature of these beasts, could you dare to disrespect their aid in the fields? Their twitching ears that warn you of strangers? Their strong legs willing to pull when your own spasm? Their welcome neighs as they greet you each morning? Nazaire's heart froze, and his taste for the chase of gold ceased.

Prospectors settled beyond the black pit, resting before the merciless climb ahead. The next morning, Nazaire raised his chin as high as it would stretch, seeking the Canadian flag that marked White Pass Summit. The prospectors faced a steep climb. The day would test everyone's legs; by nightfall, the prospectors raised a cheer when they saw the familiar colors of their Canadian flag.

———

The next morning, each man signed his name in the mounties' book. The Rockies behind them. They had reached the Cassiars, but Nazaire found no joy in arriving at this turning point. To the northwest, mountains gleamed with snow down their slopes as northern harrier hawks attacked majestic bald eagles, pulling carrion from each other's talons while in deep, sweeping dives. Nazaire's feet moved, but he was blind and mute to everything around him. Into what soulless depths must he stray in this raw wilderness? His stomach flipped, and his heart seized.

"What you say, Nazaire, we're three days to Whitehorse," Raoul said, with excitement in his voice.

Nazaire didn't answer. His ears were deaf, and his eyes dull. He was numb to his core with the sick of it.

"Nazaire, we work hard and get gold. You'll see. We'll be rich when we go home," Raoul said, a smile in every word.

Nazaire didn't move.

"Snap out of this," Raoul chided as he grabbed Nazaire's shoulder.

Nazaire raised his head and took in a long pull of fresh air.

"You're right. We're this far and it's what I want."

––––––

At Lake Bennett Nazaire and Raoul boarded separate open rafts guided by Tlingits. South of Carcross at Windy Arm, the northern route of Tagish Lake, winds blew with enough force to push men down, and many boats almost flipped. Both brothers clung to the ropes, sure that death was coming. Pools of froth shot up everywhere. Miles Canyon loomed before them, wild and unpredictable.

Beyond the high cliffs, Nazaire realized that it didn't matter if he and Raoul couldn't swim. The water was so fierce, it was a power unto itself. Nazaire held on, looking down on the other desperate humans clinging to the sides of their rafts while whitewater covered logs and dragged each man to the edges. Their duty done, the Tlingit escorts disappeared at Whitehorse.

––––––

While the prospectors rested for a day, the Sourdough found other Tlingits who would bring the group to Dawson by boat, for a dollar a man.

"Don't you want your kits off your backs? We'll arrive in a few days' time," the Sourdough encouraged.

It would take three days in restful splendor, whereas by land, almost two weeks lay before the men and four hundred hard miles. There wasn't so much a road to Dawson as there was a bushwhacked trail. The Yukon River opened and joined Lake Laberge from a narrow stream that widened to a frothing nightmare of fifteen-foot swells. Laberge was angry water and the lake, thirty-one miles long and three miles wide, possessed violent storms that arose without warning.

At its north end, the Yukon River narrowed and transformed into a ferocious pull that tossed the boats without mercy. Steep slopes that boarded rugged bluffs offered no escape.

Nazaire remained half asleep, a man weakened in spirit. What did it take for a man to be gentle? Would it bruise a man's pride to act with reason and steadfastness? Why couldn't brutes apply a tender hand? He thought of Louis and Joe, and the joy they brought him every day.

Nazaire's soul had been tested. His shoulders slumped from months of biting straps that tore at his underarms and shoulders. After two days, the river revealed a gentle bend. High on the right cliff face, a massive gouge appeared, ripped from the walls of the cliffs that bordered the Yukon River. This high bluff, known as the Moosehide Slide, marked the town of Dawson.

Nazaire and Raoul were exhausted and dirty as a bag of fleas, but they had arrived. A spark of hope grew into a hot flame that burned in Nazaire's chest. Nothing would stop him.

IN THE GOLD FIELDS

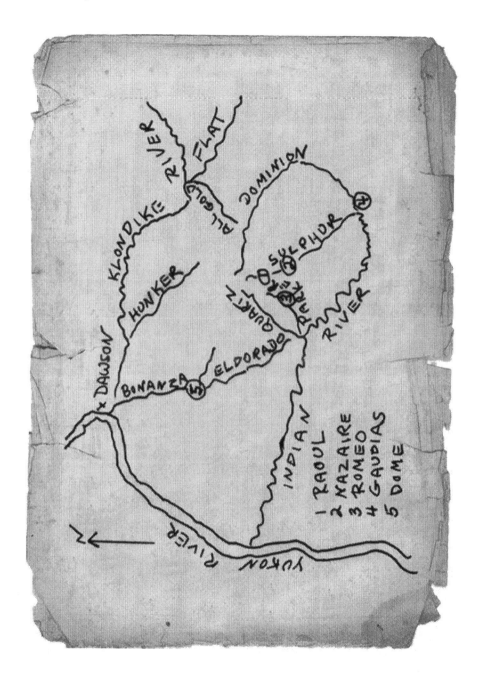

ARRIVAL

Grand Forks

The Yukon ❦ October 12, 1907

When Nazaire heard men in Dawson City speak of gold coming from Sulphur, Gold Run and Dominion creeks, his mind filled with promise. He needed to open a claim on any of these creeks.

Nazaire and Raoul had both worked asphalt mines back home in Thetford, and they knew a thing or two about asbestos mining. Nothing could have prepared them for the scale of the Dawson gold fields, however, when they rode the Klondike Mines Railway to Grand Forks, thirty-seven miles away.

The Yukon had been carved from the immense Northwest Territory, claimed by Canada a few years earlier when it was nothing short of a land grab between the U.S. and Russia. Despite a few sparks of economic growth in Hearst, Thunder Bay, Winnipeg and Vancouver, the 1896 discovery of gold thrust Canada onto the world stage. Tons of gold pulled from the Yukon lifted the country from its economic decline at a time when the world had suffered a widespread depression.

Gone were the old days of the Miners' Committee, when someone caught stealing another man's food or cache was gunned down, hung or left out in the elements to freeze. The long-ago reputation of Soapy Smith and his henchmen still painted a feeling of risk in Alaska but on the Canadian side of the gold fields, the Dawson region was tamer, with very few thefts or murders.

Every conceivable wagon and cart existed in the Yukon. Horse-pulled wagons with paneled sides, flatbeds, and misaligned plow heads fashioned onto large beams moved along muddy tracks. Farm machinery became part-mutant, part-rock excavators. Some horse teams pulled wagons with smaller carts behind, their sled rockers dragging over permafrost.

Home-made carts with mismatched wheels helped to move paydirt, bring barrels of water higher up from the creeks, all working to meter out the stubborn gold. Hand-hammered rocker skis served as dragging feet for lighter carts. Dredges with rotating belts dug up the earth as they crept forward.

The free railway carried cars filled with spools of ropes and cordage of every conceivable girth. Some rail cars hauled empty water barrels and coiled hoses. Flatbed wagons struggled to turn tight curves with overhanging boards, rough cut and weighing them down like the dragging tails of muddied peacocks.

Supply cabins dotted the creeks, each with their company name or initials painted in bright red near the roof line to be visible once the snows came. Miner cabins stood in crooked rows up the sloping sides of creek beds or set back from mine entrances.

Everywhere, miners walked, rode, pulled or were being pulled by some sort of jury-rigged conveyance. Nazaire remembered the Sourdough telling of wagons making their way among dozens of creeks in sweeping loops so that outlier miners could get transport from one creek to another. Excitement filled the air and Nazaire was a new man — ready to dig for gold, right here, right now.

———

They arrived in Grand Forks, a town that was more like a city. It included general stores, churches, eateries, a bank, a post office, a telegraph, and even a direct telephone line to Dawson from the Grand Forks Hotel. It had its own division of mounties, mail service and the dubious services of a doctor and dentist. Every hotel and saloon had a stable of good-time women available day and night. Granville provided everything a man needed.

Thousands of miners carved Grand Forks into a massive crossroads that served the major creeks. The railway brought in the heaviest equipment to Grand Forks, while most men jumped aboard any wagon with vacant space. Each creek was responsible for moving their equipment from Grand Forks to a final destination. Half the mining claims had been bought

out by Guggenheim and consolidated into
commercial operations with fifty to two hundred
miners tending his fortune. Still, there remained
hundreds of claims worked by one or more miners.
This was what Nazaire sought.

————

When Nazaire and Raoul searched out the Mine
Register Office and inquired about available claims,
the Officer said, "Got just one claim left, a pup
twenty-eight feet long.

"What does it mean, a pup?" Nazaire asked.

"You got you a creek, say fifty or seventy miles
long. Everyone's claim is 250 feet wide, so that's 250
feet across into the creek stream. A pup is a small
claim, maybe fifty feet or less off a main creek."

Nazaire and Raoul exchanged a glance.

"Maybe I wait 'til tomorrow. Don't have to take
the first thing I see," Nazaire said to Raoul.

"It's very late in the season," the Officer explained.
"You're lucky to get anything before next May. It's a
creek claim so you'll be standing in water to work it.

Might be something over in the next mining division, but it's so late in the season, I doubt it."

This was the most gut-wrenching news that Nazaire could hear.

"I'm either the luckiest or unluckiest sonofabitch here " Nazaire said. He turned to the Officer, "How do I find it?"

The Officer drew an X on a map and handed it over. "Find claim forty-one and forty-two below Discovery on Sulphur Creek. Your claim will be between them, got it? Take two stakes from back of this cabin. Sign your name and date on one of the stakes, then punch them down on both ends of the claim. Come back and pay, and it's yours."

Nazaire looked up, askance. "How do I get there?"

The Officer turned the map over and drew a circle onto the paper.

"Think of this as a pocket watch. Twelve o'clock is Grand Forks. Down at the bottom is six o'clock, so that puts you at the bottom of Quartz Creek off

Indian River. Your claim would be in the middle where the two hands meet, Granville on Dominion Creek. Wagons pick up men and drop them off all along the outside of the circle. Stand by a red pole to get a ride south, or a blue pole to go north. The trucks will stop for you."

They pulled items from the heap pile then stood by a red painted pole. Nazaire's chest swelled as a buckboard rolled to a stop before them. He was on fire.

————

When Nazaire and Raoul returned to the Mine Register Office, Nazaire slapped his ten dollars down on the counter. He and Raoul had each put grease pencil to the stakes and laughed as they drove the stakes into each end of the claim. The pup was damn small but built up with rock on both sides. How could Nazaire remain idle one more day? This opportunity was his chance for a better future. Electricity pulsed in Nazaire's chest, and his earlobes burned.

"OK, a mountie will be out in a few days to check your claim. If it's mis-measured, he'll set it to rights," the Officer said.

"Mis-measured? How could it be mis-measured? It's only twenty-eight feet, for Chrissake," Nazaire said.

The Officer continued, "Take what you want from the heap pile out back. There are pans, rockers and such. You'll be wanting rubber waders and wood."

"I heard we need to order food? We do this here?" Nazaire asked.

"Fill out these forms. You pay when it comes in. Best you figure good. You don't want to be out of food by March when mining doesn't start up again 'til the middle of May."

The Officer explained that in Dawson, warehouses were now being packed with winter provisions. At season's end, the sternwheelers arrived filled with goods to be locked up in the twenty-two dedicated warehouses. These would be, one by one, filled to capacity.

For the town's wealthy, potatoes, canned fruit,
cigarettes and snuff filled their warehoused caches.
This time of year, passengers who traveled were
outgoing — the wealthy who would winter in warm
Seattle, or the miners who would take a ship down as
far as Ketchikan to whore for a week, then return by
the Yukon and Whitehorse Railway out of Skagway.

The officer had suggested that beans, bacon, and
flour were all Nazaire and Raoul needed. They
declined a winter's worth of potatoes and the
customary twelve oranges to fight the scurvy. The
officer sniffed the air.

"You men smoke? Don't forget tobacco," the
Officer said with a wink.

Excitement colored Nazaire's cheeks as he
finished the paperwork. A tear ran down his face. His
paper read 'Creek claim 41-A below Discovery on
Sulphur Creek.'

———

Nazaire and Raoul sat their kits down in a little
eatery and spoke about their day with loud voices

and hands dancing in the air. Their conversation caught the attention of a fellow Canuck.

"I'm Broussard. Come join me," the man said.

He pushed a chair away from his table. Broussard was a Quebecer from north of Montreal. His beard was the color of rust, and his nose was too small for his face. He wore a checkered wool shirt and heavy pants rolled into his boots.

"How long you been here?" Nazaire asked.

"Since 1902. Granville was nothing then. The town was built in 1903 for Treadgold's Company. I work on Sulphur Creek ten miles away, work for good men who run the Yukon Pacific Mining Company," Broussard said.

"Are they hiring?" Nazaire asked.

Broussard continued, "Probably. They start Cheechakos, that's guys like you two, at about twenty dollars a day if you got no experience."

"What? Twenty dollars a day? Sonofabitch. I can't believe it," Raoul said. He hit the table top with his hands, smiling.

"Got a place to stay?" Broussard asked.

Nazaire and Raoul shook their heads.

"I got a cabin with a skinny Irishman, good man. We work at the same mine. I got two empty pallets. You could bunk with us."

Nazaire looked at Raoul, then nodded yes to Broussard.

"Did you order your dry goods for winter?"

"Yes," Nazaire said.

Broussard added, "Good, if you didn't tend to that, you would both be froze'd or snowed in with no food til May. Your pup is small, but it still might'a captured sparkle. You know what that is?"

"Ya, gold small like a chip of a woman's fingernail," Nazaire said.

"Right. There's no telling, you could dig all the water out, create a false dam and work it."

"And if there's no gold?" Nazaire asked.

"You got six or seven weeks before freezeup, but that'll tell you if it's worth keeping. If there's no color, give it up or sell it next summer and then come up with ten more dollars to buy another one."

"I gotta start working it right away."

"You both going to work it?"

"No, Raoul will help me for a day or two to get set up, but then he's got to get himself a job. Me, I take the long shot but Raoul, he needs to be more safe."

"I can get you in at Yukon Pacific, Raoul. It's a good crew. You'd be happy with us," Broussard said.

————

They settled into Broussard's cabin in Granville that afternoon, a luxury with four pallets, a wood-burning stove opposite the door and wooden floors providing protection from the wet come thaw. When firewood ran low, Broussard would take Nazaire and Raoul out with his team of dogs and point out girdled trees, their barks peeled the year before.

Along with the Irishman, all four took turns chopping firewood. This was how men lived in the Yukon. Nazaire and Raoul put out small snares to catch arctic hares while they chopped firewood. They brought shotguns to try their luck for lazy ptarmigans, those grouse now with their winter-white feathers, and red squirrels.

Nazaire relaxed that first night in the cabin. He had a claim and a place to sleep, but the gauntlet glove had been thrown down. He and Raoul had a few weeks to come up with six hundred dollars each to cover their victuals and tobacco for the next eight months. Nazaire was thrilled to have made it this far, but he couldn't know his test had just begun.

Sparkle

Nazaire's Claim ✒ October 17, 1907

Nazaire worked the claim with Raoul's help. They both reasoned that if they could clamp water from entering beyond half the pup's length, then dig it out, it would be manageable enough to control the claim.

Nazaire's pup was a meandering switchback that captured sediment on both sides of the creek bottom. The rocks and boulders that lined the stub of water created a draft with subtle crevasses that captured grit too dense to be swept away. The gold, since it's heavier than dirt, would have collected over time and compacted.

Boulders kept the smaller rocks in place and encouraged the muddy silt to deepen. Nazaire and Raoul worked the pup every day, building an odd dam of sorts. On the second day, the trench deepened and a wooden framework held in place. The time had come for Nazaire to set Raoul free.

"Raoul, you helped me good. Now go with Broussard and meet his big boss."

"Nazaire, you sure?"

"Yeah, go get yourself a good pay job. You need to make steady wages."

———

Nazaire sat on one edge of his claim after Raoul left. The short piece of land would be his home every day now, where he would sweat and toil for his children, his farmstead. He surveyed his domain, then walked back into the cold stream. Today was the fifth day he owned the claim, and it was time to discover what his ten dollars bought.

Nazaire stacked up extra wood and moved shovels and pails from the stream. He needed to pan for the slightest glimmer of light that announced a promise of gold. October days were dark so he lit a lantern to get a good look. With the kerosene flame shining upward, he stopped and examined his pan. He felt an odd flare in his chest.

There it was, glittering in the bottom of his pan. Again, he swirled the water lag along. The gold shone dull under gray clouds. Was it there? Was his sight precise or was his want so great that it defied truth?

Nazaire scooped up a pan of silt, tipped it and shook it to rock the paydirt as it swirled round. When he saw the faint glow for the third time, a mild warmth in his belly turned hot. A murmuring heat spread from his chest down his arms. The wallop grew into a kick, burning hot. Nazaire remembered that Sourdoughs had talked about the rush of finding sparkle.

The pieces were large, well-formed with solid edges that had endured undisturbed decades underwater, a birthing steady and true under the pressures of scraping glaciers long gone. Nazaire walked out of the water and placed his pan on the ground. His hands trembled while he picked out sparkles and laid them on a piece of wood.

He squatted, staring at them for what seemed an hour. Nazaire's shoulders rose as heaves of breath became prolonged sobs that shook his body. Long-buried tears poured from his eyes. This day was his — a glorious moment when he achieved redemption, when all the doubts and gossip of family back home could be let go, empty and without merit.

"Victoria, what do you think of this?"

Nazaire feared the sparkles might be carried away by a sudden breeze or fall onto the gritty sides of the claim. He grabbed a short length of wood and with caution, build an enclosure of sorts, surrounding the sparkles with scraps of wood, creating a defensive wall on three sides. He needed to switch pan for rocker and scoop paydirt by the shovelful. He grabbed his rocker and positioned it on one edge of the stream.

The rocker, a rectangular wooden box included a smaller box, the hopper, suspended on top. A recessed mesh screen made up the bottom of the hopper that separated paydirt. Its legs were curved like those of an infant's cradle, allowing for side-to-side shaking to distribute the paydirt.

Nazaire grabbed a shovel and fed paydirt and water into the hopper, used the vertical handle to rock the box with vigor while riffles positioned underneath the box captured gold in slanted wooden panels. The other miners had left for the day, but he continued working, the only living soul in an empty expanse of dirt and mud with not a tree visible for miles.

The pup was perfect, more perfect than he could ever have imagined. There were heavy deposits of gold in his curved twenty-eight feet of stream. The current was in Nazaire's favor because it brought gold toward him.

A surge of strength renewed his sore shoulders. Nazaire needed to pace himself, and move to solid ground to encourage water circulation. The rubber waders he had grabbed behind the Mine Register Office worked well in icy water, but now energy pulsed in every joint of his abused body, and heat flushed through his veins.

He was a man on fire.

Nazaire plunged in one shovelful, then two. The rocker shook as his shovel dug. There, caught in the riffles, he saw glints of color. Gold and Nazaire met at one and the same place. He was a man caught in the throws of fever, unable to grant good judgment one ounce of common sense.

Fatigue overtook him. He searched for a container, a discarded tin of beans, anything to hold the tiny sparkles. Nothing. He sat on the edge of his claim and pulled down his waders, removing one boot, and then a sock - the only container he had to capture the precious gold.

———

In Broussard's cabin, Nazaire talked a blue streak as he shared his good news. "You got an empty tin or jar, anything with a tight cover?"

"I'll find you something from our heap pile," the Irishman said as he walked outside to a tangled pile of trash and returned with a Beekist Honey tin and one marked Blue Ribbon Tea.

Nazaire examined the covers for a tight fit and then cleaned both tins and covers. He listened as Raoul shared his news.

"I met with Broussard's boss. He liked my 'xperience with asbesto so I start tomorrow. The Irishman'll help me settle in," Raoul said.

"So how much?" Nazaire asked.

"Twenty-two a day."

Nazaire and Raoul whooped and clapped hands. Broussard broke out whiskey while laughter filled the cabin. Each man had a shot in celebration. Nazaire jabbered throughout the meal and then became very quiet when he pulled his rolled sock from his pants pocket.

"Wait," Broussard said as he rummaged in a large pack by his pallet. He pulled out three glass vials with stoppers and two Pasteur pipettes. "Come, I show you how to get this separated."

Nazaire's and Raoul's eyes widened.

"What? I work in the Supply Shop, so whatever you need, I can get for you," Broussard said.

Nazaire poured water from the water barrel into his miner's pan, then dunked his sock with a gentle shake. The four men gathered around to inspect the pan. Nazaire grabbed his dinner knife and pushed dirt from a sparkle that looked like no more than the corner of a fingernail, thin and stiff.

"Put your sparkle in a tin, but the rest, the glitter, you need to suck them up with the pipette, the eyedropper. Put those into a vial. Any water that goes in will dry up," Broussard said.

Nazaire watched as Broussard tilted the pipette which drew in tiny pieces of glitter. He handed the pipette to Nazaire. After all the gold was cleaned from the pan, Nazaire raised his vial of gold dust and held three plates of sparkle in an open palm. The men examined the treasure.

"What you think it's worth?" Nazaire asked Broussard.

"About forty dollars. You're on the right track," he said.

"It's different this mining in running water," Nazaire said, "Not like dry mining in a three-story cavern, like asbestos."

"Best you buy more socks," the Irishman said with a wink.

Nazaire took instruction from Broussard on water flow and how often to add water to his cradle so not to wash out the precious gold. After Broussard stopped, Nazaire examined the small cabin. There were two low pallets, two high. Broussard and the Irishman occupied the high ones — being warmer than those on ground level. The wood-burning stove ticked at the back wall between the pallets. Behind the center door, the pee bucket. Hooks hung all around covered with coats, ropes and leathers. On each side of the wood-burning stove, twin shelves served as a kitchen where foodstuffs and cooking pots were stored.

Nazaire was pleased to be in Broussard's company. Yeah, he and Raoul were well situated here. He drifted off early and imagined Victoria's soft body beside him. He curled in his pallet, looking like a thin grasshopper. His long arms had looped around her body and lifted her until she nestled against his chest. Nazaire gathered her hair and tumbled it over a shoulder to reveal the delicate underbelly of her neck, white and tender, an unexplored country there for his discovery.

Her whispers cooled his chest as he reached for her golden dugs centered in their copper rings. Victoria's nipples hardened and her breath caught in tight gasps. This is what he wanted for her. He drank in her sweetness as he drifted into sleep.

Yukon Pacific Mining Company

Sulphur Creek ∾ October 18, 1907

The day before, Raoul had met Weasel, co-owner of the Yukon Pacific Mining Company. He was the big boss here at the claim and looked the part with dirty hair and a three-week stubble under his chin.

While Raoul explained asbestos mining in huge deposits in the Thetford Mines back home, Weasel had given him a slow look-over. Wide hands and muscled arms spoke of Raoul's brute strength. Weasel clarified for him that placer gold mining was digging for gold where nature had placed it, and agreed to start him at twenty-two dollars a day.

This morning, Raoul followed the Irishman as men jumped from the back of an open wagon and walked to their diggings. They stood at the entrance of bench claim #50 above Discovery on Sulphur Creek. YPMC was painted bright red across both sides of the two-team wagon.

Over half the shovel and pick-ax stampeders had departed, most ill-equipped for the harsh conditions and others seeking easier-got gold in Nome. Their absences gave way to mining companies that bought out hundreds of small claims, and with industrial equipment like heated water on hydraulic lines, processed paydirt by the ton instead of rockerful. The YPMC was one such company. It ran seven days a week in two ten-hour shifts with over a hundred miners in a network of shafts with a ladder entrance.

The back of the mine, a walk-out depot, was lined with heavy boards that created a stable platform for cartloads of paydirt pulled from the mine. Outside, the carts were emptied into connecting sluice boxes. A patchwork scaffold system of pneumatic hoses washed paydirt in raised sluice boxes that resembled the angled legs of an ugly giant centipede. The flowing action of water against the bottom of each sluice box allowed the gold, heavier than grit, to fall into riffles, the beveled slats that made recovery possible.

Raoul remembered the Irishman saying Weasel ran the whole affair with a few assistants and supervisors on a bench claim while his partner managed the smelting and assaying in Dawson. The Irishman described the old forge that melted the impurities from the gold — that part was the smelting. Classifying various weights and types of gold to establish value was the assaying. Every type of gold had a different value apart from its weight. The least valuable was gold dust, the Irishman had said, and the most valuable nuggets.

The morning was warm despite a dusty gray sky, and getting onto darker as the impact of the midnight sun lengthened. Coming out of the mine, the Cheechakos relied on the Sourdoughs to remind them of the time of day. Soon they would not distinguish noon from midnight during winter months. Raoul fell into place behind the Irishman as the line of men walked through a graveyard of short stumps toward a gaping hole in the ground. Boxes of tools and implements surrounded one edge.

The Irishman faced the day supervisor and motioned to Raoul behind him. "I'll show this one the ropes," he said.

The Irishman was skinnier than most, short and small with solid hard muscles. He wore a wool tuque and heavy canvas pants with double knees. His boots were coated with black wax.

"Grab a pick and a head torch. Take a helmet that fits your head good," the Irishman said.

As Raoul moved toward the ladder, an arm pressed across Raoul's chest. "Too many at once on the ladder. Gotta wait," the boss's assistant, McPhael said.

Raoul backed away, and then peered down the black shaft. He turned to see men lined up behind him. The shaft was one black gaping hole, not unlike the shafts in the Thetford Mines.

"He's a Johnny Newcomer, he don't know nothing," one miner said.

A stump edged one side of the hole, and miners before Raoul stretched a hand on its painted top as if to ruffle the head of a child. Raoul reached out a hand, then hesitated.

"Go ahead, rub it for good luck. We do it every morning," said the miner behind Raoul.

Raoul rubbed the stump and stepped down into the hole. At the bottom of the ladder, his feet landed on a small platform fifty-feet down. He expected the next ladder to face a different side of the shaft. He felt for a hand railing until there was none, and the shaft opened into space. His eyes adjusted enough to see the top rung of the next ladder and followed it further into the wet, moldy-smelling shaft. Rows of supplies and upright posts with lanterns flanked the platform at the base of the ladder. There, the Irishman waited for him. He looked up at Raoul's helmet.

"When you see me duck, do the same or you'll clank your head good," he warned.

Raoul tailed the Irishman all day. Mining wasn't new to him, but these shafts weren't so well shored up, and the support frames hammered onto rock face every thirty feet looked weak. Raoul stopped to inspect one frame.

"We're alright. Been working here since last year. She's solid," the Irishman said.

The hours passed with miners trying to widen the passageway without hitting a neighbor with pick or shovel. The shaft was black save for the light of three long candles stuck on the edges of a wheeled cart flickering at the crew of five. The men had head torches, an elastic band that circled the helmet with a short candle seated in a three-sided glass box.

Raoul and the Irishman pushed the groundhogs, small hand-trucks filled with paydirt, out a graded exit when they were full. Outside, men emptied the groundhogs while Raoul's eyes adjusted to the faint light. This cycle was repeated all day. When the whistle sounded at days' end, the miners dropped their tools and headed for the ladder.

The Irishman gave Raoul final instructions, "Leave your shovel and pick but keep your helmet and head torch. Tomorrow ask for a fresh candle."

Heading up through the central chamber, Raoul realized how many different side shafts there were.

"Come into the claim by ladder, you leave by ladder. That way the day supervisor knows you worked all day. Come in by the paydirt depot, you leave the same way. Different bosses for different exits. Got it?"

Raoul nodded yes.

The Irishman continued, "Do what I do, and you'll be OK."

The men went up three on the ladder like a string of circus monkeys scooting up a pole. The chill of cool, fresh air at the top filled Raoul's lungs while loose dirt from gnarled tree roots slid down his shoulder inside one wall of the shaft and slid down one side of his neck as he climbed out. Raoul watched the miners pull their helmets off and hold them upright by their waists. He did the same. Weasel grabbed a dirty flat stick and inspected each man's mouth.

"Left, right, up," Weasel instructed.

Raoul watched and when his turn came, stuck his tongue out.

"Don't need it out. Push it to the left, now right, now up," Weasel said.

McPhael, Weasel's assistant, grabbed Raoul's helmet and plunged it in a barrel of water to remove any sparkle, then shoved the wet helmet into Raoul's chest. He inspected Raoul's hands, stretched out fingers, and cleaned under Raoul's fingernails with a dirty knife. He unbuttoned Raoul's mackinaw and checked shirt pockets, then pulled out Raoul's shirttail and checked his pants pockets. Raoul fought to restrain himself, the insult heavy on his person, and a humiliation he hadn't expected.

McPhael was a big guy, thick and nervous. His face was a scattering of pox holes. He pointed to Raoul's feet and growled, "Boots and socks."

Raoul sat on a crate like the other men and unlaced his mud-caked boots, pulled off socks and presented them for inspection. He reminded himself that current wages back home were fifty-three cents a day. He remembered all the work camps across Quebec and Ontario that he and Nazaire had passed with bunkhouse crews who slept in crowded log cabins run by the Navy League of Canada. Those large projects managed by the government paid a dollar fifty per day. How often had Raoul tugged at Nazaire's coat sleeve and pleaded, "Let's stop here, ask about a job?"

"No. More money in Dawson," Nazaire had insisted.

Yes, for twenty-two dollars a day, Raoul would endure anything. He walked, tired but happy into a charcoal-gray afternoon against a cruel landscape of decapitated tree trunks, like a sea of dying men with arms skewed in a vaporous fog. Fresh miners piled out of buckboards starting their shift as Raoul, the Irishman, and others climbed into their buckboard, grateful for a ride back to their cabins.

————

That evening Raoul asked the Irishman about Weasel.

"He's a hardscrabble guy, tough but fair."

"How'd he get his name?"

"He's a slav from the Ukraine. It's Weislaw, but everyone calls him Weasel because of his sporting disposition."

The men laughed throughout dinner. Later that night, Raoul's feet hung over his canvas pallet like huge bear paws as he drifted to sleep. He had a warm cabin, a solid job with helpful friends in Broussard and the Irishman, and he was twenty-two dollars richer.

In his dreams, Raoul was a colossus, walking miles above the earth. His footsteps straddled mountains with every step. He looked up at the sky where tiny birds flew in graceful arcs around his face while his hands brushed treetops and coins fell from his pockets. He was a giant.

Flying Beans

Broussard's Cabin ❧ November 11, 1907

Nazaire awoke from a troubled sleep with his heart racing. He couldn't escape. He remembered men carrying the casket down the front aisle with wet boots as each footfall squeezed mud and snow onto the clean floor. In front of the altar, the coffin stood draped with a white cloth. The service had been a blur. Was he underwater, floating with arms that weighed nothing? He wasn't sure which way was up or down, and he couldn't breathe.

When the priest had finished, those same men picked up the coffin and carried it to the side door. He didn't want to be here, but now Nazaire was outside the church, watching as the coffin came out. He had woken with a terrible headache. By the back wall, pots rummaged against each other.

"Ready to get up? Half the day is already gone," Raoul said.

Nazaire dressed in silence while Raoul left the cabin and returned with firewood. He coaxed another log into the wood-burning stove. Now that the mines were shut down for the winter, days dragged.

"What'll it be? We've got beans or beans?" Raoul asked.

Nazaire grabbed the can from Raoul's hand and flung it to the floor.

"Sonofabitch, I can't eat those damn beans again."

"What do you want then? We have nine more days before we get our 'lotment."

Nazaire couldn't believe how much he longed for an egg or a potato. He wondered when he would taste one again?

"Raoul, when we get home, ain't nobody bringing beans into my kitchen."

December first was marked with an X on the calendar hanging on the cabin wall. That day, miners from Sulphur Creek would meet at Granville and decide if the snows were shallow enough to call for the train from Dawson. If not, they would go down by sled dog to their respective warehouses and pull out a month's worth of foodstuff, dog feed and tobacco. The mounties oversaw that each man took only his monthly allotment and thus not face starvation come March or April.

The miners would make a day of it, dropping off dirty clothes at the Dawson Laundry and a few even getting a haircut. Most would go to a saloon, have a drink and order up a large meal, usually with a generous helping of powdered potatoes. Then they'd get their provisions from the warehouse, pick up their clean clothes, pack it all up and head back on the late train. Pity the poor miner who ill-planned his tobacco. In town and at the creeks, rolled cigarettes and loose cut were valued right under gold.

"Let's go bag us a squirrel or something," Nazaire said. "I could eat a damn rat, anything but more beans. I can't wait until we go into town again."

"Heard about little Johansson? He threw up his arms and left, walked back home to Oka'oma," Raoul said.

"In this cold? Is he crazy?"

Some men did that. Just walked out, the isolation too much for those with tender spirits. He knew that would never be him, going home a failure. Nazaire couldn't think of those things. He had to focus on today and hope that come December first, he had ordered enough beans to last the month.

"Remember Broussard telling us if we didn't have good teeth, we should order potatoes and a dozen oranges against the scurvy and eat them right off the boat?" Nazaire asked. "With all these damned black days and nights, I believe he was right."

The cabin door swung open and Broussard entered in a huff, shouting, "We got us a lead on two bull moose, boys. Get dressed, we got some serious hunting to do."

Outside, Broussard's dogs howled in excitement. His two sleds were packed with tarps and his special pack of skinning knives. Nazaire and Raoul laughed as they bumped into each other, grabbing their wool overshirts and mackinaws. They pulled on their heavy work boots. Meanwhile, Broussard reached for a coil of rope and a sack of caribou gut hanging on the wall. Raoul grabbed a rucksack and packed the fry pan. Reluctantly, he packed four cans of beans.

"You leave those damn beans here," barked Nazaire with smiling eyes. We're going to have fresh liver and heart."

They would track the bulls for at least two days before the kill. To field dress the meat and haul it back was lots of work, but worth it. They could already taste it cooking.

First Reunion

Dawson ⤲ December 25, 1907

Nazaire and Raoul sat at the back of the Occidental Hotel eatery as they waited to meet with their brothers, Romeo and Gaudias. They had not seen them since the two had left home years ago, and wondered if they would recognize them. They had been boys when they left; Romeo was thirteen and Gaudias twelve. They would be seasoned men now, twenty-six and twenty-five.

Dawson was crowded with miners in town, some attending church services, most who just needed to be out of their cabins. People in the streets must have numbered over five thousand, all laughing and yelling holiday cheers. The Occidental was a favorite of French-speaking Canadians. The Irishman had assured Nazaire that his message had got through to their brothers, but would the brothers recognize each other?

A man walked through the side door, severely mustached with thick oily curls that framed a round face and a thin, short body. Romeo scanned the faces until he detected the high hairline of Nazaire, his long legs sticking out from under a table. Romeo saw Raoul and remembered the strong chin that marked their father's face. As he approached, Romeo pulled off his tuque and stood before them.

"It's been too many years," Romeo laughed.

Nazaire and Raoul stood, mouths agape while words couldn't find air. Laughter followed slaps on their shoulders as embraces caused the surrounding chairs to go askew.

Raoul looked toward the front door. "Is Gaudias not with you?"

"No, he's on Dominion Creek. The wagons use a different fork to come into town," Romeo said.

They ordered a round of whiskey and food.

"I've got a claim on Parker Creek, down off Indian River, Romeo said, "Getting over twelve dollars a pan. Where are you two working?"

"I'm with Yukon Pacific on Sulphur and Nazaire has a claim ten miles down. It goes good." Raoul said.

Talk turned to home as the three men leaned over the table, elbows sparring on the tabletop, trying to squeeze years of their lives into minutes. The oldest sister, Florence was ready to say her good-byes to the outside world and join the Little Gray Sisters of Quebec when their mother had died. In that cruel moment, Florence was no longer able to enter the convent. She would never be the big sister again but mother to her siblings, cook and charwoman to a household of thirteen. One single blow had crushed her most ardent dreams of religious life.

"Mother died two years after you and Gaudias left," Nazaire told Romeo.

"Grandmother lives still," Raoul added, "She suffered a stroke. Now Florence sleeps with a string tied to her ankle at night. It goes down the hall to Grandmother's wrist."

"How is Victoria?" Romeo asked.

Nazaire turned his eyes away from the table.

"She passed," Raoul whispered.

Nazaire and Raoul spoke of many banks in Quebec that had failed, and all the people that they knew who had lost their lifesavings overnight. Businesses were boarded up and thousands had moved to the mills of New England for higher wages. Nervous laughs and smoke from the brothers' pipes swirled above their table. They agreed to meet again at the Occidental at noon on Dominion Day, July first.

"You can always leave a message here at the hotel counter. They ask twenty-five cents for the trouble," Romeo said before he walked out the door.

Nazaire and Raoul fought the crowded streets, all permafrost and muck. They walked to the nearby Yukon Saw Mill Company and picked up a dollar bag of sawdust as fire starter for the wood-burning stove. They bought some Old Chum pipe tobacco and a fresh newspaper to fight against the coming months of idleness; they would sell the older ones in Broussard's cabin for a dollar apiece. The cold dug into Nazaire's chest as he struggled to stand upright.

He would cherish this Christmas day as bittersweet, happy to see Romeo, yet disappointed that Gaudias had not come.

"Romeo's changed," Raoul said.

"He's not thirteen anymore," Nazaire answered.

Nazaire thought of his children. Where were they this Christmas night? The thought was too much to consider with the wind pushing against him and Raoul as they waited at a blue pole for the next buckboard.

THE FIRST YEAR

The Golden Flats

Granville ❧ April 20, 1908

Nazaire and Raoul entered the Golden Flat Hotel. Nazaire stood quiet and watched, while Raoul turned and talked to anyone who would oblige. Broussard had said the town had more than four thousand people when he showed up in 1902. The hotel had remained a busy, two-story log building, pulling in dollars from the near two thousand miners who lived there.

Nazaire and Raoul had had difficulty enduring the idle months. The mines would not open until the middle of May and men were itchy with boredom. Many relieved that itch in creek roadhouses.

On the ground floor of the Golden Flats, dancehall girls gave little recitations, sketches of Shakespeare with Elysian fields of Roman palms painted in green and gold on cardboard on stage.

They sang scathing ditties followed by risqué dancers whose skirts fluttered and skunk oil lamps sputtered. Painted canvas sheets separated the eatery with a few tables and chairs from the long, stand-up bar and sour spittoons.

A large open loft of rough-cut bunks covered most of the second story. Two small rooms in the back stood behind a dividing wall of hanging canvas. The sporting women of Golden Flats used these rooms, more like narrow horse stalls, for private entertainment. One night, with men drunk and eager to brawl, one miner shoved another. Nazaire turned from his drink on the bar and tried to get out of the way, but the crowd pushed customers right off their feet. Men swayed with a sudden thrust that pinned a young woman's back against his chest.

Her crimson bow fluttered on the bar and down came flowing curls for all to witness. Sighs of surprise fell from drunken mouths. The men's eyes widened in disbelief that turned to sudden delight. Her hair, released and loosed, brushed against Nazaire's face.

He stood stunned, startled by the smell of her, exotic cinnamon and the feel of her delicate bones, the sweep of her curls against his jaw as he held her. His two large hands pressed against each soft shoulder.

Nazaire froze for a moment, recovered his senses and pulled the young woman from the angry fracas. She was thin and delicate. It surprised Nazaire how small she was, so like Victoria. Having all these thoughts jump into his head, he became displaced, unsure of his bearings in the world with a brain more addled than clear. The young woman turned her head and stretched her neck as she whispered a sultry thank you in his ear. His face turned crimson as she walked away.

"There you go, got a smile out of her," one miner said.

He thought of her but stayed away. The pull of this young woman against his loins grew. Once it became stronger, he could no longer resist. He'd find his way on the Dawson-Granville Road to the Golden Flats most Sundays while Raoul stayed in Broussard's cabin and played cards with other miners. Nazaire knew that his brother caught the attraction but to Raoul's credit, never spoke a word. Neither man could live the other's life.

Nazaire cameto the Golden Flats often on Sunday afternoons and stood without speaking for hours. He held his ale with white fingers while he waited for her to come on stage with the dancehall girls all in a row, their knees raised as they lifted their legs. The dancers displayed pearly thighs and pantaloons from flapping skirts in so cavalier a manner, he'd look up at the dazzling woman, mesmerized, unable to take his eyes off her.

After a while, Nazaire would bow his head and return to the cabin. That would be that until it hurt to stay away — hurt more than he could bear. One evening, on the quiet, he inquired about the young woman.

"Tait Negg's her name," the floor boss said, holding back a slight grin.

"Where's she from?"

"She was a maid in Seattle, but the husband of the house made advances, so she left. Signed on as a cook's assistant for one of the sternwheeler outfits, probably hired more for her small size in the galley than her cooking."

"So she's grabbing what jobs she can find, eh?" asked Nazaire.

"Wouldn't know. Tait left the ship as soon as it docked in Dawson and here she is singing before an audience of lustful men. We're happy to have her," the floor boss said.

A twinge of jealousy grew within Nazaire as he scanned the saloon, each man presumed loathsome and rapacious in his motives. Nevertheless, he grew more curious about her. Did she support herself or live off the men she met? It didn't matter. With all the strength in him, he couldn't take his eyes off her. For many months, he returned.

How could people back home understand? A man gets so lonely, it can burn out the bottom of his heart. His imagination wandered and he'd think of her outside his barn back home, fetching water at the pump, or in the kitchen, adding firewood to the stove. Just the thought of Tait back on his farmstead pleased him.

———

Home. How he longed to see the rolling green fields of the Beauce. He could leave his village, and at each hamlet he passed, soft hills appeared in front of his eyes. The gentle sweep of land with open pastures climbed in flowing curves. They were magical to him, not unlike the soft sweeping curves of Tait's hair.

In bed, Nazaire thought of Victoria and how his body had curled against her back as he lifted her up to him, her soft shoulder tucked under his chin. He took one deep breath and held it, drank in a faint scent of vanilla, the delicate locks on her neck, the swim of her hair against his face. In those moments, he'd had everything any man could want.

Victoria's face had become blurred of late, a distant visage he couldn't quite capture in his mind. He hovered between wakefulness and sleep, and in those drifting seconds, saw Tait's face looking back at him. He woke and felt guilt, so he steeled himself to stay away and remain in the cabin, safeguarded from the temptations of the Golden Flats.

When Nazaire would walk outside Broussard's cabin alone, during restless hours, he'd hum "for over twenty years you have searched for your lover." He didn't remember all the words but the song was a poem, he was sure of it; it told the story of two lovers, Evangéline and Gabriel. Wasn't it a lifetime ago since Nazaire had heard Victoria singing these words in the quiet evenings back home?

He thought of the cheerful songs that Tait sang and imagined her laughing with his sons and daughter. Often, he would return to the cabin with damp eyes and sit on his cot, silent and unmoving. If he stayed in Dawson, he might be a wealthy man, a man to whom many women would be happy to be attached. But would Tait? Nazaire was a man torn in two and didn't know which of the halves housed his heart.

Second Reunion

Dawson ❧ May 8, 1908

Nazaire didn't know what to expect, and Raoul was curious to a bruise. Romeo had sent a message to his brothers, a message passed from one miner to another along the creeks.

"Meet me at the Occidental May 6 at noon," it read. "Bring your bedroll."

After months of idleness in their cabin, the charcoal winter had turned to a bright spring. The mines readied for reopening while everyone talked about breakup and the ice lottery. First Avenue in Dawson fronted the Yukon River, where a throng of people swayed in the road. People filled all eight cross roads that spanned twelve blocks of the city. Onlookers sat on every rooftop and not one sidewalk offered space for people to climb out of the thawing permafrost.

Looking out a front window at the Occidental Hotel, Romeo spotted Nazaire and Raoul elbowing their way through the crowd. Romeo sat at a back table with his coat and bedroll holding two chairs in reserve for his brothers. Aside of him, Gaudias stood tall and gaunt, more arms and legs than anything. Romeo motioned to Nazaire and Raoul as they entered the eatery and struggled to reach the back wall.

"Glad you made it through," Romeo said, his round face framed by oily black curls, the picture of a Greek god.

Beside him, Gaudias stood, serious and stern-faced. His fine hair lay flat against a rugged scull, and an equine nose sat too large for his gaunt face. Nazaire scanned Gaudias' face, one a full reverse of the other. Where Nazaire's hair parted on the left, a severe wedge separated the right side of Gaudias' hairline. Even the chins seemed to be opposite on the two men.

Sunken cheeks cut across Gaudias' face and hinted at not enough to eat. He wore a skin mackinaw and heavy duck pants with an attached layer of waterproofing liken to cowboy chaps. Nazaire reached out to embrace Gaudias, but his brother stepped back sufficient to be out of arms' reach and remained stiff. The four brothers faced each other with conversation stalled. Romeo sat and ordered whiskey.

Nazaire licked his lips and sputtered, "Look, we do OK, Raoul and me, we're not needing any help or money. We're OK."

He gave Gaudias a strained look while Raoul nodded yes.

Nazaire didn't know what to make of Gaudias' retreat. He looked to Romeo, whose face was in full flush.

"Breakup will be here today or tomorrow," Romeo said.

The four brothers examined each other. Gaudias sat and moved his chair for a clear view out the window and stared. He kept a neutral face and said little while the other three sat and laughed. After drinks came and got tossed down, Gaudias stood and pronounced his goodbyes.

"Wait, wait a minute," Nazaire said. "We haven't seen you in so long, don't go. Let's visit awhile."

Not even a handshake was offered when Gaudias turned to leave. Nazaire and Raoul stood in stunned silence, and then sat back down. They remained quiet for a bit, all three uncomfortable in their chairs.

"Why did he go?" Raoul asked.

"Was he afraid that we would impose on him or you? We don't need money, we do OK," Nazaire insisted.

Nazaire caught the tight mouth and wrinkled brow on Romeo. What to say? Nazaire and Raoul were fresh off the farm, and accustomed to hard work but what had it done to Gaudias? Nazaire knew some men who had worked mines in Thetford for years. Maybe it took away more of a man's spirit than he realized.

Romeo scanned every wall of the eatery. He swallowed hard, then spoke as he placed two small hands on each of his brothers' shoulders.

"Gaudias has a mind of his own, that one."

"Why is he this way? What is it?" Nazaire asked.

Romeo continued, "He's had more failures than successes. He grows into an old man already, angry and stubborn. Gaudias sees his misery and not the suffering of others. With him, you can't give him nothing, and he got nothing to take."

"What do you mean?" Raoul asked.

Romeo answered with a shaking head. "Well his heart, he don't got one anymore."

Nazaire's eyes squeezed shut, then opened while a grimace sat on his face.

Romeo explained, "The world don't owe him a good living. Gaudias thinks he'll strike it big. Truth is most men make enough to live on and not much else. It's a hard life."

Romeo stood, tied a scarf around his neck and smiled, "Let's get away from this crowd where we can talk in peace. Let's walk up the slide. We can see the whole city from there."

———

They made their way outside but couldn't see beyond the crowd to the frozen riverfront until they pushed their way toward the north end of town to the base of Moosehide Slide. When they had climbed the worn trail that led to an enormous crater-sized hole at the top of Dawson cliffs, cheers rose from the crowds below.

"Breakup — this is perfect. Let's stop and watch," Romeo said as he squatted.

Halfway up the trail, they turned to see Dawson stretched out before them, with the Yukon River nudging against its graceful curve. People crowded in the streets and clapped hands as they yelled with joy. A steel tripod mounted in the middle of the pack ice had moved. At that exact moment, the month, day, hour and second had been recorded as the frozen Yukon River broke free from its stubborn grip on winter.

Romeo explained, "That's why there's such a crowd. They've all bought tickets to guess when breakup happens. Dawson also got a fresh mail delivery so today is a real big event. There's no easy way to deliver mail so some men will start yelling names. If anybody know where the man works, on which creek, he'll yell it out and the letter will get into a box going to that creek. Most men move around and don't stay on one claim for more than a year. A letter can follow a man for a year or so before it gets from Dawson into his hands."

"People say over twelve thousand miners come in off the mines today," Raoul said.

"Sounds about right," Romeo said as the three continued to climb.

"Only emergency crews work when the mines shut down. It's the only time when Sourdoughs and Cheechakos can catch up with friendships before the summer work starts."

Far below, the megaphone announcer claimed that no one had won the lottery, so the kitty would

341

build until next summer's contest. The brothers reached the top of the slide, some fifteen hundred feet above Dawson. They repeated stories from their youth and laughed. Romeo invited Nazaire and Raoul to sleep on the floor in his room at the Occidental anytime he was in town, a courtesy that anyone with a room extended to friends.

Up on the slide, everything looked unearthly. Nazaire breathed in clean mountain air. Could he ever live in a place like this? Land to be had almost anywhere. Game and fish plentiful. All the lumber you would need to build a home. It felt like heaven. Nazaire stood and admired the spectacular view of the Yukon as it snaked its way from Dawson toward the Bering Sea, some fifteen-hundred miles upriver.

Romeo stood and smiled, "Come with me to Moosehide, help some friends?"

Moosehide

Summer Camp ❧ May 8, 1908

Nazaire woke up in a tent, not sure where he was. He, Romeo and Raoul had slept in Moosehide, the summer meeting camp for the Hån Indians. The camp had a small cemetery, a wooden church and a few rough wooden cabins surrounded by dozens of canvas tents. He rousted Romeo and Raoul. Outside, women were roasting bannock; the aroma nudged all three men to join a line of others hungry for breakfast.

"I help these people every year," Romeo said. "They know everything about the land and its animals. They don't waste a thing."

"I hear these Indians know where all the gold comes from. Is that true?" Nazaire asked.

"It's no secret. They've lived here for generations. The strongest outpouring of gold is behind the Dome," Romeo said.

"They know where the gold comes from?" Nazaire asked.

"What's outpouring?" Raoul asked.

"When the earth was being born, there were huge earthquakes and explosions. These forced some land to rise and others to drop, like the Alaska coast south of here. Water sought lower areas, creating the oceans. Where the earthquakes happened, veins of minerals were crushed together with all that heat. What water remained dried up. In some places, those minerals were gold, in others copper or silver."

"How do you know all this?"

"I go to meetings when I can, the ones that explain these things. There's gold all over the area. You just gotta get it out of the ground."

After tea and hot bannocks, Romeo, Nazaire and Raoul crossed the back of the camp to a narrow trail. Many of the men wore heavy rawhide coats while the women and children dressed in caribou skin parkas with scarves around their necks. Everyone wore elk leggings, soft beaver mukluks and gloves made from caribou. The people merged into a long line where the trail narrowed.

Romeo continued, "Chief Isaac, head of the band, saw what white men were doing to the land and his people. He didn't like it, so he moved his people out of Dawson to this camp. The Håns still come every summer. It's where visiting bands trade and the young court. They fish for salmon and hunt caribou, musk ox and elk."

A few Hån greeted Romeo as they walked up a mountain trail that narrowed into a low valley

"Sam Smith, he's the first Indian Constable here. He sees that no Hån breaks the law, Håns or white man's."

The entire Moosehide community of one hundred and twelve had gathered at a small tributary off the Klondike River. The shoreline was bordered by tamarack saplings and willows. Men carried nets woven from willow stalks that sat on long wooden poles with elk gut securing the edges of the netting.

"When me and Gaudias came here, we joined the
YOOPs. That's the Yukon Order of Pioneers, so we're
constables of a sort. Not a mountie, but when needed,
we break up fights or try to make peace. Sam and I
became friends my third winter here. Food was very
low and me and Gaudias were starving. Sam gave us
meat, a big haunch of moose, and I never forgot it.
Every year, I help his people during breakup."

Some Hån had brought short, thick wooden
clubs. Others carried picks and axes, hatchets and
wooden rakes. The women and children carried bark
baskets, tarps and ropes to the frozen shoreline.

"We're going to fish today, my brothers," Romeo
said.

"What — in a frozen river?" Nazaire laughed.

"We're on a side stream of the Klondike. This time
of year, all river ice is rotten. Underneath, there are
thousands of graylings, a greasy fish not worth
eating. There'll be other kinds too, like whitefish,
maybe a few chum salmon, pike, and longnose
suckers but most will be graylings. They're pushing

against the ice and help break it apart. When they do, the Hån gather the fish for their sled dogs."

Nazaire and Raoul looked all around them at a flurry of activity. A few children stopped in front of Raoul and looked up, then walked on.

"They're going to feed their dogs?" Raoul asked.

"Yup. Always the graylings come first. They're under the ice, pushing it up," Romeo said.

Romeo led his brothers to an open spot near a pile of tarps so they could watch without interfering.

"And then we'll have us a good fish feed!" Raoul asked.

"No, not the graylings. It's the ignorant whites that eat them. Tonight the women will feed us caribou steak. You've never had better meat than caribou."

Romeo pointed to the highest mountain top where three Hån men stood on the edge, looking down at the crowd.

"These men will signal when the fish have broken through," Romeo said.

Women and children dropped their baskets and spread tarps on the ground beside the shoreline. Other women put coils of short ropes next to the tarps. Stretching across the ice, men readied net poles in a straight row.

The faint sound of drums fell from the summit of the mountain. Voices rose in shouts and whoops. The graylings had arrived. With so many people moving on the ice, Nazaire and Raoul couldn't see what was happening. Romeo gestured toward a few Hån chopping the ice at various spots, creating narrow rectangular slits.

"These men make the holes for the dipping nets. They'll stay on the ice until the fish come."

"What do we do?" Nazaire asked.

"When the tarps are heaped with fish, you two tie the tarp closed tight and pack them onto the sleds. Watch me a bit, then help when you know what you're doing."

The first sled team drove up next to the pile of tarps. Dogs barked, and excitement filled the air. Men lined up on the ice, thirty across, fighting for position on the frozen surface. They held axes, hatchets, stone spears and rakes. The rakers each began cutting a wedge of ice. Behind them, another row of men stood, holding nets.

The rakers pulled the cut pieces of ice away from the holes. Women waited with empty baskets to remove the chipped ice from the enlarging slits. They slid their full baskets to the shore, throwing the discarded ice on land, then returned. Even toddlers two and three years old helped on a special tarp set aside for children.

After the rakers cut their segment of ice out, they chopped more ice to connect their segment to the next one, creating one slit that exposed the river below. Each netter advanced, pushed his pole into the water and waited for the sudden thrust of the graylings. One by one, they raised their nets and dumped the jumping fish onto the ice as the women gathered them in empty baskets. Children helped to slide the filled baskets back to shore, struggling against the weight.

Off the ice, women spilled the fish onto the tarps and sent the children back with empty baskets. Most of the graylings froze within two seconds in the crystalline air and those that didn't got the club or someone's foot.

Nazaire looked on, amazed at the efficiency of the entire community. From the most feeble elder to the youngest toddler, the entire band worked together.

The iced water built up and chunks of new ice formed, refreezing some segments so that a net could not be lowered. The rakers chipped away the new ice that threatened to close.

Piles of fish grew on the shore. When the first tarp overflowed with catch, Romeo and a strong Hån grabbed the corners of the tarp and fed rope through the grommets, tightening up the bundle. They packed it into a sled and repeated the work.

Nazaire and Raoul nodded their heads; yes, they got it. Nazaire spread the next tarp on the ground,

Raoul grabbed a length of rope, readying himself. As one pair of men refreshed themselves and stretched out a new tarp, the other pair pulled and tied a tarp, then packed another dog sled. By late afternoon a small pile of tarps remained.

A group of women arrived with pots of hot stew and made a small fire. They grilled fresh bannocks and warmed stew, feeding women, children and elders. One by one, family groups left with sled teams pulling their toddlers or bundles of graylings.

At each village, stone caches sat deep in the permafrost. The last soft, rancid fish were a special treat for the dogs and had been cleaned out earlier by a fast broom. Men would open heavy wooden covers, and fill each cache to the very top. Down the cover would come, tied with strong caribou gut that announced the pantry bear-proof.

Nazaire asked, "Can I give it a try, this fishing with the net?"

Romeo spotted Sam Smith and nodded his head, the chin pushed up twice — the signal for a parley.

Sam made his way toward Romeo, a smile on his face. He wore a caribou mackinaw with heavy caribou skin gloves that hung from his neck by attached gut. He was a short man with a calm nature, respected by Hån and white men alike. Around his waist hung his holster and gun.

"These are my brothers from Quebec, far away. They'd like to try netting fish?" Romeo asked.

Nazaire and Raoul presented hands for a shake.

"Good you come today. My people, they thank," Sam said.

With a few jabs of Sam's fingers, a Hån led the three brothers onto the ice. They watched for a few minutes, and then Nazaire and Raoul each took a net in hand.

Romeo declined. He watched as the rush of water took Nazaire by surprise, almost pulling the net out of his hands. The net filled with fish so fast that it bulged, too full to raise through the narrow slit of ice.

The young Hån understood the problem. He smacked the wooden pole at the bottom, releasing a few fish, then helped Nazaire raise the pole. It worked. The brutal flow of water, the icy cold, and weight of the fish all surprised Nazaire and Raoul. It was hard work. From the moment the pole entered the current, lack of control overwhelmed the inexperienced men. They couldn't keep up with the merciless flow of fast water. The three brothers left the ice and stood, watching.

Nazaire said, "The cold burned my feet. I couldn't breathe with the air burning my chest. I didn't expect the fish to fight so much."

"Yeah, it was harder than it looked. No one guts the fish?" Raoul asked.

"No, the dogs eat it that way," Romeo paused and took in a long breath. "Smell that air? You'll never breathe cleaner air than this in your life."

——

The entire day had been a study in efficiency. That evening, all the men entered the largest tent at Moosehide and squatted on warm musk ox skins in front of a roaring fire. Platters of caribou steaks were off to the side, the aroma tempting everyone. Soon Hån men crowded around Romeo, some speaking broken English and introducing themselves to Nazaire and Raoul. They laughed and teased as they imitated the visitors' hauling the graylings out of the water.

"The Hån are beholding to you now," Romeo said. "Anything you need, they'll help if you ask. Just say that you're family to me."

It was a day Nazaire would cherish, hearing Romeo's familiar laugh and sharing his bright smile.

Explosion on Sulphur Creek

June 15, 1908

The blast shot up and out of the paydirt depot, settled for a second before the sound boomeranged across miles of hillsides, and careened through hundreds of claims beyond its source on Sulphur Creek.

Miners near the center of the blast clamped hands over their ears to stop the throbbing. They coughed and struggled for air in a shower of broken mud. Where was the source? Splintered wood and rocks peppered the air. The debris storm was from the Yukon Pacific Mining Company bench claim. Breathing was impossible near the flare. Air filled with dust and a gray cloud too thick to see through.

Miners ran toward the detonation, anxious to discover which claim had suffered the loss. Crumpled steel and broken helmets lay at the ladder entrance. The ends of the wooden ladder were unrecognizable, resting in segmented pieces. The paydirt depot incline, the back entrance to the mine, was strewn with frayed hoses and twisted sluice boxes, covering the hillside. Carts lay with missing wheels and hoses wrapped around broken timbers.

Two horse-drawn wagons filled with men and ropes arrived within the hour, hoping to offer aid, but the sourdoughs knew enough not to jump down an open pit until dust and air had settled. If the cause of the blast was gas caught in a vertical cut, the men in the pit would already be dead, and arriving do-gooders would join them.

Wagons in every direction climbed toward Sulphur Creek. They slowed to pick up men who jumped in the back. Nazaire crouched in one, praying for all it's worth that it wasn't the hole in which Raoul worked.

———

Nazaire jumped from a wagon and watched miners gather in small groups to argue how best to help any survivors trapped underground. They raised picks and shovels above their heads, shaking their

fists. Men everywhere pulled debris off the ground,
trying to clear a space so rescuers could work.
Nazaire ran toward a spewing cloud of dirt, scanning
left to right, trying to identify the claim. His chest
tightened into a concrete block. Could Raoul be down
there? Panic gripped his shoulders. He wouldn't
know until someone set up a working windlass and
bucket to send down a dog.

One man shouted, "It's the Yukon Pacific claim."

"My brother's in there," Nazaire shouted.

Not far from him, another man shrieked, "Here's
another one with family down there."

Hundreds of miners covered the area now, as
some fought over details. Whose dog would go
down? How much would someone pay if their dog
died of gas poison? How long before a dog could go
down safely? Nazaire had heard of the risks, along
with the outrageous value of dogs in the Yukon.
Good sled dogs brought from six hundred to a
thousand dollars each. Would YPMC put up money
for one? There were even chunks of bedrock on the

ground, the hardest layer of rock that even miners with pick axes couldn't break away.

Raoul might be dead, the Irishman too. What if the pocket was large? A seeping breach, building up pressure for another blast? Broussard should be alright. He worked inside the supply cabin two miles away.

"How can they breathe?" someone screamed.

"Get hoses and force air down?" Nazaire suggested.

Foremen and miners debated the options. Nazaire had seen it before, men arguing for hours while lives remained at risk. Over two dozen rescuers crawled around the ladder entry. They could all die if a second blast were to let loose.

Nazaire blinked, wiping dust from his eyes. The smell of rock mold lingered on the ground. What to do? How to get Raoul out? How to find his brother in the thick of broken timbers and toppled rocks?

He couldn't think. His head felt swollen as if his scalp might tear open. He searched from aces to zeds for a familiar face until, in frustration, he sat and cried. There was no vantage point, no high place from which to search, only a sea of mulling men, their clothes drab and gray.

Broussard spotted Nazaire in back of the crowd and signaled him with a wave. They walked toward each other.

"How many dead?" Broussard asked.

"I heard over a dozen at the ladder," Nazaire said.

"Does anyone know what happened?"

"Gas," said Nazaire.

Pressure built throughout the day. Weasel appeared and directed the crowd to leave. More wagons were bringing in equipment and rescuers. To Nazaire, the answer was simple. If his brother was part of the crew in a blast section, then he was more likely dead than alive. How to explain this to Raoul's young bride? Nazaire was shaken to his core. The chance of exploding methane or other gases had always hovered in Nazaire's head. Like everyone else, he pushed ghosts back into the gray and just plowed on. This is what men do. They plow on.

"Did anyone try the paydirt depot?" A man called out.

From the back of a wagon, Nazaire spotted Raoul. He gasped and took a step back.

"I thought you were dead?"

Raoul's eyes grew large. "Is that a question or a complaint?"

Nazaire hugged Raoul. His racing heart settled as tears ran down his face.

"We were in Dawson picking up nozzles for Weasel," the Irishman said, "How many hurt?"

Nazaire turned and noticed the Irishman, grabbed his shoulder and held on.

"Sixteen dead so far, all in the north tunnel, but there's more damage near the depot. Nobody knows what."

"Is Broussard OK?" The Irishman asked.

"Yea, he was in the supply cabin when it happened."

"You'll go home now," a mountie said as another mountie raised an arm in a gesture of pushing the crowd back. Empty wagons struggled to get close to the explosion site and remove debris. Despite the instruction from the police, many miners headed to their favorite roadhouse, where the blast would be the only topic of discussion.

———

That night Broussard passed around whiskey as all four men tried to relax in their cabin.

Nazaire whispered to Raoul. "Maybe it's time we leave. We've made enough money."

"It's too soon," answered Raoul. "We need to finish out this summer and work most of next."

"What if you had been in that blast? What would I tell Lucia?"

"You're rattled, Nazaire. Calm yourself. Did you forget what a damned long walk it was getting here?"

Raoul was right. They hadn't earned enough money to pick up and go home. Almost a year of walking, and all the risks they'd taken pressed on

Nazaire's mind. They had left Quebec only a year and a half ago. His head throbbed as he turned in his cot. How could he safeguard his brother's life? He couldn't.

"Romeo and Gaudias must'a heard about the blast," Nazaire said.

"They won't show their faces; they have their own lives now," Raoul said.

"You don't know that. I bet Romeo made inquiries about us. Do you think maybe Gaudias thought we needed help, needed money, and he was put off by the possibility?"

Raoul turned toward the cabin wall. "I don't know. Go to sleep."

New Hire at YPMC

Sulphur Creek ~ July 22, 1908

ochran stood broomstick straight opposite Weasel's desk at the Yukon Pacific Mining Company office in Sulphur. Despite the newspaper listing, "Sulphur Creek as a poor performer, giving up a scant 1.5 tons of gold since Discovery in 1901," he had come for a job. He wore an oily gleam on his eyebrows and the edges of his collar and coat sleeves were outlined in dirt. His frayed coat matched the shoes, all trumpery, and inadequate for working in permafrost.

"Yes, I can cipher and calculate interest," Cochran said. "I read and write too."

"You handle money before?" Weasel asked.

"Yes, carried cash and checks to the bank for my employer, Mr. Vernon Nickleson of the Nickleson Motor Car Company of Detroit. Saved the company time and provided convenience."

Cochran knew what sort of boss Weasel was as soon as the fat goat barked at his assistant, McPhael. The man had his eyes glued to the floor and his tail stuck between his legs.

Cochran grinned. He had Weasel by the short and curlies.

"I heard the going rate was twenty dollars a day."

"You got experience in the mines?" Weasel countered.

Cochran's face flushed.

Weasel scratched his head. "Thought not. OK, seventy-five dollars for a six-day week. You'll work here in my office and handle the gold swaps from the day supervisors. Want the job or no?"

Cochran shook Weasel's hand, all red-faced from the grip of steel that Weasel applied to Cochran's soft, city fingers. He's looking for the bird watcher in me, he thought, but he's hid proper. McPhael stood, shifting his weight from foot to foot.

"The job starts now. Get Broussard to advance him a pair of Wellingtons against his first wages and settle him in your cabin. Both of you be back on the job in an hour."

Weasel looked up at both men and grunted, his lecture complete. Cochran and McPhael left Weasel's office. From the corner of his eye, Cochran caught sight of Raoul Poulin as he jumped off the back of a wagon. The big Canuck walked to the ladder entrance of the mine and stretched his spine while he waited to enter the hole in the ground. Cochran couldn't believe his eyes. What luck. He could watch Raoul, maybe order the shit around. Maybe kill him, that would be better. Had Raoul seen him? No.

All those months traveling with Sherman's party and his stupid rules roiled in Cochran's mind like pinworms in fish. Cochran had taunted Raoul for no reason during the entire walk west, except that it pleased Nickleson. So often Nickleson had complained, "Them Canucks said their parts would fit my dad's cars, and they didn't. Cost my dad weeks of worry and lots of money, money that should have come my way but didn't."

Disappointment had nothing to do with Raoul or Nazaire, but Nickleson's endless needling had continued. To share sympathies, Cochran had also teased the Canucks. Now when Cochran would go to Dawson, he would put his loyalties on display for Nickleson to lap up like the dumb dog that he was.

In Skagway, Nickleson had cut him off, refusing to pay for Cochran's liquor and roadside lodgings last winter. This had killed what chance Cochran had to manipulate his golden goose. Nickleson had been the best meal ticket he had ever met.

——

That afternoon in McPhael's cabin, Cochran spoke of leaving Sherman's party, exaggerating his importance to Nickleson for McPhael's benefit.

"They left you for dead?" McPhael asked.

"Near about. Me and Nickleson, we slept through all the noise of camp breaking. Them sonofabitches slipped us some monkey juice and then stole our cash."

"What'd you do?"

"Walked all the way to Skagway. Passed the winter cutting fish. Come spring, we booked passage to Dawson."

Cochran locked eyes and smiled, exaggerating a brotherly moment.

"You wantin' to go back home?" McPhael asked.

"I got no one to go back to, but I got a severe dislike for this damn cold."

"It ain't cold yet. We still be in high summer."

Cochran vowed to get the hell out of Dawson as soon as possible. If he could gain Nickleson's favor again, he stood a chance to milk the little pissant some more. McPhael uncurled a dirty mattress on the empty bunk and threw a blanket on top.

Cochran looked at the soiled pallet. He remembered arriving in Skagway with Nickleson, hungry and wet. They had waited all winter for sternwheelers to come up from Seattle, headed to Dawson. Forced to sleep on sour pallets and work cutting fish with fishmongers, everything between them went wrong.

Nickleson had said, "I'll pay your passage to Dawson, and then we part our ways."

Those words broke Cochran's heart. He needed to reel Nickleson back in or lose the biggest mark of his life. Once Nickleson returned to Detroit, he would get his inheritance of seventy-five thousand dollars from his grandfather. Cochran meant to be the sucker-fish that cleaned up every spare dollar Nickleson would drop as he pissed it away.

"How're you gonna get home?" McPhael asked.

"Lemme think on it. In the meantime, I might be able to help you, but it'll depend on how much you're willing to help me." Cochran said.

McPhael stared Cochran straight in the face and swallowed hard.

"Gee, I'll help. I'll help out any way I can."

Cochran unpacked his dunnage bag and hung a shirt on a wooden peg.

"I sees that guy Nickleson a lot, drinking in two, maybe three saloons around town. He's always with another fella."

Cochran turned around and kicked his bag across the cabin floor. He boiled inside. No bootlicker was going to take his place in the hen house. He needed to turn this job to his advantage. His mind relaxed as the seeds of a new plan took root. Had his luck finally turned?

THE SECOND YEAR

Bad Weather

Broussard's Cabin ❦ January 22, 1909

Nazaire saw the flickering outside the cabin window. "Northern lights again," he said.

"They see them as far as Egypt. I wonder what the Pharaohs' thought of that?" Broussard asked.

Outside, Nazaire heard dogs barking. "Someone comes."

Frantic knocks shook the door, and Broussard yelled, "Come in."

A man entered with a blanket of snow on his shoulders. It was Kaine, a ruddy-cheeked machinist from Dominion Creek. He stomped his boots on the floor and bent over to regain his breath.

"Mighty cold out there," Kaine said, "Broussard? You know men by the name Poulin?"

Nazaire jumped at the question. "Yes, me, me and my brother."

Kaine stared at Nazaire and Raoul. He held one hand to his throat.

"Sit, sit," Broussard said as he pointed to his cot. Kaine searched for an even breath.

"It's got to be -26°F out there, dangerous weather," Kaine said.

Broussard turned to Nazaire and Raoul. "Let him warm up. Kaine, I'll make you some tea."

Kaine sat on a cot. "A man went missing and got caught in a snowburst. Someone said he might be family."

"Who went missing?" Nazaire asked.

"Goddy-ass Poulin, something like that. Found on Dominion Creek, where it crosses Hunter," Kaine said.

"How do you know it's him?" Broussard asked.

"The man who found him says it looks like Goddy-ass. Thin with long arms and legs. Mustache. Long face."

Nazaire sat on his cot. What to do? He searched Raoul's eyes but didn't move.

"So he's been found. He's not missing anymore. Is he hurt?" Broussard asked.

"No, not hurt," Kaine said. His eyes took in the floor of the cabin. "Sorry. He's frozen, frozen dead."

Nazaire and Raoul gasped. They stood and remained silent.

Broussard studied Nazaire and raised his hands in the air, "OK, he's dead. There's no rush to get him," he said as he passed a tin of tea to Kaine.

"Well yes and no," Kaine said. "We got us a snowburst out there."

"A what?" Raoul asked.

"It's when lots of snow falls quick in one area," Broussard said, "If you're caught in a snowburst, the wind — and there's always wind — can turn you around. It blinds you so's you don't know where you're headed."

Nazaire sat curled over, holding his head in his hands. What if Gaudias was dead and buried in heavy snow maybe until summer?

"Who found him?" Nazaire asked.

"Frank Johnnie, snowshoeing on Dominion toward his mother's cabin with fresh caribou. Found him with no coat," Kaine said.

"He was dead when Johnnie found him?" Raoul asked.

"Yeah, peed himself," Kaine said, "That's when you know they're dead. Sorry."

"Where's he now?" Nazaire asked.

"Johnnie towed him to Sulphur, where it joins Dominion. Did it on snowshoes all by himself. The body's still there."

Nazaire sat silent. Would Gaudias have been out in the cold? He knew better.

"Kaine, you got your dogs?" Broussard asked.

"Yeah, they'll need to be inside soon," Kaine said.

"Let's get your dogs packed in and fed for the night. My kennel's in back. Spend the night here and let's see what tomorrow brings."

"Makes sense," Kaine said.

"If it's good traveling, Nazaire and Raoul can follow you with my team to the body, eh?" Broussard suggested.

They agreed. The two dog teams did well with not a sound coming from the kennel all night. Temperatures had warmed by next morning with Broussard's thermometer reading 12°F. After a fast breakfast, Nazaire and Raoul took Broussard's dogs and followed Kaine's team to Sulphur where it forked with Dominion.

The high drifts were wind-blown to the North and all but obliterated the road. The sleds met the crossroads at noon with another few hours of twilight left. They spotted the dead man off to the side, propped on a high snowdrift. Frank Johnnie had used the man's belt to tie the stiff body, wrapped in a blue tarp, to the road sign.

The two teams stopped and climbed the snowdrift. The cold bit through their clothes and into their bones. Johnnie had dug for rocks at the side of the road and packed them along the base of the tarp, discouraging wolves from getting a taste. Without the blue tarp, the corpse would have remained buried in snow, a white ghost.

The body was curled over, with knees tucked under the chin, a face half covered by tight fists. They circled the poor soul, searching out ways to identify the man. One boot was unlaced, the other missing.

"Lookie here," Kaine said, "Good quality leather like this ain't to be had 'round here."

"No coat," Raoul said.

"Yeah, they do that sometimes, undress," said Kaine.

The mustache and clenched fingers were frozen together. How could they see the man's face? If Nazaire could get one good glimpse, he would know if it was Gaudias. Snow covered one ear, the other a black pancake glued to the side of the head. Nazaire grasped the hands and pulled, forcing the body to follow while he examined an unfamiliar earlobe.

"Let's get his hands off the face," Nazaire said.

Both thumbs were hidden under cover of sealed fingers. The shirttail clung to the back of his pants, while one swollen eye followed them with suspicion. Kaine held the corpse by the shoulders while Nazaire and Raoul each grabbed a forearm and pulled. Each hair on the corpse's face was white and standing stiff. Next, Kaine placed a foot on the man's chest and pulled. The stubborn hands wouldn't dislodge from the icy body.

"Why one eye open?" Raoul asked.

"Unusual," Kaine explained. "Most times, the eyelashes freeze together, and you're as good as blind. No fire's gonna unstick frozen eyeballs."

Crack. The three men jumped at once and stopped pulling.

"What'd we do?" Raoul asked.

"Broke a shoulder, I think," Kaine said.

The corpse's face revealed blackened lips and nose. They turned the body on its side and from the buttocks, discovered the yellowed stain covering the man's upper thighs. An unbuttoned shirt displayed chest hairs turned blue like an angry sea.

"Can't make out if it's him," Nazaire said.

They maneuvered around the body while their feet fought the drift for balance. Nazaire grabbed the inside of the elbow and pulled. A crusted line appeared where the lips should have been.

Kaine held the back of the man's head while Raoul rolled the body to free the opposite arm and pulled down. Crack.

"I think we broke an arm this time," Kaine said.

The three men stopped and peered at each other.

"We can't stay in this cold much longer," Kaine said.

Nazaire's feet shuffled while Raoul remained silent, looking wide-eyed.

Kaine instructed, "check his pockets."

Nazaire pulled off his mittens and struggled to search the dead man's pants pockets.

"Nothing," he said.

No ring on the fingers, no cross or cloth scapula around the neck. A real lost soul.

"I don't want no widow upset with me for desecrating her man," Kaine bellowed in the howling wind.

The body was almost angelic, with hoarfrost covering his bare chest. Under the legs, a slab of stained ice had been chiseled to free the body from the ground. He lay in a partial round the way young children sometimes did, collapsing elbows and knees in want to disappear. That one open eye followed the men no matter how they twisted and turned the body.

"Is it your brother or no?" Kaine asked.

Nazaire's heart pounded. He bent to get closer to the face and almost fell on top of the ashen man. "Don't think so."

Raoul studied the face from a side angle.

"Look, the nose," Raoul said.

Nazaire approached the face again, scanned the nose, the forehead, and back to the nose.

"Not him, not Gaudias," Nazaire said.

"You sure?" Kaine asked.

"Ya." Nazaire looked at Raoul, grinned and turned back to Kaine. "Six generations of Poulin men and not one hook nose in the bunch."

Raoul pushed the body onto the tarp while Kaine got rope. They trussed the man tight and packed him into Kaine's sled.

———

In Broussard's cabin everyone warmed up by the wood-burning stove with Kaine's dogs back in Broussard's kennel and the corpse secure in the dog's food cache.

"Sorry to drag you guys out," Kaine said.

"It's OK. What you do with him now?" Nazaire asked.

"I'll take him to Grand Forks, let the mounties or Saint Mary's Hospital sort it out."

379

Nazaire pulled out a bottle of whiskey and passed it around. Thoughts of Gaudias flooded his mind. He had been an impatient boy of twelve when he had left home. Nazaire remembered a time Florence, their oldest sister, baked cookies, a special treat with cinnamon and pearl sugar on top. Gaudias had run into the farmhouse and stopped short at the sight of the heaping plate. He reached out a hand.

"No you don't young man," Florence said.

His smile vanished and his head hung low.

"Oh, go 'head. Don't say anything to the others."

Nazaire had seen it all from the summer kitchen and had smiled at the joy one simple cookie had brought Gaudias. How often had Gaudias helped brush the horses' withers and flanks, check legs for prickles, maybe plait their tails?

In Dawson, Gaudias could scarce give thirty minutes to sit with him and Raoul after an eleven-year absence. What a fine how-do-you-do. Why would he be this way? It was an undeserved slap in

the face. Is this what this country does to a man —
replaces a heart with stone?

Weeks later, Nazaire found out the frozen man
was from Finland, come to work on the Indian River.
He'd gone into Dawson for supplies.

"Only two miles from his brother's cabin when
Johnnie found him,"Broussard said.

If the frozen man were Gaudias, what would he
do? Bury him here? No taking a body back home.

This winter passed like spreading molasses.
Miners walked between nearby cabins, visiting for an
afternoon. They played their musical instruments, re-
read old newspapers and letters — anything to chase
the grayness away. When the food got low, the
miners hunted moose or caribou, dividing the meat
among many cabins. They learned to sing new songs,
cut paper labels from canned goods into a fresh deck
of cards, and how to bring fur to a shiny gleam.

The winter was long but Nazaire knew he could
tough it out now. His nights were filled with happy
dreams of a full house back on his homestead.

The Ride Along

Lookout near Bear Creek ❧ May 30, 1909

Raoul couldn't very well refuse to go once Cochran ordered him onto the buckboard. He sat in great discomfort, wondering why Cochran would want him along. They were in Grand Forks, in front of a supply depot. His mind still reeled from finding Cochran in his life again — Cochran!

"Wanna see where all the gold comes from?" Cochran asked Raoul Poulin.

He didn't wait for an answer, just snapped the horses' leathers and they were off. The buckboard headed toward Dawson with the team struggling in the mud and melting permafrost for twenty miles when it veered off onto Bear Creek Road, nothing more than a circle for supply wagons to switch directions. At the back of the turn-around, a leg of plowed road rose two thousand feet up to a lookout. The top of the lookout was a flat promontory, a dead end that offered a panoramic view of the thrashing Klondike River below.

The press of the river created a rising froth that saturated the lookout and its one majestic fir whose base included exposed tree roots. Stunted trees bordered the back end of the lookout, struggling to thrive in scant, depleted soil.

At the front of this flat pancake, the Klondike River flowed next to a sheer, two thousand feet drop-off onto rock slopes. Any rescue would be impossible if anyone ever fell off.

To the east, rough roads led to the head of Bear Creek, and to the west, plateaus transformed into steeper gullies, water carried tons of rock and silt, creating canyons that stretched beyond. Wind, rain, arctic cold, and snow widened the gaps into great seams of water and gold, gold and water that meandered for miles and became creeks of gold.

Cochran swung the buckboard wide and circled, facing the direction they had come. He jumped down and took in the view. Raoul remained on the bench with his arms stiff at his sides. He dragged the palms of his hands down his pants' legs. After all the bullshit that Cochran and Nickleson had pulled on Nazaire and others during Sherman's journey, Raoul remained on high alert.

"Poulin, come see how pretty this looks," Cochran said as he walked toward the sheer drop-off.

Raoul hesitated to answer, He turned to face Cochran and then said, "Yeah, I see."

"No, no. Come down here. I want you to see this."

Cochran turned and pointed beyond Raoul. "This is where the gold first came out of the ground. Got it told to me by a mining geologist."

"I thought it came from the Dome?"

"No. Well yes and no. The Dome is just one place where gold peeked out of these rocks.

Cochran stood at the edge, lit a cigarette and stared out. "Come see this. It ain't a sight you see every day."

Raoul hesitated, then dismounted, focusing on the horses and their leathers. His heart raced. Sweat began to form on his forehead. He took a few steps forward, one hand on the hind rump of one of the horses, the other trembling. His throat grated, dry with itch. He didn't want to be here, not for anything in the world.

Raoul walked toward the trunk of the massive fir, stealing a look into the back of the wagon for any weapon, a blade, maybe a pry bar. What was the sonofabitch up to? Raoul couldn't work it out, but he sensed danger lurking in this isolated place. The roar of fast water blocked out the sound of every living thing. Not one raven or buzzing mosquito could be heard, not even the hooves of the impatient horses as they stomped in place.

Cochran remained rooted near the edge of the cliff face. "What's the matter, country boy? You afraid of a little water? Look, you can see where the Yukon sucks up the Klondike from here."

Raoul dragged his feet at each step. "Looks real picturesque."

Raoul walked to the right of Cochran but stayed behind him. He remained as close to the back of the buckboard as possible and looked up at the sky.

"Where're the eagles?"

He saw dozens of eagles make downward spirals every day. They flew with wings outstretched as the air currents lifted them in lazy rings.

While Raoul searched the sky, Cochran backed up and hovered a hand on Raoul's shoulder. Raoul sensed the proximity and slid a few steps away. The hairs on his neck stood in protest. Did the bastard mean to kill him?

At that exact moment, three Hån men walked out from the stunted trees. They stood beside the horses, staring at the two men. Cochran and Raoul had seen them at the same time, their presence giving Raoul his chance to add distance from his boss. Raoul clenched his teeth while his eyes followed the Hån turning down the rough trail. His heart pounded as he made his way to the buckboard and climbed up, his eyes locked on the direction that the Hån took.

"Let's go," Raoul said.

He hid his shaking knees by squeezing them together and sat on both hands all the way to Sulphur. Where had the Hån come from? He didn't care. He'd never been so happy to see Indians before. Maybe they had saved his life. He felt sure of it.

Tonight, in Broussard's cabin, Raoul would borrow Nazaire's short boning knife for protection. He would speak to Nazaire and Broussard about how to make himself scarce from the clutches of Cochran and McPhael. He didn't trust either of them. This ride along was something he wouldn't forget.

Hoffmeyer's Mistake

Dawson ✌ July 1, 1909

Dominion Day was Canada's national holiday and Dawson all but exploded with the sweep of twenty thousand Sourdoughs, Cheechakos, and sporting women, all crammed into the city over a three-day celebration with more whiskey flowing than throughout the rest of the year. Flags and regalia hung outside every building.

Nazaire and Raoul settled in at the saloon of the Occidental Hotel where Nazaire mentioned his fallow acres and plans to arrive back in Quebec to one of the stagecoach drivers. Nazaire asked how best to leave the region and when. He needed to get back in time so as not to lose his land.

"Some of those laws have changed," the driver said. "You can't be absent from your farm until seed day like before. Now you gotta be back earlier."

"When?" Nazaire asked.

"Ask Hoffmeyer. His kid brother lost a piece of land because he didn't get back home in time."

Nazaire searched out the miner at the straight and found him down a few saloons on Second Avenue. He pulled Hoffmeyer aside and inquired about the law.

"Yeah, my brother worked with me on Eldorado Creek, got back home, and his little ten-acre pasture farm had been reported as abandoned. Law changed a few years back. You got to report to some authority by the last of April, let them know you've arrived. What a sweet piece of land he had up in Vermilion Bay," Hoffmeyer said, "and he lost it."

Nazaire held his breath. Were his deepest dreams in jeopardy? Would his sweat these past two years come to nothing? Nazaire rushed to tell Raoul of Hoffmeyer's words, and then they both sought out Broussard to check this new information as truth.

"If you read the Prairie newspapers instead of Dawson's, you might of picked up on this. Theys full of farming news. Do some back planning. Grab you paper and pencil and use my calendar to work it out."

Nazaire pulled a tattered piece of paper from his pants pocket and sat with Raoul, pencil in hand. Broussard opened his wallet and offered the calendar. They spoke in low voices with Nazaire swallowing his anger. How could he not have heard of this before? With all his careful planning, how could this one particular detail have escaped him?

"Well?" Broussard asked.

"I can't do it, I'm too damned mad to think straight," Nazaire said. His face colored tomato-red. With paper at a premium, he entered the back room of the eatery and ripped a label from a can of peaches, turned it over and prayed to God that he had not outstayed his time.

"You need to get through at least half the Rockies before freezeup, or you'll get froze'd in 'til next May," Broussard said. "That's one thing you best get right."

Worry lined Nazaire's face as he took the calendar in shaking hands and thought of the many towns he and Raoul must pass through to reach Quebec. After check and re-check, they couldn't come up with a date to leave. Nazaire couldn't focus on so burdensome a task as he and Raoul sat next to Broussard.

"Relax. Have yourselves a drink, then return to this problem with a clear head," Broussard said.

———

Outside, banners hung from every rooftop on Dawson's First Avenue. People whooped it up with whiskey and food in the one square mile town. Even the Hån celebrated with two days and nights of song and dance. Men and women filled every rooftop and windowsill with not one inch of road or sidewalk absent from a body occupying space.

Nazaire and Raoul searched for Romeo and Gaudias with no luck. They couldn't resolve which date to leave Dawson while pinned against the throng of people in the streets. They rode the free train back to Grand Forks and returned to Broussard's cabin, the one place that offered quiet.

Tomorrow, Nazaire must go over plans again for their retreat out of the Yukon; it was the most important decision of his life.

Tait Negg

Granville ❧ July 23, 1909

Nazaire sat at the bar of the Golden Flats Hotel in Granville. He ordered a whiskey, drank up, and then asked for Tait by name. Today was his third visit to the roadhouse this month. His hands shook as he paid a dollar to the floor boss, who pointed to the stairs running behind the long, stand-up bar.

"She'll be up in five minutes. Door number two," he said.

He made his way from the ground floor to the second story, an open expanse of bunk beds and a few rank spittoons. Next to an open window, a piss bucket pulsed with yellow.

He walked to one end of the open loft where a small hallway marked off private rooms. Behind a hanging canvas, he found an ill-set door with '2' painted in black. He entered, and turned to face a small bed, and a wooden chair. An empty fruit crate stood on end and served as a small dressing table with a woman's hand mirror lying on top. He sat down, stood, and stepped away, all red-faced with the back of his legs hitting the chair. Plop, he went down.

He heard loud footsteps through the door and pulled out his pocket watch. He snapped the cover shut before he marked the time. The latch slid up, and his mouth went dry as Tait entered the room.

She stopped as Nazaire took in a sharp breath and slowly raised his head. He saw her shoes, the hem of her emerald skirt, and a glimpse of her red petticoat. He took in her cinched waist, the narrow shoulders and plunging cut of her gown. Her pearl-colored breasts shivered when she sat.

All these delights filled his eyes and rushed to his head. The necklace heavy with gold nuggets, sparkle earrings and lips opened into a welcome smile. His eyes fell to her breasts. Would he ever nestle his head against those ivory mounds? His throat caught at the sight of her sparkling eyes, the totality of perfection.

"I know you," Tait said.

The pulse of blood warmed his neck as heat spread to his face, and the blush burned his earlobes. She clasped her hands on her lap and waited. He crossed his arms and pulled in his long legs to allow her space. One knee brushed against her skirt, and he flushed scarlet.

She lifted her hand to a hairpin at the back of her head and pulled. A cascade of curls fell like splashed water behind her neck. She loosened the top button of her bodice and released a hanky from the cuff of her sleeve. One delicate tap liberated a wisp of perfume, an exotic bouquet of cinnamon.

He raised his hands in surprise. "No, no, don't," he whispered.

She placed her hands back on her lap as he lowered his eyes to the floor. He hadn't planned how to act or what to say. He found himself much unacquainted with the situation.

"My, my spouse," he stammered.

"Tell me about her."

He relaxed and talked in shallow whispers with his head down and both hands animated as he spoke of Victoria and her delicate fingers.

"She knit sweaters and scarves, slippers crocheted tight so's the cold don't go through when you go to the outhouse," he said.

Tait tilted her head and curled her lips inward. A hall lamp outside the room threw soft shadows against her gown and moist lips while the skunk oil sat heavy in the air.

"Even our sheets got lace on the edges," Nazaire said. "Those lace sheets went in the coffin with her two years ago."

He spoke of how he worked in the barns, repairing the horses' tack and leathers using hammers and awls, the tools used to solve problems on a farm. It's what farmers did, fixed worn leathers using the brute strength of their hands. His long fingers cut the air as he spoke while his legs fidgeted in his chair. He told Tait about the maple sugar evaporator he had built from metal sheets the railroad had thrown away.

He explained how he tapped his maple trees, a strong tradition in Quebec and planned to replace the inclined entry to his barn for his cows and horses.

He didn't come for a poke. Didn't she see he was solid? He wanted her to understand. A lull grew in the room and not wanting to give it importance, Nazaire asked, "What do you say? Are you happy here?"

Her eyes widened at the question. She paused and flashed her eyelashes before she spoke. "The Dawson gold fields have been good to me. I'm pleased to sing and dance for the hard-working men of Granville."

He hadn't expected these words to come from her soft lips. He crossed and uncrossed his arms when two soft knocks on the door announced his time up. She stood and extended her hand palm up toward him. He examined the open hand, and then took a step back. She withdrew her palm, turned and walked out. In the hallway, the floor boss opened the door painted with '1' in black, and she disappeared inside.

———

Nazaire left as if in a dream walk. He followed the Dawson-Granville Road back to Broussard's cabin. His thoughts of Tait mingled with memories of Victoria. His insides churned with indecision. Was it time to leave the Yukon? Maybe, but but why go home to an empty farmhouse? A cold bed? At least with Tait, a woman who warmed his insides, a woman who could make him happy, he had a chance for a fresh start. Was he wrong?

If he returned to Quebec, didn't his children deserve a fresh mother? Someone always happy and gay, singing cheerful songs? She'd learn how to milk the cows and pick up eggs while avoiding his ornery rooster. Couldn't he go back with a new bride? Create a future with no-say-so from relatives or the church? He kicked anything his boots found on the ground. Nazaire sucked in a hard breath while a spark of anger grew in his chest.

The look on Tait's face when she threw open her hand lingered in his head. Beyond the dollar he had given to the floor boss, Tait wanted a handout. How stupid he didn't pick up on her wanting fingers. What should he do now? He couldn't decide.

Nazaire grew angrier with every mile he walked. What did he think, that she'd warm to a chance of spending private time with him? She was nothing, a hussy, the most beautiful, grand whore he knew.

Discord

Broussard's Cabin ❧ July 25, 1909

Sunday morning, Nazaire turned in his cot, arms and legs coiled up like a dead bug. He scanned the cabin and caught a stream of cold air on his neck and a glimpse of Raoul carrying the piss bucket out as he slammed the door. When Raoul returned, he threw the empty bucket on the cabin floor. Nazaire jumped from his cot. The bucket rolled to a stop in the corner.

"I'm giving my notice," Raoul said.

"What?"

Nazaire sat on his cot, putting on his socks and pants.

Raoul stomped a foot on the floor and pointed an angry finger against Nazaire's chest. "You're the one who wanted to come here. Have you forgotten? I miss my spouse and children. I wanna go home ... NOW"!

"Why?"

"Why? If you stay and give up your land, you're as good as a bum. All this time you talk about going home, and now you drag your feet? You're nothing without your land. What are you waiting for, Nazaire?"

"Why leave so soon?" Nazaire answered.

"We have enough gold. Winter's coming, snow and ice. You heard Broussard. We need to leave now or be trapped 'til spring. Let's go now."

"Yes, you're right, it's time to think ..."

Raoul screamed. "NO THINKING. I came here to make you happy, goddamn it."

"What?" Nazaire held his hands at his waist, then lowered them to his sides.

Raoul turned with his fists opening and then closing. Froth sat in the corners of his mouth.

"It's coming on freezeup, damn it, time to go. You gonna stay here and forget about your children? Give up the farm to mine gold?

Nazaire's eyes widened at the question. "No."

"What's going on? It's that whore, isn't it. Are you attached to this woman?"

"No."

"What's this woman to you?" Raoul yelled as he flung tin plates and a bottle of blackstrap to the floor.

"She's nothing to me. A simple distraction," Nazaire mumbled with downcast eyes.

"How is it going to end? Are you gonna bring her home with you?"

"No," Nazaire swayed from one foot to the other like an ambushed animal.

Raoul leaned into Nazaire and whispered, "What're you thinking? No one's gonna accept her."

"What? I'm not thinking anything."

"Sonofabitch, that's right. You're not thinking at all. Every Friday, men talk about her and the other broken women at the Golden Flats. Think she's gonna leave her rich life for you?"

A blush of scarlet flashed across Nazaire's face. "No."

"Let me knock that idea off your shoulders. She'll never be happy on the farm, raising your children. Come home and find yourself a village girl to marry."

Nazaire remained stiff, blinked and looked at the floor.

"Is this how it is? Your spouse dies and so do you? Aren't you still a parent? Don't you still have children? Did you forget your promise to Thomas? Your promise to return in the spring of the fourth year? Tomorrow's my last day to work, then I pack to leave."

Raoul stood with clenched fists, turned and slammed the cabin door behind him. Nazaire wanted to run from the cabin and make his way to the Golden Flats. Stand outside and yell for Tait to come out. What would he say if he saw her? Would she even care? In his heart, Nazaire wasn't happy in the Yukon. He had seen too much cruelty here among men filled with limitless greed. Even Romeo and Gaudias wore a mantle of bitterness. They had stayed too long in this queer place and had become indifferent to a strange

403

world at odds with the natural rhythms of life. Romeo and Gaudias would never come back home, but had bound themselves to Dawson in their gold-blindness.

Everything fought against Nazaire's mind and body, men's natural instincts. Even eating battled against his insides. Beans went from steaming hot in the fire to near-frozen bullets away from the flame. Icy spears would cut into his throat and stomach, like swallowing nails. His guts cramped when he forced a stinker from his sour ass. There was little different in Broussard's cabin with his meager stove than it was crossing the Rockies.

Working hard from sunup to sundown in honest labor, this is what being a man was. But to watch men work like ants in four warm months, then lay in drunken idleness during the cold eight was unbalanced and not natural.

The gray of the twilight months pulled at a man's soul until it was wind-hollowed. Deep inside, his stomach fought a tug-o-war. All he knew for certain was he missed his children.

Could he remove Tait from her depraved life and make a spouse and mother of her? Wouldn't his family recognize all the warmth and goodness he saw in her? Put her in acceptable clothes, and she'd be fine in Quebec with her delicate smile and sweet songs.

Raoul's words swirled in Nazaire's head. Was Tait a soiled dove? Beyond help? Could he dismiss thoughts of her and return home to where relatives believed him to have misused Victoria and kept a wanting table for her and their children?

Nazaire walked from Broussard's cabin to a tributary of the Klondike. He needed to clear his head, and the soft sounds of the water calmed him as he stood staring at the surface of the stream. The current moved in gentle swirls, twisting in spirals. The water swayed near the further edge, forming designs and odd twists in the slow current.

He wasn't looking at water, but the discarded ginger hairs from a solitary musk ox, some twenty pounds of wet fibers each beast left behind when it crossed the water. These soft hairs coiled in the wet

405

gurgle as they separated into two long clumps, mimicking the open wings of Victoria's swan barrette.

Nazaire's shoulders rose and fell in sobs. "Victoria, forgive me. I never said good-bye."

Nazaire thought back to the day he and Raoul packed to leave home. Each brother had given their father a solemn oath to return together. He walked across the shallow stream and grabbed a handful of the guard hairs, gathered up their silk and with a fresh resolve, knew what he must do.

YPMC Office on Sulphur

July 26, 1909

Cochran sat behind Weasel's desk in the Yukon Pacific Mining Company office on Sulphur Creek. The large desk and chair made the room smaller, with a wooden floor that didn't do much to keep out the cold. A small chest stood next to a camping stove as it heaved out smoke. It sputtered to life from a piece of frozen wood in the firebox.

"You sure you heard right?" Cochran asked.

"Yeah. They're both talking about going home," McPhael said.

"If you ain't in on this a hundred, McPhael, say it now."

"I said I am. Stop your damned badgering."

When Weasel entered the office, Cochran moved posthaste from Weasel's chair. Would he suspect anything, what with him and McPhael in the office this early? Cochran smothered a cringe as Weasel inspected him head to toe. "What's on your dirty mind?" Weasel asked.

"Nothin' boss, getting a jump on the day is all," Cochran said.

The week had had its challenges because a broken water pump had left eleven days' worth of gold uncleaned. It had to be cleaned a bit before leaving the claim, otherwise the smelter in Dawson would have double the work before the gold could be assayed.

Sparkle and everything finer got packed in delicate glass vials and secured inside padded slots in a special wooden box. Crates of backlogged gold filled the cabin with a few covers stacked on the floor.

The two-horse YPMC buckboard arrived with the payroll and Weasel's lunch, hot in its cast iron pot. The old Hån woman in Moosehide prepared caribou stew and bannock for her family and always set aside a portion for Weasel, husband to her youngest granddaughter.

The buckboard driver knocked at Weasel's office door. He'd leave in a few moments for his end-of-the-week ritual — spent at the cabin of one of Grand Forks' girls — which he'd prolong until late afternoon.

At the sound of a knock, Cochran and McPhael walked out to the buckboard. McPhael removed the payroll bag and carried it inside while Cochran lifted the lid of Weasel's hot stew and underhandedly added brown liquid from the glass vial. He stirred the concoction with a dirty finger, shook the burn away as best he could, and took in the delicate aromas before opening the cabin door. He carried the pot inside, careful not to spill any and incite one of Weasel's rants.

McPhael put the payroll bag on the desk and stood idle while Cochran counted out the final sum. Because it matched the amount listed in the payroll book, he added his initials against the book entry. Weasel sent McPhael to get some items from the supply cabin a few miles away. McPhael hesitated at the door, searched Cochran's face for what to do, but left as instructed. Next, Weasel wrote out a note and sealed it in an envelope.

"I want a written report on the pump flow. Put this in the hands of the day supervisor yourself," Weasel said as he thrust the envelope into Cochran's chest.

The morning wasn't going as planned and Cochran remained frozen to the spot. Did Weasel suspect something? Cochran couldn't be sure. What if Weasel were to lock his office from the inside once he left? Then Cochran wouldn't be able to come back in and his plans would be for naught. What to do? Tell Weasel the day supervisor was out sick? That wouldn't work. No, he mustn't do anything to delay Weasel's normal routine.

"Well?" Weasel barked as he set himself to his steaming caribou stew and bannock.

Cochran snapped from his reverie and left as instructed. Thirty minutes later, Cochran and McPhael walked back into the office together. Weasel sat in a stupor, eyes closed and gravy dripping from a slack mouth. They remained silent as Weasel slumped over in his chair, insensible.

Cochran breathed a sigh of relief. He had done it, and his plan would succeed. He would show Nickleson he needed him to get out of the god-forsaken Yukon and return to Detroit and the easy life they had both enjoyed.

McPhael locked the office door while Cochran gathered the cash and logbooks, throwing them all into the payroll bag. Three times the usual amount of raw gold would leave for Dawson today, and Cochran intended to have it all. A spark of giddiness grew in his chest.

Cochran threw the payroll bag into the box with all the fine glassed gold, and secured the cover while Cochran kept watch over Weasel. McPhael stacked the sealed crates in the YPMC buckboard outside and secured them in place. Had Cochran underestimated the total weight? The heavier the load, the longer it would take to make a clean getaway.

After McPhael returned to the office, Cochran sent him out. "Time to get Poulin."

———

Raoul sat in line with the other men on break, the typical Friday talk of Saturday rendezvous with the strumpets at the Golden Flats and other roadhouses along the creeks.

A booming voice broke the calm atmosphere, "Poulin, to the office," McPhael said.

Cochran was in a black mood when Raoul walked up to the YPMC office. Cochran stepped outside and faced Raoul before the Canuck put his hand on the door latch. Cochran pushed Raoul back one step into the road.

"Take the buckboard to Grand Forks and pick up a small bundle for YPMC. It's at the cargo station there. Then go to that lookout near Bear Creek. Remember where it is?" Cochran asked.

"Yeah," Raoul said.

"McPhael's gonna show up. Wait for him and unload some crates from your buckboard onto his wagon. Got it?"

Raoul nodded.

"And look to McPhael for your pay."

"OK," Raoul said. "But I need to talk to Weasel."

Cochran's face colored. He pushed a pointed finger into Raoul's chest.

"Do it when you come back," he growled.

Cochran disappeared into the office.

After Raoul had driven off, he and McPhael left in another buckboard by an east-turning road toward Bear Creek. They needed to be in place before Raoul showed up. Cochran locked up Weasel's office and the pair left.

Cochran would get everything he wanted: a chance to take care of Raoul Poulin once and for all, gold enough to buy passage out of the harsh North. If successful, Nickleson should be in his debt for sharing the take.

Cochran had made a gross error in judgment two years ago, and he knew it now. In every way, Cochran had agreed with Nickleson. He adapted the youth's dislikes and prejudices, like this stupid hate for all Canucks. He ate foods he didn't care for just to be agreeable, admiring the same women, even if they weren't to his liking.

After Sherman had left them no alternative but to follow the rail tracks to Skagway and endure that terrible winter cutting fish to pay for food and a pallet, Cochran had become sullen and hateful. He was lucky Nickleson agreed to pay for both their ship's passage to Dawson. But that was all — Nickleson declared that Dawson would be the end of their time together.

Nickleson had sent telegrams to his mother, begging for more money, and then had sent others to his father at his workplace. Nickleson played the meek innocent, the down-in-the-dumps son, unworthy of disturbing his giving and loving father. All these ploys Cochran had taught Nickleson. Now

414

the kid was pouring all his bucks into every watering hole in Dawson.

All Cochran's hopes and dreams hinged on getting on Nickleson's good side once again. After the gold switch, he would drop McPhael damned quick, and then he and Nickleson could move the gold to Whitehorse. They would book passage to Seattle by boat and then onward to Detroit. He took a deep breath and chuckled at his accomplishments. Yes, his plan was perfect.

Fool's Errand

July 26, 1909

Nazaire gasped in surprise as Raoul barged into Broussard's cabin out of breath.

"I'm supposed to take the company buckboard out near Bear Creek and meet McPhael. Something about a broken wagon. That sonofabitch Cochran took me there once, and I swear he was gonna push me over the edge. Will you come with me?" Raoul asked.

Something about this didn't seem right. Nazaire could see that going to Bear Creek made the hairs on the back of Raoul's neck rise.

What was Cochran playing at now? Why would he give Raoul this kind of errand when it was Weasel who ran the bench claim?

"OK, but how's about we bring rifles and shot," Nazaire said.

"I'm thinking that this here buckboard has all the week's gold in it."

Raoul pulled the covers off a few crates. One box had a bag of cash and the YPMC log books. Two crates held raw gold.

"He's setting you up. He wants you for a fool's errand. Damn him."

"I bet all the other crates are gold. I knew Cochran was up to no good," Raoul said.

Nazaire scratched his head. "It made no sense. If there's some wagon broke, why not take an empty buckboard and load up a spare wheel or some tools first?"

"Ever since we met up with that sonofabitch, he's been picking on me, on the both of us," Raoul said.

A bead of sweat sat across Nazaire's forehead. Whatever Cochran planned, he was sure trickery would be at the root of it. Nazaire guided the horses through the icy mud to Grand Forks. The time had come to face Cochran once and for all.

Raoul picked up the bundle waiting at Grand Forks and Nazaire drove the open buckboard toward Bear Creek and up that lookout trail. The two brothers hadn't covered five miles when a scraping sounds came from behind them. Was someone coming up the coastal trail? Who could it be? Raoul panicked. His eyes grew large as he grabbed his rifle and took aim. In an instant the sound was upon them. It was a man, a Hån Indian walking with a shoulder bag and pack strapped to his back.

"It's Sam, Romeo's friend from Moosehide," Raoul said.

Sam had small eyes that took in everything or so people said. He wore a caribou mackinaw and moose boots tied with pieces of leather. His gun and holster were tied at the waist. His skin was smooth, his complexion ruddy. Even his hands, often uncovered in the severe cold, held the cast of a person much younger.

Raoul stopped Sam and repeated the story of his odd errand while Nazaire pried open one of the crates to give Sam a look-see.

"This smells bad to me. I ain't never met a man so hateful as Cochran. He's harangued us since we joined up with Sherman and the shaman," Nazaire said.

"Shaman? Who shaman?" Sam asked.

"My friend, Coppaway, an Ojibway. He traveled with me and Raoul to Edmonton, more than two thousand miles together. He was my good friend. Cochran would'a killed me if it weren't for Coppaway stopping him. He saved my life," Nazaire said.

Sam looked the two brothers in the eyes. "Have idea."

Sam carried six round pails nested on his back with matching covers packed in his shoulder bag.

"Put gold into pails, then fill boxes with rocks. We hide pails, then go Bear Creek," Sam said.

Nazaire and Raoul worked the covers off the crates of gold, made the transfer and then banged the

419

covers in place. They hid the pails in thick brush behind a large boulder.

"Cochran'll see red when he finds out," Raoul said.

"Too bad. The sonofabitch's abused us ever since we laid eyes on him," Nazaire said.

Sam looked at Nazaire. "This man bad long time?"

"Yes sir. He insulted another Indian, Longfox. Just a scared boy, he was," Raoul said.

Sam's eyes widened, then he nodded.

"Bring buckboard slow to lookout, make next to big tree, wheels near edge. You can do?" Sam instructed.

Nazaire nodded at Sam as all three men boarded the open buckboard, with Sam sitting stiff on the end.

"Don't need to fret. The horses ain't gonna hurt you," Raoul said.

Nazaire looked across to Sam and flashed a quick smile. "You know your dogs, I'll give you that, but we know our horses."

Nazaire's face relaxed for a moment. After the fight he and Raoul had had yesterday, he wasn't sure if he might stay, with the pull of Tait Negg strong. His life wasn't supposed to go this way, but this fool's errand topped everything. Cochran intended bloodshed; he felt it in his bones.

Both brothers knew Cochran to be a lousy shot, impatient and foolish. But what about McPhael? Nazaire wasn't a man to tolerate fools. Now he was hell bent on getting out of this godforsaken wilderness alive. The open buckboard pushed on, dust rising behind the wheels like some chariot riding into a hell storm.

Lookout near Bear Creek

July 26, 1909

Nazaire shivered as he swung the open buckboard wide on the precipice at the lookout above Bear Creek, crossed the open area and rested the rear wheels beside the huge balsam fir.

He and Raoul followed Sam as the three peered over the edge of the cliff face. Two thousand feet below, the Klondike roared. Now Nazaire understood how Raoul felt when Cochran had lured him to this edge. Sam led the men behind the tree line where one hidden, elongated rock gave cover. Nazaire's heart raced.

Why would Sam insist on hiding in such a spot with barely a few stunted trees separating them from whatever mischief Cochran had planned? Nazaire scanned the periphery looking for means of escape. There were none. Sam's plan was meant to shock.

McPhael would be expecting one man to await him, not three.

"He's coming," Raoul said.

Slipping wheels announced another conveyance approaching. The driver gasped in surprise at the open buckboard already there with no possible room for another on the small plateau. A horse and covered wagon remained on the trail.

Nazaire and Raoul recognized McPhael as he stepped from the driver's seat and stood to examine the small plateau. He held an open hand against a belly gun tucked in his belt. What kind of trap had Cochran planned for Raoul?

McPhael looked around. "Raoul Poulin, show yourself."

Murmurs sounded from the wagon.

"Get out here and start moving boxes," McPhael insisted.

He walked to the rear of the covered wagon, out of sight. Nazaire's heart quickened. What was he doing now? Nazaire heard murmurs and noticed the business end of a rifle cut into the air as the wagon body lowered, then rose. Cochran jumped down from the back. Nazaire felt sick to his stomach when he heard a rifle hammer cock. His breakfast climbed up his throat as he gasped and swallowed a chunk of beans.

"Poulin, get to work. We're in a hurry, damn you," McPhael ordered.

Nazaire wondered if he should come out from behind cover and face Cochran once and for all? When Cochran walked out onto the precipice and fired a blast toward the trees, Nazaire had his answer. Cochran intended mortal harm.

Something pushed McPhael out from behind the wagon. He turned and said, "You didn't say nothin' bout killing nobody."

"You said you'd do anything to help me. You promised," Cochran seethed.

"If you want him dead, you kill him," McPhael said.

Nazaire's face drained gray. Cochran's handgun was more pop than firearm, but McPhael's rifle might plug a man into eternity. Shots whizzed by Nazaire's shoulder, making his throat run dry. He worried the buckboard horses might spook and run into the trees.

Nazaire, Raoul, and Sam spread out as much as possible behind the elongated rock that gave them cover.

With lips stretched tight, Nazaire aimed and returned fire. Nazaire remembered his father's words when he left.

"Bring your brother back home safe," Varis had said.

Nazaire had his Winchester, and Raoul his Remington, but neither brother wanted to hurt anyone. From his belt, Sam pulled out a .45. Cochran and McPhael couldn't know how many men were shooting at them. Nazaire's ears throbbed as each bullet fired into the trees. Gunfire ricocheted off a rock and burned white powder across Raoul's face.

He blinked and stifled a cough as more shots rang out and one hit the bottom axle of the wagon.

"Damn you, Poulin. I should have killed you when I had the chance," Cochran yelled.

Could Cochran have planned that both conveyances would sit side-by-side? Both would never fit, making any switch in cargo all the more difficult. What the hell was he thinking?

Cochran aimed and fired. One blast tore through the air and skinned a small rock, grazing Nazaire's ear. He jumped up in surprise, holding a bloody hand to the side of his face.

Raoul moved next to Nazaire and inspected the wound. He pulled a rag from his pocket and handed it to him. Cochran rushed to the far edge of the wagon under cover, holding his firearm with both hands. Before he could take fresh aim, Sam returned fire.

Would Cochran think the men firing at him were from the mine or maybe Indians who disappeared into the trees like wild game? The hairs on Nazaire's neck stood stiff. He feared discovery, his and Raoul's.

Would the shooters claim Raoul was stealing the gold? He was ordered to drive the YPMC buckboard here. Would the authorities believe Raoul over Cochran and McPhael?

Nazaire looked over at his brother. An angry welt had risen on Raoul's forehead, dotted with fresh blood. One side of his face looked to be covered in flour.

Did Sam expect a shoot-out to the death or even have a plan of escape? They were tucked against one edge of a cliff with nowhere to go but down.

Gunpowder girdled the scrubby trees so thick that Nazaire clutched his throat, tasting lead and salt. Fearful thoughts raced through his mind. Would he die today, his body buried in some god-forsaken grave? How could God have put him at such mortal risk?

He didn't deserve this. He was an honest man. A hard-working man. If something happened to him, who would look after his children? Who would raise them? Who would teach his boys to fell a tree or dig a

"We're getting the hell out of here after this. Ain't no country to be living in with the likes of this pissant. My place is where my heart is, back home," Nazaire told Raoul.

Cochran pointed his rifle at McPhael. "Earn your keep and pull the gold off the buckboard."

Would Cochran kill McPhael and blame it on Raoul? McPhael hesitated, then walked into the open toward the buckboard and pulled three crates to the ground. He punched the air with a finger as he took a count.

"Looks like it's all here," McPhael said, twitching his eyes as he scanned the trees.

Sam aimed and hit McPhael in the leg. He screamed in pain and limped behind the front end of the buckboard. He was pinned down.

Sam fired at Cochran and then motioned for Nazaire and Raoul to stop shooting. Cochran reloaded and fired blind into the greenery. McPhael crab-walked to the nearest crate on the ground and sat, his face twisted in pain. He tied his neck scarf around his bleeding leg.

Nazaire licked his dry lips. He trusted the slug in McPhael's leg would keep him occupied.

———

Cochran's words electrified the air as he swore a blue streak. He walked into the open toward the open buckboard and climbed up, struggling to move the horses away from the tree. Crates blocked the path.

"Damn you, Poulin, I can't have you or anything else block me now," Cochran yelled. "I mean to have this payroll and gold and return with my sweet meal ticket by my side."

Cochran's hands shook with rage. Try as he might, Cochran couldn't get the horses on the open buckboard to align and back up. Cochran threw his coat to the ground in a huff. He was done.

The horses fought against Cochran's rough handling while McPhael whimpered, a hand pressed against his leg. Cochran pulled the crates to the side for clearance to maneuver the open buckboard. He leaned against the wood siding and peered over the cliff edge.

Through all his machinations pulling the horses' halters and screaming, the buckboard remained stuck. Gnarled roots caught on the wheels in deep ruts. In a huff, Cochran threw the horses' leathers to the ground. He ran to the back of the buckboard, slipping on the drenched blanket of moss. At the same moment, the back wheels released, freeing the horses and pulling backward with a jolt toward the edge.

Cochran's eyes bulged. His face squeezed into a contorted mask, fighting the consequences of his actions. He dug at the air with curled fingers, frantic to grab anything. Behind the elongated rock, all three men watched as Cochran screamed and fell.

———

"We go," Sam whispered.

He pushed some tree branches behind him and searched the ground. He dropped down to his waist as he pointed to his feet.

"Look like bad spot, but not. Steps under, bring you quick away," Sam said in a whisper.

He was standing on an ancient animal trail. Nazaire and Raoul watched Sam take a step aside, then drop lower into the ground. Was he in a hole? Yes. The path opened below them into a series of steep, hard-packed ridges that led down the cliff face. Their shirts and faces were awash in sweat and gunpowder when they walked into Bear Creek and caught a wagon going to Dawson. They made their way to the Royal North-West Mounted Police barracks in Dawson, where Sam reported to the commander.

Nazaire and Raoul sat outside. Adrenaline coursed through Nazaire's veins as he put a hand to his chest, breathing in the clean, quiet air. He was alive, and so was Raoul. Nazaire examined his fingertips, still white from clutching his rifle trigger.

It was time to get the hell out of the Yukon.

COMING HOME

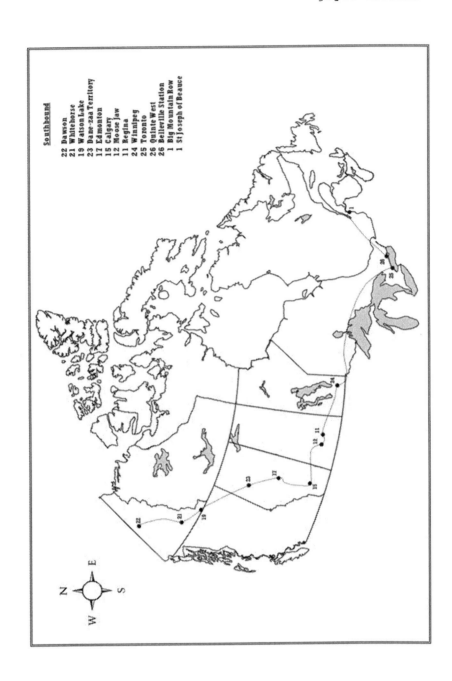

Southbound

22 Dawson
21 Whitehorse
19 Watson Lake
23 Dane-Zaa Territory
17 Edmonton
15 Calgary
12 Moose Jaw
11 Regina
24 Winnipeg
25 Toronto
26 Quinte West
26 Belleville Station
1 Big Mountain Row
1 St Joseph of Beauce

433

CHASING ICE

Closing the Claim

Dawson ❦ July 28, 1909

Nazaire and Raoul made their way to First Avenue in Dawson with their rucksacks sitting on thin arms and bundles tied to their walking sticks. Both brothers were gaunt in the face with round shoulders. Their dirty fingernails and cut up hands spoke of a miner's life.

Nazaire entered the Yukon Mining Register Office and relinquished his claim to the Crown. He got a grunt for his trouble and at last was a free man, unattached to the cold north and happy to be going home. He breathed a sigh of relief and waited outside the Occidental Hotel while Raoul left a note for Romeo and Gaudias.

Nazaire had never experienced excitement the likes of the last two days — using a hidden game trail to get off the lookout and riding the strong Klondike current in a caribou skin boat. He, Raoul and Sam arrived at the mounties' barracks on the riverfront with hands and faces peppered with gunpowder and ears throbbing.

Weasel offered Raoul and Nazaire a one hundred fifty-dollar reward each for safeguarding Yukon Pacific Mining's gold and payroll. They couldn't believe their luck. Since the *Dawson Daily Sun* and the *Whitehorse Star* had posted details of the robbery, everyone saluted the heroes wherever they went. They planned to board a six-day ride in an open-air, overland coach to Whitehorse with the fare all but eating up the bulk of their reward.

Yukon justice had prevailed. The mounties found Cochran's body caught in a fish wheel while Nickleson and McPhael had been tried in the Queen's Court and found guilty of premeditated theft and intent to do mortal harm. Their sentence? Two years in the Dawson jail, and a transfer to Whitehorse for eight more. McPhael was a hardened man who knew justice in the territory, but how would the soft-skinned Nickleson survive? Under Territory law, prisoners must cut a cord of wood each day. Come up short and you wouldn't be fed until you chopped.

Sam Smith walked down the street with his daughter Mary by his side. He wore his town clothes — a black serge suit with vest and black, wide-brimmed Stetson. Little Mary looked so proud in a calico dress and deerhide leggings. Beads decorated her pretty vest. Nazaire's eyes met Sam's.

"We're going back to Quebec. Thanks for all your help."

"It long way? How you go?"

"We're not sure. But we got to get through the Rockies before freezeup," Nazaire said.

They agreed to meet later. Nazaire's stomach was knotted. No one, not even the Hån could predict freezeup. He and Raoul must cross most of the Rockies before the snows and ice or face certain starvation.

———

Nazaire and Raoul entered the Bank of British North America and stood in line with stiff hands at their sides, staring straight ahead. A counterman beckoned them forward.

"We got gold to sell," Nazaire said.

"Assayer's Office," the counterman pointed to the corner staircase.

Down the stairwell, a young man stood behind a small counter with a few posters hanging opposite him on the wall, with one certificate that read 'Steven Blondine, Assayer General for the Bank of British North America' in elaborate script.

Nazaire surveyed the tight office space, scanned every box, the scales, a row of shiny weights peeking from an open drawer underneath. A metallic pinch hung heavy in the cramped space from bottles of quicksilver and other washes set off to the side and used to clean gold. A classifier stood on a stand, its mesh screens ready to separate dust and sparkle from small nuggets.

"We got dust to sell," Nazaire said as he pulled thirteen tins and two glass bottles from his worn rucksack.

The assayer placed a telegram in front of him.

"Today's gold is valued at $12.90 per hundredweight. The Assayer's Office takes 2% as a fee for the bank, as stated on the poster behind you."

He took a curved scoop and placed it in the cradle of the scale and reset the bar above as he poured Nazaire's gold into the scoop, a few tins at a time.

"You've no nuggets but lots of sparkle," the assayer said.

He grabbed a fresh receipt and wrote out some numbers. The assayer didn't speak the value out loud. Instead, he pointed to the dollar amount written on the receipt.

"This is what your gold's valued at today."

With big eyes, Nazaire turned and looked at Raoul, his mouth gaping wide. The assayer opened a drawer and counted out Nazaire's cash, a huge payout. Raoul stepped up to the counter next. Deep in his rucksack, he held back two gold nuggets wrapped in ermine intestines. They were not for sale but promised, the larger was for himself and the smaller for his spouse, Lucia.

The assayer repeated the steps, writing out a receipt to trade Raoul's few vials of dust for crisp dollars. Raoul smiled as he pushed the cash in his pocket along with his YPMC earnings that he had collected from Weasel the day before. The brothers smiled, and their faces colored pink. This was the moment Nazaire had dreamed of since leaving home. He and Raoul would return, both victorious and gleaming. Nazaire turned back toward the counter.

"We read in the papers many banks fail. How do we protect our money?"

"Upstairs, the bank could give you a check."

"No, not everything on one piece of paper."

In their mud-caked boots, worn mackinaws soiled and patched at the elbows and under the arms, Raoul and Nazaire were a sight.

The assayer lowered his voice. "You've nine thousand dollars. Change some of your cash upstairs to larger denominations, so it's less bulk to carry. Buy fresh balbriggans; you only need the bottoms. See Mrs. Blondine at number twelve Third Street. She'll sew hidden pockets in them so's they hide the bulk of your cash. She's discreet."

The brothers whispered together for a moment.

"Don't have her sew up all your money. You'll need some for transport and food until you get home."

"Wait," blurted Raoul. "She keeps secrets, this Mrs. Blondine? Not talk about what she sees?"

"Yes."

They climbed the stairs, leaving the assayer with a slight grin below his pencil mustache.

Out on the street, Nazaire turned to Raoul and hugged him. "We did good to come here, we did damn good."

———

After buying cut tobacco, Nazaire and Raoul
stopped at the Dawson Bath where they caught soap,
a rich dark brown made from bear fat that left a
greasy coating on their skin. Later, they rendezvoused
with Sam who had arranged an escort to ride with
them to Whitehorse. This arrangement saved them
three days' travel plus their reward money.

"Sam, how did you make this happen?" Nazaire
asked.

"White men call 'moccasin news.' My words go by
horse, and then with runner. Words come back quick-
quick by water."

The three men shook hands and parted. Nazaire
would never see Sam again. He thought of Coppaway
and his easy ways, his words had been few, but his
actions generous. Sam shared the same qualities in a
style perhaps more subtle but no less gracious.

Nazaire glowed euphoric at thoughts of returning
home with such a fortune. Now he and Raoul must
make good time. They had been away two and a half
years, too long to be separated from what both men

loved and cherished. After an overnight in Whitehorse, a party of five mounties and two Tlingits would escort them more than two hundred fifty miles southeast to Watson Lake.

With no spring and fall in the Yukon, summer would turn to winter like the flip of an electric light switch. All Nazaire's hopes and dreams hinged upon the weather. If Watson Lake was already icing up, would the mounties have any other choice but to turn back?

Watson Lake

The Yukon ❧ September 8, 1909

Eleven hours of daylight made for hard riding with the mounties as the Tlingit guides headed for Watson Lake.

The small trading village was not what Nazaire remembered. Instead it was a lonely place with a few dozen Kaska Dena living in bark huts. They carved ice sculptures with half faces of eagles or masks of monster warriors, totems of the Kaska Dena. The sculptures cast an ominous cloud over Nazaire's mind while the horse-riding wrenched stamina from his body as he longed for darker days with less sun. The party had little sleep, but these mild inconveniences didn't faze their escorts, only Nazaire and Raoul. Caribou meat in rich gravy and late-summer onions were a bonus shared over evening fires.

Fresh orders took the mounties northeast, out of the subarctic dip that was Watson Lake. Nazaire and Raoul were now left with the Tlingits, some two hundred fifty miles from their home. The Tlingits wanted to turn back.

The head Tlingit proposed a plan. "Mounties gone. Now you go with Kaska Dena at Liard. They take you to far side territory. Many sleds. Much climb. They have little food. No eat much or they be angry."

With the promise of two fresh bull moose come summer, they were passed to a party of southbound Kaska Dena near the Liard River. Tlingit territory teemed with moose each spring and the Kaska Dena found the promise irresistible. This exchange would meet the Tlingits' obligation to Sam Smith and the Kaska Dena.

The small party of Kaska Dena were handsome men with iodine skin who thrived in the wild north of the lower Yukon. After years in hiding, they remained suspicious and belligerent with all strangers, especially whites. Critical to their way of life was protecting dwindling resources and camouflaged gorges. They harangued Nazaire and

Raoul every day, no doubt aiming to keep their suspicious guests off guard.

These skilled hunters survived on little more than wolf, grouse, and arctic hare. Nazaire thought that even in their isolated territory, the Kaska Dena were being trespassed upon each year. The same thing was happening to the Hån of Moosehide and in some measure, to the Quebecers back home. Why did the government and the church meddle in peoples' lives?

The Kaska Dena played games at night, and sang songs. At one camp, someone poured warmed bear grease onto a stick while two Kaska Dena struggled to grasp it. Sometimes they would gamble all night by hiding small rocks in their closed hands and snapping their fingers as their wrists shook in odd patterns.

Nazaire turned to Raoul. "See how they enjoy themselves?"

Hearing laughter in such a coarse setting was a jolt. Intolerant of anyone different, Raoul remained fearful for his life and possessions as a barrage of angry words continued from their hosts. One night,

Raoul grabbed his ermine intestines and swallowed it. For the next three days, Nazaire tried to distract the Kaska Dena while they laughed at Raoul intent on examining his droppings.

"No one wants to steal from you. Relax." Nazaire said.

The Kaska Dena continued to curse Nazaire and Raoul as the party tobogganed through hidden passes and skirted the spines of mountain tops. Dahl sheep hid among the rocks. After Nazaire pointed them out, two hunters left the group and returned that night with fresh mutton. Nazaire enjoyed a fuller plate of meat that night for his help.

The Dreamers

The Rockies ❧ October 12, 1909

Nine Dane-zaa Indians appeared one morning in front of the Kaska Dena camp, looking askance at the two white faces sitting by the camp fire. The Dane-zaa were a small hunting party patrolling the western edge of their territory. Beaver mittens and fur cloaks covered the Dane-zaa's braided hair which they wore greased to a shine. Beads and shells decorated their tunics. This encounter was exactly what the Kaska Dena had hoped for; it was a chance to negotiate transport for Nazaire and Raoul over the remaining distance across the Rockies.

The Dane-zaa, better known as the Dreamers, would expect a high price, and the Kaska Dena would pay it. If a few young Kaska Dena men left their female-poor territory, took a Dreamer bride and lived among them, the Dreamers would welcome the infusion of new blood into their band.

447

The three Kaska Dena who agreed expected any union to include accepting his bride's moiety. By their giving up their Kaska Dena spirit allegiance to adopt their bride's, the Dreamers would accept the new grooms as committed members of their new band.

Both parties reached an agreement that would come to pass at the coming spring gathering. The head Kaska Dena faced Nazaire and Raoul.

"They take you Edmon," he said as they turned to leave.

———

Nazaire and Raoul were passed to the Dreamers, running each day among dangerous muskegs and through icy forests. The Dreamers covered their faces in bear grease against the harsh cold and smeared it on the two white men. Most of the Dreamers wore fur hats that kept their braids in place. Heavy bison robes covered their shoulders, and they wore caribou-skin tunics, leggings and trousers. Each night they built rigid pole huts with brush cover, packing the poles up each morning. The sunlight dimmed, visible eight hours a day now as the group traveled through a cloak of gray.

Each white face was assigned an escort. Nazaire's escort had a black tattoo that all but covered his face and made him all the more menacing, and he blindfolded Nazaire each day with heavy bindings. An older Dreamer did the same to Raoul. The bindings remained until the days' travel had ended, and the sounds of making camp rose around them. Resistance was of no use. Nazaire once pulled his blindfold off and was struck in the mouth. Both men became resigned to this strange treatment. They lowered their voices to whispers so as not to gain attention. Nazaire reached for an arm for support but was struck behind the knees for the attempt. The Dreamers were a fierce people, intent on giving away no secrets.

While they climbed steep mountains, Dreamers pushed the white faces ahead, often grabbing them by the arm or shoving them in the shoulder. Nazaire and Raoul fell often until they became accustomed to the daily ritual. When the Dreamers made camp at night, the bindings came off and angry words started. Nazaire and Raoul tried to be useful by clearing the forest floor to build their brush huts for the night.

A boy about eight years old walked among the campfires each night. He carried a lined pouch across his chest. One Dreamer filled the pouch with fresh meat which the boy offered at each campfire. He wore a combination trouser and boot suit that kept out the snow. This duty, providing meat at the fires, was an honor given him after his parents died of the pox.

Nazaire remembered hearing of these traditions. The boy would learn what it was to be a man while being taught by dozens of uncles. Once the bindings were removed, if Nazaire and Raoul scanned their surroundings, the young boy hit them with sticks across their backs. Nazaire's stomach turned rock hard while Raoul jumped at any sound near him. The comforting heat of the sun shrunk to four hours a day, leaving Nazaire and Raoul miserable. If only they could get warm.

When the Dreamers bent tamarack branches into snowshoes, Nazaire and Raoul mimicked them. They traded all their cut tobacco for two dirty blankets made from Dahl sheep, a welcome replacement for their thin bedrolls. Every morning, Nazaire cringed each time the group broke camp, sure that the Dreamers might abandon them in the wilderness. Would they dare kill them? Raoul whimpered in their hut at night, while Nazaire slept curled up, holding his stomach in a protective stance.

At one encampment, the Dreamers switched from snowshoes to sled dogs. One night, the tattooed Dreamer pulled Nazaire and Raoul's gumboots off their feet. In their bewilderment and panic, Nazaire and Raoul dared not sleep. The next morning, the tattooed Dreamer walked past their hut and threw down beaver mukluks that reached their kneecaps. With warm feet, Nazaire and Raoul could better tolerate the cold. They were grateful but not a gleam of sentiment lay upon Nazaire's face.

The Dreamers made Nazaire and Raoul sleep
near the dogs. The constant growls confirmed their
own low status. They kept their gaze downward and
flinched when anyone walked nearby. Every night
among the Dreamers bred terror in Nazaire's mind as
he closed his eyes and wondered if he might be killed
in his sleep. He curled his shoulders inward as he
waited for the boy to swat his head. Why had Nazaire
agreed to this? Would the abuse end before each
brother became weakened from the lack of food and
sleep?

One morning Raoul reached out to stroke the lead
dog's head and the animal snapped, almost biting off
his fingers. The Dreamers laughed at him, but Raoul
noticed the lead dog's eyes. One was blue, and the
other gray. He saw something else.

"This dog has double eyelids," Raoul said.

Raoul tried to confirm his discovery through sign
language, but the Dreamers yelled at his efforts. The
young boy stiffened his back as he passed, spitting at
him with proud sneers. Some days, Nazaire lost all

patience and growled at the abuse, spitting and swearing at the tattooed Dreamer while Raoul curled into a ball, silent and shielding his eyes.

With unbound eyes, each white face was prodded to stand on the back runner of a sled with a Dreamer escort on the opposite runner with both men grasping the handrail. Each time they fell, they were dragged a few feet and slapped. The bindings would be re-tied, and the ride would resume again. Working the sled team was exhausting for the white faces. Their hands, stiff with cold, often slipped from the runner, slowing down the entire group. One evening, a Dreamer pulled Nazaire and Raoul's coarse leather gloves off their hands. In the morning, he gave them warm, beaver mittens that extended to their elbows.

Their arms ached from holding onto the sled rails, so they were sometimes pushed into the sleds to ride like dead cargo, curled up among the warm furs. The pair struggled to hide their fatigue, fearing the Dreamers might abandon them. The possibility gnawed at Nazaire's mind every day. The sun was visible three or four hours each day now.

One Dreamer fresh in camp grabbed Nazaire's kit and pulled everything apart, inspecting each item. His curiosity led him to put on Nazaire's shirt, then from his waistband, the Dreamer threw down a bone carving shaped like a wolf. Nazaire scrambled to repack his kit and hoped no one would notice the cash in his balbriggans.

Long weeks had passed and the days and nights grew colder. At their campfire, Nazaire rubbed his hands on his pant legs for hours while Raoul crossed and uncrossed his arms and legs. They whispered to each other with pinched lips. Nazaire woke during the night, cold and stiff. He walked out of the brush lodge and tried warming his legs by the fire when the head Dreamer approached him, a knife in his hands. Nazaire turned back to his hut, teeth chattering. The cold had become severe, biting his face and earlobes.

When the trail turned due east, Nazaire and Raoul mimicked the Dreamers as they scrambled for pieces of bark to make sun-blocking masks. The words of old man Connolly rang in Nazaire's head, 'Watch the Indians and do what they do.'

Two runners appeared in camp one night with fresh bear meat. The young boy slapped Nazaire and Raoul on their backs with switches as he cursed them, threw their meat to the dogs and gave them little kindling. The dogs supped better. Another night, two Dreamers pushed Raoul down. The tattooed Dreamer took Raoul's kit while the older one watched with interest.

"They want my gold," Raoul whispered to Nazaire, his face pale as he remained seated and silent.

The tattooed Dreamer unfurled Raoul's kit, laughing as he threw items to the ground. The ermine-intestine pouch tumbled into view with two frayed wool shirts. He grabbed Raoul's shirt, smelled it and then pushed it into the snow-covered ground with his foot. One sleeve landed near the camp fire and began to scorch at the cuff. He struck Raoul on the shoulder. Raoul stiffened and began to rise.

"Stay down," Nazaire said.

The tattooed Dreamer picked up Raoul's two pipes and examined them. The older Dreamer grabbed Raoul's old tuque, turning it in his hands, unable to work out its purpose. He stood in front of Raoul, snorting a dare.

Raoul's hands shook. He looked to Nazaire with imploring eyes. Nazaire had had it. He needed to do something about these attacks. If it was a mistake, at least Nazaire and Raoul would die with dignity. Nazaire took a deep breath, stood and pulled the hat from the older Dreamer's hands. Nazaire pivoted in front of the items on the ground, blocking off both Dreamers. Raoul retrieved his ermine-intestine pouch. The tattooed Dreamer and Nazaire faced each other with hard gazes that bore in upon the other. Nazaire stood his ground with his chest thrown out, but his lips quivering.

"Leave our things alone," Nazaire screamed with a ferrous shard in his voice. His hands shook from the cold.

The tattooed Dreamer pulled Raoul's pipes from his waistband and selected one to keep. He pulled out a small bone carving from his rawhide possibilities bag and threw it at Raoul's legs. With palms down, the tattooed Dreamer crossed his open hands, a gesture that sealed their trade complete.

That night, Raoul swallowed his ermine-intestine pouch again. Days later, one Dreamer caught Raoul examining his scat but said nothing. How could anyone explain why a white face would break apart his own feces? The days were long and hard. In the evenings, Nazaire rocked back and forth, clawing his hands with shaky laughter from his throat and his face ashen. He wondered if the Dreamers would accept money to abandon them. Would he and Raoul be better off if they did? Would they even understand what money was?

From Watson Lake to Edmonton was over a thousand miles. How far had they come? Nazaire had no idea, but one late afternoon, it hit him. At their fire that night, he faced Raoul and said, "The sun is brighter now and it stays in the sky longer each day."

"What's that mean?" Raoul asked.

"We're coming out of the Yukon, getting lower than the 60th Parallel, closer to civilization."

The next morning a burly Dreamer woke Nazaire and Raoul with angry insults. He threw their gumboots and thin gloves down. He pushed them to the ground and pulled the mukluks from their feet and grabbed the beaver gloves from their hands. The Dreamer removed the poles and brush cover that made up the hut roof, and packed them in his sled. With an angry huff, the burly Dreamer raised an arm and pointed to a distinct trail head then left.

"They've released us. Thank goodness," Nazaire said.

"Where the hell are we?"

"Damn if I know."

Nazaire and Raoul emerged at a small trapper village called Whitecourt on the banks of the Athabasca River. They were some one hundred miles north of Edmonton, as close as the Dreamers were wont to come to civilization.

They were out of the Rockies and alive to tell of it.

A NEW WORLD RUSHES BY

Edmonton

Alberta ❧ February 6, 1910

Both men looked haggard, with creased cheeks and worn work pants that hung from their thin frames.

They had each eaten two meals in the Sagitawah settlement before inquiring as to their whereabouts. A ride south in a trapper's wagon dropped them three days later into a world where people, horses and automobiles rushed by. Their relief at being among civilized men transcended spoken words.

———

Edmonton had grown into a new world, the likes of which they had never experienced. Automobiles were everywhere, whizzing by with little regard for people. Few horses shared the road with the autos. The pioneer town Nazaire remembered had grown up. New brick buildings lined many streets. Gone were the tents, replaced by handsome wooden houses and storefronts. They bought a newspaper and discovered the date — already February had begun. Nazaire puzzled it out.

"We'll never make it home in time by walking. We need to ride the train."

"OK. We use our reward and don't touch what we sweat for," Raoul said.

They stood inside the Grand Trunk Pacific station in Edmonton. They had enjoyed another large breakfast of eggs and Cheechako potatoes, the real stuff and not powder, but now were eager to buy tickets to the end of the Prairies, Winnipeg. They heard rumors of fires and worried over their cousin Julia Fraser and her family.

Nazaire asked a man sitting on a long bench, "Any fires in Red Deer?"

"Dunno. There's plenty come up from Montana and North Dakota. The Big Blowout the newspapers call it. Millions of acres burnt," one man said.

"Wonder if the trains could be delayed? I'm gonna ask," Nazaire said.

Nazaire and Raoul wandered across the terminal with its gleaming marble floors and polished spittoons.

"Do you see that? Women here in this big hall with men. They should be in the women's waiting room," Raoul said.

Nazaire looked around. Raoul was right, both men and women were mixed in the spacious hall with no separation of sexes.

"I suppose it's what some call progress."

They learned that Dawson newspapers had reported devastating blazes throughout the summer. Why hadn't December snows stopped the fires? Nazaire scuffed his feet across the polished floor, the bite of butcher's wax up his nose while he bought tickets.

There was a broadside against one wall. Nazaire read aloud.

"FREE-160-acre farmsteads. It's not the land that holds value, it's your blood upon it."

Raoul wore a neutral face as he regarded it.

His feelings had changed considerably since leaving Quebec. All across the Prairies, he had seen one broadside after another where the government first gave a hundred-sixty acres to immigrants for ten dollars. The next broadside Nazaire saw offered three-hundred-twenty acres for twenty dollars. A third broadside offered a hundred-sixty-acre homestead to any British citizen new to the country for free. Now this fourth broadside offered anyone free land — a one-hundred-sixty-acre homestead. So many emotions ratcheted inside Nazaire's body. It was glorious to be alive, grateful for a full belly and no longer resenting men with easy-got land or those more prosperous as he.

"I can't be fretting about a government if it's generous," Nazaire said.

He was headed home to his farmstead, eager to collect his children, with enough money to make right his family and his land against any debts. Nothing else mattered. Outside on the train platform, Nazaire and Raoul waited behind a collection of better dressed people. They didn't take to the notion of conductors leading second-class passengers to a separate entrance at the back of the train. Instead, Nazaire and Raoul boarded the front with first class.

As they walked from one car to another, passengers viewed them as uncouth and objectionable. Their dirty clothes raised noses when they entered the dining car and stood, inspecting paper doilies under dinner plates. At the kitchen, the dividing line between the classes, an attendant herded Nazaire and Raoul to their proper seats in second class. They sat on hard wooden benches that faced rows pressing upon each other as they thought back to what the rail line offered the privileged in first class.

———

Once the train left the station, Nazaire's shoulders slipped down, and he breathed a sigh. He stared at the date on the front page of a newspaper. "My birthday, we passed it. I turned thirty-six two months ago," he said.

Raoul extended a hand with curled fingers. "I'm twenty-five. That makes Gaudias twenty-six and Romeo twenty-seven," he said.

Nazaire remembered a Cheekanos telling how rail travel had changed, with excursion fares no longer attracting the idle rich, and colony cars with their sinks and stoves gone forever. A few passengers read about the conflagrations in the newspapers and asked hard questions, followed by loud discussions that brought womenfolk and children to a fearful quiver.

Nazaire opened a brochure that outlined the route to Winnipeg. His lips curled out as he struggled to understand the numbered columns and unfamiliar names. A young priest offered an outstretched hand.

"Trying to figure out where you'll get off?" The young priest asked.

"Winnipeg," Nazaire said.

The young priest circled a cipher next to Calgary-three.

"The railroad claims this train will arrive in Calgary in three days," the young priest said.

Tapping each fingertip against his thumbs, Nazaire worked out the stops ahead.

"We get to Winnipeg by maybe February eleven. If the weather is good, we can walk the rest," Nazaire said with a wink.

"How many miles we walk?" Raoul asked.

"Fifteen hundred. Little more, little less. We have the time, and feet don't cost us anything, right? We see what snow there is in Winnipeg."

Raoul nodded.

Nazaire continued to read his issue of the *Edmonton Capital*, its headline warning of the fires spreading across southern Alberta. The train was headed bang straight toward the inferno. With their money spent on fare all the way to Winnipeg, what could Nazaire do? Get off with Raoul at the next stop and travel on foot? Would these infernos slow them down? Nazaire's face burned, and his lips stretched tight as he folded his newspaper and slid it into his mackinaw pocket.

At dinnertime, the conductor entered the coach car and slapped his hands, rousting people like a farmer calling a gaggle of geese.

"Chow time, ladies and gents," he said with both arms flopping up and down as he packed everyone in tight on long benches in one cold car. The slop arrived, steam rising from large bowls while hands shot forward to grab buns — too few for those seated at the table. Everyone ate thin stews with small spoons and drank tea resembling stained water. Four men seated across from Nazaire and Raoul remained capped with their wool hats over flattened hair, greasy and smelling of charcoal. They were furnace workers who ate with fingers, their stained palms and dirty fingertips resembling black gloves.

Before light's out, Nazaire and Raoul walked to another car and looked over the second-class berths that cost an additional fifty cents a night. They found the berths awkward to maneuver, with scant space to stand and untie a man's boots. The clean slept next to the filthy in a single row of doubled-up narrow bunks. Women slept together with small children in a cot with a thin sheet giving privacy between bunks. Some men grinned at the break in propriety, but Nazaire and Raoul looked straight ahead and dared not risk embarrassment coloring their faces.

They decided to save money and sleep sitting up on the wooden benches. Facilities for every two cars were limited to one toilet, with a small basin used for a wash-up station, insufficient for the number of people.

That first night, Nazaire felt the bruises on his elbows. He figured that from Watson Lake, where the mounties left, to Edmonton had taken all of twenty-one weeks. He and Raoul had spent five weeks with the Kaska Dena, who shouted at them every day, and sixteen weeks with the Dreamers, who blindfolded and nearly starved them. Their clothes hung off their bodies, and each had the sharp look of a tramp.

Without the guides, alone and untested in so harsh a country, they would have perished. Frightened all those days and nights, Nazaire's mind had begun to slip in a queer manner. Even Raoul acted odd, muddling words and bobbing his chin to the ground when anyone came near.

Nazaire hated those men and their abuses. He understood why the Dreamers were desperate to accept an agreement with the Kaska Dena; they were a fierce people. Despite the rough handling, Nazaire smarted from the offenses he and his brother had endured.

He envied the Dreamers' evenings spent content by small fires, playing simple hand games. They carved wild animals from moose antlers while the northern lights flashed above. Theirs was a simple life with challenges that fought against their survival. Food, water, shelter — all the things that blurred what a good life was — these were what the Dreamers struggled for each day. He hated them for the rough treatment he and Raoul received, but in one edge of his mind, he could see their way of thinking. Those sixteen weeks with the Dreamers had turned something in him that would never be the same. He finally understood what it was to be an Injun.

Calgary

February 8, 1910

As the train pulled out of Calgary, Nazaire
spied a group of men in a large alleyway.
"Who are these men?" he asked aloud.

A cheeky woman said, "They're members of the
Salvation Army. See their gabardine uniforms and
white gloves? I love the pilot caps."

The musicians crowded into the small space,
trying not to bump into each other's trombones,
bugles, cornets, and top-heavy suzzaphones.

Calgary had become the largest horse distribution
center in the Prairies, with a series of switching
stations and corrals holding livestock ready to be
trained out. From open doors, Nazaire could see
warehouses and rail sheds brimming with tack and
animal feed.

At one switching station, a corral held Shire
horses looking like giants, wide-chested with thick

legs and tufted ankles. Their muzzles rocked up as they bolted in complete joy in the open corrals.

"I never seen so many horses," Nazaire said to Raoul.

A grin crossed Nazaire's face. Most were solid black, similar to the coats on Louis and Joe. A cow wrangler with leather chaps looked out his window.

"Those are Shires, 'bout eighteen or nineteen hands. Theys taller than Clydesdales and stockier, with shorter bodies. Those damn tails could cut a good cigarette in two for walking too close behind."

Further down the rails, a dog herded a flock of ewes in another corral. Beyond them, a team of Clydesdales had gathered, most liver chestnuts and roans. Their bodies were sleeker than Shires, stretching at the shoulders and standing sixteen to eighteen hands, with tight tails in fancy braids.

"Who would believe there's so many horses in one place?" Nazaire said.

He pointed to the hump yard they had walked by in 1907 in Alyth as they watched one car being

472

pushed over a hill into the downgrade where it would be set into cuts ready to join outbound trains. The Grand Trunk gained speed as it skimmed the outer boundary of the city where dozens of tepees spread across an open expanse. In the distance, two young Indian boys led a herd of what looked like a hundred untethered horses toward a slow stream.

"That's the Blackfoot Reserve," a man said.

Three days out of Calgary, Nazaire noticed a yardman flagging the train and a few thousand feet beyond, another yardman.

Nazaire nudged Raoul, "What's this about?"

The windows rattled as the brakes beneath the coach car squealed and hissed. Nazaire rushed to stand, and stepped across the aisle, brushing his head against the pressed metal ceiling. He placed two long arms against the high baggage rack and leaned toward the window. Raoul stood and did the same. The train slowed and its engine chuntered as a Signalman appeared near the tracks, sawing the air with signal colors. The train veered into a siding and forked right onto a spur, where it came to a labored stop. Passengers leaned toward the glass while a buzz of questions filled the car.

A conductor opened the forward coach car door. "Ladies and Gents, we'll move to the side so's another train can pass. It'll be a ten-minute delay."

He walked out the back door of the car, letting in a rush of frigid air.

"Probably a silkie is all," a grizzled old-timer said. He fidgeted on his bench while eyeballing the goings on outside.

Nazaire turned to him. "A silkie?"

"Silk train, out of Vancouver. Pushing the other trains off the main line on accounta the cargo theys carrying."

Surrounding passengers stopped talking and leaned an ear closer.

The old-timer continued. "Not supposed to say. Railroad don't like people finding out."

He let fly a wad of chaw that hit the edge of one wooden bench with a twang.

"Silkworms come into Vancouver Harbor di-rect from Hong Kong in Jay-pan to the rail yards. Thems gets loaded onto special heated cars. Under guard with orders shoot to kill anyone who delays the packing and training out. Each train worth mebbe five, six million dollars."

"Hong Kong is in China, not Japan," a well-dressed man said.

"Don't make no never mind," the old-timer said.

"Sounds like a story," a woman commented.

"No story, lady. Them silkies run from Vancouver to New York in 'bout thirty hours. Theys go without stopping except for putting on water an' food with fresh crews. Coal for the engine."

A cargo train barreled down the track parallel to the Grand Trunk Pacific, its engine roaring louder than Jehovah. The coach car swayed in the wake of displaced pressure as the faster train whizzed by like a herd of buffalo outracing an idle animal, rattling each window pane. It pulled fourteen cars.

Females jumped when the whistle from the cargo train blasted, the sound dissipating while a black plume from its chimney threw a smattering of inky spots on the windows. Some men had counted the cars and debated how powerful an engine must be used to haul the worms.

"That train don't stop for no stations?" Raoul asked.

"Cor-rect. It's gonna stop mebbe four times before it gets to New York. Mebbe change engine once or twice for a fresh one."

"We're on the wrong train," Raoul said.

"It don't take no passengers, only worms. Ain't that a hellofa thing?"

The coal stink of the cargo train found crevasses and cracks from which to abuse the uneasy passengers waiting on the spur.

"They shoot to kill, you say?" A young man asked.

"Yessum, theys do. You watch. Every time a silkie comes through a station, you'll see two riflemen come

476

outside of the Engineer's Walk an' two others stand on each side o' the caboose, leaning out far, watching for trouble, damned ready to shoot anybody who tries to board. Them worms must be real finicky."

The old-timer's eyes passed from one passenger to another, then back out his window.

"What do they do with those worms?" A young boy asked.

"Delicates, boy, fancy unmentionables. For women."

Nazaire felt the silence in the car built up like a pot ready to boil when a sudden jolt tossed everyone forward on their benches. The Grand Trunk Pacific pulled out of its siding and followed the Moose Jaw River across what looked like virgin land with thousands of acres of browned stubble shrub. The ten-minute delay had stretched to two hours.

"Damn, when are we gonna get going? We could almost make better time with our legs," Nazaire complained.

His thoughts turned to God and what he'd thought of while creating a world with the vastness of the Prairies. Their incomprehensible reach coursed through his mind. Here in a sweeping valley surrounded by towering mountains, the insignificant train chugged along passing miles of barbed wire and thousands of shorthorns — stocky white-faced cattle.

This land could make a man weep for want of it. Some little piece, maybe a pitiful hundred and sixty acres to start over would be enough to fill his heart. But not without his children. His mind turned to Thomas, his eldest son. How would he look now? Growing into his legs and getting tall like all his boy cousins? All the Poulin men were long in the bone. How he missed Thomas' gentle ways and helpful attitude, always by his side when the team returned to the barn at day's end, opening the stable doors, pushing the mare over to make room for Louis and Joe. Nazaire sighed and uncurled tight shoulders as he lay his head on the back of the hard bench.

"I'd feel better if we were on that silkie."

Moose Jaw

Saskatchewan ❧ February 11, 1910

Nazaire smelled soot and burned vegetation seeping inside the rail car for days after leaving Moose Jaw Station. Shriveled saplings outside Nazaire's window resembled gnarled fingers stretching to the sky, seeking mercy. Six Indians pulled out stakes, dismantling tepees and packing belongings into two carts by the side of the tracks.

"Sarcees gettin' out while they can," a young woman said, "moving toward the Saskatchewan River to the Athabaskan."

Narrow canyon walls pressed against the train as it labored, the engine belching while it fought steep climbs out of gorges choked with ash.

When the train slowed to a stop, the coach car door opened, and the conductor announced, "Ladies and Gents, we'd like volunteers, vigorous menfolk to lend a hand. We got us some trees on the tracks. Ten men ought to do it."

Nazaire and Raoul pressed against the glass, searching for what industry required volunteers. They glanced at each other and knew the answer before they stood.

"Mind your cash," Nazaire whispered to Raoul.

The stench of burn snaked up Nazaire's nostrils as soon as he set foot outside. The volunteers walked a few thousand feet in front of the engine where embers flickered in some of the trees. Railwaymen ran up from the caboose with shovels and tools while volunteers offered nervous hands ready to help.

The Yardmaster, his red badge visible on his hat, shouted instructions, moving one group of volunteers ahead where more trees lay across the tracks. Embers from black spruce popped, while a group of volunteers ran back and forth with buckets of water. Across the railroad ties, Nazaire spotted strangulated squirrels, their coats fluffy and untorched.

"The fire was damn fast. See the squirrels? They're not even burned," Nazaire said.

"Sonofabitch, that fast!?" Raoul said.

Nazaire coughed, anxiety reddening his face as he turned to see the pilot standing on the engineer's walk. It took picks and axes, straps and sometimes saws to remove larger trees. First-class men in their day jackets and felt hats stretched their necks outside their windows to watch volunteers sweat in the hazy air. Railwaymen located and doused tree trunks with live sparks inside. Everywhere pointsmen and engineers worked next to boilermen.

Section men with their blue denim caps patrolled the tracks from the back of the train followed by twenty soot-covered Chinese. A section man approached the Yardmaster.

"I found this lot by Pasqua. Can you imagine, still hiding in the caves, afraid the government will demand their Head Tax."

"Did you get them all out?" The Yardmaster asked.

481

"I believe so. I told them there's nothing to be afraid of, but they are, of course."

"Bring them over to the Mission. They'll sort them out there."

The Chinese huddled together, whispering and pointing to the burnt trees surrounding them.

Nazaire stopped and turned back to watch the group. "They're so small," he said, cringing at the lot.

"Who? Those children?" Raoul asked.

"Those aren't children, they're grown men. They look to be starving."

The Yardmaster sent two boys with rags and pails of water to walk along the tracks offering refreshment for eyes and faces streaked with sweat and lampblack. Smoke hovered above the tracks, creating apparitions of gray ghouls fighting to draw breath. Tree trunks had burned and tumbled down from the high ravine walls, dragging sediment and animal carcasses, some part fur and part char. A pair of eleven-point antlers pushed up under blacked brush, jaundiced with its rack in peeled layers. The stench coiled down the men's throats and a few vomited on the side of the tracks. Nazaire's mouth worked to catch saliva in the smoke-choked gorge.

"If we left last summer, we would'a walked into this," Nazaire whispered.

"And never lived," Raoul finished the thought.

The conductor gathered the volunteers in an empty storage car with a barrel of water jury-rigged above a drainage platform. Torn dish towels and bars of Peet's soap helped remove the stink of burn. The men were treated to a free meal during a special late-dinner seating, the thanks for volunteering. Five hours had passed before Nazaire and Raoul returned to their car and reassured the passengers everyone was safe.

The next afternoon, someone read from an article in the *Edmonton Capital,* 'The fires started in Idaho's great western white pine forests, whose trees held large amounts of resinous sap that boiled out and formed a cloud of explosive gas. With their great numbers, trees exploded and pushed flaming tongues in the air for thousands of feet. Waves of rolling fires burned west into Montana and Washington, with winds that pushed the inferno north across southern Alberta.'

Everyone stiffened on their benches and many of the women wore frightened faces. As the train moved ahead, anxious eyes watched out the glass. Menfolk gentled their women and children with calm voices. Thoughts of home built up in Nazaire's head and throbbed in his throat like a frog in full swell, watering his eyes. Sonofabitch, what else would delay the train?

Regina

February 13, 1910

T he coach car bustled with activity as Raoul put on his boots and stretched in the aisle. Nazaire joined him.

"Where we stop next?" Raoul asked Nazaire.

"Regina."

"How many delays we gonna have?" Raoul whispered as he sat down, and pressed his nose to the glass.

Collapsed grain elevators and charred pastures appeared in the windows. Black acres were level against the curve of the land with not a hollow hidden, every bump and mound exposed with blue gray dust swirling in a frantic dance. Silent hours dragged with catarrh burning in Raoul's mouth, the phlegm sticking against his throat, refusing to rise.

Would there be more fires ahead? It was hard enough to sleep sitting up on the wooden benches than to worry about night-time fires. Raoul felt the bruises on his shoulders from the motion of the train.

"Morning gents," the young priest said when he entered the car.

"Where'd he go last night?" Raoul whispered.

"He rented a berth. Wouldn't think a priest could pay extra to sleep," Nazaire said in a low voice.

Raoul cocked his head. Something had changed outside the window. Gone were the clickety-clacks, those throbbing, flat sounds replaced by a light hum echoing with vibrations no longer pushed into the ground but released through the air. The children were the first to jump to the windows and squeal.

The train slowed to a crawl as Raoul struggled to open his window and pushed his head outside. His knuckles gripped the armrest and turned white. The train was on a trestle, one long curl. Hundreds of feet below, a contradictory sight revealed itself. The entire valley floor was black with charred trunks, victims of the Big Blowout. The inferno had moved from the summit down into the basin and traveled through coulees and troughs before it swung further west.

"Look, the fire follows us," Raoul said.

Nazaire switched places with Raoul and peered out the window.

"It's behind us. Everything to the east is untouched. See the snow? It's covering green trees, not dead trunks."

Raoul switched places and again pushed his head outside. Nazaire was right; the fires had traveled west but to the east, mountains were mottled green with light snow cover. Low clouds looked to be no more than wisps of ghosts.

The sounds of the tracks changed again as the train moved onto solid ground. Raoul sighed and shook out his stiff legs. He stretched his sore back from cramped quarters. Some children cried with impatience, their feet stomping on the dirty floor. When the conductor entered the coach car, Raoul asked.

"Can I walk to another car? My legs are so tight."

"No, just stand and stretch. We're just two days from the next stop."

Passengers heard the question and began complaining in angry voices. The requests to disembark and stretch continued for many hours until all the passengers were allowed to exit and stretch at the next stop. Men shook out arms and cramped shoulders. Some people removed shoes and socks to feel the icy ground and push light snow between their swollen toes.

The passengers returned to their seats in reluctant agony. Hooligans had pilfered an old man's knapsack during the stop. The news of the theft traveled when the old man called for a conductor and shook an angry fist in the air. The young priest tried to comfort the old man, but with no success. Passengers in the car searched their belongings for possible missing items while the old man sat with tears filling his eyes as he clutched his dirty cap.

"Let's sleep with our boots hanging on our necks, tied together," Raoul said.

"Ya, and maybe we hug our rucksacks during the night," Nazaire suggested.

Raoul unbuttoned his shirt and sucked in his stomach to check the cloth pockets that the seamstress in Dawson had sewn in his balbriggans.

"Don't do that. You call attention to yourself," Nazaire whispered. He pivoted in his seat, trying to hide Raoul's actions.

Hooligans, usually in pairs, shifted from one car to another, seeking a game of Faro and hoping to clean up every spare penny. One brought a filthy can of burnt matchsticks with him, their sulfur heads chewed off in boredom.

That night, the land swallowed a moon so wide it scarce fit across two windows, its reach blinding as if an explosion were burning Raoul's vision, maybe erasing memories.

Outside Regina, cars were added ahead of the caboose and created a sluggish drag. The engine screamed with strain when the train pulled out in a swirl of snow like a cocooned moth emerging black and glistening gray. Nevertheless, the press of the glass continued to mesmerize Raoul.

"Look, wolves," he said.

Children crowded to his small square of glass. The engine lurched on as it charged into deep tunnels where roots and rocks scratched the outer walls of the cars until the Grand Trunk Pacific spewed out into a bright, blue sky.

"Look, the caboose," Raoul said while a few children pushed toward him to discover the last car at the rear of another long curve.

Dead end canyons gave Raoul wonder as to which mountain pass would swallow the train next. Rail tracks off in the distance resembled the scratchings of crows' feet in new snow.

"Look, Indians," Raoul said as he watched poorly dressed Indians stand by a few rag shacks on uneven ground, their doorways littered with empty tins and bottles. The train stopped at one-room stations and sometimes discharged exhausted staff as they brought in a fresh crew. Station workers replaced wood, water, and foodstuffs that served both classes.

Raoul amused the children by pointing out the next stop listed on Nazaire's fold-out brochure and laughed as they grew excited over approaching destinations. The conductor came into the car carrying the missing boots in his hands. Passengers applauded and smiled in approval once the old man and his boots were reunited.

A man with a crutch picked up discarded newspapers from the kitchen crew and read aloud. Every page asked for help in large headlines: help to haul water, bury the dead, fix telegraph wires. The world, it seemed, was desperate for help after the latest flareups destroyed towns from Calgary to Regina.

Raoul let out a deep breath on learning that the fires were behind them. Damn if anything got in his way now. Whatever lay ahead, he'd fight with everything he had to get back home. He missed his spouse and wanted to hold his daughter and son.

491

Raoul thought of his father, Varis, and wondered how he was holding up. What would he find when he got home? Would his children remember him? Had his absence pitted his father against impossible hardships managing the dairy farm? Forty cows were a lot of work for two neighbor farm hands and the sixty-eight-year-old Varis.

Raoul thought back to what Varis had said when he and Nazaire left. Wasn't it the same thing that all fathers said when their sons went off on promenade or to some job far from home?

"You best come back with your brother," Varis had said to one son, and then the other.

Like dutiful sons, both had promised 'yes' to Varis.

Every day that passed brought Raoul closer to home and this alone was cause to smile. How Raoul passed idle days with ease and laughed at a toddler across from him. Sometimes he picked the boy up to give the mother a few moments' rest. Raoul sat like a bear, allowing the little cub to climb him and find pockets for his paws in Raoul's ears. The giant laughed while tiny hands painted horses and Indians on the window until one gray morning, under three feet of fresh snow, Winnipeg presented herself.

Winnipeg

Manitoba ❧ February 20,1910

Nazaire woke during the night on the hard seat of another Grand Trunk Railway train, this one headed for Toronto.

From Edmonton to Winnipeg and out of the Prairies had taken all of two weeks. Yes, he would be home in plenty of time. Perhaps he and Raoul should walk the rest of the way from Toronto. They would be close, maybe less than a hundred miles. It made sense; walking cost you nothing.

When would he sleep again lying down? He made his way to the water closet and shut the door. The sounds of feet scuffling caught his attention.

"What — sonofabitch," Raoul yelled.

Nazaire heard the commotion and recognized Raoul's voice. What could be happening? Nazaire raised the bent horseshoe nail that served as a latch, and pushed against the commode door. It felt blocked from the outside. Someone was pushing against it. Nazaire heard the faint intake of air. He gave the door a shove and caught a glimpse of two men who disappeared toward the rear of the car into darkness.

A wrangler stood in front of Raoul with a blade in his hand that flashed against the moonlight coming through the windows. The wrangler was short but his heeled boots gave him more height and an advantage. Nazaire remembered him by the indigo kerchief around his neck. Nazaire made out the silver tip of his knife as it pivoted to the side. The wrangler cut Raoul's top trouser button and tugged on his balbriggans.

"Sonofabitch," Raoul screamed.

Raoul's trouser opened to reveal packets of cash peeking out at his waist. The wrangler faced Raoul, still in a stupor from sleep. Could Nazaire get the knife? He sized up the situation in seconds, and seized the wrangler's hand from behind. The coach car door opened and a beam of light brightened the interior. The conductor entered with a small lantern.

Behind him, Nazaire felt hands at his shoulders, ready to grab his arms.

The wrangler cut the air in an arc and a two-inch smear of blood appeared on Raoul's chest. Raoul gasped as he pushed the wrangler away. He rose from the bench, towering over the short thief. Behind Raoul, the conductor turned his lantern to full brightness and blew his whistle. Nazaire struggled to gain the knife and give Raoul free space.

Raoul clenched his hand to land a punch when the wrangler yanked at one of the cash pockets. Raoul's fist connected with the wrangler's face. The wrangler spun in a half circle and fell to the floor. The conductor rushed the wrangler, holding his arms from behind. The knife flew under several wooden seats and men scuffled between Nazaire's legs in the dark to possess it.

"Pass the blade forward, or I'll throw the lot of ya off," the conductor threatened.

With reluctance, a hand came forward with the knife. How many men had intended to benefit was unclear, but most seemed awake. They were quick to point a finger at the wrangler, red-faced and standing alone with a bloodied nose and chin, one streak reaching the bottom of his dirty chaps. The indigo kerchief remained on the floor. Raoul clutched at his chest with one hand, grasping his kit with the other. He struggled to gain breath. A second conductor opened the rear coach car door.

Nazaire stepped up to him. "We need safe passage. There's none for us here."

"You sonofabitch," Raoul said to the wrangler as he winced at the blood on his undershirt.

"Everyone back to your seats," the second conductor said, then turned to Nazaire and Raoul, "You two come with me."

———

He led Nazaire and Raoul to the sleeper berths in the first-class section. A medic sought Raoul out and tended his cut with Mercurochrome and bandages.

"Your yellowed night shirt gave you away. The cut's shallow. Try not to get the bandages wet when you wash," the medic said.

In the first-class berths, soft sheets hinted of rosewater and cradled the brothers' shoulders while thick pallets almost long enough for their legs wrapped them in delicious comfort. What a joy to sleep flat, their bones against the thick mattress.

The next morning, Raoul caught sight of the wrangler and two men outside the train. They were in the back of a buckboard with their hands shackled and heads held low in shame. A sheriff drove the buckboard away from the small railroad station.

The supervising conductor approached Nazaire and Raoul. "The Grand Trunk Railway expresses its apologies and hopes you can forget this unfortunate experience. Feel free to enter the dining car after lunch hours to enjoy complimentary tobacco and teas. Take meals in the coach car behind you with the women and children. Otherwise, meals in the dining car are a la carte."

498

Although the chefs prepared plates of speckled rainbow trout and other delicacies, Nazaire and Raoul ate with the women and children. They didn't trust the word 'a la carte' and wouldn't entertain any reason to spend more cash. Their second-class ticket included meals in the slops' car.

In the smoking car that first afternoon gentlemen passed, tipping their fur hats while ladies gave shy smiles. Nazaire and Raoul were heroes, but unaware of their status. They sat stiff and cautious, relishing uncreased, clean newspapers and coveting small tins of complimentary pipe tobacco.

The pair sat in cushioned comfort with ample room for long legs and without elbows digging at their sides. They watched elegant ladies take afternoon tea with biscuits and once joined the gentlemen who drank ale in posh stuffed chairs in the men's Smoking Salon.

From their windows, they watched a train run parallel to theirs with a bright red snow plow in front of a single engine. The plow blocked the pilot's view

with its towering height and girth as split scoops
hurled ice in twin violent arcs, shattering in a shower
of diamonds at each side of the tracks. Every snow
plow that fronted a train engine frightened Nazaire.
Could some odd event or an act of God cause another
delay? What else in God's name could hold them up?

A few curious men invited Nazaire and Raoul to
brandies one evening and asked after the goings on
that brought them to their part of the train.

"What do you think of first class?" A bearded
gentleman asked.

"It's the second class that railway barons are in
love with now," a wiry gentleman said.

"How so?" Nazaire asked.

"Travel, my boy. It marks a man or woman as
cosmopolitan and a person of substance."

"Why is that?" Raoul asked.

"It's not just the rich that travel. Now the poor
move about as well. The riff-raff are spending money
and they've captured the hearts of the railroad

owners," the wiry man said with a wink. The
conversation sat awkward, so Nazaire and Raoul left.

During their remaining time in first class, they
enjoyed nights of easy sleeping in framed, wooden
berths that were spread lengthwise across both sides
of the sleeper coach cars. Rich drapery provided
privacy for every upper and lower berth. The Men's
Emporium proved a welcome improvement, with its
closeted toilets in private alcoves, each with fresh
towels, a large wash basin and pitcher. Even the
wooden seats gleamed with oil. Samples of Bay Rum
and scented soaps completed the aura of these
splendors, not lost to simple folk like Nazaire and
Raoul.

In their berths, Nazaire and Raoul would lean out
toward each other over the aisle and speak of
theirtime with Sherman and all the haggard men that
walked into camp, smelling the cooked food, and how
Sherman and Lennox led them out.

"Sorry, we're provisioned to feed our party of
paying men. There's none extra," Sherman would say

with one hand on his pistol grip. They wondered about the tent cities they had walked by, a few smelling foul and one with an open flap, the inside a shambles with two children dead on the dirt floor, bloated with the pox.

Under his sheets, Nazaire could no longer remember Victoria's face. His mind held one vague image, that of her holding and hugging his children. Victoria had managed the children, but now that she was gone, so was that connection. Nazaire needed to devise something for the children. How often did she coddle them? Every morning, it seemed. And at bedtime too. Menfolk might consider him soft, but maybe he should continue Victoria's gentle ways. In the morning, they left the train.

FOOT TRAVEL

Toronto

Ontario ❧ February 27, 1910

Two feet on solid ground felt wonderful to Nazaire after the last week of travel that brought him from Winnipeg to Toronto.

The city was filled with brick buildings and wood shanties that pushed against one another as stores lined busy streets and workers crowded sidewalks and roads, all fighting for space.

It took the remainder of the day to escape Cabbagetown, with its lilting Irish brogue, and reach the outskirts of the city proper as it fell away to fields of thinned black birches, revealing a vaulted sky. Nazaire and Raoul filled their chests with clean, fresh air as Lake Ontario stretched before them to the horizon.

They followed the rail tracks east and tucked in at night in one shantytown after another. One morning a roaring noise awakened them. Thousands of birds flocked above: gulls and ducks, herons and jays, nuthatches and red-tailed hawks, every kind of bird a man might know. At the back of the armada, a pair of swans took up the rear guard.

Nazaire thought of Victoria, and with such a welcoming omen, he couldn't keep his eyes on the road.

A passing hobo commented. "Thems going to the Oshawa Marshlands north of here to court other birdies with head bobs and dancing that don't stop. It's a wonder a man can sleep with all the noise coming from the swamps."

They passed watermen in rubber pants as they dug for scallops and clams along the shoreline with the sharp cut of ammonia drifting onto the road. Watermen stood with bent backs and swept claw tools across the mud like the strikes of a metronome. Briny scallop and oyster shells painted the shoreline a mottled gray while on the water, oystermen raised twin tongs to push their boggy catch into the net dredges floating behind their small boats.

Each day, Nazaire perked up with talk of what he must do. He needed to use the extra days before planting to accomplish all manner of chores.

"I need to go to the village and buy food, flour and salt for the cupboard, fresh churned butter and maybe a jar of store-bought jam. I should get the farrier to put new shoes on all my horses and rasp their teeth. Maybe buy a young sow to fatten until winter. I gotta chop firewood to warm the house, clean out the barns, mix feed for the animals, make sure that all the water barrels are full."

He couldn't contain the excitement coursing through his body. He had been taught not to sell the skin before you've killed the bear, but his happiness was too great. After all, what was it to be a man — to protect what is yours — and when required, to be a stone, cold and unyielding, to push away the frivolities of childhood and take up the burdens of manhood.

Nazaire's entire life was his homestead, his family, his extended family. Not one touched by wanderlust, he had always stayed close to home. Never had he ventured so far away, and never for so long. All the worries that swirled in his head he could now count as banished with home only two or three days' away. Every waking hour brought more chores to the forefront of his mind, plans he had pushed away until now. But he needed this burst of happiness, this carefree time to pierce the air with his hopes and dreams.

"I gotta get cleaned up, maybe even buy a new shirt and dungarees before gathering my children. Gotta buy seed for planting, and settle my debts with the regional government, square things with our father, then with Victoria's family."

Nazaire paused and touched Raoul on the shoulder. "I did it. I dared to believe in me. I didn't see it at first, but now I'm grateful Victoria's family took my children. You were right, Raoul, I need to find myself another spouse. It's the only way I'll get my children back."

Tears of satisfaction welled in Nazaire's eyes. A huge smile crossed his face. At night, Nazaire cried in his bedroll. He cried at the thought of seeing his children again, laughing with them, examining their faces while he searched for a hint of Victoria, her easy laugh and bright eyes. All would be restored to him now. He imagined brushing Louis and Joe again, rubbing behind their jaws. He woke refreshed and happy.

A sign at Kingston alerted them that they were halfway between Toronto and Montreal when a rising fog blanketed the road. Nazaire and Raoul could scarce see from their knees down and fell into walking Indian file.

"Aghhh. Stop Raoul," Nazaire yelled. "Don't fall on me."

Raoul's legs stuck fast. One second Nazaire had been in front of him, and the next he was gone.

"Where'd you go?" Raoul asked.

"The side of the road gave way. I'm in a gully to the right. Aghhh."

"Stay put. I'll get you out."

Nazaire yelled in pain. Raoul knelt down and felt the road with his hands, sweeping wide arcs with his fingers until his thumb caught the edge of a hole, and with both hands he reached out to learn the size and direction of the cavity.

"I'm in sand and mud. My leg's hurt bad."

Raoul leaned over and stretched a shoulder over the black hole, grasping at anything he could. As the fog dissolved enough for Raoul to see the road, he flagged down a truck driver's help.

———

Raoul and the truck driver pulled Nazaire from the decayed ditch and drove to the nearest medical clinic, no more than a one-room affair used more for storing ointments and crutches. The clinic was managed by an apprentice doctor who made house calls in surrounding towns.

When Raoul had dosed Nazaire with enough whiskey, the doctor cut one leg of the balbriggans from ankle to kneecap, applied black ointments to draw the inflammation from the leg and wrapped it in waxed paper. Nazaire screamed at the doctor's slightest touch as he covered his right leg with a cotton splint.

"You've got a broken fibula. You'll not be walking for eight weeks," the doctor said.

Beads of sweat formed on Nazaire's forehead. He looked at Raoul, unsure what to say. The doctor turned to Raoul, "The ambulance can take him to the hospital in Toronto or Montreal. Or I can treat him at a widow's cottage in the next village where I send many of my patients."

"Can't I take him home by train? It's not more than a hundred miles?" Raoul asked.

"Move him now," said the doctor, "and he'll be a cripple for life."

———

In the widow's cottage, Raoul settled Nazaire in his bedroom, helping him out of his cash-laden balbriggans. Raoul removed his as well, replacing them with his old, worn underwear. They removed what cash each might need before Raoul repacked their rucksacks with both balbriggans wrapped in a core surrounded by more layers of clothing.

Raoul secured the bundles by cordage in a manner to best announce mischief; all their earnings were in those two bundles. Just shy of three years of sweat and sore muscles, their hopes for a brighter future.

Raoul bit his bottom lip, then looked at Nazaire.

"OK, I stay close by and get a job. When we leave for home, we leave the both of us."

Quinte West

March 2, 1910

The sunlight forced Raoul to cover his eyes, and as his vision adjusted, sheets of gauze covered trees. Arbors and shrubs emerged around him as acres of apple trees filled his view.

"Told you you'd smell it before you see it. Quinte West, they call it. Biggest fruit station in Ontario," a stocky man said. "I worked here before. Come June there'll be two thousand pickers in the steam rooms making jams and jellies, crating them up in the rail cars."

Raoul stood next to the stocky man. A foreman on horseback approached them, his leather work belt the sign of his position. Out on the road, the Quinte West Fruit Station sign hung from the main cabin wall, six miles east of the widow's cottage.

The foreman's horse turned to face the men.

"I remember you," the foreman said to the stocky man. He looked at Raoul. "Experience?"

"Blueberries, low and high bush, apples, and tapping maple trees," Raoul said.

The scent of turned soil filled the air. The land rose, and people came into view while their voices carried like warblers' cries in a dying wind. Beyond the fruit trees, white pines edged the property. The voices grew louder as Raoul followed the foreman down a cart trail to a double-wide row with a railroad spur cutting north. Men and women worked, bent over, but most stood in the rows. Every few feet wooden boxes filled with tools, poles and cordage sat in the center of each row. The women wore cotton mesh hats with a brim while the men had wound strips of white cloth around their heads.

Quinte West grew large varieties of peaches and pears, prunes and cherries, but the specialty of this experimental station was strawberries, raspberries and apples — in particular, apples that were grafted to strengthen their resistance to bugs.

On one side, a long warehouse buzzed with activity as women with hair pinned up looked like

angels while corner fans rotated high on the walls,
pulled heat up from barrel fires. Tiny wisps of hair
danced by the necks of the women and Raoul stood
mesmerized, succumbing to carnal thoughts. As the
weeks passed, these images haunted his nights in his
tent as he longed for his spouse, Lucia, so close He
wondered if he could take a night train home, and
return to Quinte West the next morning. Some men,
he had heard, did that.

Raoul worked with a team of three men, digging
holes and planting young trees. One boss, the bug
expert, took great pains to record everything about
each tree and shrub in his journal as the men seated
saplings straight and true. He tended rows of Trenton
apples, the Royal Duchesses, rose-smelling
Gravensteins, Seek-no-Furthers, Starks, the
Alexanders, Fameuse apples, and the King Greenings
as the station grew and recorded information on
every kind of apple tree known to Canada.

"That's the science part, recording everything in
journals. You wait 'til hot weather and watch the big

boss count bugs every third day. We even got salt experts tending the Quakenboss and Japanese plum trees," one worker said.

Raoul thought it strange to count bugs, but if the government wanted to know these things, then who was he to object?

"Come full season, the whole town of Quinte West works for the station. That's over four thousand, with all the pickers, grafters, arborists and the head supervisor. He's a soil expert. Edaphologist they call him, from London," the graft foreman explained.

Raoul developed a delicacy when grafting buds onto young trees. Who would think that a man with hands like bear paws could be so delicate? His foreman started to reserve Raoul's labor for Herculean projects that befitted those large hands and brute strength.

As a regular worker and not a 'seasonal picker,' Raoul enjoyed room and board plus whatever canned items he wanted from one of three long refectories. Shelves lined one wall filled with last years' jams and jellies, and every meal was a feast as men and women opened up one delicacy after another and passed it down long, bench tables. Along with hearty soups and hard-grain breads, Raoul ate his share of canned berries with exotic names on colorful paper labels.

In the men's quarters, Raoul slept in a canvas tent and enjoyed the luxury of a weekly cold shower. He worked in glorious sunshine as he moved crates or dug irrigation gutters, happy to be off the trains and on firm ground. The work was easy but didn't dampen his frustrations.

"Playing a hand or two tonight?" one worker asked Raoul.

Raoul nodded. The card games were held in one of the men's tents after supper. Many men played a penny hand — more to look at the naked ladies on the cards than for the camaraderie offered. Those nights taunted Raoul as he thought of the lovely angels working the rows of saplings each day. Some young ladies didn't even wear stockings or pantaloons, and their hitched skirts offered a good look-see. Ivory ankles and long legs fell into languid curves up to their thighs. This was the most troublesome part of the job.

At the canning stations. angels cinched their long white skirts to their belts, preparing for a season-long production line. Tables fronted the fires, each one identified with the fruit to be canned. Ladles remained at the ready with boxes of paper labels, a paint brush and bottles of glue at one end. Behind the canning stations, crates of tin cans rested against the walls and hand carts waited for the season to begin. More women would arrive and each, Raoul knew, would taunt him at night.

In the darkness under his blankets, he thought of that black hole on Sulphur Creek where he had sweated for months. The one truth he had learned while there was that although each man was responsible for himself, always Nazaire would be close by to help him in any manner necessary. Raoul missed his spouse with a fierceness new to him, and longed to have her in his arms, but he wouldn't

516

abandon Nazaire. He had no choice but to swallow his randiness another few weeks until Nazaire was mended. They'd left home together and dammit, they would return the same way.

Belleville Station

April 18, 1910

The car pulled up at 5 a.m. and Nazaire walked out of the widow's cottage with kits packed and his old work clothes hanging from his thin frame. He might be home by late afternoon. Nazaire stretched his long legs and arms in the back seat while in the front, Raoul squeezed his shoulders together.

While Raoul's friend drove, Nazaire asked questions.

"What kind of job did you find?"

"Chopping branches. They call it grafting. I worked with a lot of angels, the female kind," Raoul said with a glimmer in his eyes.

"You and your angels? What more?"

"I set up trellis supports, stretched out hoses and checked nozzles for water lines. Last week, I moved mattresses and blankets from a rail car into an open-air warehouse. Two thousand pickers will sleep there this summer."

Nazaire looked at the driver. "How far is the station?"

"Belleville — it's a few miles, but first he's got to collect his last pay," the driver said, nudging a chin toward Raoul.

The car turned down a dirt road, closed in on both sides by large hemlocks whose long branches reached across the road and held hands with their sisters, blocking out sunlight.

The excitement coursing through Nazaire's body couldn't be contained. The car stopped at the Quinte West sign. Raoul got out and headed for the foreman's office. Everything looked so bright. The sight of so luminous a horizon pulled at Nazaire, and he couldn't resist — he stepped from the car to look up in awe.

Rows of trees and shrubs were draped in white in every direction. The gauze-covered women, Raoul's pale angels in mesh hats and flowing skirts, seemed like a dream. There were angels everywhere, in every row, behind every wheelbarrow, their white gauge skirts moving like flashes of whitefish in water.

Nazaire's chest filled like a river bursting from its bed. Grateful sobs pierced the air and cut through the quiet morning, causing flight in hundreds of birds, singing birds and terns, gulls and egrets that crowded the tall border trees like sentinels. Everything around him glowed in new growth, young seedlings and exploding buds. Nazaire felt a sense of steadfast belonging.

He thought of the miles he had walked and the long days running in Indian file through the Rockies, and the gold he had wrenched from the ground. In Sulphur Creek, he had violently split rocks, rapaciously clawing in slush and mud. All his sweat and toil had led him to this sweetness, a moment of spectacular clarity. He would be home in less than a day. What could be more glorious to any man than this sense of belonging, his rightful place?

FAMILIAR FIELDS

Back to Big Mountain Row

Quebec ❧ April 18, 1910

Raoul slid off the back of the open wagon and stretched as Nazaire followed. They were in front of the old wayside cross recessed in the gully by Big Mountain Row. It had the same splintered, knee rest. The weathered oak cross remained perfectly straight. Raoul had passed here countless times and would return again to say a prayer of thanks, but not today.

Nazaire dropped his rucksack and turned toward the village, away from his farmhouse. Raoul knew that Nazaire hid his feelings deep inside, hidden like a stone under water; you reach for it, but it's always farther away. Raoul picked up Nazaire's rucksack and kit, then said, "When you're ready, come to Papa's for the evening meal."

———

A pulse of nerves spread through Raoul's large chest and up his shoulders. He smelled dirty and looked worn out as he walked across three farmsteads to his father's farmhouse. He could feel Lucia next to him, her soft curves and full buttocks. He lifted the latched door, the excitement of being here electric.

"I'm home," he announced with pride as his eyes swept across the kitchen.

He dropped the rucksacks and kits to the floor and breathed in a lingering curl of cinnamon above the wood-burning stove. The rough-cut oak table, with its inset copper ring, threw the familiar tang of sour salt under his tongue. Thoughts of his childhood, eating meals with his large family where there were never enough chairs to sit on, popped in his head. Often, a sibling had held him in their lap.

Raoul searched the cupboard for a bottle of whiskey and a glass. He poured a generous shot as boots and socks fell to the floor. His toes buzzed with throbbing as he massaged the bruises on his feet.

The farmhouse was too quiet. Where was everybody? Where was Lucia? He pulled a galvanized tub from the back hallway into the kitchen and filled it with bubbling water that heated in pots in the fireplace. One by one, he dropped his clothes on the floor with total disregard. It hurt to stretch each toe apart from its neighbor.

He stepped into the welcoming water. How long had it been since he had felt the comfort of a hot bath? He had had some cold ones, but they were not the same. Indentations from his rucksack straps revealed scabbed skin on his scapulae and dimpled hips. The soles of his feet were fleshy like the white underbelly of a dead perch. A broad smile spread across his face as the water softened him and his eyelids dropped.

The kitchen door latch suddenly slapped open. Lucia entered the room, followed by three children who trailed behind, a line of wobbling goslings. Raoul perked up. Lucia stood with arms raised, shocked at the sight of him. She searched his face, the strong Abenaki chin and nose. He was gaunt and rawboned, his overgrown beard and hair darker than she remembered, his face ruddy with windburn.

"It's me, I'm back," Raoul said with a smile wider than his sunken cheeks.

Lucia released a held breath as the smallest child cried out. All the children stood stiff and stared.

"You're home, finally home and safe." Lucia ran to him, bent over the tub and opened her arms. Raoul reached up and pulled her down to him as they kissed. Gray water splashed on her smock and the floorboards. They hugged for a long time.

"Put the children down to nap," he whispered as he cradled her backside with two big paws.

Lucia stepped away and hushed the crying child.

He examined the faces of his two children, then to the youngest child, a toddler clinging to Lucia's skirts.

"Who's that?" He asked.

"Meet your daughter, Lucienne."

"How? When did she come?"

"What do you think? After you dropped your load and left."

"Lucienne, that's a pretty name you gave her."
Raoul looked at the child as she whimpered.

"My father, where is he?"

"At the neighbors. He comes in a bit. Nazaire, he's
not with you?"

"He left for the village. He's not ready to face his
empty house."

Lucia stood behind the tub, examining Raoul's
shoulders, checking the scars at the joints of his
elbows. She glided her fingers through his long hair,
looking at his scalp.

"I make you a poultice for your shoulders," she
said.

From one cupboard in the kitchen, she removed a
box of bicarbonate of soda and bottles — witch hazel,
castor oil and borage oil. Raoul watched as Lucia
made a potion, mixing and smelling the concoction.
She returned and faced Raoul in the tub.

She gently placed her two hands on his ruddy
cheeks, bent down and whispered, "And gold?"

Raoul had rehearsed this moment since leaving

Dawson. He planned to shuffle his feet and look left,

then right, and maybe lower sad eyes to the floor. He

had so many things to tell her about their journey: the

ugly, stark gold fields; the beauty of sprawling

canyons; and a sky that could swallow a man; it was

so immense. He would tell her of wild horses, and

hidden muskegs and pole netting fish with the

Moosehide Hån. He would tell about the Dreamers

who pushed and kicked him, of waiting for his gold

nuggets to reappear. How he wanted to share all

these things and more, but right now, he couldn't stop

the smile escaping across his face.

Lucia thrust a foot hard on the floor, and stood

with hands on her hips, her lips a thin line.

Raoul remembered that wonderful, playful pout

which Lucia could give you if she didn't get her way.

"And gold? Did you find gold?" She asked again.

"I worked in a mine with forty other men. The

first season, they paid me twenty-two dollars. The

next, twenty-four dollars, and this last year, I worked

for twenty-six. I even picked up two nuggets on the ground."

"Twenty-six dollars a week? That's wonderful."

Raoul motioned that she bend down to hear him whisper.

"No, not each week, but each day. We did good, excellent good. Now, woman, put the children to nap and give me my real come-home kiss."

Back to Saint Joseph of Beauce

Village Center ☙ April 18, 1910

Threhe air in Nazaire's chest caught in his throat as he walked toward the village gates. He felt Victoria beckon him and he came knowing it would break his heart. Was he ready now? He was dizzy with thoughts that circled his brain.

He recognized the solid wall covered with budding ivy as it wound around the two stone arches. The left arch was the village entrance, and the right an exit. Nothing had changed. He could see down the short street to the back of the church and across the Chaudière River. On the opposite shore, not a mile beyond, fields of prime acreage rolled upward from the water's edge as the valley opened up in front of him, an unwinding carpet of fresh stubble. He drank in the sweetness of the spring meadows and the smell of rich, black soil that made the Beauce Valley home.

He walked down the hill to the back of the church with its cemetery enclosed by a wrought-iron fence and thought of the last time he had stood here with snow covering everything in a ghostly veil. He gritted his teeth and palmed his cheeks with the back of one hand to wipe away tears.

Nazaire had not thought out how to find Victoria. Passing through the cemetery gates, he didn't know which row would hold her resting place. Would she even have a tombstone? He had no idea. These questions seized upon his heart.

He scanned the cemetery grounds for a full minute, then walked to the last row. With each step tiny droplets of sweat beaded his forehead. She must be here. Slight trembles radiated from his fingers and up his forearms as he began to cry. The weight of so lengthy a journey, more than eight thousand miles, had not yet registered through his swollen shoulders and blistered feet that pained his heels and toes.

Nazaire couldn't read the names through his tears, so he willed himself to be calm. He paused, then started again, reading from the last row. He was patient, showed respect and bent with purpose and dignity as he passed one headstone after another reading the names. Something was off. The dates were wrong. He couldn't figure out why; then it came to him.

Nazaire needed to find the newer part of the cemetery. He circled to the outer perimeter to restart his search at the opposite end. He walked in front of the first row, bent as he read the names. Where was she? He had so many things to tell her, resolutions he had made, decisions about the children.

A robin alighted above the next grave as Nazaire's eyes focused on her name cut across the bottom of the stone. The hairs on his arms prickled. He stumbled on his knees toward her grave, the shock of seeing it difficult to take in. He bowed his head and curled his shoulders into his chest when the heavy tears came. He couldn't control his breathing. Nazaire straightened his long spine and raised his head. He began to weep with a faint wail, then in elongated sobs. It was a release so long in coming.

Was he once and for all here, in front of his spouse's grave? Perhaps it was the want of home, the despair of not being back sooner that came from his throat.

He leaned one arm against the stone and slowed his breathing as he read the name again at the bottom edge all green black with mold, then whispered, "I'm here."

His eyes widened, and then he looked away. Taking a deep breath, Nazaire started: "I didn't abandon you, Victoria. I couldn't bear to think of you in the stone shed until spring. We had to leave so as to arrive in the gold fields by the start of summer. It was my only chance."

Nazaire's voice wavered as he spoke aloud.

"I risked everything, and it paid off. I found gold. I can erase our debts, pay back your family all their generosities. Our children are safe. The farm and land is ours to keep. I want to gather up our children, hold them close to me and never leave them again."

He felt the weight of the promenade beginning to lift from his shoulders. He was a new man, strong and able to look everybody in the eye with pride.

Nazaire stood and noticed movement on the main road. People walked by but one figure stood idle, a child lanky and thin, and after a few moments, began a tentative step toward the climb up the village hill. Nazaire needed to go home now. He longed for his children around him. He felt a gentle touch on one shoulder.

"Father?" A voice whispered.

Nazaire turned and laid eyes on the lanky boy. They each stood motionless, then Nazaire reached out with two long arms that enveloped Thomas in a tight embrace.

"My son, my grown man."

After a long minute, Nazaire pushed Thomas to arms' length and took in the new look of his boy.

"See, Thomas. Papa keeps his promises."

END NOTES

Gaudias Nazaire Arthur Raoul Romeo

The Poulin Brothers – All Farmers, Trappers, and Loggers by 8 or 9 and considered Men at 10

Translations, Interpretations, & Archaic Language

In some of my scenes, archaic language or phrases are direct translations from French whereas, in a few instances, a character's speech mimics a reasonable interpretation of common speech of the time. Here is a listing of some peculiar wording, some of which might still be heard today:

BRUISE ON MY TIME from the scene Call the Doctor — Call the Priest

The priest is complaining that Victoria Poulin is taking too long to die. He has been called there to give the farmer's spouse Last Rights, but she's still in the midst of giving birth, an exasperatingly lengthy process. The priest complains of missing his afternoon port served in a crystal glass. He's not in his usual comfortable seat in front of a roaring fire back at the Presbytery, a handsome residence with many comforts. Instead, he is miles away in a drafty peasant's roughshod farmhouse and dreading the

535

ride home that will be slow and cold. The priest's phrase that his uncle will hear of this "bruise on my time" is how the priest speaks his frustration.

TELL BROTHERS COME from the scene The Letter
In the letter dated 1900, Gaudias, who can barely read and write states that "If things bad at home tell brothers come." He is explaining the opportunity to earn excellent money in the gold fields. He knows that there are still open claims to be had in Dawson.

LECTURE from various scenes
Lecture is used in six scenes. In Catholic reporting for marriages, baptisms and last rites, priests finish their written report with the words "The Lecture Complete" before affixing their signature and those of any witnesses. Over time, it became a euphemism in homes for "I have spoken. There'll be no further discussion of this."

In the scene Seeking Advice, Connolly squinted while he worked his mouth, and caught saliva "for the lecture," means that Connolly was readying himself to give a series of instructions.

In the scene Carlington, when Sherman "took over the lecture," he continues to give rules and expectations of the journey.

In the scene Cookie's Concoction, Lennox turned to join Sherman in his tent for an uneasy parley about Longfox's "lecture." Lennox enters Sherman's tent to discuss what Longfox' tirade could mean.

In the 1907 scene Edmonton, Peck had "started his lecture" means that Peck had is already speaking to the crowd. Later after the grizzled man spoke, Peck "took over the lecture" means that he continued with the cautions to the crowd.

In the scene New Hire at YPMC, when Weasel hires Cochran, he grunts, a sure sign that "his lecture is complete," meaning that this is the end of the discussion and Cochran and McPhael are dismissed.

MAMA'S GREEN SOAP from the scene The Letter Gaudias requests that if his brothers did come to Dawson, they "Bring mamas green soap." When Romeo and Gaudias left home in 1884, they each carried a bar of this green soap. Customarily made with wintergreen or mint leaves crushed and mixed with pine needle oil, this strong soap wasn't used to wash with. Instead, when someone spit on the soap, they rubbed the wet soap on broken skin, cuts or bruises on hands, elbows, knees or feet. Because the soap was never submerged in water, a bar would last a long time, and its healing properties were highly valued.

PURCHASE from various scenes

Purchase is an old-fashioned word that means steady on one's feet or having a strong grasp. It is used in four scenes. In the scene Winchester, with tracks that followed higher ground with dry, sure "purchase" for their steps.

In the scene Portage la Prairie with unable to focus his feet for sure "purchase".

In the scene Blind Swale where Raoul found it difficult to maneuver out of clumps of devil's club with no "purchase" touching firm soil.

In the scene Summit Pass where Nazaire tied his gumboots together, happy to let his toes grab "purchase" where they could.

REPEAT THE MASS FOR THE DEAF from the scene
Carlington
While Sherman is explaining important information,
Raoul is not listening. Nazaire reprimands him with
the words "I don't repeat the mass for the deaf,"
meaning that if you didn't catch it the first time, you
wouldn't hear it a second.

THE SLEEPING MAN from the scene Thunder Bay
In Coppaway's band, the legend of the 'sleeping man'
is very sacred. It is a rock formation that looks like a
giant man reposed along the shore of Lake Superior.
The monolith has helped men navigate the large lake
for thousands of years.

THE DOG BARK and PRAIRIE ITCH from the scene
Kenora
The Ojibways numbered sixty-one and most suffered
terrible from the "dog bark," a few from the "prairie
itch."Whooping cough was called the dog bark by the
Indians. The symptoms are a cough that continues

day and night, exhausting and dehydrating. Eventually, the ribs are so bruised from the constant coughing that the sick person can go into cardiac arrest from so much internal bruising. Prairie itch was a constant itch that allows for no sleep. Most often, prairie itch was caused by mites under the skin or No See Ums.

SHINPLASTER from the scene Brandon

In the scene Brandon, Nazaire and Raoul present a twenty-five cent Canadian note known as a "shinplaster" for payment for a barrel of hot water where they could each bath, clothes and all. The notes were no longer distributed by the government but still circulated. Like other countries at this time, Canada switched currencies from bronze to copper to silver, and eventually gold. The currencies themselves, as well as their values, fluctuated until more stability came not only to the country, but also the world.

JUMPIFIED from the scene Moose Jaw and 1907 Calgary

In the scene Moose Jaw, when everyone was "jumpified" with excitement over the size of the kill, jumpified is meant to show excitement.

Jumpified has the same tone in the 1907 scene Calgary when the wolfhound has something in its mouth and becomes "jumpified" as a result.

HEAD-SMASHED-IN RIDGE from the scene Cookie's Concoction

Longfox praised the great herds of buffalo who met their death at "Head-Smashed-In" ridge during his rant the night before he left Sherman's party. The ridge was a buffalo jump that the Blackfoot used where the buffalo were driven off a thirty-six-foot cliff near Fort Macleod, Alberta. Although the thirteen-year-old Coppaway would not have known details of the ridge, he knew that he was near it and had heard many stories in his childhood about the prowess of the great Blackfoot nation.

MOCCASIN NEWS from the scenes Richer and Closing the Claim

Sam Smith has sent a message from Dawson to the Tlingit band in Whitehorse, asking for an escort for two white men across the Rocky Mountains. His request left Dawson by horseback, then with runners. The reply returned to Sam Smith by boat via the Yukon River whose 5.8 MPH current would pull the boat for the 438-mile trip. To First Nation peoples, "moccasin news" is news carried by foot, on horse or over water. The term "moccasin news" also appeared in the scene Richer to indicate that Indians beyond the town of Richer were now aware of the actions of Cochran and Nickleson.

BEAT ANOTHER MAN'S DRUM from the scene
Richer

First Nation peoples have a belief that when a man
makes a drum, he is the only living person destined to
beat it. No one should "beat another man's drum."
Rawhide drums represented the spirit of the drum
maker, an embodiment of the maker's character. That
Cochran dared to tap an old Indian's drum was a
betrayal which the Ojibway's would not tolerate. The
insult demanded justice.

FLUENZE from the scene Portage la Prairie
Coppaway said, "I had a beautiful squaw and young
daughter, two summers. Lost them to the "fluenze."
Coppaway is saying that his wife and daughter died
from influenza.

ACQUAINT THEMSELVES WITH SOAP from the scene Brandon

A few men cared not to "acquaint themselves with soap" means that some men didn't want to pay five cents for a bath. It was cheaper to jump into a barrel of warm water clothes and all, getting two jobs done for the price of one.

HUNDEN KOMMER HER from the 1907 scene Calgary

The Norwegian traveling with Sherman has a wolfhound and like most dogs, has learned commands from his master's native language. In Norwegian, "Hundenkommer her" means "Dog, come here."

'LOTMENT from the scene Flying Beans

"We have nine more days before we get our "'lotment," Raoul said. He is referring to the monthly allotment of provisions that all the people working in and around the gold fields had access to one day a month. Following the news of the gold rush, the government of Canada mandated that the mounties control storage and access to provisions in the isolated Yukon to minimize the risk of starvation.

CURIOUS TO A BRUISE from the scene Second Reunion
A note reaches Nazaire and Raoul but the message is a bit odd. Bring warm clothes and bedrolls? This instruction from Romeo left Raoul "curious to a bruise" which means very curious.

MONKEY JUICE form the scene New Hire at YPMC
"The sonofabitches slipped us some "monkey juice." Cochran is claiming that he and Nickleson were duped with a few drops of monkey juice. Historically, monkey juice was a form of liquid heroin used to quiet victims. Usually applied to the membranes in the eye, it would trigger an instant high. In this case, Cochran claims that he and Nickleson were given some concoction to make them sleep through camp.

WANTING FINGERS from the scene Tait Negg

"How stupid he didn't pick up on her "wanting fingers", Nazaire thought. After Nazaire had paid one dollar to the floor boss for a visit with Tait Negg, she had the audacity to present an open palm, those "wanting fingers" that pleaded for more coin.

WANTING TABLE from the scene Discord

Nazaire's table was found "wanting." Victoria Poulin's brothers gather during her home viewing. As the talk in the kitchen becomes more gossip than chatter, it becomes clear that her siblings felt their sister's life was hard, and the food on the table so little that one left the table wanting more.

CAUGHT SOAP from the scene Closing the Claim

In the early 1900s, perfumed soap was outrageously expensive in Dawson and reserved for dancehall girls and prostitutes. All items then were brought in from outside, the major cause for such inflated prices. Most people used bear soap made from bear fat, dark brown and despite the greasy afterfeel, it did its job well. In the scene Closing the Claim, Nazaire and Raoul stopped at the Dawson Bath and "caught soap," means that they stopped for a bath.

NEVER SELL THE SKIN BEFORE YOU KILL THE BEAR from the scene Winchester and Toronto
The words "You don't sell the skin before you kill the bear" resonate in Nazaire's head. Many children were taught not to count your chicken's before they hatch.

BEST ANNOUNCE MISCHIEF from the scene Toronto
Raoul secured the bundle by cordage in a manner to "best announce mischief" if unbound. Raoul has wrapped their new, cash-laden balbriggans at the center of a bundle, further surrounded by tin cups and cutlery. If untied, the bundle would make plenty of noise, alerting Nazaire to any thievery.

Liberties

I apologize for the liberties I have taken, and for misleading my readers with the following confessions:

There are many purposely misspelled words in the dialog of some characters. For example, the letter of 1900 written by Gaudias Poulin includes misspellings from a person who couldn't read, nor write and was unfamiliar with place names.

The scope of this story is 1907 to 1910. In those years, First Nations people were called "Indians," therefore, I used this term in my book. However, it does make me flinch as I wouldn't refer to any First Nations person as such today. This novel is based heavily on facts, and in a few cases, I have woven in everyday experiences men would have shared on the wagon trails, corduroy roads, old Indian trails, animal paths, in the bush and on the creeks in the gold fields.

I did not investigate the exact law of untilled land being at risk for abandonment in the 1910s, however, when many Canadians left for the Yukon, they followed the rule of being back home by 'seeding' day of the 4th year.

What I know as fact is that in 1910, Nazaire Poulin did return to his fields, fallowed from 1907 through 1909, did come back with gold, did pay whatever fees or charges had accumulated and did retain ownership of his land. This pressure of returning home on time was greatly pressed upon him.

As the Seigneurial System of land ownership, usage, assignment of habitants (tenant farmers) and inheritance were phased out in Quebec, it took time for legal changes and specially attitudes to cascade to outlier villages such as Saint Joseph of Beauce and for the old customs based on Napoleonic Code to pass out of memory.

I wholeheartedly apologize to the Gros Ventre First Nations people concerning Longfox's behavior. He was the product of my imagination, a frightened and lonely teenager who had lost his uncle while visiting a strange area, and felt abandoned and isolated for many weeks among First Nations people he didn't know. I imagine he was relieved to be traveling with Sherman yet resentment of the verbal abuse from Cochran and Nickleson grew. He is by no means representative of the proud Gros Ventre First Nation peoples of Fort Belknap, Montana.

Again, I owe huge apologies to the Dane-zaa First Nations people of the Rocky Mountains. I have tried to portray people who had suffered deaths by contact with white faces, and who struggled with scant resources in their hostile environment.

When my research revealed sixty woodland Anishinaabe living at Kenora, all suffering from the 'dog bark' or whooping cough, and all sixty had succumbed by the end of 1907, I felt that Coppaway's visit would have been enough encouragement for their Shaman, also sick, to disclose the Turtle band's secret cache of cowrie shells. How else could these sacred items be preserved? I resisted the temptation of having the Turtle band's shaman give Coppaway his band's stick — a way of transferring custody, usually temporary, of a band's history, songs, dances, and stories — the most sacred objects a band possessed. Sadly, Coppaway realized that the Turtle band would die out, thus the reason for weeks of sorrowful wailings and sage cleansing on his part.

There are many First Nations' bands represented in this novel. I apologize if I have misassigned the territories of these bands or their traditional clothing or customs. In this novel, I wrote about the Ojibway First Nation peoples of Curve Lake at Peterborough, where Coppaway grew up.

Coppaway met the Ojibway First Nation peoples of Kenora, part of the Turtle Band who, research had stated, perished by the end of 1907 from the dog bark.

The Americans insulted the Ojibway First Nation peoples at Curve Lake, Roseau River near Richer.

Guides across the Rockies included the Doig River First Nation peoples of Rose Prairie, and the Blueberry First Nation peoples north of Fort Saint John in Buick. Next, readers met the Tlingit First Nation peoples in the Cassiar Mountains and at Carcross.

We met a Kaska Dena First Nation guide from Fort Nelson who led Sherman's party up Summit Pass, and a group of Kaska Dena at Watson Lake and in the Kaska mountain range.

Sam Smith was a Constable for the Tr'ondëk Hwëch'in First Nation peoples of Moosehide, Yukon.

The Dane-zaa First Nation peoples or Dreamers lived in the Peace River areas of Alberta and BC, while many Blackfoot First Nation peoples appeared in Saskatchewan and Alberta.

There is a passing mention of Ojib-Crees near the WahgoshigFirst Nation in the Great Clay Belt, the Cree and Sarcee.

The fires of 1910 across most of southwest and southeast Alberta were started in 1909 below the Medicine Line in the states and spread north. These were real. My imaginings spread these fires to the railroad segments where the train had to stop frequently to remove dead and burned cattle or brush. These fires ravaged millions of acres in Manitoba, Saskatchewan, and Alberta. In Canada, the conflagrations were called the 'Big Blowout' in the Peel Prairie Newspaper Archives, and in the U.S, the 'Big Blow Up.'

Many of the American fires were reignited from 1909
to 1910 and were extinguished by U.S. Afro-American
firefighters, Buffalo Soldiers, who often crossed from
the states into Canada. In 1909, many First Nations
people of the Rockiesa who had never seen an Afro-
American before referred to these firefighters as
'Midnight Men' and were grateful for their help.

The old-timer who informed passengers of the silk
trains was added to explain silk trains that did carry
outlawed silkworms from the piers of Vancouver
under secret cover in customized, heated rail cars
through Canada into New York and New Jersey.
These trains had priority to pass before all other trains
in Canada, even the royal train. Personnel on these
trains did have "shoot to kill" orders if anyone
delayed or interfered with their passing.

Snowfall in February 1910 was sourced from 1909
data.

The Fruit Station in Quint West was one of five fruit stations that the Canadian government established on which to harvest and strengthen various seeds, shrubs and fruit trees with the most disease-resistant stock. Each fruit stations was headed by 1) a soil specialist, 2) an entomologist, 3) a master arborist, 4) a seed tester, and 5) a tree and shrub graft specialist.

To the present-day Fraser family of Whitehorse, Yukon, I enjoyed imagining Cameron Fraser and his handsome horse ranch. I purposely misassigned Fraser's wife to the Poulin men.

I moved the Oshawa Second Marsh a few miles closer to Quinte West than it actually is.

Undoubtedly, there are other misrepresentations that I have not mentioned, and for these, I am genuinely sorry.

Thanks

There are many professionals from whom I've asked questions, and I thank them all for pointing me in the right direction. My questions ran the gamut from how heavy are western wolves to which routes did the silk trains follow. I needed to know about gold, mining, the saturation of electric cars in major cities. While reading about the consequences of a world depression from the 1880s through to the 1920s, I found that Quebec suffered many economic failures. The entire country lacked a stable banking infrastructure. I needed to ferret out where sparks of a growing economy were and how these contributed to a rising second class.

To my mentor, author Rich Marcello, I appreciate so much your generosity, patience, and instruction. What a champion teacher you are. To my editor, Ann Frantz, your guidance helped my work to shine. To my critique group at Seven Bridge Writers'

Collaborative in Lancaster, I am honored to be a member. To my beta-reader, I appreciate the tough love.

In Quebec, to the infamous Marcel Cliché, noted genealogist and prestigious Historic Researcher at the Musée Marius-Barbeau and to the generous Mr. Daniel Carrier, Art Historian and distinguished author at the Société du Patrimoine des Beaucerons, both heritage collections in St-Joseph of Beauce, Quebec, you have both helped me remain steadfast in my goals. Thank you for your patience with my research. To Stephan Vachon, President of Musée Ferroviaire de Beauce at Vallée-Jonction, Quebec, I appreciate hearing about the history of the rail line and how it impacted peoples' lives in the Beauce Valley.

In the Yukon, to Ed Jones, thank you for your generosity and kindness during my Dawson trip and with my numerous emails. I loved the walk in the

Dawson YOOP (Yukon Order of Pioneers) Cemetery
as we searched for Romeo Poulin's grave, my
granduncle. To the Yukon Archives in Whitehorse,
the Klondike Library of Dawson, the Dawson
Museum and the McBride Museum, many thanks for
all your help during my research stay in Whitehorse
and Dawson. To the Heritage Department of the First
Nations People of Dawson, I owe you a debt of
gratitude as you honored me with a visit to
Moosehide where I found the graves of my HÅN
grandaunt, Mary Smith Poulin and her father, Sam
Smith. To my newfound relatives, George Poulin of
Carcross, Yukon and Roch Fraser of Whitehorse,
Yukon, I am delighted to have connected with both of
you.

In British Columbia, to my Poulin double-second
cousins, Gloria Hamilton and Norma Poulin-Riddall,
I am grateful for your encouragement and for sharing
your memories as they crossed into mine. The
grandfather of these two sisters was a sibling of my

grandfather. The grandmother of these sisters was also a sibling of my grandmother. Brothers marrying sisters was a common occurrence among Quebecers. To my Vachon second cousins, Paul Tremblay, Diane Tremblay-Savage and Nicole Tremblay, thanks for all your stories that paint our family histories richer.

In the U.S., to my first cousins, your recollections and photos have been a wonderful encouragement for me.

At Coursera.com, I received an eye-opening education from an Associate Professor of the University of Toronto, Jean-Paul Restoule, who taught "Aboriginal Worldviews and Education." Your teaching style and amazing course content was just what I was looking for.

I owe a special thank you to Mrs. Pierrette Pépin-Roy of Saint Georges, Quebec for her friendship and letters of encouragement. The story of her entrepreneurial father-in-law was delightful, and accurate. Saskatchewan was a source of many horse sales during the late 1890s. It is the rich details she generously shared with me in our correspondence that bring the past to life.

One story starts:

He drove his car to the Quebec rail yard and left it, going by train up to Saskatchewan. He bought his horses: one stallion and his many mares. They were packed into boxcars and headed down to Quebec. The train often stopped, allowing the horses to exit the cars into enclosed corrals, drink fresh water and stretch their legs before arriving at the next stop. Handlers unloaded the horses every four hours.

Once in Quebec, he tied the stallion to the back of his car. Meanwhile, all the mares were released from their corral. As he drove slowly in busy streets, the mares needed no encouragement to follow. So unusual a sight was this that people stopped and lined the sidewalks as if a circus performance was unfolding before their eyes. This is how the horses were led back to Saint Georges, ready to be calmed and then sold.

Tell me What you Think

I'm delighted that you've read *the long shot*, and I hope you enjoyed it. I'm back home, spending hours each day, writing Book 2 in this series. Please consider leaving a review of *the long shot* on Amazon or Goodreads. I'd love to hear from you and learn what you liked and didn't like. Thank you for reading my work, and I hope you are moved to write down your own stories; they are the real gold in your life.

Book Club Guide To the long shot

For any group that would like to feature *the long shot: a french canadian saga – Book 1* as a book of their month selection, send a request to replythelongshot@gmail.com for a PDF version. The *Book Club Guide to the long shot* is also displayed at joycederenas.com/resources.

Other Documents of Interest

I have also written stand-alone documents that describe the time period of *the long shot*.

Roads in the Prairies is a document that explains the difficulties of travel in the early 1900s.

Roads No More is a document that gives the art of bushwhacking a good looking-over inside the mysterious Rockies.

First Nations People of the Yukon is a document that presents some of the Aboriginal Canadians featured in this novel.

These are available if you send a request to replythelongshot@gmail.com and specify which document you want. They are also displayed on my website under joycederenas.com/resources.

Want to keep up with Joyce?

To keep up with Joyce and all her frenchiness, visit joycederenas.com to learn about book signings or book talks near you.

Have something interesting to share?

Joyce loves to hear about the Beauce or Dawson. She would love to hear from you in English or French. Contact her at replythelongshot@gmail.com.

Author Biography

Joyce Derenas wrote User Guides and created Help systems for technology companies around Boston for fifteen years, retired, and then decided to have some fun. She loves the details of daily life in earlier times. She writes in her debut novel, *the long shot*, about Nazaire Poulin, a poor grain grower in the village of Saint Joseph of Beauce, Quebec. All of Joyce's stories are based on the real lives of her Quebecois relatives, some pioneers to the Beauce Valley.

Decades earlier, Joyce started building her family's genealogical tree, and her love of the past grew from that interest. She has visited the village of her mother's birth often, and has also researched in the rich collection of the National Archives of Canada in Ottawa, but in the back of her heart, she had always harbored a dream to find some footprint of her French-Canadian relatives in the deep north of Canada's wilderness.

Once retired, a love for primary research led Joyce to the Yukon for a two-month visit, searching for the footprints of her grandfather and his gold-mining brothers.

> "I left for the Yukon knowing that I had a connectionto four brothers and two wives, and returned with knowledgeof twenty-two deceased relatives and six living relatives,"Joyce said.

She received her BA in English with a Concentration in Writing from Worcester State College. While there, Joyce wrote her first, short biography of Ichabod Washburn, a steel magnate and one of the founding fathers of the Worcester Polytechnic Institute in Worcester, Massachusetts. This short biography remains in the permanent collection of the prestigious American Antiquarian Society.

Made in the USA
Middletown, DE
30 April 2019